The
LINCOLN
LETTER

BOOKS BY WILLIAM MARTIN

City of Dreams
The Lost Constitution
Harvard Yard
Citizen Washington
Annapolis
Cape Cod
The Rising of the Moon
Nerve Endings
Back Bay

The

LINCOLN
LETTER

...

WILLIAM MARTIN

FORGE®

A TOM DOHERTY ASSOCIATES BOOK
New York

THE LINCOLN LETTER

Copyright © 2012 by William Martin

Map by Jon Lansberg

Design by Mary A. Wirth

A Forge Book
Published by Tom Doherty Associates, LLC
175 Fifth Avenue
New York, NY 10010

www.tor-forge.com

Forge® is a registered trademark of Tom Doherty Associates, LLC.

Library of Congress Cataloging-in-Publication Data

Martin, William, 1950–
    The Lincoln letter / William Martin.—1st ed.
        p. cm.
    "A Tom Doherty Associates book."
    ISBN 978-0-7653-2198-5 (hardcover)
    ISBN 978-1-4299-4713-8 (e-book)
    1. Lincoln, Abraham, 1809–1865—Collectibles—Fiction.   2. Historians—
Washington (D.C.)—Fiction.   3. Washington (D.C.)—History—Civil War,
1861–1865—Fiction.   4. Political fiction.   I. Title.
    PS3563.A7297L56 2012
    813'.54—dc23

                                                                    2012019934

First Edition: August 2012

Printed in the United States of America

0   9   8   7   6   5   4   3   2   1

FOR CHRIS

I could have dedicated all my books to her.
And in some way, I have.

Acknowledgments

In the foyer of the new Ford's Theatre Center for Education and Leadership, a tower rises. It's thirty-four feet high and built of books, fifteen thousand books. It represents the work of many lifetimes, all devoted to a single life, Abraham Lincoln's. Reading those books could easily become the work of a lifetime, too.

But Lincoln is there. You'll find him in those books. You'll find him in the many photographs of his presidential years, a remarkable human portrait of a nation's agony written in one face. When you enter his presence in print or pictures, you feel as if you can reach out and touch him. His deeds and death may make him the most revered figure in American history, but he always seems accessible.

However, there's not much left of the Washington that Lincoln inhabited during the years when the nation's future turned on his every decision. Time has paved the muddy streets, covered the filthy canal, and replaced all but the most famous of the buildings that Lincoln would have known.

And if you're telling a story set in Lincoln's Washington, you want your readers to smell that canal, scrape the mud from their boots, and see the skyline that Lincoln saw. You want them to embrace the details of a time long past so that they will live the story with your characters, both the historical and the fictional. To do that, you'll need help. And I have gotten help in many ways, from many generous people.

Peter Drummey, librarian of the Massachusetts Historical Society, has a knowledge of history's facts and a love of its drama that make him an invaluable resource for the historical novelist who balances fact and drama in every scene. He is also a great student of the Twentieth Massachusetts Volunteer Infantry. Ron Egalka provided extensive expertise on the handguns and weaponry of the era. Madeline "Nonnie" Mullin, curator of the town history room at the Weston Public Library, is a former Washingtonian filled with insights into the history and the geography of her native city. And the library staff made certain that whatever reading material I needed, I got.

Many others took the time to send me information, answer questions, offer hospitality, and challenge my assumptions about the Civil War: Robert Ablondi, James Bartlett, H. W. Brands, David Brno, Lorraine Chickering, Justin Dietz, Josh Henson, Gina and Dennis Podlesak, John Riley of the White House Historical Association, Vivian Spiro, Mark Svrcek and the staff at the Antietam Overlook Farm, and Martin Weinkle.

My daughter, Elizabeth, a long-distance runner who has trained along most of Washington's streets, served as tour guide on my explorations of the city, past and present. She led me to the Eastern Market, the National Greenhouse, Ford's Theatre, the Lincoln Gallery at the Smithsonian Museum of American Art, the Lincoln Cottage at the Soldiers' Home, the Renwick Gallery, the towpath along the C&O Canal in Georgetown, Rock Creek Park, and Fort C. F. Smith Park in Arlington.

My wife, Chris, played many roles, as always. She cooked some of the dishes that my characters ate. (She now makes a delicious she-crab soup, though she drew the line at "sloosh.") She drove while I took notes on our research journeys. And she was a stalwart companion in the field. She plunged willingly into the West Woods at Antietam, led our mile-long march from Robert E. Lee's statue to the Angle at Gettysburg, and braved the mud when I decided to see Ball's Bluff from the Potomac riverbank. She also waited patiently through more than her share of "writing" weekends.

Of course, we couldn't have visited those places and walked the ground of history if not for the efforts of so many to preserve the sites and restore the buildings: nonprofit groups like the Civil War Trust, the National Museum of Civil War Medicine, and the National Trust for Historic Preservation; the various municipalities and the states of Maryland, Pennsylvania, and Virginia; and perhaps most importantly, the U.S. National Park

Service. Visit, as we did, Manassas, Ball's Bluff, Harper's Ferry, Bolivar Heights, the turnout at Grove Farm (site of the famous photograph of Lincoln with McClellan in the field), the town of Frederick, Maryland, the Pry House, the Antietam battlefield, or Gettysburg, and you'll appreciate their efforts.

Also, anyone seeking to bring the world of the 1860s to life should thank the men who hauled their huge cameras and fragile glass negatives across that rutted American landscape. They left the first photographic record of a nation at war. Some of their names are familiar: Mathew Brady and Alexander Gardner. But I owe thanks to the lesser-known Titian Peale, son of Rembrandt Peale, grandson of Charles Willson Peale. He climbed into the tower of the Smithsonian castle one August afternoon in 1863 and made a 360-degree panorama of Washington. I referred to it hundreds of times. How much of the Mall did the Armory Square Hospital cover? See the Peale panorama. Was the bridge across the canal at Tenth Street a footbridge? See Peale. Want to see it yourself? Go to the Smithsonian Web site: www.civilwar.si.edu/smithsonian_castle.html.

And though there may be fifteen thousand books about Lincoln and as many about the Civil War, and I have read my share of them, let me mention just a few on Washington itself: a pair of primary sources, Louisa May Alcott's *Hospital Sketches* and Walt Whitman's *Memoranda During the War;* and two excellent social histories, *Freedom Rising,* by Ernest B. Ferguson, and *Reveille in Washington,* the 1942 Pulitzer Prize winner by Margaret Leech.

Thanks also to my agent, Robert Gottlieb, who has been saying for twenty years that I should write a novel about Lincoln, and to my editor at Forge, Bob Gleason, who has been talking since we first met of a novel about the Emancipation Proclamation. I always listen to both of them.

And finally, thanks to family and friends not mentioned here. They leave me alone when I need solitude. They join me for dinner when I need conversation. They read my books, too.

WILLIAM MARTIN
March 2012

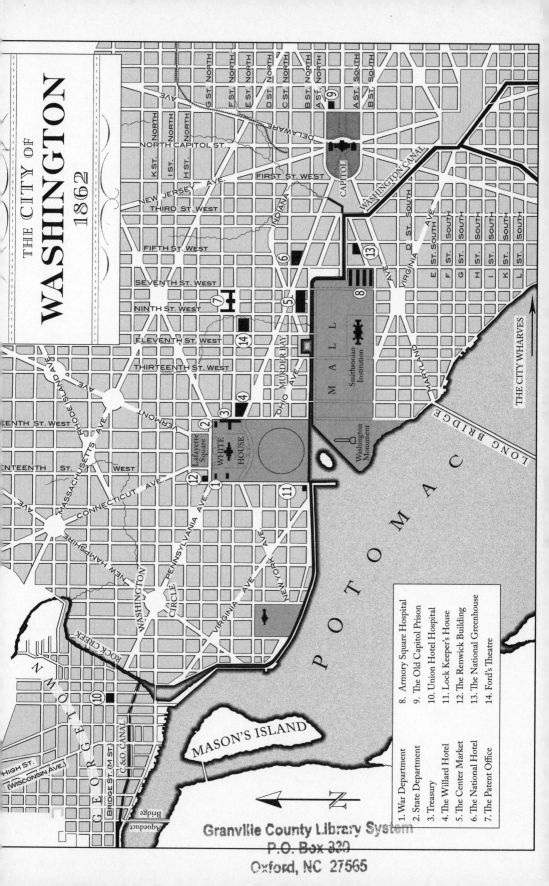

THE CITY OF
WASHINGTON
1862

NORTH CAPITOL ST.

FIRST ST. WEST

THIRD ST. WEST

FIFTH ST. WEST

SEVENTH ST. WEST

NINTH ST. WEST

ELEVENTH ST. WEST

THIRTEENTH ST. WEST

EENTH ST. WEST

ENTEENTH ST.

CAPITOL

MALL

Smithsonian Institution

Washington Monument

POTOMAC

LONG BRIDGE

THE CITY WHARVES

GEORGETOWN

ROCK CREEK

MASON'S ISLAND

Aqueduct
Bridge

C.&O. CANAL

BRIDGE ST. (M ST.)

HIGH ST.
(WISCONSIN AVE.)

NEW HAMPSHIRE

MASSACHUSETTS

RHODE ISLAND AVE.

CONNECTICUT AVE.

VERMONT

CIRCLE

WASHINGTON

PENNSYLVANIA AVE.

VIRGINIA AVE.

NEW YORK AVE.

Lafayette Square

WHITE HOUSE

MURDER BAY

OHIO AVE.

INDIANA

NEW JERSEY AVE.

WASHINGTON CANAL

DELAWARE AVE.

VIRGINIA AVE.

MARYLAND

K ST. NORTH

I ST. NORTH

H ST. NORTH

G ST. NORTH

F ST. NORTH

E ST. NORTH

D ST. NORTH

C ST. NORTH

B ST. NORTH

A ST. NORTH

A ST. SOUTH

B ST. SOUTH

C ST. SOUTH

D ST. SOUTH

E ST. SOUTH

F ST. SOUTH

G ST. SOUTH

H ST. SOUTH

I ST. SOUTH

K ST. SOUTH

L ST. SOUTH

N

1. War Department	8. Armory Square Hospital
2. State Department	9. The Old Capitol Prison
3. Treasury	10. Union Hotel Hospital
4. The Willard Hotel	11. Lock Keeper's House
5. The Center Market	12. The Renwick Building
6. The National Hotel	13. The National Greenhouse
7. The Patent Office	14. Ford's Theatre

PROLOGUE

April 1865

On the last day of his life, Abraham Lincoln wrote a letter.

If he was angry, anger did not reveal itself in his handwriting, which was typically clean and open. If he was euphoric, and those who observed him that day attested later that he was, euphoria did not express itself either.

The letter lacked the poetry of his best speeches and demonstrated none of the cold and relentless logic of his political writing.

It was as simple, direct, and blunt as a cannonball:

> *Dear Lieutenant Hutchinson,*
>
> *It comes to my attention that you are still alive. This means that you may still be in possession of something that I believe fell into your hands in the telegraph office three years ago. It would be best if you returned it, considering its potential to alter opinions regarding the difficulties just ended and those that lie ahead. If you do, a presidential pardon will be considered.*
>
> *A. Lincoln.*

Lincoln did not inform his secretary about the letter.

It was unlikely that he wanted questions regarding correspondence with an officer who had served not only in the field but also in the War Department telegraph office, before coming into significant personal difficulty.

It would also have appeared strange that Lincoln did not address the letter to Lieutenant Hutchinson. He sent it instead to Corporal Jeremiah Murphy at the Armory Square Hospital on Seventh Street.

But even a president had his secrets.

Lincoln sealed the letter and slipped it into a pile of outgoing correspondence, some to be mailed, some to be hand delivered around the city.

It was just after eight when his wife appeared in the doorway to his office. She was wearing a white dress with black stripes and a bonnet adorned with pink silk flowers. She had always favored flowers. But she had worn them less and less in the last four years. No woman who had lost a son and two half brothers, no woman who had watched her husband grow old under history's heaviest burden, would be inclined to wear anything but black. Still, flowers and dress did nothing to soften her voice. "Mr. Lincoln, would you have us be late?"

He said, "Tonight, we shall laugh."

Then he called for his carriage, and they went to the theater.

ONE

Friday Night

Peter Fallon received a copy of that letter as an attachment to an e-mail on the third Friday night of September.

He would not have read it, except that it came from Diana Wilmington, an assistant professor at the George Washington University and author of a controversial new book, *The Racism and Resolve of Abraham Lincoln*. The book had gotten her onto television, radio, magazine covers, and made her one of the most recognizable African American scholars in the country. Peter had also dated her when she was an assistant professor at the University of Massachusetts.

"I've been thinking of you," she wrote. "I still read the Boston gossip pages. (How could I not, after the gossip we inspired?) So that bit about you and Evangeline caught my eye. Not getting married but still having a reception . . . genius."

Yes, thought Peter. *Genius.* The hall had been rented and the champagne was cold. It was a great party. As for the decision not to get married . . . he was not so sure.

He took a sip of wine and kept reading:

"I really liked Evangeline. I thought she was good for you."

True. Peter couldn't remember which of them first said, "If it works don't fix it." But now, Evangeline was prepping a new project in New York, and Peter was guest-curating a new exhibit in Boston.

"However," Diana went on, "I'm not writing about your love life. I'd like you to take a look at this attachment."

Peter clicked to the scanned image of a letter. He glanced first at the header, printed in an Old English typeface: "Executive Mansion." Beneath it was the word "Washington," the date April 14, 1865, and to the side, the word "Private" handwritten and circled. Then Peter's eye dropped to the signature, to the clear and characteristic cursive that was the Holy Grail of autograph collectors everywhere: *A. Lincoln.*

In an instant, he knew that whatever this was, it was worth seven figures: a Lincoln signature, on a Lincoln letter, written from the Lincoln White House.

Then he looked again at the date and felt a chill: *the day Lincoln was shot.*

He wiped the sweat from his palms, as if he were touching the original instead of seeing it on a computer screen. He almost went looking for white cotton curatorial gloves.

Could this be Lincoln's last letter? A last insight into the most analyzed, adulated, biographied, beloved, and, in a few places, detested man in American history? And what did this anonymous lieutenant have that mattered so much at the end of the Civil War?

Peter clicked again on the e-mail:

I held this letter in my hands a week ago, along with the envelope addressed to a Corporal Jeremiah Murphy. A man was offering it for sale to the American Museum of Emancipation. I told him we were very small, hoping to consolidate with the Smithsonian Museum of African American History and Culture when it opens in 2015, but that I would talk to our board. When I tried to contact him two days ago, he had gone incommunicado. I had been planning to ask you to appraise the letter. Would you be willing to put your skills to finding it, or at least uncovering the story behind it?

Peter lifted the wine bottle. One more tip into the glass would bring him to the bottom of the label. When he drank alone—something he'd been doing more since the wedding that wasn't—he had a rule: Drink to the bottom of the label and no farther. Stopper the bottle. And every few nights, finish the high-quality dregs. So he poured a bit more, swirled, and sipped.

Then he wrote back:

The last big Lincoln letter to come on the market was his answer to the so-called Little People's Petition. It went for 3.2m in '09. That's where the bidding starts on this, if it's authentic. So call me. I'm up until midnight.

Then he drank the wine with a little wedge of Époisses: a big cab with a big cheese, an excellent nightcap. And NESN was nightcapping an excellent Red Sox game, which he missed because he had been working on a new exhibit for the Boston Public Library: "A Northern City and the Civil War."

It was opening on September 22, the 150th anniversary of the day Lincoln announced the Emancipation Proclamation. The Leventhal Center was providing battle maps. Rare Books was delivering journals and photos from the famed Twentieth Regiment Collection. Peter was contributing a few things from his Antiquaria catalog, including a presentation copy of Walt Whitman's *Memoranda During the War*, inscribed to Ralph Waldo Emerson. And an anonymous lender was offering a signed copy of the Emancipation Proclamation itself.

Peter was doing more than guest curators usually did. He considered it a signal honor from his city, so he wanted to earn it.

And Boston was more than his city. It was his *town*.

He had his roots in Southie. He'd gone to BC High and Harvard. He ran his business from the third floor of a Newbury Street bowfront that was above an art gallery that was above a restaurant. He had Red Sox season tickets and sat on the boards of two Boston museums. And he could never imagine moving to New York, no matter how much he liked to visit.

Evangeline had decided that she didn't want to live anywhere *but* New York, which made marriage a problem and led them to face a hard truth: They both liked their independence, no matter how much they loved each other.

So they'd had a party instead of a wedding and settled for status quo ante. No sharing of utility bills or toothpaste, no extracurricular sharing of themselves, either.

While he waited for Diana Wilmington to call, Peter e-mailed Evangeline:

See you Sunday. We'll have fun on the battlefields.

Then he poured the rest of the wine.

.   .   .

How did we decide that a little thing like a city would keep us apart?

That was what Evangeline Carrington was thinking as she rode a taxi down the West Side the next morning. But she didn't think long, because she was catching the 8 A.M. Acela to Washington for her biggest professional adventure yet.

The travel writer was trying television.

She had always written—for satisfaction, for pay, for therapy. She wrote in her attic when she was a girl. She wrote for the *Crimson* when she went to Harvard. She wrote her way through Columbia School of Journalism after her first breakup with Peter. And after her first marriage fell apart, she wrote about the places she went to escape.

She had built a nice career, but every year, there were fewer travel magazines and fewer travel sections in fewer newspapers. So it was time for the next step. She'd thought about a blog. But Peter urged her to think big: television.

And she had an idea for a show, but not for the Travel Channel or PBS. No, when she thought television, she thought History Network.

Her idea: a photogenic journalist takes you to fun places. Sure, it had been done before. But Evangeline was planning to explore the best sites, restaurants, and hotels for the history-oriented traveler, and each bundle of shows would have a theme: Revolutionary New England, the Oregon Trail, New York in the Ragtime era. . . .

The network fell in love . . . with her, with her pitch, and with her plan for the first bundle: *Travels in Civil War Country,* yet another angle for their wall-to-wall Civil War sesquicentennial programming.

So Evangeline was off to D.C. to shoot locations, and Peter would join her Sunday afternoon for a driving tour to Manassas, Antietam, and Gettysburg.

She got out of the cab at the Eighth Avenue entrance to Penn Station, rolled her suitcase onto the escalator, and rode down to the miserable waiting area. Hundreds of people were always standing there, watching the giant message board, waiting for a track announcement so they could stampede to the gate and stumble down the stairs to the platform, because no one wanted to be the last aboard a crowded train and end up standing all the way to Providence or Trenton.

There was an article in all that, she thought, a nuts-and-bolts piece about riding Amtrak. She'd be sure to mention the separate Acela waiting area. She showed her ticket at the Acela gate and rolled her bag to a seat as far as possible from all the cell-phoners.

No greater convenience than the cell phone, but one of the miseries of modern life was hearing other people's phone conversations in restaurants, movie theaters, and Acela waiting areas. If you were on your way to D.C., did you care if some stockbroker wanted to move his clients out of Microsoft at the opening bell on Monday? Or that a handsome young man was going home to Allentown because he hadn't even had a call-back in six months? Or that a business-traveling mom wanted her stay-at-home hubby to stop serving Pop-Tarts to the kids for breakfast? No, no, and no.

Evangeline found a quiet spot, took out her iPad, and checked her e-mail. First she dumped the spam. Then she glanced at several notes from her producer. Then she read the messages from Peter.

She had answered his midnight e-mail when she got up:

Leaving on Acela. We'll have fun when you get to DC. And this was the right move.

He had written back around seven:

Can't wait. All those battlefields. Better to be traveling to battle-fields than turning our lives into one.

A wise response, she thought, though they seldom argued. Sure, they disagreed plenty and wisecracked all the time. But they never had one of those long-running, scorched-earth kinds of fights that had turned her marriage into its own private Gettysburg.

Then she noticed a new e-mail from Peter. It had come in at seven thirty. The subject line read:

HACKED/Call me

She pulled out her cell, pressed his number, and heard him say, "Where are you?"

"Peter, it's customary to say good morning in the morning."

"Okay. Good morning. Where are you?"

Evangeline noticed the business-traveling mom give *her* a look, so she lowered her voice. "I'm at Penn Station. What's going on?"

"I got an e-mail last night. Now the sender tells me she thinks she's been hacked."

"And why is that my problem?"

"If the hacker went through the sender's address book, he knows the sender's been communicating with me and with you, too, since you're interviewing her in D.C."

"Diana? Diana Wilmington?"

"Right."

"Who's hacking her?"

"Who knows? But when someone sends me the scan of a newly discovered Lincoln letter, and the next morning she tells me she's been hacked—"

"You do what you always do."

"What's that?"

"Get suspicious."

"Is that why we're not getting married?"

"Because you're suspicious?"

"No. Because I'm predictable."

"A little bit of both and . . . Peter, you sound kind of woolly. Are you hungover?"

"Of course not. And don't open any strange e-mails. Whoever is reading Diana's stuff, we don't want them reading ours, especially if this is about a Lincoln letter."

"Now receiving passengers at Gate 9E, train 2109, Acela Express to Washington—"

"Peter, I have to go. Drink some water. Hydrate. You'll feel better. See you tomorrow."

After she hung up, Evangeline looked down to put the phone into her purse and saw the shoes of that cell-phoning business mom right next to hers.

The shoes were red patent leather, half-heeled, stylish but sensible. The legs were well shaped if a bit muscular. The suit was blue pinstripe, with a skirt just short enough to be stylish but sensible, too. The body in the suit was trim, fit, tight.

Evangeline didn't like anyone invading her personal space, but as she raised her head, the woman smiled and said, "I want to show you something."

"Yes?"

She put her iPhone in front of Evangeline's nose. And there was a picture of Evangeline in a linen sport coat, blue jeans, and oxblood cowboy boots, in front of the famous bas-relief of the Massachusetts Fifty-fourth, the first black regiment in the Union Army, in a publicity shot for her new show.

"I read your articles all the time," the woman said. "I look up and here you are."

Evangeline felt a little jolt. It was the first time anyone had ever recognized her in a public place. So she stood and offered her hand.

The woman took it. "I'm Kathi. Kathi Morganti. I'm a fan."

"Thank you. Are you going to Washington?"

"Going home. I've been in New York all week meeting clients. I'm a lobbyist, and reading your travel articles always reminds me of what I'm working for."

"What's that?"

"Vacations."

They laughed and headed together for the train.

Evangeline hoped that she hadn't made a three-hour friend, someone who'd talk the whole way to Washington. She had work to do. But she liked to think she had fans, and maybe this one might offer a business card. Knowing lobbyists in D.C. was a good way to get to know everyone.

As they started down the stairs, Kathi Morganti said, "Acela to Washington. A literal power trip. You never know who you'll meet."

.   .   .

Peter had been lying.

He *was* a bit hungover. So he took two more aspirin and took Evangeline's advice. He hydrated, inside and out, with a can of seltzer and a
shower.

When he got out of the shower, he cursed. He had put the towels in
the laundry and forgotten to replace them. So he threw on his terry cloth
robe, wiped his feet on the bath mat, and padded down the hallway to the
linen closet.

He lived in a two-story condo in a five-story Back Bay brownstone.
The master bedroom and attached study were at the front. The guest/TV
room was at the rear. The linen closet was in the hallway between.

He opened the door, grabbed a thick towel, and decided that since he
was so close, he would surrender to temptation. He would visit his sanctum sanctorum.

It always cheered him when he needed cheering, and since the wedding that wasn't, he'd needed plenty. If business was slow, it reminded
him of his assets. And when he questioned himself altogether, when he
wondered if he should have pursued some sane profession like business or
law rather than brokering rare books and documents, a visit to the sanctum sanctorum reminded him that what he did mattered.

He knelt and pressed a sequence of floor tiles in the linen closet; then
he gripped the doorframe on either side and pulled. With a hydraulic
whoosh, the whole closet slid out of the wall and pivoted into the hallway.

In front of him now was a stainless steel door with a combination lock.

He spun the dial, and the door opened. The space beyond was not
much wider than the linen closet, not much deeper than the shower stalls
in the bathrooms on either side. Walls, floor, and ceiling were steel lined.
Temperature and humidity were strictly controlled. And in case of fire, the
room would fill with halon gas to kill the flames and preserve the contents.

He kept most of his collection in the Antiquaria office on Newbury
Street, where he did the daily work of buying and selling everything from
Shakespeare Second Folios to signed first editions of the complete James
Bond. But here was where he kept the things that mattered most, the

treasures he hoped never to part with until the time came to bequeath them to his son or give them to the Massachusetts Historical Society.

Aside from his contractor brother, who had installed this room, the only people who knew about it were Evangeline and his silent partner, Orson Lunt.

He flipped on the lights. To the left was a wall of tray-type stainless filing cases, all alphabetized. The *S* drawer held a quarto of Shakespeare's *Love's Labor's Lost*, printed in 1598. In the *W* file was George Washington's letter of March 5, 1775, ordering the army to go on to Dorchester Heights.

And when Peter pulled out the *L* file, he was looking into the eyes of Abraham Lincoln, forthright, confident, careworn. The picture had been taken by Alexander Gardner in November 1863, a few weeks before the Gettysburg Address. It had been printed on a carte de visite and signed by Lincoln himself. As far as Peter knew, it was one of only a few authentically signed Lincoln cartes in existence.

But the real treasure lay to the left of the picture.

In 1864, Lincoln had signed forty-eight printed copies of the Emancipation Proclamation, to be auctioned at a Philadelphia fund-raiser for the United States Sanitary Commission. They were known as the Leland-Boker editions, after the printer, and only half were known to exist. Peter Fallon was looking at one of them.

He would be the anonymous donor at his own show, and he would insist on high security. After all, Robert F. Kennedy's signed Leland-Boker had recently sold for $3,700,000, the most money ever paid for a presidential document. Peter and Orson Lunt had bought theirs from an Illinois dentist in 1990 for $300,000. It was not as valuable as Kennedy's, nor as good a deal. Kennedy had paid only $9,500 for his in 1961, and the Kennedy name had given it a provenance that added a premium to any price.

In the humming quiet of the secret room, Peter studied the single column of type and the confident signature, *A. Lincoln*. In the Emancipation Proclamation, Lincoln had decreed that those who had been held in bondage for generations would "be then, thenceforward, and forever free" . . . at least in the rebellious states. He had not freed the slaves in loyal states, because he did not believe the Constitution gave him that right, and he feared that they would secede if he tried, but he had taken the first step toward racial equality in America.

Peter considered it an act of enormous moral and political courage.

After the Proclamation, the war was no longer a struggle between the ideologies competing in America since its birth, between those who wanted a strong central government and those who wished, as Jefferson Davis had said, simply "to be left alone." Lincoln had transformed the war into a struggle over the very meaning of America.

But like so many in those days, Lincoln would pay for his beliefs with his life.

Peter glanced at the document to the right of the Gardner photograph, one of the most poignant letters ever penned in America.

A surgeon named Curtis, of the U.S. Army Medical Corps, had written it to his mother in April 1865. He had gone to the White House on the morning after Lincoln had kept his appointment with the assassin. He had gone to perform the autopsy.

The letter described a room on the second floor, across the hall from Mrs. Lincoln's bedroom: a bed, heavy draperies, a wardrobe, sofas occupied by military officers and civilian officials in stunned, grief-stricken silence . . . and the naked body of the president, covered with a sheet and towels, lying cold and dead on a board suspended between two sawhorses.

It was a letter of stark clinical detail. The doctor had been performing a primitive forensic analysis, after all. He described the removal and dissection of Lincoln's brain and the search for the bullet, which he could not find until, "suddenly, it dropped through my fingers and fell, breaking the silence of the room with its clatter into an empty basin beneath. There it lay upon the white china, a little black mass no bigger than the end of my finger—dull, motionless, and harmless, yet the cause of such mighty changes in the world's history as perhaps we may never realize."

How true, thought Peter Fallon.

The man who fired that bullet, John Wilkes Booth, had heard Lincoln suggest four nights earlier that the nation's renewal and reconstruction would mean extending the vote to some—but not all—Negro freedmen.

"That means nigger citizenship," Booth had been heard to growl. "That is the last speech he will ever give. I will put him through."

And so he had.

Since then, historians had sifted every Lincoln document and observation, searching for meanings and meanings within meanings. They had relived for one generation after another every moment of that terrible Easter weekend. And they had agreed with the young surgeon that the world had seen mighty changes, some because of what Lincoln had done, some because of what he had not lived to do.

So . . . was the history now settled?

How could it be, when an enigmatic letter might emerge a century and a half later, referencing a certain "something" that Lincoln wanted returned. What was it? What changes had it wrought? And how much, Peter had to wonder, would it be worth?

Time, he decided, for a whole weekend in Washington.

But before he packed, he texted Antoine Scarborough, his research assistant:

Abraham Lincoln, a lieutenant named Hutchinson in the telegraph office, a corporal named Jeremiah Murphy. That's all I got. See what you can find. We'll talk later.

Two

April 1862

꧁ That night the Negroes sang.

They sang in the churches where they worshipped the white Jesus. They sang in the hammer-nail hovels where they lived. They even sang on Pennsylvania Avenue, where Uncle Abe might hear them in his fancy white house.

From the second-floor windows of the War Department telegraph office, Lieutenant Halsey Hutchinson watched them go by.

They were singing spirituals and minstrel songs and marching songs, too, songs that climbed Jacob's ladder and raised a ruckus and blessed John Brown, whose body by then had been three years a-molderin' in the grave, but whose truth was surely marching on through that warm spring night, because Congress had passed an emancipation act for the District of Columbia. And after five days of rumination, the president had signed the bill, freeing three thousand slaves with the stroke of a pen . . . and the promise of restitution to the District slave owners.

So the Negroes sang.

Halsey Hutchinson did not much care about them. He had joined the army to preserve the Union. But he could not blame them for celebrating.

He even hummed a bit of "John Brown's Body" himself. It was a tune with a stir to it. It made a man want to march. It made him want to sing out from deep in his chest. It had even inspired a Massachusetts lady to write new lyrics that she called a battle hymn. Halsey had read the lyrics in the *Atlantic Monthly,* but he had not yet committed them to memory. It would not have mattered, because he could not sing . . . anymore.

A year earlier, when he gathered with his wine-punching friends in Boston clubs or performed for adoring females in fancy parlors, he could give out with the voice of a baritone angel. And no lieutenant had ever offered a sweeter hymn at Camp Massasoit, where the Twentieth Massachusetts Volunteer Infantry had mustered and trained and worshipped through six weeks of summer Sabbaths. And during those long autumn nights of tenting on the Potomac, his songs had made the waiting easier for any who heard him . . . Billy Yank or Johnny Reb across the river.

Now it was a wonder that he could even talk.

A rebel bullet had struck him in the throat, leaving his voice a graveled whisper, perfectly distinct but no longer loud enough to be heard by men in the midst of battle.

That same bullet had also damaged his resolve. One moment he had been rallying his men at the base of a promontory called Ball's Bluff, the next he was sprawled in the mud with blood gushing from a wound at his collar. By the grace of God, it had been a glancing wound, but a wound nonetheless, as if someone had struck him in the neck with a ball-peen hammer.

He still believed in the sanctity of the Union. But after Ball's Bluff, he had begun to wonder if the Lord believed otherwise. Brave men wasted on a worthless objective, hundreds slaughtered on a Potomac riverbank, half his fine regiment killed, wounded, or captured . . . all because of blundering leaders, bad intelligence, and the belief that nine hundred men could make a riverborne assault with three rowboats and a barge. . . .

Perhaps the Lord had been telling them something at Ball's Bluff. Perhaps the dissolution of the Union was foreordained, so best end the bloodshed quickly.

Halsey drove that thought from his mind whenever it surfaced like a blue-clad body floating in the Potomac. It would never do for a man who now worked in the very brainpan of the war to believe that the war was unwinnable.

Besides, like Bull Run before it, Ball's Bluff had turned out to be no more than a little pantomime before the play, something to amuse the theater patrons as they made their way to their seats. The real show had begun that spring, when General McClellan took the army south to the Virginia Peninsula. And the biggest scene yet had unfolded at a Tennessee crossroads called Shiloh Meeting House, where more Americans had fallen in two days than in all the previous *wars* that Americans had fought.

Halsey brought a hand to the scar at his neck and tried to feel some vibration in his broken voice.

Instead, he felt . . . *something* . . . behind him, a movement, a force, a presence. Without turning, he knew what it was: Abraham Lincoln, on his nightly visit. Then he heard the high, reedy voice and sharp prairie accent:

"That sure is a fine song they're singin'." Lincoln looked down at the Negroes splashing through the pools of gaslight on Pennsylvania Avenue.

Halsey glanced at the clock over the mantel. "It's barely ten, sir. You're out early."

"And *they're* out late." Lincoln kept his eyes on the Negroes below, though he stayed back so they could not see him. "When I signed the District emancipation, I did not rescind the curfew against coloreds on the streets after ten o'clock."

"But some would say that tonight, you've given them reason to break curfew, sir."

"Some would."

From the corner of his eye, Halsey looked up at the president for a clue as to what he was thinking. Of course, no one in Washington looked *down* on Lincoln, not literally anyway. No one was tall enough. And no one ever really knew what he was thinking until he decided to make his thoughts plain.

Halsey admired the face that so many called "homely" or worse. The features had a masculine strength—bushy black brows, a nose as straight-ahead as the point of a plow, neat furrows cut from the nostrils to the beard. And the skin—permanently browned and leathered—gave evidence that the strength was hard earned, honestly come by in a lifetime of frontier laboring and horseback lawyering.

And just then, Lincoln was smiling.

People said that his little half smile seemed to describe a dozen different benevolent emotions at once. But when a man's expression could convey so much, it might also be good for conveying nothing at all. Halsey thought that Lincoln's smile concealed things, too, deep things, mysterious things.

After a moment, Lincoln said, "So, what do we hear from our generals?"

"Dispatches are in the usual place, sir." Halsey gestured to the desk between the windows: a work surface supported by spindly legs on one side, office safe on the other, a superstructure of pigeonholes, shelves, locking drawers . . . the beating heart of the brainpan, if there could be such a thing.

All the dispatches from all the battlefronts passed first through the War Department telegraph office . . . and that desk.

They arrived in cipher on sounding keys that clattered away day and night and even then were setting up a racket in the adjoining room. A key operator translated the dots and dashes into a series of seemingly unrelated words, apparent gibberish. Then he brought them into the cipher room and placed them on the desk by the door. A cipher operator—working from charts, templates, and keywords—made sense of the gibberish. Then he placed the finished message in the top drawer of that desk.

By day, Major Thomas Eckert sat at the desk and ran the office. He cataloged the dispatches, then delivered them to Secretary of War Stanton, whose office adjoined through a screened door on the other side. The irascible and autocratic Stanton would then determine what information he would release to the world and what he would withhold, and since so much of the news was bad, he withheld a great deal. But at night, Eckert and Stanton went home.

Lincoln was usually wide awake and wandering.

He might amble over from the White House at ten or at midnight or in the small hours when the rest of the world was wrapped in sleep. Sometimes he came in shirtsleeves with a gray plaid shawl over his shoulders. Sometimes he wore an old linen duster and floppy felt hat, as if they might disguise Washington's most recognizable figure. But usually he wore his familiar black suit.

If the wires were buzzing, he would raise the gas in the lamp above Eckert's desk, take out a book, and wait. If all was quiet, he would soon be on his way back to the White House. But whenever he finished reading through the messages, he would always say, "So, boys, I'm down to the raisins. Anything else?"

That night, cipher operator David Homer Bates looked up from his desk and said, "I'm working on something from General McClellan, sir, if you'd like to wait."

"Well, I don't feel much like sleepin'—" Lincoln pulled out the chair. "—so cipher on. Maybe it's the casualty numbers."

Earlier dispatches from McClellan had described an attack across a dam on the Warwick River, an attempt to pierce rebel positions before Yorktown, but it seemed that McClellan had lost his nerve once the Vermonters who led the attack gained a toehold. This did not surprise Halsey. Back in October, McClellan had not even bothered himself about the crossing at Ball's Bluff. Maybe it was something about rivers. . . .

But Halsey did not share his thoughts with the president. It was not his place. Instead he busied himself with paperwork at his desk in the corner.

Bates put his head to the work in front of him.

Lincoln took a pencil and small red leather-bound notebook from his pocket and began to write.

Then Bates looked up. "Mr. President, I've been working in this office for the better part of a year, and I'm puzzled about something."

Lincoln said, "What is it?"

"Whenever you read through the telegrams, sir, when you get to the last one, you always say you're 'down to the raisins.' Why is that?"

Lincoln chuckled and cocked his head.

Halsey sensed a story coming on.

"Well, now—" Lincoln tossed the notebook onto the desk, then leaned back in the chair and unfolded those long legs, so that they seemed to travel halfway across the room.

Yes, thought Halsey, another story.

"There was this little girl back in Springfield," Lincoln began. "And it was her birthday. And she ate so much raisin-and-spice cake—the kind with the thick white butter-frostin'—that she looked like a foundered horse, with a belly so full, she could barely move and sickly-white skin the same color as that frostin'. And right after her little friends left, she took to castin' up her accounts."

"You mean she vomited?" asked Halsey.

"Lieutenant, you do make me wonder what my son can be learning at that Harvard College. Castin', pukin', chuckin', tossin' . . . all fine euphemisms for the act of vomiting."

"If my experience with the Harvard punch bowl is any indication, sir, your son will be familiar enough with the act if not with the terminology."

"Well, every boy must learn his lessons," said Lincoln, "though I have to admit that the taste of spirits never held much interest for me."

"But, sir," said Homer Bates, "the raisins?"

"Oh, yes," said Lincoln. "The little girl kept pukin' for so long, her parents thought she might cast up her very own stomach and die right then, right on her birthday. So they sent for the doctor. He came and gave her belly a listen, then he asked to see the last thing she'd tossed. So they brought him the chamber pot. He took one look at the little black bits floatin' in the pot bottom, and said, 'Folks, don't you worry none at all. She'll be better and better soon, 'cause she's down to the raisins.'"

After a moment Bates's moon face brightened and he laughed.

Halsey managed a smile. "'Down to the raisins.' That means her stomach's empty . . . nothing more to see."

"Just that," said Lincoln. "So . . . when I read through the pile to the message I saw on my last visit, I know that I need go no further, because I'm down to the raisins."

"Well, sir—" Bates got up and gave him a sheet of yellow paper. "—have a raisin."

Lincoln laughed, took the dispatch, and read.

First, his little smile fell off. Then his voice lost all good humor. "Three Vermont companies. Thirty-nine casualties. Thirty-nine more sons with grieving mothers. And the position abandoned." He held the dispatch for a moment; then he let it flutter to the floor, as if it were simply too heavy.

Halsey and Bates looked at each other and waited for Lincoln to speak again. It was several minutes.

Then Lincoln raised his head from contemplation of the carpet pattern and said, "Is there anything else?"

Bates whispered, "Not for a while, sir."

Lincoln stood. "Then I'm off to bed."

Halsey got up and followed Lincoln to the door. "Mr. President, wait."

Lincoln stopped. "What else, Lieutenant?"

"I'm supposed to see you downstairs and delegate an escort."

Lincoln stepped into the hallway. "I'll find my own way out."

"But, sir"—Halsey hurried after him—"Secretary Stanton insists."

Gas lamps lit their way to the top of the stairs, to the landing at the duty desk, and down to the first floor. The gas was always burning in the War Department.

Lincoln bounded down, two steps at a time, and his voice echoed with annoyance: "Lieutenant, I walk over here every night by myself. Most nights, I carry a cane to fend off the shadows. Mrs. Lincoln feels better if I do—"

"She's right, sir," said Halsey. "There are people abroad who . . . who . . ." Halsey did not want to state the obvious.

So Lincoln stated it for him: "Would do me harm?"

"Well, yes, sir."

Lincoln turned for the east exit. He was moving quickly, as if running away from the bad news that always seemed to be arriving on the wires.

At the exit, two soldiers stood guard, two who had been wounded badly enough that door duty in the capital was the best service they could render. One snapped to attention. The other, whose left sleeve was pinned at the elbow, opened the door.

Lincoln stopped on the threshold and looked out at the White House, glimmering beyond the trees. "If a man is determined to bring me down between here and my front door, Lieutenant, it will be impossible to protect me."

"It's still our job, sir," said Halsey.

"So it is." Lincoln seemed to soften. "So it is. And we wouldn't want the secretary angry." Lincoln looked at Halsey and the two soldiers. "He'd have you all shot if he found out I was walking home alone."

"You know him better than I, sir," said Halsey.

Lincoln pointed to Halsey's armpit. "Is that one of those newfangled shoulder holsters under your coat? The kind with the spring-loaded clip?"

"Yes, sir." Since military officers attached to the civilian telegraph office did not wear their uniforms, Halsey wore a Brooks Brothers tweed suit. He lifted a lapel to reveal holster and pistol. "Adams thirty-one-caliber, double action."

"So," said Lincoln, "if we're attacked between here and my front door, we'll have no worries."

"No, sir." Halsey did not add that he was a dead shot, though he was.

"Then lead on," said Lincoln.

And together they stepped into the darkness, following a path through the trees to the crescent-shaped carriage drive. Lincoln moved quickly on those long legs. Halsey hurried to keep up.

"So tell me, Lieutenant," said Lincoln as they went, "did you know my son?"

"No, sir. I was in the Law School. He was a freshman, but I noticed him on occasion in the Yard. He became something of a celebrity at election time, as you can imagine."

"I can," said Lincoln a bit ruefully. "So did I."

Gas lanterns illuminated the great portico of the Executive Mansion. A light burned in the bedroom of Lincoln's secretaries, Nicolay and Hay, another in Mrs. Lincoln's room.

"I've heard," said the president, "that I did not win a straw poll at Harvard."

"You've heard correctly, sir."

"Do you think the young men were expressing their parents' opinions?"

"Well, the Hutchinsons of Massachusetts are in textiles, sir, so—"

"So you voted for cheap cotton?"

Halsey sensed movement out on Pennsylvania Avenue. Someone was watching them from the shadows. He stopped and put his hand inside his coat.

But a voice from the street, a Negro voice in timbre and tone, cried out: "God Bless you, Mr. President."

Lincoln raised his hand in a little wave and went on up the flagstone walk.

The shadow watched a moment longer, then moved away.

Halsey watched the shadow a moment longer, then hurried after the president.

And Lincoln said, "You haven't answered my question, Lieutenant. How did you vote in Harvard's straw poll?"

"Well, sir—" Halsey decided right there that he would not be intimidated by any man. "—I'm old enough to vote legally."

"And—"

"I voted for Senator Douglas, sir."

"So, you and your family are not Abolitionist, then?"

Halsey said, "Massachusetts is the seat of abolition, but my father and uncle—"

"Your uncle? Hutchinson of American Telegraph? You thank him for your new position in the War Department, don't you?"

"After Ball's Bluff, my uncle told Secretary Stanton that I had worked for him in Boston. I had learned the telegraph business from the bottom up, so I knew about wires and batteries and resonators and such, so I still had much to offer, despite my wound."

Lincoln stopped and looked Halsey in the eye. "I believe you do, Lieutenant." Then he turned his gaze to the front of the mansion. "I believe all you wounded boys still have much to offer, and all the boys who've died had much to offer, too, even . . . even my own boy."

The president's middle son, twelve-year-old Willie, had been carried off by fever in early March. His youngest, Tad, had barely survived. His wife was said to have gone insane with grief. But Lincoln had soldiered on, through crisis after crisis. . . . How to persuade McClellan to use the mighty army that he had built? How to make sense of the slaughter at Shiloh? How to justify the freeing of the District slaves?

Lincoln stared up at the great portico, as if he expected it to fall on his head. Then he said, "I've enjoyed our talk, Lieutenant. I will look forward to seeing more of you on my nightly passages."

And Halsey Hutchinson watched the long black shadow ascend the stairs, push open the unlocked White House door, and step inside.

There, he thought, went the loneliest man in the world.

. . .

Just before dawn, the telegraphs stopped clattering. So Bates and the key operators retired to a basement room where a pot of coffee always boiled.

Alone in the office, Halsey relished the morning quiet, a small reward for passing the night in labor. He signed an order for a new key word to be transmitted to all federal stations, hidden in a message about a requisition of shoes for army mules. He lowered the gas in the ring of lights hanging from the ceiling. Then he gathered up his papers and stepped to Eckert's desk to put them into the assigned pigeonhole.

And that was when he saw it: *the president's notebook.*

Lincoln had tossed it onto the desk when he began the raisin story. It had slid under the pigeonholes, where it lay forgotten as news arrived of McClellan's retreat.

Halsey's first thought was to put it in the dispatch drawer.

But what if the contents were private, so private that the president would not want Major Eckert or Stanton reading it? Perhaps he should examine it, just to be certain.

So he took the book and stepped to the window.

The sun was appearing somewhere over Maryland. The slanting rays etched patterns of light onto the buildings of Pennsylvania Avenue and created long shadows at the feet of passersby—men riding horses, washerwomen carrying mops and pails, drunks staggering home, mattress maids heading for work or few hours of rest on mattresses of their own.

Washington was an early town . . . and a late one.

Halsey flipped to the last pages and saw a date, April 16. *A diary?* He read the entry written in Lincoln's large, well-practiced hand:

Signed this day: emancipation for DC. I have ever desired to see city freed from slavery in some satisfactory way. Only question, expediency: What of border state reaction? Would they fear a similar move and secede? This concern stayed my hand until Sen. Sumner asked if I knew the identity of the largest slave holder in Washington. He said, "It is yourself, sir . . now that the Senate has passed the bill to free the District slaves." So I signed. But . . . is $300 a head sufficient restitution to preserve loyalty of District slaveholders? And what of more general emancipation?

General emancipation? Could the president actually be thinking such thoughts? Opposing slavery was hardly the same as freeing more than four million ignorant Negroes. Of course, the president was talking to himself here, clarifying ideas in his own mind. Halsey thought about closing the book, but he read on:

What of freed Negroes? Black man will never be mental equal of white man, so full citizenship significant problem. Citizenship means suffrage. Black suffrage? Radical Repubs insist it must follow a general emancipation. I will seek another path when this war is over. Whether it lasts three more months or three more years, we will face great challenges in rebuilding trust between the sections, challenges best met by removing the Negroes from the debate. I will seek a solution that benefits all, North and South, black and white: Negro colonization. I support amendment to District emancipation, providing funds for such purpose. But to where? Africa? Central America? Must discuss with their leaders. Immediate general emancipation is a thing I consider but am not ready to do. The real problem with a general emancipation is—

There the writing stopped, at the place where Bates had asked about the raisins.

Again Halsey thought about shoving this diary into one of the locking drawers, but he could not resist turning to the front page.

The first entry was dated March 3, 1861, the eve of Lincoln's inauguration.

Congress proposes Constitutional amend't, stating federal gov't "shall never interfere with the domestic institutions of the states." I am for the old ship and the chart of the old pilots. There is no need for amend't to protect interests of slave owners. It is not now and never will be my intention to interfere with them in their own states, as I'll say t'morrow.

Halsey flipped through a few more pages, read a few more entries. Each one revealed some new bit of the president's thinking about slavery and his attitude toward the Negroes, whose existence in bondage may have been the catalyst for the war but was not, in the eyes of thinking men like himself, the true reason for fighting it.

In an entry for early March 1861, Lincoln jotted down calculations:

$400 per slave x number of slaves in Border States = cost of how many days of war? Compensated emancipation cheaper than fighting.

In April, a week after the war had begun, Lincoln wrote:

Gloom and torment. Await troops, but only Mass. answers call. Do we have any army but what comes from Mass. Where are the rest?

Do they hesitate, thinking this is war to free the Negro? This is not a war to free the Negro. The central idea pervading this struggle is the necessity of proving that popular gov't is not an absurdity. We must settle this question now, whether in a free government the minority may break away whenever they choose. If we fail, it will go far to prove incapability of people to govern themselves.

Halsey heard echoes. . . . Lincoln had said much of this publicly, but not all of it. And though he could appear the gloomiest of men—until he told a story—he could not have wanted Americans to know that their leader had ever been afflicted by "gloom and torment."

Halsey realized that his mouth had gone dry. *Spittin' cotton.* That's what the soldiers called it when a man's tongue clove to the roof of his mouth before battle. But for Halsey it happened as he read the thoughts of the man whose election had *caused* all the battles . . . or so some claimed.

And he decided, right then, that he would not betray those thoughts. Those that were private and unspoken might also be incendiary. Best return them to the president as soon as possible. But when?

Now.

Though Halsey was not supposed to leave his post, he would rather answer questions about a brief absence than about a small leather-bound diary. So he slipped it into his breast pocket, turned, and . . .

. . . bumped into a slope-shouldered man dressed mostly in brown— brown suit, brown vest, brown tie, brown porkpie hat, thick brown beard, stubby brown cigar.

"Leavin' early, Lieutenant?" Even his voice sounded brown, low pitched and dark.

"I'll be back."

"Wouldn't want you sneakin' off before your shift ends, not after stuffin' government property in your pocket."

Halsey looked into the brown eyes beneath the thick brown brow. The color described the man. Halsey hoped the color red did not describe his own face. He said, "Detective Joseph Albert McNealy, you are a suspicious man."

"So there's nothin' in your pocket?"

"What's in my pocket's my own business."

McNealy flashed a smile, tobacco-stain yellow in that nest of brown facial hair. "We live in a city under siege, Lieutenant. There's rebel spies on every corner. There's rebel sympathizers in every family. There's even rebels in this building, I suspect."

"Is that why you're sneaking around at six in the morning?"

There came a commotion in the hall—shuffling feet, snapping heels, muskets presenting, and a single voice rising. It was the sound that always preceded the puffed-up man in the swallowtail coat. Then he appeared:

Secretary of War Edwin Stanton, already in high dudgeon, and the day hadn't even begun yet. He stomped along the hallway, stopped at the cipher room door, and scowled through tiny spectacles at Halsey and the detective. The scowl, the long graying beard, and the shaven upper lip gave him the look of a prophet who believed in a god of vengeance, not of love. "What dispatches have come in overnight?"

Halsey pulled himself to attention: "Three from Tennessee, sir, two from Manassas, and—"

"The Peninsula! What news from the Peninsula? From McClellan?"

"Just a moment, sir." Halsey went to the desk and got the pile of dispatches.

Stanton snatched them and hurried on. "Stay close, Lieutenant. I'll be answering to these presently."

"Yes, sir."

McNealy watched Stanton step into his office; then he said to Halsey, "The secretary cannot abide General McClellan."

Stanton's disembodied voice boomed out, "I also cannot abide War Department detectives wasting time here when the whole city is crawling with no-gooders."

"Yes, sir," answered McNealy, "I'm heading out now, sir." Then he turned back to Halsey and whispered, "The only thing he can abide less is a man who works for him who is *not* working for him. You follow?"

"No."

"A man who may be working for himself. A man who may be pocketing War Department information when everyone's off drinking coffee. Something worth a pretty penny to some rebel spy, maybe."

Halsey reddened now. He could feel it in his cheeks. It wasn't embarrassment but anger. He knew how to draw a perfect five-pointed star with five pistol shots at a hundred paces. He knew what it felt like to take a bullet for his country. He knew what the generals were thinking before the president did. He would not brook the suspicions of this Chicago door-peeper. But as he grabbed McNealy's lapel, he heard Stanton's voice echo down the hallway: "Lieutenant Hutchinson. Come in here!"

McNealy's eyes shifted. "Best see what your boss wants."

Halsey brought his face close to the detective's. "No man questions my integrity."

"Integrity is a young man's luxury, Lieutenant. My job is too important for integrity." McNealy then peeled Halsey's fingers one-by-one from his lapel. "I'll be watching." And one of the most accomplished rebel-catchers in the War Department detective service set out to catch a few more.

II.

It was not until an hour later that Halsey's shift ended and he could hurry down the stairs and step into the sunshine.

Ordinarily he relished April mornings on the Potomac. No New England chill in the air, no east wind puffing the last exhalations of winter off the Atlantic. Here spring days came in gentle and warm and could make a man forget for a few moments the cataclysm engulfing the nation. But not that morning.

Halsey looked around to make sure that McNealy was not watching from behind some pillar or post. Then he took the path through the trees to the White House carriage drive, where he was reminded that one man's cataclysm could be another man's opportunity . . . . . . or another woman's.

They were already lining up, as they did each dawn—office seekers, favor seekers, friends, relatives, relatives of relatives, men bearing letters of introduction, women bearing petitions of mercy, widows, orphans, inventors, scoundrels, scalawags, the sons of scalawags, and the sons of rich men, too—all waiting for nine o'clock, when the White House would officially open and they would crowd in under the portico, into the foyer, up the stairs, and if they were lucky, all the way to the reception room outside the president's office, their petitions in one hand, their business cards in the other, their expectations high that before the day ended, the president himself would summon them to a personal audience and satisfy their petition or solve their problem.

It was said that at the beginning, Lincoln had spent most of his day with these people.

His secretaries had imposed some order on the process, so that he could put in a proper day's work. But he still insisted on seeing them. He called it his "public opinion bath."

Halsey ignored the dirty looks as he bypassed the line and went up to Edward McManus, the doddering majordomo who had been answering the White House door since the days of Andy Jackson.

McManus had a fringe of chin whiskers like the president's and a florid Irish face. "The gates open at nine," he said. "The line forms at the back. Just give me your card and go to the back. The president decides who he sees and who he don't, but the back is where the line forms."

"Official business. Tell the president Lieutenant Halsey Hutchinson requests a moment of his time."

"Well, son, the president's off inspectin' the forts across the river. Won't be back till noon. If you have dispatches, leave them with me."

At noon, Halsey would be escorting a young woman to the Smithsonian. He was not about to miss that. So he considered surrendering the diary to McManus. But he had decided that he would put the president's private thoughts into the president's hands and nowhere else. So, with the diary still in his breast pocket, he turned and headed down the other side of the carriage drive.

He was halfway to Pennsylvania Avenue when he heard his name.

"Halsey! Halsey, old boy! Halsey Hutchinson!" A slender man in his late thirties was hurrying down the walk. He wore a checkered suit, polished brown boots, and a fresh-trimmed Vandyke: John Charles Robey, distant cousin.

Halsey wished that he had kept walking.

"I heard that you'd been wounded, Halz."

"You heard right." Halsey let his voice croak a bit more than usual.

"But you're looking excellent. And still aiding in the war effort, I see."

Halsey started walking again. "And what is it that you're up to?"

"I'm aiding the war effort, too."

"I'll bet you are."

"Once more into the breach, dear friends." Halsey's cousin was fond of quoting Shakespeare in a big honking voice and bad British accent.

The family called him John Charles, to distinguish him from Plain John, another cousin. Plain John owned a newspaper in Pittsfield, Massachusetts, and was a radical Abolitionist, the sort who believed that Lincoln was a malingerer on the question of race. The family believed that John Charles was a malingerer in general, a fast-talking buck-passer whose presence in the patronage line meant that he saw an opportunity for himself, not for the nation.

At least he was no Abolitionist. Those people gave Halsey an itch.

"I've been trying for a week, Halz, but I haven't gotten beyond the first landing. And if what I just heard is true—that the president won't be back till noon—I'm for a leisurely breakfast. Care to join me?"

"Not particularly."

"I'll buy. In exchange, you can offer me a few pointers for when I meet the Original Ape."

"Original Ape?"

"Why, Lincoln, of course. That's what the papers are calling him, even in the North."

"Calling him that won't get you very far in the patronage line." Halsey picked up his pace. "As my father says, he's the only president we've got, so we should speak well of him."

"Your father's a wise man. But I've heard that Lincoln spends a lot of time in the telegraph office. So my favorite cousin must get to speak *to* him, as well as *of* him."

"I speak only when spoken to," answered Halsey.

"When you speak, could you just mention your cousin and his fine shoe factory in Brockton, Massachusetts?"

"Why?"

"Because there are shoe factories all across the goddamn Union, Halz, all vying for government contracts."

They reached Pennsylvania Avenue.

The trees in Lafayette Park were leafing out. Carriages and horses were clattering by. And somewhere in the distance, drums were thrumming. But in Washington, drums were always thrumming. They set up a constant cadence that echoed off the buildings around the park and bounced back to create a counterpoint, so that everyone on the street seemed to be moving to one beat or the other.

Halsey turned east and went with the cadence.

John Charles followed on the counterpoint. "This war is the chance of a lifetime, Halz."

"Tell that to the boys in the lime pits around Shiloh."

"Shiloh? Oh, yes. Terrible thing, that. But . . . but you know what I mean."

"Not really."

"Well, you must hear things."

"Things?"

"Conversation. Talk. The president and the secretary, putting their heads together over some telegram or better yet, some requisition for shoes. That sort of thing."

If you only knew, thought Halsey.

"Or maybe you just hear the president thinking out loud."

If you only knew, thought Halsey again.

"And if you were to tell such as myself what you hear, I might be able to use it to the advantage of the family."

Halsey had to laugh. "You mean to the advantage of yourself, don't you?"

"You know me too well, gentle cuz."

As they passed the State Department, two Negroes approached. The taller one was carrying a shovel. The fatter one had a mule harness over his shoulder. They both looked at Halsey and tipped their hats.

Halsey passed them every morning and always tipped his bowler in return.

His cousin watched and said in amazement, "Halsey, they're niggers."

"A man tips his hat, you tip yours. It's a sign of respect, no matter his color."

John Charles glanced over his shoulder. "Now you've done it. They've stopped. They're watching. Show them respect, the next thing you know, they're following you through the street, looking to cadge coppers or beg some menial job."

Halsey looked back and sure enough, the Negroes had turned. His eyes met theirs, then they went on their way.

John Charles said, "The great thing about this city, gentle cuz, is that the niggers are *expected* to tip their hats and make way on the street. It wouldn't be a bad lesson to teach them in Boston, either."

"I'm no Abolitionist," answered Halsey. "It's just good manners to tip your hat."

"And good sense not to. Those damnable Abolitionists want to turn this into a war to free the nigger. But the nigger isn't the issue. It's saving the Union that matters, saving our businesses."

Halsey had had enough of this.

At the corner of Fifteenth, he stopped. "I am very tired just now, so I don't care about saving the negroes or the Union or you. And I don't want breakfast. I'm going home to sleep. If you follow me or use my name in the presence of Mr. Lincoln, I will shoot you, *gentle cuz*." And to make the point, he flipped open his jacket.

John Charles looked at the pistol. Then he looked at his cousin. Then he took out a calling card and pressed it into his cousin's hand. "You can find me in the lobby of the Willard Hotel every afternoon at four o'clock, along with every other man-on-the-make in Washington. Between eight and midnight I'm at Squeaker McDillon's on Twelfth."

"McDillon's? The gambling hell?"

"I prefer to call it a faro parlor."

"At least you're not dallying with whores."

"In this city, gentle cuz, we're *all* dallying with whores, except some of them wear suits instead of dresses. So"—now he tipped his hat—"excuse me while I dabble."

. . .

Halsey watched John Charles go north; then he went south to the place where Pennsylvania Avenue left the Executive Branch and resumed its diagonal run toward Capitol Hill. And as the panoply opened before him, his thought was always the same: If this was the grandest thoroughfare in Washington, it did not bode well for the republic.

Its width befit a street of high ambition in the capital of an ambitious nation. And it was lined with trees and buildings. And it was angled so as to draw the eye toward that fine distant prospect—the hill atop which sat the national legislature.

But width merely afforded more room for mud to spurt up through cracked cobblestones, for pigs and fowl to run wild, for wagons and omnibuses to break down. It also separated the respectable activities of the north side—hotels, theaters, businesses—from the area called Murder Bay, a triangle of land formed by Pennsylvania on the north, the canal on the south, and Fifteenth Street on the west, and into which were crammed enough saloons, dance halls, gambling hells, and whorehouses to satisfy every corps in the Army of the Potomac, should they all go on leave at once. And the best that could be said of the trees was that when they leafed out, they performed the aesthetic miracle of blocking most of the ramshackle buildings from view.

As for the pillared Capitol, it appeared as if someone had stuck a giant eggbeater in its roof to mix up whatever was inside. Construction of a dome had begun in 1859, but the war had stopped it. Now the crane holding up the cast-iron ribs resembled the beater handle, and the ribs looked like the paddles. But the work had resumed. The president had insisted. He said that finishing the dome would symbolize the continuity of the nation.

In a city of bleak reality, thought Halsey, hopeful symbols had their place.

He took to the north side of the Avenue. It was the "good" side, which meant it would be safer for a man carrying a valuable diary, and it boasted a fine brick sidewalk.

But the peddlers were already crowding it. An organ grinder was playing and his little monkey was dancing. A tonic salesman was hanging a sign on his stand—DR. PHILBERT'S HEALTH JUICE. PERTECTS FROM KOLERA, TYPHOID, AND POXES OF ANY KIND. And the candy vendors and soap sellers were jockeying for the best spots near the entrance to the Willard Hotel, which wrapped around the corner of Fourteenth Street.

Halsey often stopped for breakfast at Willard's buffet and stuffed himself with bacon, poached eggs, and tureens of duck-liver pâté. But not this morning. The importance of what he carried, the responsibility he had impulsively taken onto himself, had also taken his appetite. So he kept on.

And he kept a quick pace, because as the morning crowd grew, the chances of meeting pickpockets grew as well. He held his jacket tight and watched for the reach-and-runners who worked boldly, or the excuse-me-sirs, who operated in tandem, one bumping and apologizing while the other picked, or the lightfoots who came up quietly behind and were gone in an instant.

Around Ninth Street, the crowd thickened with cross traffic and wagons and people laden down by sacks of sundries. The Center Market, a great shed sheltering scores of smaller sheds and stalls, dominated the south side of the Avenue and covered the whole triangular block down to the canal. It was noisy, raucous, and smelly, but the true stink of the city rose from that canal, which ran up from the East Branch of the Potomac, skirted the base of Capitol Hill, then turned to form the northern boundary of the dust pit called, on more optimistic maps, the Mall. The canal had been dug to improve river trade. But once railroad cars replaced canal boats, it became no more than a trench for sewage, garbage, and a few feet of slow-flowing water.

Halsey went with his head on a swivel . . . left, right, center, and back.

He passed Brady's National Photographic Portrait Studio and Art Gallery. He went by Hannassey's Undertaking. Against the doorjamb stood a white pine coffin. Above it a sign: THE DEARLY DEPARTED RENDERED LIFELIKE AFTER DEATH. SHIPMENT ARRANGED TO ALL UNION STATES. STEP INTO OUR BOX AND TEST ITS STURDINESS.

By then, the diary felt like a lead weight in his pocket. He wished that he had left it on Eckert's desk. But he could not go back now. Besides, he was almost home.

For him, as for the other military men who worked in the War Department, home was the National Hotel, at the corner of Sixth. It was one of the finest buildings on the Avenue, red brick, five stories, a shade-giving portico above the sidewalk, and the most modern of conveniences, a telegraph office at the street corner.

Halsey gave another look behind, then crossed Sixth.

And the Negro bootblack named Noah Bone called to him: "Mornin', Mr. Lieutenant Hutchi'son, sir. Glorious mornin', ain't it?"

"Morning, Noah." Halsey hurried by the twin shoeshine chairs.

"Shine, sir?" said Noah.

"Not today." Halsey barely glanced at the Negro, who was somewhere in his forties, with a bald head and a shoeshine-stained apron.

"I think you need a shine, sir. I think you *really* need a shine."

That made Halsey stop.

Noah winked. "I even give it to you for free, sir."

Halsey sensed that something was up, so he climbed into a chair and put his feet on the braces.

Noah took a brush and knocked the mud from around the soles of Halsey's boots. "I just thought you might want to know, they's two men lookin' for you."

"Men?"

"Yes, sir." Noah kept brushing. "One of 'em follow you down the Avenue."

Halsey glanced back along the sidewalk, expecting to see John Charles.

"Don't bother lookin'." Noah kept brushing. "He step in a storefront when you look back, just 'fore you cross Sixth."

"How do you know?"

"Well, this here's my place in the world, sir. I make sure I know what all's happenin' 'round me. I keep my eyes peeled and my ear to the ground. And I know the feller followin' you. He's one of the watchers."

"Watchers?"

"They go about watchin' for deserters and Secesh spies and such."

"I think you mean detectives. What's he look like?"

"Like someone drop him in a manure pile and he come up all brown. All brown all over, 'cept for his itty-bitty white face."

So, thought Halsey, McNealy had decided to tail him.

"Thank you, Noah."

"You treat me good, sir, I treat you good." Noah put down the brush. "Now—"

"You said there were two men?"

"Oh, you like the other gent. He's famous." Noah spread polish on Halsey's boots. "Yes, sir, when Mr. De-tective see you talkin' to this gent, he think better of you."

"When will he see that?"

Without raising his head, Noah said, "In about five second. 'Cause the other gent jess steppin' out the hotel telegraph office."

Halsey recognized the young man coming along the sidewalk. He was slender, well tailored, handsome. He perched his hat just so, at an angle that was not too jaunty, not too dull. His mustache curled symmetrically around the corners of his mouth. And he sauntered toward them with the kind of athletic grace that could not be taught but could certainly be refined.

"Mornin', Mr. Booth, sir," said Noah Bone.

John Wilkes Booth stopped, looked down at the Negro crouched before the white man's boots, and said, "Mornin', boy."

Noah stood up. "This here's the gent I was tellin' you 'bout, sir. This here's Lieutenant Hutchi'son of Boston, Massachusetts."

Booth reached over Noah and offered Halsey his hand. "I asked the boy here if any of my neighbors in the hotel hailed from Boston. He mentioned yourself, sir."

Noah went back to work with a pair of polishing brushes.

Booth said, "I promised him a nice gratuity, should a Boston man direct me to places where young ladies of good character might be found in his city."

"Mr. Booth goin' to Boston to play in a show," said Noah.

Booth said, "Next month, I'll be appearing as Romeo at the Boston Museum."

"There's a performance I'd like to see," said Halsey. "I admired you in *Richard the Third*."

That seemed to please Booth, who climbed up and settled into the vacant shining chair.

Had anyone else done it, Halsey might have pulled the pistol right then to protect the diary. But here sat theatrical royalty. Halsey was so honored that he forgot his other worries, at least for the moment.

Booth said, "I'll be assaying *Richard the Third* in Boston as well."

Halsey had played a few amateur theatricals in college, so a line from *Richard the Third* came quickly to his mind: "Now is the winter of our discontent made glorious summer by this son of—"

Booth raised a finger. "Do not say 'son of Kentucky,' sir, or I shall be forced to look elsewhere for my Boston acquaintances."

"Kentucky?" asked Halsey, momentarily confused.

"This nation lies in perpetual winter," said Booth, "until the next election removes Kentucky from the seat of power."

Now Halsey understood. Lincoln was a son of Kentucky, and as his campaign song went, "the hero of Hoosierdom, too, the pride of those suckers so lucky . . ." For some reason, people from Illinois were called "suckers."

Booth leaned closer. "I would not speak so frankly, but the boy here—"

Halsey noticed Noah shift his eyes upward, though his hands kept working.

"—the boy here tells me that your family is in textiles."

"They are."

"Then I might infer that your family business relies on a supply of cheap cotton?"

"You might."

"And therefore I might infer that you are not Abolitionist?"

"I'm not," said Halsey, and he noticed Noah's eyes shift again.

"Well, then—" Booth stood, pulled out his card, and handed it to Halsey. "—I would be most appreciative of a letter of introduction from you, sir. I shall repay your kindness with the dress circle upon request."

Halsey read: JOHN WILKES BOOTH, NATIONAL HOTEL, WASHINGTON.

"I'm in room two twenty-eight when I'm not traveling the highways and byways, bringing the wonders of the Bard to the masses. I look forward to further conversation, sir, before I leave." And with a half bow, Booth excused himself.

Noah put the two polish brushes into the box under the seat and pulled out the buffing rag. "Mr. Booth, he don't like Abolitionists much."

"Sounds as if he doesn't like the president much, either," said Halsey.

"Well, sir"—Noah started his rag *pop-plopping* on Halsey's boot—"I shine any man's shoes who pay my price, Abolitionist, Union Democrat, or outright Secesh."

"A wise philosophy," answered Halsey.

"So—" Noah stopped shining a moment. "—spit, sir?"

"Spit?"

"Ain't no Abolitionist care if a colored man spit-shine his shoes, and no Secesh want to go around with colored spit on his boot. You say you ain't Abolitionist, and I know you ain't Secesh. Do Union Democrats from Boston mind a little spit shine?"

Halsey said, "I want your best work."

So Noah gave a neat spit to each of Halsey's boots and applied the last buff.

Halsey gave him a whole Yankee dollar as a tip.

Noah grinned and said, "I keep my eye peeled, sir."

III.

Halsey Hutchinson could lie down to sleep and tell himself that he would awaken in two hours, or four, or five, and no matter how exhausted he might be, his eyes would pop open at the appointed moment. So he awoke precisely at noon in the narrow fifth-floor room overlooking the alley behind the hotel. His pistol was in his hand. Lincoln's diary was under his pillow.

He used the chamber pot. Then he pulled his room bell three times.

A colored servant soon appeared with a pitcher of hot water, which he exchanged for the chamber pot, which was emptied down a pipe at the end of the hallway. Where it went, Halsey did not want to know.

As he shaved, Halsey faced two decisions:

Uniform or Brooks Brothers? Carry the diary or hide it in the room?

Uniform. That was easy. Women liked uniforms, and while men in uniform were as common in Washington as men on the make, Halsey knew that he looked good in his.

As for the diary, he would have left it under his pillow, but he suspected that McNealy might be visiting the room while he was out, so he'd keep it with him. It would spoil the line of the uniform, but better that than losing it to a man who sought spies everywhere.

Instead of the diary, Halsey left a little note under the pillow for McNealy.

Then he smoothed his uniform and took his kepi, which bore the "Bugle and 20th" insignia of his old regiment. Inside the crown was a carte de visite in a small tin frame, the image of the young lady of the day.

Her name was Constance Wood, and she had been the prettiest girl at the United States Sanitary Commission levee, held in the Patent Office gallery a few weeks before.

Along with just about every other young officer in attendance, Halsey had been drawn to her. However, he had not pursued her. He had not hovered. He had not hurried to the punch bowl to fetch her a drink. He had not stood waiting for a sign that he might approach and talk to her.

Perhaps that was why *she* had been drawn to *him*.

In truth, he had gone because of another girl.

Samantha Simpson of Wellesley, Massachusetts, served in the Sanitary Commission volunteer office in Boston. She had sent Halsey a note:

> If you appreciate my correspondence, as you did my company when you were convalescing, you will make an appearance at the fundraising levee in Washington, present yourself to the committee organizers, and speak a good word for the Boston volunteers.

And so he had.

And then Miss Wood had approached, saying that the heat of the reception had quite tired her out and she would be ever so thankful for an escort back to the Willard Hotel. He had considered this to be rather forward, especially for a young woman so generously gifted by nature with a long, graceful neck, strawberry blond hair, and a smile that was as much a challenge as an invitation. But he had offered his arm.

And they had walked chastely back to the hotel and chastely bid good-bye.

Since then, he had left his calling card twice at the Willard, and the second time, she had responded with a note:

> Lieut. Hutchinson, I should like to visit the exhibit of photographs of Red Indians at the Smithsonian on April 17. As the Smithsonian Park is an unsavory place for ladies, even in daylight, a gentlemanly escort would be most welcome. I hope that you will be so kind as to meet me in the ladies' parlor at the Willard, at half past twelve. We might dine together and walk from there.

And if Miss Samantha Simpson objected, well, she was in Wellesley, Massachusetts, and Miss Wood was here, and a young man who had faced death on the battlefield came quickly to understand that life's pleasures should be savored whenever the fates presented them.

. . .

If a man wanted to know what the world was thinking—about any-thing—in the uncertain spring of 1862, he could find out at the Willard Hotel . . . because the world went to Willard's.

It was a short walk for the clerks who worked in the Executive Branch, as it was for the office seekers who needed liquid sustenance after a day in the patronage line. It was an even shorter walk for the reporters who merely had to stroll across Fourteenth Street from Newspaper Row. And a quick carriage ride brought senators and congressmen down from the hill, secure in the knowledge that there would always be someone to buy them a meal.

Halsey stopped at the entrance to let his eyes adjust after the noonday sunshine.

His other senses adjusted as well . . . to the smell of cigar smoke, bay rum, and bodies . . . to the sound of raised voices and roaring laughter . . . to the feel of the machine-made carpet crunching with all the dried mud and cigar ash ground into it . . . to the sight of fifty faces, then a hundred, then a hundred more, all turning in his direction, to see if this young uni-form was worthy of a business card or a beer or a bit of blather . . . and to the taste of ambition—metallic, acidic, burning—that flavored the very air.

Several men approached immediately. They came from the right and the left. Flanking parties, followed by a frontal assault, lobbyists on the attack.

That was the new word for them—*lobbyists*—because they spent so much time in the Willard lobby, lurking in the corners, lounging on the circular settee, leaning into conversations, looking for information or in-fluence with any decision maker or power broker who might pass on his way to dinner, drinks, or assignation in an upstairs room.

But they did not care about Halsey. They were not even looking at him.

One of them said, "Congressman Wood! A word, sir. A word if you please."

Another said, "My card, Congressman. Please accept my card, sir!"

"Congressman, did you read my proposal to outfit the New York regi-ments in the uniform of the Fire Zouaves? I can offer a deal on fabric for those baggy red trousers!"

"Not interested. Not interested in any of you."

Halsey turned to see a tall, cadaverous man with long black hair and mustache moving straight toward him.

"Are you Hutchinson?" asked the man.

"Yes, sir."

"Then you're the one I've come to dine with."

"But, sir—"

"No man squires my niece about Washington who hasn't passed muster with me."

And Halsey realized that he should have asked a few more questions about Miss Constance Wood. In Boston, a young man and woman of the same class were formally introduced. Backgrounds were known. Pedigrees were familiar. Families were friends. There was no opportunity for an unpleasant surprise like this because . . .

. . . in addition to being a Democratic congressman from New York's third district, Benjamin Wood owned the *New York Daily News,* the most rabidly anti-Lincoln paper in the North, so rabid that the postal service refused to accept it for mailing. So Wood had shipped his paper on express trains, but government detectives had boarded the trains and confiscated the paper. So Wood had put the paper on hiatus. But he had continued his Congressional attacks on an administration that he said was bent on Abolitionist rule and the destruction of the Constitution. And when he could no longer editorialize in his paper, he had written a melodramatic novel called *Fort Lafayette,* about Secession and Southern honor.

In short, Halsey could not have chosen a worse congressman to dine with. But he did not have time to retreat. He was overwhelmed by a superior enemy, a man who knew how to take a room and hold it.

Wood boomed out, "Are you armed, Lieutenant?"

"Yes, sir."

"Well, then, unless these jackals give us a path, I authorize you to shoot your way to lunch."

Immediately, a sea of broadcloth and facial hair parted before them.

· · ·

In the dining room, a harpist strummed tunes that added a bit of gentility to the din of conversation echoing off the high ceiling. Halsey noticed some heads turn, while many eyes simply shifted. Who was walking in behind the maître d'?

Look and be seen, but look without seeming to. That was the rule of the Willard dining room . . . and eat all you could, because tomorrow, Stonewall Jackson might arrive.

Halsey followed Wood and the maître d' to what must have been Wood's usual table, given Wood's proprietary attitude toward it and the maître d' and the room in general. The table perched on a raised platform, overlooking both the room and the Avenue, so Wood had a fine view of the ladies and gentlemen already seated and those just arriving.

A pitcher of ale appeared on the table.

"We'll take the buffet, Jester," said Wood to the Negro waiter.

"You come on a good day, sir," said Jester. "We got fine fried Chesapeake oysters, and what we call George Washington beef, 'cause it grazed around the Washington Monument, so it's tender and juicy."

Wood watched the waiter go off. Then he turned back to Halsey. "There's a darkie who loves his job and does it well, no matter how many of his brethren are held in chains on the other side of the river. But if Lincoln gets his way, we'll have free darkies swarming around us thicker than blackberries. And that is a thing I mean to stop."

"So I've heard."

"I'll bet you've heard plenty about me in the War Department—"

"How do you know that I work in the War Department?"

"The Confederates may be fighting us, Lieutenant, but we Peace Democrats have plenty of enemies right here in Washington. So we have our spies, as well." Wood raised his mug. "To my beautiful niece."

Halsey answered: "To Constance *Wood*. I should have known."

Wood leaned across the table. "Now, what are your intentions?"

"Intentions?" Halsey knew where that question was aimed, but he would make the congressman clarify . . . and squirm a bit. "Intentions, sir?"

"Toward my niece, of course. Are you a young man of honor or just lookin' for a quick kiss behind some pillar in the Smithsonian?"

In truth, Halsey was hoping for a kiss or two, but he placed his mug on the table with an indignant thunk and said, "I resent that question, sir."

To Halsey's surprise and faint disappointment, Wood smiled, which gave his gaunt face the appearance of a skull. "The answer I was hoping for."

After a moment, Halsey picked up his mug again.

Wood raised his. "I salute your bravery, sir, and your good sense."

"Good sense?"

"Good sense to be here, courting my niece before returning to a desk in the War Department, a far better fate than what awaits your friends in the field."

"I believe I still have much to offer, sir, despite my wound."

"A noble sentiment." Wood pulled a card from his vest pocket and wrote a note on the back, then called the waiter and told him to see that it was delivered to room 444.

Meanwhile, another diner was returning from the buffet, his plate heaped high with fried oysters and steamed greens.

Halsey watched the food go by, and his mouth began to water.

Wood grinned at him. "Hungry, are you?"

"I haven't eaten since last night, so . . . yes, sir."

"Hungry for a lot of things, I'd bet . . . I just sent my niece a note. She'll wait on you at one o'clock in the ladies' parlor. So you have time to calm your hunger for food *and* your hunger for makin' a difference, before you satisfy your . . . *other* . . . hungers."

"How do I make a difference in less than an hour, except to the fried oysters?"

Wood took a swallow of beer. "Are you Abolitionist or Unionist?"

"Unionist," said Halsey, "I believe that the preservation of the Union is our primary goal. But if the abolition of slavery follows—"

"What about reunion without abolition?"

"If that would stop the bloodshed and preserve the Union, absolutely."

"Union without abolition would do just that, *and* save us from Niggerocracy."

"I have not heard that word before, sir."

"You wouldn't among your Republican friends, but . . . have you heard our motto?"

"What's that, sir?"

"'The Constitution as it is, the Union as it was.'" Wood took another sip. "They call us Copperheads in the Republican press. They mean to call us snakes in the grass. But look here—" He pulled out a penny and pointed to the liberty head. "—this is the copperhead we believe in. Liberty. And the sooner we get this war over with, the better for the Constitution, the Union, and liberty, too."

"That's something we can all agree on, sir," said Halsey, maintaining his neutrality.

"You could help to achieve it, and save lives as well, should you offer information that you think pertinent."

"Pertinent?" Halsey looked around to see if anyone in the room was paying particular attention—War Department spies, perhaps. Halsey decided to say nothing more. He had learned in his law classes that sometimes, nothing was the best thing to say.

"Come now, Lieutenant. You must hear things."

And for the second time that morning, Halsey said, "Things?"

"Discussions between the president and Stanton. What are they planning? What provisions of the Constitution will they trample next? How far will Lincoln push for Niggerocracy?" Wood gave a disgusted laugh. "After the bill he signed yesterday, I wouldn't be surprised if he's planning to free every nigger in the country."

And for the third time that morning, Halsey thought, *If you only knew.*

"General emancipation"—Wood shook his head—"the worst disaster that could befall us. If it happens, the South will fight even harder. There'll be slave rebellions, waves of darkies pouring north, hungry, dirty, ignorant. We'll have to start shooting them at some point. The bloodshed will never end."

With each sentence from Wood's mouth, Halsey resolved more firmly to protect himself and the presidential thoughts in his pocket.

Wood said, "If we knew beforehand that Lincoln was planning a general emancipation, we might head it off. Save the nation before it's too late. And you, young man, you see the president almost nightly."

"I speak only when spoken to," said Halsey.

"All the better. Just listen. And should you hear that Lincoln is considering something that would make Abolitionists rejoice, tell your allies . . . political or personal."

"Personal?"

Congressman Wood drilled his dark gaze into Halsey. "Such a service would put you in good with not one but *two* proud uncles of Miss

Constance—myself and my brother, Fernando, formerly the mayor of New York. And certain female favors might follow."

So Benjamin Wood was not above using his niece. Halsey remembered his cousin's words about dallying with Washington whores. Some wore dresses. Some were congressmen.

And what would Halsey say to this . . . *use* . . . of a young lady's charms?

What he said was that he could not wait another moment for a plate of fried oysters. Then he got up and headed for the buffet table.

.   .   .

Once Halsey had been seen in public with the uncle, he might as well enjoy his time with the political streetwalker. So he escorted Miss Constance Wood to the Smithsonian. He was, however, the perfect gentleman. And she appeared the perfect lady.

She admitted that she had sought him out at the levee because of his position in the War Department. But she added that she admired his bravery at Ball's Bluff.

Her honesty disarmed him . . . her flattery, too . . . not to mention the aroma of her dusting powder.

And he told himself that if he had to be seen in public with a Peace Democrat's niece, there was none in Washington he would choose over her.

They walked down Tenth Street toward Smithsonian Park, stopped on the cast-iron footbridge across the City Canal and looked east, then west, first at the skeletal dome of the Capitol, then at the stub of the Washington Monument, half built and topped with an awning.

Miss Wood called it, "A city as unfinished as the nation itself."

Halsey said, "And so it will remain, until the question of Union is settled."

"Union," she asked with a tease in her voice, "or slavery?"

But they did not stay to debate. The stink from the canal was too strong.

As they entered the circle of woods around the Smithsonian Castle, Halsey put his right hand on his holster and she clutched his left arm. Three thuggish-looking men lounging against a tree trunk gave them the once-over. But they were too lazy for trouble in broad daylight . . . or perhaps too intimidated when Halsey unsnapped the holster flap.

Constance said how happy she was that such a resolute young man would squire her. And they passed from the bright sunshine into the cool shadows of the red sandstone castle, a towered fortress built, it would seem, to protect knowledge from the vandals of ignorance. And since Halsey had toured Europe and studied the great buildings, he could throw around architectural terms like "Gothic" and "crenellation" and "keystone" to impress her.

They started in the Great Hall, where they saw the skeleton of the *Megatherium*, a giant sloth long extinct. Then they went into the West Range, the magnificent pillared passage connecting the central building with the library. There, hundreds of Plains Indians stared at them from walls and display cases, frozen forever in chemically rendered shadow and light, bronze-colored men and women who, said Constance, "will soon be pushed aside to accommodate the march of a great nation."

"Not so great," Halsey said, "until our immediate issues are settled."

"Resolute," she whispered, "and well spoken, too. A man to make a girl swoon."

He felt the excitement tighten his chest . . . and other parts. He was fit, firm jawed, and went with a seriousness of purpose that men seemed to admire. He also wore a mustache and chin strap that some said made him look like General McClellan himself. But no young woman, not even Miss Samantha Simpson of Wellesley, Massachusetts, had ever suggested that he made her swoon.

He looked up the gallery and down, and it seemed that they were alone with the unblinking Indians. So he determined to extend her swoon. He took her hand and led her behind a pillar.

She giggled and said, "Why, Lieutenant Hutchinson, whatever are you doing?"

He said, "You know right well."

And she did. She raised her face to his and closed her eyes.

He brought his mouth to hers in an exquisite kiss.

And there came the expected responses . . . the deep breaths, the deeper breaths, the momentary pauses, the meeting gazes, the touching hands, the twining hands, the roving hands . . . hers to his collar, to his neck, to the buttons across the front of his uniform . . . his along her smooth uncorseted back and down to the hooped crinolines of her skirt, protection for her and for him, too, since her skirt saved her from feeling the most obvious of his responses.

So he was shocked and embarrassed when she whispered, "What's this hard thing spoiling the line of your uniform?"

Then he realized that she was feeling the diary in his breast pocket.

As he told her it was his daybook, she slid her hand so that somehow the book lifted from the inner pocket, and he felt it slip across the front of his uniform, out between the single row of buttons, and then, to his shock, it flopped onto the floor.

She looked down. "Your daybook?" She leaned closer, squinting in the half light behind the pillar. "But a name is written there, on the end-paper. It says, 'A. Lincoln.'"

Halsey snatched up the book, shoved it back into his inner pocket.

She whispered, "That looked like Lincoln's very own hand."

"I admire the man. I asked him for his signature."

Her eyes narrowed. He expected another question about the diary. Instead she said, "You *admire* the man? Is that what you told my uncle?"

"No. I didn't think that was something your uncle wanted to hear."

"But you said what you had to in order to spend time with me?"

"Guilty as charged."

"Well"—her smile invited another kiss—"that's what *I* wanted to hear."

So he kissed her, first on the lips, then on the cheek, and then, with an exquisite inhalation of her scent, on the side of her neck.

And she whispered, "Write today's events in your daybook, sir, in red letters."

Just then, there was a commotion at the end of the gallery. A group of officers and their wives was arriving with Dr. Henry himself, director of the Smithsonian.

The two young people scurried off.

. . .

Return the diary. Return the diary. Return the diary.

That became Halsey's only thought after he had escorted Constance back to the Willard. The sooner the diary was out of his possession, the better.

So he hurried up Fifteenth Street, along the pillared side of the Treasury Building and reached the Pennsylvania Avenue corner just as an open carriage came rattling along.

It carried the president in his stovepipe and a tiny woman in a black dress, black bonnet, and black veil.

Mary Todd Lincoln turned her face toward him. And Halsey saw a visage of inexpressible sorrow, a mother who had lost a child just six weeks earlier.

Before that awful event, an afternoon carriage ride had been part of the daily routine for the Lincolns, a small escape from the White House. If this was her first ride since then, Halsey could not intrude. So he did not call out.

The little woman turned away. The president whispered something in her ear. The carriage rolled north onto New York Avenue.

Halsey stood there a moment, wondering what to do. An appearance in the War Department, four hours before his shift began, would arouse far too much suspicion. So he returned to the National Hotel.

. . .

It had been a good day, all things considered. He had eaten well at the Willard. He had enjoyed a kiss from a young woman who had been smiling in his daydreams for weeks. And he had kept the diary safe, if not entirely secret. All that remained before he returned to the War Department was a bit more sleep.

But the note under his pillow—*Look elsewhere for what you seek*—had been replaced with this:

Today, the president told Major Eckert that he had lost his daybook, with notes and addresses. He believed that he left it in the telegraph office. Is that what you were stuffing into your pocket this morning?

Halsey felt his mouth go dry again. McNealy had been there. McNealy was on to him.

He poured himself a glass of water and took a swallow. He would have to think. But he needed a bit more sleep to think clearly. So he put the diary under the pillow. Then he stripped off his uniform and opened the wardrobe.

And a hand burst through the hanging suits and shirts. The hand held a pistol. The pistol pressed against Halsey's forehead.

Then a face appeared from the folds of fabric within the wardrobe. Halsey could not make out features, except for a bushy black beard. "Hands up, gentle cuz."

Before Halsey could react, something crashed down on the back of his head. . . .

. . .

When he awoke, the room was dark. He had a lump the size of a grape-shot on his skull. He staggered to his feet and grabbed for his watch. *Gone.*

He reached for his pistol. *Gone.*

For his wallet. *Gone.*

He stumbled over to the bed, took a deep breath, and reached under the pillow for the diary. *Gone.*

He perched on the edge of the bed and put his throbbing head in his hands. He tried not to vomit as he remembered the words "gentle cuz."

That son of a bitch.

He threw on his civilian suit. He reached under the wardrobe, where he had taped a second Adams pistol. His father had given him a matched pair as a gift. He holstered it and left.

At the hotel telegraph office, he wired his father:

NEED FUNDS. SEND DRAFT AUTHORIZATION, HH.

His father would not question. Since Halsey's return from Ball's Bluff, the elder Hutchinson had grown warmer, more paternal, more will-ing to see to the needs of a young man who had demonstrated both cour-age and responsibility. Halsey lived frugally and still had some money in a Washington bank, but this robbery had severely depleted him.

Then he hurried to the Willard, cursing his sense of responsibility as he went. He had taken the diary because he thought that protecting it was the right thing to do. Now, he had lost it, with what consequences for Lincoln and the Union, he could not imagine.

He had half an hour to find his stupid cousin, confront him, and get on to work. He could not report late to the War Department. Major Eckert insisted on punctuality. And Halsey had always been punctual. If he reported late, suspicions would rise.

At the Willard, he passed quickly through the lobby bar but did not see John Charles. So he followed the sound of the harp to the dining room and peered in.

Jester the waiter was approaching with a tray of dirty dishes. "Evenin', sir. Mr. Congressman Wood ain't here if that's who you lookin' for."

"I'm looking for a tall man in a checkered suit. Fond of quoting Shakespeare and acting like he's British."

"I think I know who you speakin' of, sir, but I ain't seen him." Then Jester scurried on to the kitchen.

Halsey took the stairs three flights to his cousin's room and knocked. No answer. So he tried the door, and it swung slowly open.

He peered into the darkened room. It was similar to his own in the National: long and narrow, a single window, bed to the left, wardrobe against the wall to the right.

It took a moment for his eyes to adjust to the faint light. Then Halsey noticed that the wardrobe was open. But he was puzzled. There seemed to be a dark mass hanging from the door.

He stepped in, stepped closer to the mass, and felt his insides wither.

The mass had a head . . . and a body.

Halsey pulled out a box of matches and struck one.

And though he had seen many horrors at Ball's Bluff, what he saw in the match light sickened him. The head had a face, but just barely. The face had eyes, but just barely. The eyes had been pounded until they resembled large, ripe, purple grapes. Blood dripped in long saliva strings from the spaces where the teeth had been. It ran down the front of the waistcoat, down along the trousers, down to the tops of the expensive boots.

Halsey touched the hand, then brought his ear to the bloody mouth. The hand was ice, and the mouth offered not a whisper of breath. The belt around the neck suspended the body and cut so deep into the flesh that blood was seeping through the notches.

Halsey felt the fried oysters rising in his throat. He backed out into the hallway. He closed the door. He looked up and down and saw no one.

He heard in the distance the whooshing and snorting of the steam elevator. He took the stairs instead.

.   .   .

That night, the soldiers defied their curfew and sang their songs of joy . . . or of drunkenness . . . or of whore-sated debauchery. . . .

They were passing the windows of the War Department, moving west, toward the camps by the river. They were singing the new lyrics to "John Brown's Body."

Halsey wondered briefly if he could give out with a "Glory hallelujah!" But he had other things to worry about. Then he sensed movement.

"More singin'," said Lincoln.

Halsey glanced at the clock: 1 A.M. "You're up late, sir."

"Up late . . . puzzlin', frettin'."

Bates had gone off to the privy, so the president and Halsey were alone.

Lincoln said, "Did you happen to find a daybook on the major's desk last night?"

Halsey had turned over in his head what he would say to that. It might be better for the president to think that he had lost the book on the White House grounds. It might afford him a bit more peace of mind than the truth: that it had been stolen by men who were probably looking for other things. And more important, the lie might give Halsey the time to find it.

So he lied. And he hoped that his face did not redden.

"Well," said Lincoln, "I've thought long and hard about where I might have left it and I have to say, I'm down to the raisins."

THREE

Saturday Morning

Evangeline wanted to read her book: *Reveille in Washington*, the 1942 Pulitzer Prize winner by Margaret Leech, about a city that was almost always in peril between 1861 and 1865.

But her new lobbyist friend had followed her onto the train and hadn't stopped talking yet.

Evangeline took the window seat and pulled out her book. Kathi Morganti dropped her laptop bag on the aisle seat and stowed her things.

Evangeline hoped that any woman in a pinstripe suit and pageboy, riding the power corridor on a Saturday morning, would have better things to do than chitchat. But Kathi sat down and said, "You know my mother wanted something distinctive, so she named me Kathi with an *i*. But there's nothing more distinctive than 'Evangeline.'"

"Thanks." Evangeline opened the book to the part about the D.C. Emancipation. The reaction of the Washington Board of Aldermen had amazed her. She had even underlined it: "We urge Congress to offer safeguards against turning this city into an asylum for free Negroes, a population undesirable in every American community."

For Evangeline, educating herself about the Civil War had also been an education in the history of American racism.

But Kathi kept talking. "What do they call you for short?"

"They don't."

Kathi raised a brow, as if to say, *Oh, a snob who prefers to be left alone.*

Evangeline didn't want her thinking that, at least not the snob part. She was going to be sitting next to this woman for three hours. Best keep it friendly. So she added. "Ever since I was a girl, people have tried to call me Eve, Evie, Vange, Vangie, Angie—"

"I like Evie." Kathi warmed up again.

"—but it's always been Evangeline. My mother liked the poem by Longfellow. 'This is the forest primeval.' And so on."

"You don't hear that name too often, 'Evangeline.' It's very nineteenth century. Perfect name for somebody doing a series on the Civil War."

And though she didn't want to keep talking, Evangeline had to ask, "How did you hear about the series? Press release? E-mail blast? Tweet? What?"

Kathi leaned closer. "I'm a lobbyist at Hamill and Associates. We work on tax policy, health care, energy issues . . . and we do a lot of work for nonprofits, like museums, colleges, historical organizations. So I keep my ear to the ground, which means that every History Network press release shows up on my computer."

Just then, a conductor stepped into the front and announced, "This is the quiet car! No cell phones, no music, and no loud conversations. Tickets, please!"

Kathi said, "We'd better shut up."

Thank God, thought Evangeline.

"But let me buy you coffee once we leave Philly," said Kathi.

. . .

An hour or so later, they were sitting in the café car, drinking Green Mountain, the Amtrak house brand. Evangeline was having a blueberry muffin, Kathi a cheese Danish. The morning sunlight was streaming in the east windows, flickering and strobing as the train passed trees, telegraph poles, and bridge abutments. So they'd both put on their sunglasses. Evangeline wore wraparound Ray-Bans. Kathi wore Prada. Evangeline's did the job. Kathi's did, too, and announced that she could afford Prada.

And she could. When she wasn't looking, Evangeline had Googled her and learned that Hamill and Associates had billings in excess of $25 million a year.

The founder, Suzanne Hamill, had been a two-term congresswoman from Maryland whose legislative specialty had been tax policy. The other partners came from power centers all around the Beltway. Kathi had begun as a staffer for a New York congressman on the House Appropriations Committee.

Kathi took a bite of Danish. "You are one of my heroines."

"Heroines? Me? Why?"

"The way you handled your wedding."

Evangeline stared through her sunglasses. First the scene in the Amtrak lounge, then the chitchat about her TV show . . . now the wedding that wasn't. She was starting to feel a little creeped out. Her wedding—or lack of it—was not fodder for her friends and certainly not for strangers. "How do you know about that?"

Kathi said, "Well, there was a lot on the Boston gossip pages, you know."

"Do I ever."

"And once your TV project was on our radar, any reference to you popped up—"

"With little notes, I imagine—" Evangeline took a sip of coffee. "—like, 'Oh, hey, here's how to do a wedding when you've decided you don't want to get married.'"

"I have two wonderful kids." Kathi tapped a button on her iPad and a pair of smiling little boys popped up on the screen.

"Very nice," said Evangeline.

"But—" Kathi slipped off the sunglasses to show her sincerity, and the flickering light also showed the mid-forties crow's-feet. "—somewhere between the time the invitations go out and the vows are taken, a lot of girls figure out that they're making a big mistake, and—"

"That's not quite how it happened with Peter and me."

"Peter Fallon. The antiquarian, right?"

"You know about him, too?"

Kathi put on the sunglasses again. "As I said, our firm represents a lot of institutions. Colleges seeking funds will try to establish the importance of a new building by putting something important into it, like a Shakespeare folio or a copy of the Emancipation Proclamation, and your former boyfriend—"

"Current boyfriend."

"Oh, you stayed friends," said Kathi. "That's nice."

Evangeline just stared and let this Kathi Morganti keep talking:

"Sometimes Peter Fallon may compete with one of our clients. Sometimes he collaborates. So he pops up in our research briefings, too. Some coincidence."

Was it? Evangeline was beginning to wonder. She said, "You're very thorough."

"It's part of the job," said Kathi. "Lobbying is all about connections, about knowing the right people, and if you don't know them, knowing the right people to tell you who the right people are. Your boyfriend is one of the right people's right people."

"I'm sure he'll be thrilled to know that."

"I mean it, sincerely, and in this business, being sincere is almost as good as knowing the right people."

"Sincere . . . I'll drink to that." Evangeline brought her cup to her lips just as a man entered the car and walked past them. She noticed him because everything about him was designed to impress: ramrod posture, silver hair pushed straight back, porcelain white skin, white shirt, black suit, silver and black tie, a half-smile that proclaimed confidence rather than happiness.

When he ordered coffee, the deep voice gave him away: New York Democratic Congressman Max Milbury. He had been representing an upstate district for years and was facing his first November challenge in a decade.

Evangeline turned back to Kathi. "Hey, that's—"

Kathi was shoving the last of her Danish into her mouth. "Time to get back."

But before they could clear out, Milbury was standing over them with a steaming cup of coffee in his hand.

"Ms. Morganti," he said, "I hope you haven't followed me onto the train."

"You flatter yourself, Congressman."

He looked down from under those gray eyebrows. "Usually it's the lobbyists doing the flattering."

Kathi Morganti smiled, a tight rictus that said a lot without saying a word. Evangeline had seen that smile on a lot of female faces in the business world. The woman who did not want to cause controversy, or make a scene, or destroy an opportunity in the presence of an obnoxious male colleague often . . . simply . . . smiled.

We both know you're an asshole, but I'm smiling. I'd rather stick pins in my eyes than talk to you, but I'm smiling. Nothing you say will change my mind about you, but I'm smiling.

The train rocked slightly, causing the coffee in the congressman's cup to slosh. Most people put lids on their cups. This looked to Evangeline like a liquid threat.

"Shouldn't you be spending the weekend kissing babies in Albany?" said Kathi. "Considering the polls?"

"I never trust the polls." Milbury could give a shit-eating grin as good as he got. "In that respect, polls are like lobbyists."

"Lobbyists write half our legislation, Congressman."

"That's why I'm headed to Washington. Big hearings this week on tax policy. I'm introducing an important bill, something truly earthshaking. I want to be there to control the spin once the lobbyists start whining." Then he looked at Evangeline. "And I like to be in Washington for the start of the fall session, no matter what's happening in the district, Ms. . . ."

"Carrington, Evangeline Carrington."

The congressman's eyes brightened beneath groomed brows. "The travel writer?"

And for the second time that morning, Evangeline got a nice little ego-boost.

"I enjoy your columns," said Milbury. "I travel a bit myself, being on the House Committee on Natural Resources. We have oversight for the National Parks."

Evangeline said, "I'm planning to visit a few."

"So I've heard."

Evangeline looked at Kathi. "Does everyone know my business on this train?"

"When it comes to filming at NPS sites," said the congressman, "I make it my business to know, especially the battlefields. I have an affinity for battlefields."

"Like the one you're on now," cracked Kathi, "right in your own district."

He ignored that and gave Evangeline his card. "I'm at your service."

As she took it, she noticed one of the other passengers, a bearded guy wearing a blue baseball cap with a blue patch and white star insignia on the crown. He was sitting at a table on the other side of the car and scrolling through the messages on his iPhone.

And . . . did he just take a picture of them? Yes. Evangeline gave him a glare.

Milbury turned to see what she was looking at. So the guy raised his iPhone, and this time he was blatant about it. *Click. Click.*

"I hope you don't mind, sir." The guy stood and offered his hand. "I guess I'm excited to see a real congressman, especially one I always vote for."

"Not at all," said the congressman in a big voice with a big grin, as if he could sense that a lot of people in the club car were now checking him out and perhaps recognizing a powerful New York Democrat.

The man with the camera said, "I teach high school history and this is just a great treat. I'd love to show my kids that congresspeople are just ordinary folks."

Kathi Morganti said, "Yeah, Congressman. Show him how ordinary you are."

Max Milbury stepped back and said, "If you promise to e-mail me the photos, I'll pose with the host of a new History Network series, and with one of my favorite Washington players."

The man said, "Oh, this is wonderful. Thanks, Mr. Congressman." *Click. Click.*

Milbury said, "Great. Remember to e-mail my office. And what's your name?"

"Steve. Steve Burke."

"Well, thank you, Steve Burke." The congressman shook his hand.

"Thank *you,* Congressman." The man grabbed his coffee and left the car.

Then Milbury swung back to Evangeline. "Always nice to meet the people. And may I say, Ms. Carrington . . . you have some fine representation. We may have our disagreements, but Ms. Morganti's firm has my utmost respect."

Evangeline sensed the atmosphere changing. In Washington—or on the train to it—a little schmoozing made everyone friends again.

"Thank you," said Evangeline, "but I'm not in business with Ms. Morganti."

"No," said Kathi, "this meeting is entirely coincidental."

"Kathi, you never do anything by coincidence." Milbury winked at Evangeline. "She may say she's not doing business with you, but she's always doing business."

"That's me," said Kathi. "Just a lonely wanderer on the Northeast power corridor, another common nightwalker on K Street—" Kathi glanced at Evangeline. "—where the lobbying firms are."

"Common nightwalker," said Milbury. "Interesting choice of words. Will I see you tonight?"

"You might." Kathi batted her eyes, as if she were flirting.

"I look forward to it." And Milbury excused himself.

Then Evangeline said to Kathi, "Did he wink at me? I hate a man winking at me."

"He does a lot of things people hate, starting with his tax policies." Kathi looked around at the people still casting sidelong glances at them, then whispered, "One of our clients is supporting a Republican lawyer who may just beat him in November."

"A Tea Party challenge?"

"More like a libertarian."

"A libertarian? With a lobbyist?" said Evangeline.

"They don't believe in government," said Kathi, "until they need something. So they need lobbyists ready to argue their case in Washington, just like everybody else."

They finished their coffee and went back to the quiet car.

The stop in Philadelphia had opened up three seats, and Kathi admitted that she had to prepare for an afternoon meeting, even though it was a Saturday. So they exchanged business cards and agreed to talk again.

Evangeline figured that was the last she would see of Kathi Morganti, the congressman, and the bearded man named Steve Burke.

.   .   .

Union Station greeted travelers the right way, thought Evangeline, with a massive barrel-vaulted ceiling and hundreds of pounds of gold leaf decorating thousands of medallions, all brilliantly restored and gleaming.

Welcome to the national capital, a city of power, wealth, and public drama . . . but mostly power.

By the information desk, a young woman in blue jeans and T-shirt was waving: Abigail Lynne Simon, the producer of *History Travels*.

She was in her thirties, slender verging on skinny, with the driven look that all young producers had . . . driven because of their bosses and driven because of their ambition to be bosses. The money in television— network, affiliate, or cable—was concentrated at the top. Smart young people like Abigail had to work hard and hope for a break.

After some "how was your trip" chitchat, Abigail got to business. "We're scheduled in Ford's Theatre this afternoon. Tomorrow, we shoot at the Lincoln Memorial. We'll start early, catch the sun hitting Abe's face, grab some B-roll. Or we may change plans and drive to Antietam tomorrow, to catch some of the anniversary events. . . ."

The production van was waiting just beyond the arched doorways. The Capitol dome gleamed through trees. The traffic swirled on Massachusetts Avenue. It was hot, and the forecast promised more heat and humidity. Typical late summer on the Potomac.

As Evangeline climbed into the van, she noticed her coffee companions: the congressman was meeting a black Chevy Tahoe; Kathi Morganti was hailing a cab; and history teacher Steve Burke was jumping into a black Chrysler 200.

Abigail introduced the girl behind the wheel: Mary Knapik, PA, which stood for production assistant, which stood for van driver, coffee-brewer, cable puller, anything-er . . . the bottom of the filmmaking food chain. She was younger than Abigail, but wore the same jeans-and-T-shirt uniform. She said, "Willard Hotel, right?"

"Yes, on the site of the original," said Evangeline. "I want to feel the ghosts."

Washington had two styles of monumental architecture: Greco-Roman pillared power and fancy French grandeur. The 1904 Willard was beaux arts, a turreted French classic on the corner of Fourteenth and Pennsylvania, two blocks east of the White House.

The lobby had so much marble, it looked like the Vatican Library . . . marble pillars, marble floors, marble concierge desk, and Peacock Alley, the long marbled, palm-lined hallway that led through the hotel to an exit on F Street.

Evangeline stopped to admire it all, glanced at the guy smiling up at her from a lobby chair, looked again, and said, "You?"

"A pleasure to see you, Miss Carrington." Peter Fallon put down his copy of *Washingtonian,* got up, and came toward her.

She said, "This better be good."

. . .

They knew her at the Willard and offered to comp her, but she never took freebies. So they gave her a nice suite with a view of the Federal Triangle: all those big, blocky buildings housing the ICC, the DOC, the IRS, the FTC, the EPA, and a lot of other letters from federal city alphabet.

She tipped the bellman, then turned to Peter. "What are you doing here?"

"Do you realize we haven't been alone in a hotel room since the wedding that wasn't?"

She took off her jacket and threw it on a chair. "How did you get here and why?"

"I flew down." Peter dropped his shoulder bag and took off his blazer. "Grabbed a flight this morning to Reagan. Just made it."

"That's the 'how.' And the 'why'?"

"We have a lunch date." He opened the wrapping around the complimentary fruit basket on the coffee table and poked through it.

"We?"

"We're meeting Diana Wilmington at the Eastern Market."

"What's this about? And stop touching the fruit."

He grabbed a sprig of grapes. "The Lincoln letter was bought at the flea market there—"

"Flea market? You came all the way down here to go to a flea market?"

He popped a few grapes in his mouth. "Diana sounded worried about the hacking business. The man who brought her the Lincoln letter was supposed to contact her, but he seems to have gone underground."

"Figuratively?"

"Let's hope so." He held the sprig in front of her. "Grapes?"

"Oh, Peter—" She shook her head and stalked to the window. "—no!"

"What? You love grapes."

"*No* to all of this. I do *not* have the time for this."

"C'mon. You don't start filming till—"

"I'm heading in a new direction—" She snatched the sprig and pulled off a grape and popped it in her mouth. "—and you're just trying to pull me back."

"But you have to admit it. When we go after something, we always grow closer."

"I thought we *were* close." She ate another grape and looked out at the low-slung city that, for all its pretensions, had a human scale, because nothing could rise higher than the Capitol dome. "I thought we understood each other. I thought we had an arrangement."

He put his hands on her arms. "I can live with the arrangement . . . me in Boston, you in New York, but I need my sidekick when I'm—"

"Sidekick?" She handed him the sprig. One little raisin-sized grape remained.

"Er"—he dropped the sprig in the trash—"how about 'partner'?"

She looked out the window again.

He massaged her shoulders. "I need your—"

"Women's intuition?" She was trying to resist his touch, but she was always more susceptible in a hotel room. Something romantic about private moments in new places, something exciting, something that promised more than just sex, but *drama* . . . and sex.

He whispered, "I was going to call it your instinctive yet analytical intelligence, but—" He felt his iPhone vibrate in his pocket. He took his hands away.

She turned. "What now?"

He was reading the phone.

Another thing that cell phones were good for, she thought—breaking the mood.

He said, "She wants us to meet her now. There's a presentation at GWU that she has to attend later, needs to prepare for it. So we can go and be back here by one thirty."

"One thirty? No one thirtyers, Peter."

Some people had nooners. Peter and Evangeline had a private joke about one thirtyers.

He said, "Plenty of time to freshen up and—"

"Forget it. You're trying to sweet-talk me into trouble. And I need to rehearse." She tossed the phone on the sofa and tossed herself after it. She pulled off her boots and undid her blouse. She was wearing a powder blue bra the same color as the blouse. She noticed him staring and said, "What? *What?*"

"Sometimes, you unbutton your blouse, it means yes. Today, I'll take it as a no."

"I'm showering. And I'm not going with you."

"Well . . . can I stay here tonight?"

"You weren't supposed to be here till *tomorrow* night. That was our deal."

He grinned. "Expecting someone else?"

"No. No boyfriends. No girlfriends. No distractions, which is what you are."

"So you're turning me out in the cold cruel capital?"

She sighed. She almost laughed. He could almost always make her laugh, even when he was exasperating her. She pulled the second credit card key from her purse and flipped it to him. "Don't charge anything to the room."

. . .

That went well, he thought.

Now to get to the bottom of this Lincoln business. He had a feeling that whatever was going on, he was coming to it just as it sped out of control.

He took a cab over the Hill to the East Capitol Metro stop on Pennsylvania, got out and glanced back at the great white dome. It dominated Washington. It defined what Dickens had called the city of magnificent distances. Locate the Capitol, and you knew how far you were from anything. And usually, you knew how magnificent the distance was.

Peter had friends who said that walking anywhere east of the Capitol, you should carry a twenty-dollar bill and just give it up when the junkie stuck his gun in your face. That was an exaggeration. There were tough sections in the District, sure, places where the power of the federal government had never made an impact, where the problems of any big American city existed.

But this was one of the oldest Washington neighborhoods . . . nice town houses interspersed with a few dumps, nice front yards, some filled with children's toys, some with gardens, places where people lived and worked and raised families . . . a nice urban neighborhood half a mile from where they ground up the national sausage every day.

And after a few blocks, he came to that magnificent old market.

It dated from the 1870s and resembled a brick Victorian train station. Outdoor stalls overflowed with color—red apples, green lettuce, orange carrots, pink melons. And one look at the cast-iron skylights on the roof told Peter that inside was an enormous market hall filled with wonders. On a bright Saturday morning, the place was swarming with shoppers.

Diana Wilmington stood under a canopy near an apple stand. She was wearing tight jeans and a white silk jersey. Her big gold hoops flashed against her skin. She looked more like the lead singer in some Motown girl-group than a college professor.

She threw Peter big come-on-over wave. If she seemed worried about hackers or watchers, she didn't show it. Instead, she laughed.

It was the laugh that had first attracted him. He had heard it at a gallery opening in Boston ten years earlier. Then he had noticed the graceful legs and coffee-colored skin. Then he had watched her move, relaxed yet regal, as if the whole room were moving around her. Even though she was a lot younger, he'd made a move of his own. They'd had some good fun at Celtics games and over a few nice nice dinners in his Back Bay condo. Then they'd moved on.

He gave her a quick hug. "We have to stop meeting like this."

"Welcome to one of the crossroads of the capital," said Diana. "White and black, rich and poor, young and old, lobbyist and welfare mom. They all come here because if you can't find it in the Eastern Market, you can't find it."

"Even letters from Lincoln to forgotten lieutenants?"

She gave a jerk of the head and led him toward a basketball court across the street. That was where they ran the weekend flea market. Dozens of tables and stalls had been set up, and people were selling . . . selling . . . selling . . . old furniture, from mahogany to lawn . . . new rugs, both hot and legal . . . prints and paintings, beautiful reproductions and bad originals . . . rare books, old books, and paperbacks without covers . . . DVDs and videocassettes . . . tables full of tchotchkes, knickknacks, junk, trash . . . and treasures.

As they crossed the basketball baseline, Diana said, "The man who offered me the letter—his name was Jefferson Sorrel—he told me he found the letter and envelope here, inside an engraving of 'First Reading of the Emancipation Proclamation.'"

"Why did Sorrel come to you?" asked Peter.

"He said he liked my book, and he liked the idea of the African American Museum of Emancipation."

"Did he know how much a letter like this can be worth?" asked Peter.

"I think so." Diana was leading him through the crowd, toward a stall in the corner under the shading branches of a magnolia. She stopped about ten feet away. "I think that's the guy who sold it to him. His name is Donald Dawkins."

"So . . . what to you want me to do?"

"You've dealt with people like this. He may know something without even knowing it. I'll do the talking. You just jump in anywhere."

The man was reading a book beside a table of Civil War memorabilia. He was black, about sixty, with a potbelly and the look of hard work ground into his big hands. Peter noticed that the book was Eric Foner's *The Fiery Trial: Abraham Lincoln and American Slavery*. Appropriate.

"Afternoon," said Diana.

"Afternoon." Dawkins barely raised his head.

"This sure is a fine collection of Civil War material you have," said Peter.

Dawkins looked it over as if seeing it for the first time himself. Framed engravings of Civil War scenes, cut from old copies of *Harper's Weekly*; porcelain statues of Frederick Douglass; bobble heads of Lincoln; a framed repro of the Emancipation Proclamation; and piles of books, including an unjacketed *Killer Angels*. Peter picked it up: first edition. The price, written in pencil on the flap, suggested that Mr. Dawkins didn't know his book values: *$15*. With a jacket, it would have been worth $915.

Diana said, "We're Lincoln fans."

"Mmmhm." He nodded and went back to his reading.

There were three types of sellers at flea markets. One gave you a cheery "Can I help you?" and started pitching you straight off. One said hello, busied himself with something else until you asked a question, then oozed all over you. And one acted as if he didn't care whether you bought or not, even though he watched you the whole time from the corner of his eye. Dawkins appeared to be the last kind.

"Always looking for Old Abe material," Diana went on. "And I heard, about a week ago, you had a nice repro of the Ritchie engraving, *First Reading of the Emancipation Proclamation.*"

Dawkins raised his head. "Where'd you hear that?"

"From the buyer," said Diana.

"Why'd he tell you?"

Diana looked at Peter for a bit of help.

Peter said, "Occasionally we buy for the African American Museum of Emancipation."

"We?" Dawkins gave Peter a squint. "You ain't black."

"I'm Black Irish."

"Yeah, and we's all brothers under the skin," said Dawkins. "Did you buy it?"

"No."

"Well, if you see that feller, tell him I want to buy it back. Tell him to return my phone calls. Tell him I'll pay him another fifty dollars for it."

"Why?" asked Diana.

"Because I sold it late in the day. I wanted to go home with somethin' in my pocket, so I made a bum deal. The next weekend, I could've sold it for more."

Now Peter cocked an eye at Diana. *How much more?* Did someone know what had been in the backing of that engraving? Someone who had come late?

Peter asked, "Where did you get it?"

Dawkins scowled. "What do I look like? A chump? I'm a dealer in Civil War memorabilia, tellin' the African American story. What's here is for sale. But don't be asking me where-all I bought or who-all I bought from or—"

"You can't blame me for trying," said Peter. "I'm in the business, too."

"Then you ought to know better." Dawkins picked up his book again. "I find things everywhere . . . flea markets in Virginia, book bins in Baltimore, barn shops in Pennsylvania. I don't tell folks where I find stuff, and neither do you, I'm bettin'."

"You got me there."

"All right, then," said Dawkins. "Now, if you ain't buyin', I'm readin'."

Diana said to Dawkins, "Do you have a receipt for the engraving?"

"Now *you're* playin' me for a chump," said Dawkins. "And you're a sistah."

Peter winked at Diana, as if to say that she was on her own, and he moved over to the next table.

The proprietor gave Peter a yellow-toothed grin. He was white, wore shorts and sandals with socks. His gray T-shirt had a picture of Robert E. Lee and Stonewall Jackson above a caption, VIRGINIA HERITAGE. He said, "A fine collection of books here, sir."

Peter glanced at a trade paperback of Grant's *Memoirs.* Then he picked up a much older volume: *Fort Lafayette*, by Benjamin C. Wood, published in New York, 1862.

Meanwhile, Diana was asking Dawkins, "Why do you think someone else wanted that engraving."

"So *now* what do I look like? Bill Cosby or somebody, givin' up the daddy-talk to anybody who asks? We got the Proclamation anniversary comin' up. We got a big museum show openin' at the Smithsonian. So anything connected with it ought to get premium price. So buy somethin' or leave me alone."

"I'm not buying today, but—" She picked up another book from his table.

Peter saw the title: *The Racism and Resolve of Abraham Lincoln.* He folded his arms and waited for the reaction when Diana said, "I'll be glad to sign this."

"Sign it? What do you mean, sign it?" Then it dawned on him. "You wrote it? You're Diana Wilmington?" Dawkins smiled for the first time. "I seen you on TV. That's one damn fine book. I didn't want to resell it after I read it, but it's got a message folks ought to hear. Even Lincoln had his blind spots."

Now, thought Peter, she had him.

Dawkins pulled out a pen and said, "Make it out to Dick and Savannah."

After a bit more conversation, they had the address of the buyer, the man named Jefferson Sorrel. Then they tried to get the address of the seller, too, but Dawkins was not *that* impressed.

"You just tell that Sorrel he took me," said Dawkins, "and I don't like being took. See if you can convince him to sell it back."

"We'll do our best," said Peter. He did not add that the law of the flea market was as simple as the law of the jungle: No refunds, no exchanges. If you bought it, you owned it. If you sold it, you didn't, even if it included a hidden letter worth seven figures.

As they turned to leave, the guy in the next stall said, "So I can't interest you in *Fort Lafayette*? It's a good value."

"It's dogshit," said Dawkins. "That's why I sold it to you."

"It's historical," said the other dealer, "a first edition of a book written by an anti-Lincoln congressman."

"Racist garbage," said Dawkins. "It justifies secession. It justifies slavery. But it came with the Proclamation picture."

That remark got Peter's attention. He picked up the book again.

And the guy in the ponytail kept talking . . . kept selling. "Yes, sir, that's the oldest book in my collection."

Peter's curiosity was piqued, so he went into bargaining mode. "You want five hundred for a book with worn headbands and torn endpapers, printed on acidic paper?"

"But it's rare."

"But it's from the mid-nineteenth century, so it's burning."

"Burning?" said the guy. "It's not burning."

"Someone ought to burn it," said Dawkins.

Peter held the book up to his nose. "You can smell combustion, a slow motion burn as the acid they used to break down the fibers of wood pulp keeps working a hundred and fifty years later, except now it's breaking down the paper itself."

The guy with the ponytail said, "But can't you conserve it or somethin'?"

Peter shook his head. "Not worth it."

"Gotcha, Dougie." Dawkins laughed and said to Peter, "Sold it to him for a C-note, now he thinks he can talk you into five hundred."

"Because," said the guy, "it's a real rare book."

"Rare because it sucks," said Dawkins. "No one even knows who that Wood dude was."

"A New York congressman," said Diana. "He opposed Secession and Emancipation, too. He also owned the *New York Daily News*. Wrote awful things about Lincoln, got shut down. He's obscure today, but more interesting than people know."

"So," said the guy with the ponytail, "what do you think of that, Mr. Big-Deal Boston book buyer?"

"How do you know I'm from Boston?" said Peter.

"Everybody in the book business knows Peter Fallon, even flea market paperback peddlers like me." He offered his card. His name was Douglas Bryant. "I love your catalog. Never had the money to buy anything from it, but—"

"Thanks." Peter flipped through the book again. There were a few names on the endpapers, but little else.

"And even if I didn't know who you were," Bryant continued, "I might be wondering what kind of big deal you were, considering the guy taking pictures of you."

"Pictures?" said Peter and Diana at the same time.

"Yeah," said Bryant. "A big guy in a blue T-shirt and a blue ball cap with a white star on it, white star and blue patch. It looks like the Bonnie Blue Flag, one of the first symbols of Confederate resistance. That's why I noticed him. I thought it was a cool cap. I thought he was taking candids for a photo spread on how the smartest book man in the business skins the little guys. That's why I've been smiling like an ass."

"No," said Dawkins. "That ain't why."

"Where did he go?" asked Peter.

"He headed for the market."

Peter gestured for Diana to follow and then he picked up the pace and shouted over his shoulder, "Five hundred bucks for that book . . . *that's* a skinning."

He led Diana past the flea market stalls, past the baseline, and as they stepped through the chain-link fence, they saw the guy. And he saw them.

Diana shouted, "Hey, you!" And suddenly, she was running. "Hey!"

The man looked at them for another second, then turned and ran up the ramp that led through swinging doors into the market itself.

Diana took off right after him.

Peter cursed. He'd been in Washington two hours and already he was in a scramble. He decided to go in the far end and come at the guy from the opposite direction. So he began to run.

Someone shouted, "Hey, slow down there."

A dog walker with two pit bulls pulled on his dogs. One of them started to bark.

Peter sprinted past the dogs and all the way to the far end of the long brick building. He dodged a dozen people who were leaving with bundles and pushcarts of food. He went in by the west door. He all but leaped over a little girl holding her mother's hand. He bumped through the inner doors and burst onto the market floor itself. Then he stopped for a second to survey the place.

A cheese vendor said, "Fontina?"

"What?"

"We have a nice fontina today."

Peter shook his head. He saw nobody wearing a blue cap with a white star, nobody with a camera. He could see Diana, however, standing tall in the middle of the market, her eyes scanning the crowd.

Peter went up to her. "Why did you chase him? I was going to play it subtle."

"Subtle is when you're watching your back in the halls of academe and no one has it," she said. "On the street, be *street*."

And on the street, someone was watching. Someone was in competition.

She said, "So, what's next?"

"This." Peter pulled out his cell phone and texted Antoine Scarborough in Boston:

Any word on Lincoln, Hutchinson, Murphy, telegraph office? Need info NOW.

Four

April 1862

As dawn approached, Halsey Hutchinson was dreading the day. Dread came to life when he sensed a presence at the office door: Detective McNealy.

Halsey kept his eyes on his work as McNealy's shoes crossed the carpet and stopped beside the desk. Then Halsey inclined his head slightly, glanced at the tracked-in mud, and said, "There are boot scrapers at all the entries, Detective. You should use them."

"Treat me with respect, Lieutenant. I may be your best friend. I may be your only friend."

"Every man is my friend, until he's not."

"Did you get my note?"

"Did you get mine?"

McNealy pulled it out of his pocket. "'Whatever you seek, you will find it elsewhere.' Very pithy. The story of a man's life could be written in those words."

Halsey had not expected philosophy. On reflex, he offered a bit of his own: "'Do not go where the path may lead; go instead where there is no path and leave a trail.' Ralph Waldo Emerson."

"A family friend I suppose?"

"Actually, yes, even though he's an Abolitionist."

"You like to flash your Boston friends and your book-learnin', don't you?"

Halsey reminded himself not to goad. It would do no good to goad. He put down his pen and sat back. "How can I help you, Detective?"

"You know the power I wield?"

"I know you can arrest a man on almost any suspicion and call it treasonous."

"That power derives from the man who works on the other side of that screen door." McNealy jerked his head toward Stanton's office. "He gets it from the president."

"It certainly doesn't derive from the Constitution."

"You forget, Lieutenant—" McNealy brought his face close. "—we are at war."

Halsey angled his head to show the scar at his neck. "I need no reminding."

That caused McNealy to settle back. "I'll ask you plain, Lieutenant: What the president says he lost—his daybook—was that what I saw you stuff in your pocket yesterday morning?"

"It was my own daybook." Halsey thought that was a good lie. "I assume you read it when you rifled my room."

"I did." McNealy grinned. "So you can also assume that I know about your stroll to the Smithsonian with the niece of the most anti-Lincoln legislator in Washington."

Halsey turned to his work, pretended to finish a requisition, and planned his next reaction. A bullet in the neck was a shock for which one could not prepare. But an interrogation could be like a line of bait leading to a leg hold. Proceed cautiously and avoid the trap.

"So," said McNealy, "when you walked past Lafayette Park with a man in a checkered suit, when you indulged a disloyal congressman in talk over fried oysters"—he cocked his head for better eye contact—"you must have known I'd be watching."

Halsey stood and tugged his vest. "I told you yesterday—"

"Yes, yes . . . your integrity." McNealy took off his porkpie and wiped the sweat from the hatband. His hair was thinning into what they called a widow's peak.

Halsey folded his arms. "If you have a question, Detective, ask it."

"Who was he?"

"Who?"

"The man in the checkered suit?"

Halsey had already decided there would be no dissembling over this. "He was my cousin, John Charles Robey, a contract seeker from Boston."

"Did you say *was?*"

Be careful, Halsey told himself. "*Was,* yes. You asked me, who *was* that man."

McNealy nodded. "He's now a permanent *was.*"

Halsey steadied himself against his chair, looked out the window, then back into McNealy's face . . . all planned gestures, such as Booth might have used, were he playing this scene on the stage. *"Was?"*

McNealy told of the discovery of the body while Halsey sat and feigned shock.

McNealy seemed to buy the act. He said, "Can you think of anyone who might have wanted to do your cousin harm?"

"Next to himself, my cousin loved faro, females, and whiskey, in that order."

"There are hundreds of gambling hells in Murder Bay, and by the latest count, four hundred and fifty-three whorehouses in the District. You need to be more specific."

"My cousin and I are not close, so that's the best I can do."

"All right." McNealy pulled out a business card and gave it to Halsey: HANNASSEY UNDERTAKING, PENNSYLVANIA AND 6TH. "When the body is released, we'll send him here. Hannassey prices fair, but he charges double for a colonel over a captain, double for a lieutenant over an enlisted man. Don't know what he'll charge for a war profiteer, but he'll do his best with your cousin's face—have you seen the face?"

Halsey looked up slowly. "Before or after you say he was pistol whipped?"

"Hannassey'll fix the face and put your cousin on a fast train to Boston." McNealy turned, then stopped and said, "But one more thing, Lieutenant."

"What's that?"

"Why did you show him your sidearm yesterday? You opened your coat and showed him that little Adams popgun."

"He wanted me to introduce him to the president. I told him the president has bigger worries. I told him I'd shoot him if he kept bothering me . . . or the president."

"Shoot him?"

"A figure of speech."

"Well," said McNealy, "he showed no bullet holes, so I reckon you're in the clear on that, but . . . do you have your pistol with you?"

Halsey knew that if he could not have produced a pistol, the beam passing through the magnifying glass of McNealy's brain would have been a light of pure suspicion. But Halsey pulled out the second Adams and put it into McNealy's hand.

McNealy looked at the barrel. "No blood or hair." Then he smelled it. "Hasn't been fired lately." He handed the gun back. "You're in the clear, for now."

Just then, Major Eckert stepped into the office. He looked at McNealy the way soldiers looked at maggoty meat. "What are you doing here?"

"Asking a few questions. Lieutenant Hutchinson says that he doesn't know anything about the book the president lost, or about the murder of his cousin last night."

"Murder?" Eckert looked at Halsey.

"We found him in the Willard," said McNealy, "hanging from a hook in his own wardrobe. Beaten so bad, he looked like uncased sausage. As dead as Andy Jackson."

"My cousin had high hopes but low tastes," explained Halsey.

"That's it, then," said Eckert to McNealy. "Can't be stated more clearly than that. Are we done here, Detective?"

"For now."

"Make it for good," said Eckert. "There's no disloyalty here. So don't be bothering my men. In fact, stay the hell out of this office."

McNealy pulled out a cigar, bit the tip, spit it toward the spittoon, and left.

Eckert said, "That man is a pain in the ass. I prefer detectives who do all their work undercover. At least you don't know when they're bothering you."

He was more than a pain, thought Halsey. He was pure danger, so best change the subject before it infected Halsey's relations with the man he respected most in the office.

Major Eckert wore a trimmed mustache and a neat suit, but he had the bulk of a man who could bend a fireplace poker in his bare hands.

Halsey had seen him do it, just to prove the poor quality of War Department pokers. But Eckert's best feature was his calm. He appeared calm in the morning, remained calm in front of Secretary Stanton's tirades, and would surely display calm in a crisis.

But before Halsey spoke, a tall figure appeared in the doorway, shrouded in a white canvas duster and floppy felt hat. He pulled off the hat and said, "Favor seekers are out early."

"I'm sure they won't recognize you in that getup, Mr. President," said Eckert.

"It helps." Lincoln handed Eckert a paper. "Get this off to General McClellan."

Eckert called Homer Bates into the cipher room, gave him the message, and set him to work. Then he said to Lincoln, "Anything else, sir?"

"Any word on that daybook I seem to have lost?"

Eckert shook his head.

"Oh, well, no matter." Lincoln asked for the overnight traffic, flipped through the pile without any comment, then glanced at the clock and said, "Major, I'll beg an escort from Lieutenant Hutchinson. His shift must be nearly over."

Lincoln gave Halsey that benevolent, inscrutable smile.

He knows more than he is letting on, thought Halsey.

. . .

In the daylight, Halsey and the president did not have to keep to the path. They could pick their way through the trees and head for the side door of the White House.

Lincoln went with the felt hat pulled low and his head hunched down so that he looked considerably shorter than his six feet and four.

But voices were soon echoing through the trees. "Mr. President, sir, my petition. Did it reach you yesterday?" "Mr. President! My cousin, Orvis, from Illinois, he said I should tell you that he sent me!" "Mr. President, I need just a minute of your time!" "Mr. President, please, sir!" "Mr. President!" "Mr. President!"

Lincoln whispered to Halsey, "If any of 'em come too close, show 'em your pistol."

"Yes, sir." Halsey put his hand into his coat.

"These people just don't seem to understand that there are too many pigs and not enough teats."

They legged it all the way to the door at the west side, the one that led onto the ground level, out of sight of the carriage drive and the crowd.

Lincoln pulled off the hat and ran a hand through his wiry black hair. He meant to straighten it but did no more than tousle it. Then he tugged his vest and said, "McManus tells me a young officer came to the door yesterday. Said he came on official business. Had a first name that sounded like a last name. Wore a fine tweed suit. Was it you?"

"It wasn't really official business, sir."

Lincoln furrowed his brow. "Unofficial, then?"

"I wanted to apologize to you for—" *Come up with something*, thought Halsey, anything. "—speaking my mind the night before."

"What about?"

Keep lying, Halsey told himself. "Why . . . the coloreds . . . how I thought you were giving them extra reason to break curfew. I may have sounded a bit disapproving and—"

Lincoln laughed, as if he knew where Halsey was headed. "These days, Lieutenant, I feel like a man walkin' along the top rail of a rickety fence between two fields. There's wild dogs in one field and snakes in the other. So I step as careful as I can. I only tell people what I think it's time for them to hear, and I try not to lose my balance by sayin' too much . . . or not enough . . . or the wrong thing."

"Well, sir—"

"So I don't take offense at what people say to me, not my enemies, and certainly not my friends. Have a good day's sleep, Lieutenant."

II.

Find the daybook. Find the daybook. Find the daybook.

That's what Halsey was thinking as he left the White House grounds.

As usual, he passed the two Negro laborers, one carrying a shovel, the other a mule harness, on their way to wherever they worked. They tipped their hats. He tipped his and kept walking.

Lincoln's trust had made him feel even worse. Whatever the president was thinking about slavery, it would not do him or the country any good to reveal his thoughts too soon.

So Halsey decided to find the daybook, perhaps right then, because he thought he knew where it was. He took to the bad side of Pennsylvania and at Twelfth turned south into Murder Bay. He went half a block and met two women.

Their faces were painted and powdered, and one of them was wearing a dress that showed the tops of her breasts. She said, "Lookin' for friendship, mister?"

"I'm looking to play a bit of faro."

The girl put a hand under each breast. "You can play with these. Faro, Twenty-one, even poker."

"Yeah," laughed the other one. "Poker all you want."

"Poker." Halsey just looked at them . . . first at the breasts, then at the women. "Not this morning. Faro."

They both pulled long faces.

He said, "Now, a faro parlor? Is there one around here called Squeaker's?"

"You mean Squeaker McDillon's?" She jerked her head to a line of row houses and seven-stair stoops on the other side of the street. "The middle one."

He tipped his hat. "Thank you, ladies."

"Ooh, ladies, he calls us. Ain't we gettin' fancy?"

He left them and crossed the muddy street. There was little business at that hour. The all-nighters had gone home, the day-timers had not come out. A man in a red kepi sat outside McDillon's door. He was whittling with a huge Bowie knife.

As Halsey approached, the man extended a leg, so that Halsey could not climb the stoop. Without taking his eye from his whittling he said, "You want somethin'?"

"Is this Squeaker McDillon's?"

"Who's askin'?"

"I'm lookin' for faro."

The man looked up. "I said who's askin'."

Halsey thought about pulling his pistol. But he was here to scout, not battle. So he said, "Are you open for business? Or do I ask the Superintendant of the Metropolitan Police about your hours?"

"You a soldier boy? Or the law?"

"So you're not open?"

The man just went back to his whittling, then he shouted, "Hey, Shag!"

At the top of the stoop, the front door opened. "Yeah?" said Shag.

Halsey recognized the beard and the voice. He held his breath and hoped that his tweed suit and hat would be disguise enough.

"This feller wants to know, do we got gamblin'?"

Shag was wearing a suit of long white underwear and a gun belt holding a brace of Navy sixes. He gave Halsey a look.

Halsey decided that if he saw a flicker of recognition on either face, he would step back and start shooting.

But Shag said, "No faro till two o'clock. Find someplace else." And he slammed the door.

Halsey released his breath. But he would not be walking into McDillon's, flashing a pocket pistol, and finding out what he wanted to know, not with those Navy sixes waiting.

"Anything else?" grunted the Whittler.

Halsey looked up at the building, then noticed the alleys at either end of the row, separating the joined façades from freestanding houses.

"I asked you a question," growled the Whittler. "Anything else? If not, move along or I may just bop you off the head with the handle of my knife."

"Better than stickin' me with it."

"That's the first right thing you've said."

Halsey tipped his hat and went on his way. And he went quickly because most likely, it was the Whittler who had bopped him in his hotel room the night before.

But as he went, he heard a door open. Then he heard a voice, like a gate turning on a rusty hinge: "You're in line for some extra scratch. That was one damn good get."

"Man should pay his gamblin' debts. Not lay 'em off on his cousin."

Halsey glanced over his shoulder:

Two men were coming down the front stairs of Squeaker McDillon's.

The one called Shag had put on his pants and hidden his guns under his coat.

The other one was shorter, cleaner. His blue suit and neat beard made him look more like a barrister than a gambling boss. But those eyes gave him away. They were nervous squirrel's eyes set in a nervous squirrel's face. They flicked at Halsey, then flicked away, then flicked back again. They said that this was a man always looking for an advantage . . . or a buried nut.

Halsey pulled his hat low and crossed the street. When he reached Pennsylvania he stopped, as though trying to decide which way to go.

Squeaker and Shag did not give him another glance. They dodged a passing omnibus and crossed to the good side of the Avenue.

Halsey shadowed them, and their trail led straight to the Willard.

.   .   .

If a man did not have the smell of money or power about him, he could easily lose himself in Willard's lobby. He could drift from one conversation to another, disappear behind a newspaper, pretend to snooze on the settee, or sidle up to the bar and order a brandy and scan the room.

Halsey ordered, sipped, and enjoyed the pleasant burn on his tongue. But where were Squeaker and Shag?

At first, he feared that they had retreated to some upstairs room to peddle what they had stolen from him. Then, through the dining room doors, he noticed Shag at the breakfast buffet. So he took his brandy and sauntered over for a better look.

And what he saw reminded him that while the world might go to Willard's, the world was truly a small place: Squeaker McDillon was sitting with a woman, sitting boldly, sitting in plain sight.

Harriet Dunbar, widow of a Maryland tobacco planter, had been known before the war as one of the most gracious hostesses in the city, a lady who welcomed politicians and opinionators from all sides. She still entertained, though her salons were now attended mostly by men wearing blue uniforms. She had even entertained Halsey, though he doubted that she remembered him. In the morning light falling through the front window, her face looked severe, pale, all heavy brow and tightened jaw.

Squeaker casually reached into his pocket, took out a piece of paper, and slid it across the table to her.

Jester the waiter came by and said to Halsey, "Mornin', sir. Y'all need a seat?"

"No. But . . . that Mrs. Dunbar, does she come here often?"

Jester looked over the bobbing heads. "You mean the lady talkin' to Squeaker?"

"You know Squeaker?"

"Everybody know Squeaker. And Miz Dunbar, she used to be a reg'lar, but she don't come here too often no more."

"Because of the war?"

"I reckon," said the black man. "And on account of so many of her friends leavin' when Secession start. They left. She stayed behind."

So, wondered Halsey, was Squeaker offering something to a Southern spy? More than one Washington lady had come under the eye of government detectives. Some now resided in the Old Capitol Prison, and some were still out there stealing Union secrets, sneaking them south in the strands of their hair or the folds of their skirts.

Mrs. Dunbar glanced at Halsey. Her brow furrowed as if she recognized him.

So he turned, finished his brandy, and left.

. . .

The lobby of the National was smaller and quieter. Halsey preferred it.

Harvey, the desk man, greeted him and asked if he cared for breakfast.

Halsey then heard a voice from a chair by the lobby fireplace: "Or would you join me in a coffee, Lieutenant?"

A curl of smoke rose from behind a newspaper. The headline announced: VAST MOVEMENT OF TROOPS UNDER WAY IN VIRGINIA. That was a lie. There were vast numbers of troops in Virginia, but none of them seemed to be moving.

Halsey said, "Good morning, Mr. Booth."

"Call me Wilkes." Booth lowered the paper. "Coffee?"

"I don't mind if I do." Halsey sat in the chair on the other side of the fireplace. The flames crackled and took the morning chill off the lobby.

Booth filled a cup from the china pot beside him and handed it to Halsey. "A hard night, Lieutenant?"

"Every night is a hard night, Wilkes. And call me Halsey."

"I hear that the Original Ape comes by your office every night."

"You mean the president?" Halsey sipped the coffee.

"Don't play coy with me. You know the line of my talk."

"The president visits most every night. I also hear he visits the theater."

"For all his flaws, he is a student of the Bard," said Booth.

"And you? A hard night for you?"

"I was excellent onstage, less so at the faro table."

Right then, Halsey decide that stopping to talk to Booth was most fortuitous. "Where do you gamble?"

Booth looked around and lowered his voice, as if revealing an intimate secret. "I have visited half the gambling hells in this city. An actor should observe many people and play many roles."

"Ever been to Squeaker McDillon's?"

"A clip shop," snapped Booth. "If you have a taste for cards, there are far more reputable places."

"I have a taste for danger," said Halsey, letting that croaking voice croak a bit more, as if to put some conviction into his words. "I hear it's a dangerous place."

Booth grinned. He seemed to enjoy danger, too, or at least the promise of it.

"Can you tell me, Wilkes, what their parlor looks like?"

"I think you can imagine. They call them 'gambling hells,' not 'gambling halls.'"

"Do you remember the layout? Faro tables in the front or the back?"

"What difference does it make?" asked Booth.

"I like to enter by the front and leave by the back. That way I can't be tracked."

"Tracked? By whom?"

"The men who know that I win. I tend to win."

Booth thought that over and nodded, as if he approved. "You can't leave directly by the back, because the tables are in the upper parlor, at the top of the front entrance. The back door is on ground level and opens on an alley."

Then Booth pulled a small book from his pocket. It was the same size, the same thickness, and had the same red leather covering as Lincoln's daybook. For a crazy moment, Halsey thought that it *was* Lincoln's daybook. But it was a common thing. There were probably thousands like it.

Booth took a pencil and began to sketch. "I'll give you a map of the establishment in question. In exchange, you will go with me and show me how you win."

"But I'll go early, before my shift at the War Department. You'll be on the stage."

"So I will." Booth looked at Halsey a moment, then tore out the sheet and handed it over. "I'll expect that list of Boston ladies, then. I leave soon."

Halsey took the sheet, put it into his pocket, and said, "I shall ask Miss Samantha Simpson of Wellesley, Massachusetts, to see to your welcome."

"You could also ask your sister."

"Sister? My sister is in Boston."

Booth looked to the man at the desk. "Did you hear that, Harvey? He says his sister is in Boston."

"Perhaps I should call for the house detective, then," said Harvey.

Halsey felt the heat rising around his collar. "House detective?"

"A young lady came in a while ago and presented herself as your sister," said Booth. "I was tempted to show her to your room, with perhaps a stop in Two Twenty-eight to read her a few of my notices. Would you like for me to help you now?"

"I'll see to this myself."

.   .   .

Upstairs, Halsey put a hand on his pistol and pushed open his door.

The silhouette of a woman blocked the light from the window. Her hands lay folded on the front of her hooped skirt. Her hat sat primly on her head, as if to announce that she did not intend to stay and would admit of no activity but business.

Halsey said, "Miss Wood?"

"I am appalled that I was kissing a thief yesterday, a spy, right in the War Department."

"I don't know what you're talking about."

Out of her purse she pulled an envelope. Out of the envelope she pulled a page—diary sized—on which were written the words: *The real problem with a general emancipation is*—

"Does that look familiar?" she asked.

Halsey felt his stomach clench. He had read this page the morning before, the last page in the Lincoln daybook. He said, "Where did you get this?"

"It came to my uncle's suite and was slipped under the door."

"Has he seen it?"

"No. Nor has he seen this." She pulled a note from the envelope. It read:

Recognize the handwriting? Torn from a diary. There's more. It'll cost you. Send word if you're interested. McD.

She snatched the page. "This is the exact size of the book you had yesterday, the book with Lincoln's signature on it, the book you dropped."

"You mean my daybook, which slipped from my pocket as we embraced?"

She looked down at the floor, then into his eyes. "It was a very pleasant embrace."

He thought about embracing her again and turning this in a new direction. After all, she had come without chaperone, and she was a powerful temptation, even as she stood motionless before the window, like some Renaissance Madonna . . . with her hat on. He stepped closer. "I've been thinking about it ever since."

"Think about this instead: Someone has betrayed the president, someone who knows that my uncle would do anything to damage him. Was it you?"

"Why would you think that?"

"Because you won my uncle's approval. I was your reward. What did you promise him?" She held up the page. "Lincoln's diary?"

Halsey stepped back. "I promised him nothing."

"Then what did you say to him?"

"I said nothing."

"Not even that Union without abolition would be preferable to no Union at all?"

"That's what Lincoln believes," answered Halsey. "He also believes that to preserve the Union, he will do what he must. He'll call for more troops. He'll suspend habeas corpus. I assume you know what that is."

"Don't patronize me, Halsey. The right of every person to be presented before a judge when accused of a crime, a right that may be suspended in times of rebellion."

"Lincoln suspended it without Congressional approval. And he had your uncle's paper shut down simply by denying him postage, and—"

"You work for a man you disagree with, then?"

"I've made a choice to fight for union, just as Lincoln has."

"Then you believe that the Negroes are not the issue?"

"There would be no war without the slaves," he said, "but they're not the issue."

"Some of us believe they're the *only* issue, and we'll do anything to free them."

Halsey laughed. "You're an Abolitionist, then?"

"Not just an Abolitionist. An absolute Douglass-ite."

"Douglass-ite?"

"It's my own word. A disciple of Frederick Douglass."

"The runaway slave?"

"The editor of a newspaper, the author of a mighty autobiography, an orator of amazing power."

"I've heard of him," said Halsey.

"You must not simply hear *of* him. You must *hear* him." She came across the room and put her hand on his arm. "Oh, Halsey, the sound of his voice and the perfect logic of his reasoning turned me from a silly girl to a crusader for truth in an afternoon. You must hear him and you must *read* him. Do you know his book?"

"I have not read it."

"Any Unionist who does will become an Abolitionist overnight. Read of a boy torn from his mother. Read of a beloved aunt trussed to a pillar and flogged until the blood runs in rivers down her back. Read of the destruction of manhood, of womanhood, of family. Read of the enforced ignorance that only superhuman effort can overcome. Do you know that it is a crime to teach a slave to read in most Southern states? Why do you think that is?"

Halsey shrugged. "It has never been my concern."

"Because you can read. A man who can read can think, not simply react. And a man who can think can understand his world and the evil perpetrated upon him, and perhaps he can rebel."

"One rebellion at a time is enough." Halsey tried to make a joke.

But Miss Constance was boring in on an uncomfortable truth. "We are a foolish nation to deny the mental capacity of ten percent of our people, because we wish to steal their sweat and tears. What godly nation would do such a thing?"

Halsey shrugged again.

"Read Douglass and hear the whip whistle, hear the chains clank, see the blood of innocents splatter, and know that a greedy nation, north and south, has done evil. And once you've read it—"

Halsey said, "If Douglass is an Abolitionist, he can't be too happy with Lincoln."

"What Abolitionist is?" She took her hand away. "Lincoln moves too slowly. But who is the alternative? My uncle? Do you know what he said in his last editorial?"

Halsey shook his head.

"He said that Lincoln would encourage servile insurrection."

"A fear in many parts of the country, even among the businessmen of Boston."

"So they oppose Lincoln, too?"

"They are happiest when they and the nation are enjoying the fruits of their prosperity," answered Halsey, "thanks to a supply of cheap cotton."

"It makes you wonder how Lincoln ever got elected," she said.

"Now then, your uncle will be angry if he knows you're here, or if he discovers that you're stealing notes slipped under his door."

"And I will be angry if you're lying to me about this diary."

"I know nothing of the diary or of someone who calls himself McD."

"Just prove that you're not part of this. And restore the book to the president. If you do, the nation—and I—shall be indebted to you. And if we go to the Smithsonian again, perhaps we'll look for that pillar and—"

Halsey heard a voice behind him:

"I am disappointed." Booth was standing in the doorway, shaking his head melodramatically. "A man and woman in a hotel room in midmorning, and the door left chastely ajar." He looked at Constance. "I would have closed it."

Constance looked at Booth, then at Halsey. "You have famous friends, Lieutenant, but fame does not guarantee a gentleman."

She stepped past Halsey and pushed by Booth, who took off his hat and executed a deep bow.

The men watched her walk down the hall; then Booth said to Halsey, "Strange seduction practices you Boston men have."

"Were you eavesdropping?"

"Contrary to what your lady friend thinks, I *am* a gentleman."

Did she believe that he could simply go to some hiding place and retrieve the book, all for the promise of another kiss? Was she that calculating? Or did she really like him?

Halsey could not deny that he had enjoyed that kiss in the Smithsonian. And if there were more to be had, he would enjoy them, too. He had no intention, however, of showing her Lincoln's daybook. He might tell her about it, perhaps in the Smithsonian, in front of that pillar, just as he led her into its shadow. But first, he had to find it, before Squeaker McDillon peddled it to the highest bidder.

Halsey considered going to McNealy with the truth. Then he might be able to walk into McDillon's with a flanking party of Provost Guards, demand the book, and identify his cousin's murderer in the process. But questions would arise. Why hadn't he turned them in earlier? Why had he removed the president's daybook . . . then lied about it? And why this? And why that? It would take him days to explain, by which time the daybook would be on its way to Richmond or New York.

So he would do his best himself, and if he failed, he would pray that he hadn't damaged the president. He would ask help of only one man.

. . .

"Shine." Halsey dropped into Noah's chair.

"You sure is a good customer, sir." Noah went to work.

Halsey asked, "Seen any watchers today?"

"I don't see the brown white man, if that's what you askin'."

"Good. Anyone else?"

While his hands worked, Noah glanced over his shoulder at two women strolling by. One carried a wicker basket; the other held a parasol. "Them ladies could be watchers, but their voices is too happy. They's on their way to market. And you see the feller with the big belly and stovepipe hat, just crossin' Seventh? He could be a rebel spy. But he's a congressman. And they's the two painters goin' in the hotel just now. They could be goin' to rob a room, but I seen 'em enough to know they's just painters."

"You're not answering my question," said Halsey.

"I'm sayin' I watch everyone. And whoever been watchin' you . . . ain't just now."

Halsey studied the back of the black man's head and wished that he could enjoy a bit of careless happiness himself, just a man doing manual labor in the morning sun. He also noticed, through the back of Noah's shirt, ridges of raised skin, crossed and crisscrossed. He had noticed them before. Whenever Noah worked, the sweat appeared first in fabric lines on the shirt. Halsey knew they were whip scars. But he never asked about them. It was not his place. And this morning, he had other things on his mind. He said, "Noah, how tall are you?"

"Five-feet-ten, one hundred and sixty-seven pounds, if it's all the same to you."

"Do you have any old clothes?"

Noah straightened up. "Well, sir, all my life I been tryin' not to dress like a congressman, and I think I succeeded right well."

"Would you sell me a pair of old trousers and a shirt. Maybe an old coat and hat?"

"What for?"

"Never mind what for." Halsey reached into his pocket and pulled out a dollar coin, withdrawn from the bank that morning. "Bring them to my room before noon." He put the money into the black man's hands. Then he stood.

"But I ain't finished shinin'."

"No time." For what he was planning, Halsey would want dirty shoes.

Back in his room, he rang his bell for hot water to shave. Then he decided a little black stubble filling in the spaces would be a good thing, too, and his beard grew fast.

. . .

An hour later, as he was memorizing the map that Booth had drawn, he was startled by a knock on his door. He put a hand on his pistol. "Who's there?"

"Jacob Bone." The boy looked to be about eighteen and met Halsey's gaze directly, which was unusual among the blacks that Halsey had encountered. "My pa said for me to bring you this." He handed over a package wrapped in brown paper.

Halsey gave the boy a tip and sent him on his way.

Then he put on the clothes—rough linsey-woolsey shirt, moth-eaten old jacket, floppy, sweat-stained brown felt hat. He also put on a pair of uniform trousers. Plenty of men were walking around Washington in uniform trousers . . . some who had been discharged or mustered out for wounds, some who had simply deserted. With a knapsack over his shoulder, he went down the back stairs and out through the hotel's basement.

He walked up to D Street, then turned south on Eighth, crossed Pennsylvania, and went into the great shed at the Center Market. Hundreds of people were milling about, bargaining, shouting, selling, buying. It was a good place for a man dressed as a worker to lose himself or anyone who might be following him.

He meandered a bit, checked the price of flour, paid a penny for a cellar apple that still had a satisfying snap when he bit into it. Then he found his way to a butcher's stall because he had an idea. He bought a large beef roast for eighteen cents.

Then he spied a butcher's helper pushing a wheel barrow filled with offal. He followed the fellow down Ninth to B Street and across to the low parapet beside the canal, where the helper dumped intestines, stomachs, and other innards into the brown water.

Halsey said, "I'll pay you a dollar for your apron."

"A dollar? I got a whole day's work ahead of me. I ain't splatterin' guts on my clothes. You know how bad they stink?" The butcher's helper pivoted the wheelbarrow and almost knocked Halsey over.

Halsey jumped back and pulled out a coin. "Ten dollars, then . . . gold."

The young man looked at the gold, at Halsey, and then at the apron.

. . .

A short time later, Halsey Hutchinson, dressed as a butcher's helper, carried a paper-wrapped piece of beef past the Whittler, who was still whittling at the front stoop. Then he turned down the alley at the end of the row on Twelfth Street and followed it to the alley along the back.

A stray cat rattled out from a pile of tin cans.

Two men rolled a flour barrel off a wagon and into a yard.

A woman hung clothes on a line.

A curtain fluttered from the front of a privy.

Halsey walked along the back alley until he came to the little yard behind Squeaker McDillon's. From Booth's map, he knew that the windows of Squeaker's office were on ground level. So he looked up at the building, pretending to look for an address, then pushed open the little gate and stepped past the McDillon privy.

He would have preferred to be doing this at night. But McDillon's would be packed at night. He would have preferred not be doing it at all, or doing it in a more legal way, since he was—almost—a lawyer. But he was also a soldier with a duty and a responsibility.

So he peered inside. He saw a desk, a safe, a spittoon, a sofa.

And stretched on a sofa was Squeaker . . . asleep. Open on his chest, as if he had been reading it all morning, lay the small red leather-bound book.

Halsey decided to move. He looked up and down the alley. The flour men had gone off. The clothesline woman and her laundry basket had disappeared, leaving smallclothes and sheets fluttering like ghosts in the sun. Even the cat had left.

So he tried McDillon's door. To his surprise, it was unlocked. No need to talk his way in with a story about a gift from the butcher. He simply pushed, the door swung open, and he stepped into the back hall. In front of him, a narrow flight of stairs led up to the main floor. A narrow passage led into a kitchen beyond the stairs. And Squeaker's office was to the right.

Halsey stood and listened . . . no shuffling of cards or feet, no voices, not even the sound of a Bowie knife whittling.

So he stepped into the office.

Squeaker awoke the instant the floor creaked. "What the hell is this?"

Halsey dropped the beef and pulled the pistol. "Be quiet."

Squeaker started to rise.

Halsey told him to stay still.

Squeaker stopped in midmotion. He was leaning on his elbows. The book was still open on his chest. His voice squeaked: "You shoot that gun and—"

"Just give me the book. All I want is the book."

"Who wouldn't? I got more—"

While holding the gun on Squeaker, Halsey crossed the room and snatched it.

And he noticed Squeaker's eyes shift to something behind him. He whirled, looked into the muzzle of Shag's Navy six, and fired.

At the same moment, Squeaker reached up and grabbed Halsey's arm.

Halsey swung the pistol and smashed Squeaker across the bridge of the nose.

But Squeaker was hard-nosed and pushed Halsey away and knocked the book onto the floor. Then he reached under his desk and grabbed for his scatter gun, but before he could clear it, Halsey put a bullet right into the middle of his forehead.

Squeaker fell backwards, hit the wall, and dropped into a sitting position on the sofa, as dead as the piece of beef.

And Shag lay facedown, a pool of blood expanding beneath his head and rolling quickly across the floor toward the book.

Halsey snatched the book before the blood reached it.

Then he heard someone moving through the room above. He stepped into the hallway, looked up the stairs, saw the Whittler with his Bowie knife.

"Hey! Stop!" shouted the Whittler.

Halsey fired twice. He had won more shooting competitions than anyone at Harvard. So it was skill and instinct that put two perfect shots into the Whittler. Chest first, forehead second, like a paper target. But no paper target ever came tumbling down a narrow staircase, straight at him.

He jumped back so the body wouldn't hit him. Then he shoved the book into his knapsack and stepped out, past the open door of the Mc-Dillon outhouse, where—he now realized—Shag had been busy when Halsey arrived.

.   .   .

The sounds of the city—the distant thrumming of drums, the nearby rumbling of wagons—were enough to muffle four shots from a small handgun in a closed space. After a short distance, Halsey slipped into an outhouse along the alley and pulled off the butcher's apron and floppy felt hat and shoved them into the knapsack. Then he took out his blue officer's tunic and kepi and put them on. Then he headed for C Street.

But he did not turn north for the National Hotel, not yet.

He had to walk.

He had to walk because he feared that someone might be following him.

And he had to walk until he stopped shaking. He had just killed three men. They were not the first men he had killed. He had shot two rebels at Ball's Bluff. But he had never before killed men as he looked them in the eye.

He told himself that they had it coming. But he was not yet ready to stroll into the hotel lobby as if nothing had happened.

So he had to walk.

He walked west on C, then south to B, then west to Seventh. Across the canal, on the Mall, rows of blue-clad soldiers were marching, maneuvering, moving to bugle calls, keeping cadence with the drums. The Army of the Potomac had gone south. But there were still troops in Washington, and the Mall was a perfect place to drill them.

On the Seventh Street Bridge, Halsey stopped, dropped his knapsack at his feet, and looked down at a boat tethered to the rock wall of the canal. Then he looked up and out, at the ribs of the Capitol dome, at the dust that tramping feet sent high into the sky, at the half-built Washington Monument, shimmering in the sunlight like a shard of reality in an unfinished dream.

A wagon went by carrying lumber for the new Armory Square Hospital, under construction in the middle of the Mall. The driver nodded, and Halsey gave a jaunty salute. He waited until the wagon rolled off the bridge. Then he moved his foot and pushed the knapsack through the cast-iron balusters into the canal.

Then he kept walking south, onto the Mall.

He went past the training field toward the hospital that fronted on Seventh. As an officer of the War Department Telegraph Service, he could get into any military establishment in the city. As he knew the names of the officers in command, he could tell the guard that he was there to see Major So-and-So. And if anyone was following him, he could easily lose them in the maze of tents and barrackslike wards.

He hurried past the first patients, soldiers lolling in the sun, some leg-less, others armless, some reading, others playing cards, others staring into space. The sight of these men reminded him of the cost of this war and made him think, yet again, that Peace Democrats like Benjamin Wood might be right when they said that we should forget slavery and bring the South back into the fold on whatever terms they wanted.

He went out onto Maryland Avenue, then over Capitol Hill. Then he headed for the National, confident that he had finally gotten control of himself.

III.

That night, Lincoln ambled into the telegraph office around eleven thirty.

More bad news awaited him.

McClellan reported that Detective Pinkerton's network of informants had spied large numbers of troops reinforcing the rebels behind the same Yorktown works that the British had defended eighty years before. So McClellan was asking for more men.

Lincoln read through the message, pursed his lips, chewed his cheek.

"Down to the raisins, sir?" asked Bates.

Lincoln nodded.

"Well," said Bates, "not much more coming in."

Lincoln looked at Halsey. "I'll take your escort home, then, Lieuten-ant."

On the walk back, neither Lincoln nor Halsey mentioned the day-book . . . or much of anything else.

However, if the president had asked Halsey about the betting activities of Benjamin Wood, whose reputation as a gambler was well deserved, or the sexual proclivities of a certain member of the Senate who liked boys more than girls, Halsey could have expounded all night, because what he had found and stolen was not the president's personal daybook, but Squeaker McDillon's ledger, a compendium of the ways in which a man could tap, trap, swindle, and blackmail the most powerful people in Washington. It even contained what Halsey hoped was the only record of his cousin's gambling debts, with the note: *Gets drunk, brags on Lieut. Halsey Hutchinson of War Dep't, his "gentle cuz." Talks like a poof.*

As for the president's daybook, it was still out there . . . somewhere.

When they reached the White House, Lincoln said, "Lieutenant, you're a fine walking companion. You know when to speak and when to keep silent."

"I only speak when spoken to, sir."

"A true skill. It will help you go a long way . . . in the military or in the law."

"Thank you, sir."

"General McClellan can outtalk a country preacher on a Sunday mornin', but when it comes time to do something, he catches a case of the slows."

"The slows, sir?"

"It was hard enough to get him to move. Once he hatched his plan for the Peninsula, taking the whole army south by boat, then marching them north against Richmond, I had my doubts, but I said, 'at least he's in motion.' Then—" Lincoln caught himself. "I would not share my thinking with you, Lieutenant, except that I trust you will keep it to yourself."

"I will, sir."

"Folks don't need to know *what* I'm thinking until I'm ready to tell them."

"No, sir. That would not be a good thing. But I must warn you, sir—"

Lincoln cocked a brow and fixed an eye on Halsey's face.

Halsey saw no benevolence, no playful humor in the president's gaze. He thought he saw suspicion. And his damaged throat tightened around his words, stopping them on the way out. He stammered and fell silent. His momentary resolve to tell Lincoln the truth, that the presidential

daybook had fallen into the hands of an enemy, either military or political, passed as quickly as it came.

He would not submit to the embarrassment of his own stupidity. He
could not admit to the president that he had killed three men and still
failed to rectify his mistake.

"Warn me of what?" asked Lincoln.

"Warn you that the soldiers like McClellan, despite the 'slows.' At
least that's what I've heard."

"I like him, too," said Lincoln. "If he delivers us the rebel capital, I
shall like him all the more. Good night, Lieutenant."

. . .

On his way home the next morning, Halsey left a card at the Willard for
Miss Constance Wood. He wrote on the back of it, *Viewing* Megatherium
today, with previously planned preliminaries.

Then he stepped to the bar, ordered a brandy, and sauntered to the
doorway of the dining room. Harriet Dunbar was sitting at the same
table, sipping coffee. She looked as if she was waiting for someone. The
Squeaker? He would not be coming. But she raised her head and studied
each man who entered, then looked away in disappointment.

Halsey was back in the Willard at noon, and Constance was waiting in
the ladies' parlor on the second floor. The room was not reserved for ladies.
But certain male activities—drinking (anything but tea), cussing, and
spitting—were frowned upon. Gentlemen were expected to be gentlemen.

Constance was sitting at a table by the south window. The Washington *Daily Republican* was spread out in front of her.

"Miss Wood." He took a seat opposite her.

She looked at the newspaper. "It says here that a gambling den called
Squeaker McDillon's was invaded yesterday by a gunman who killed
three men, including one whose initials are—" She looked up. "—McD."

"That, I assume, would be the owner," said Halsey.

She pointed to his shoulder. "If I were to ask you to lift the flap of
your suit, I would see a holster. If I asked for the pistol, would I smell
gunpowder?"

"You would smell gun oil. I keep my weapons in excellent working
order. All of them." He did not think she would catch the extra meaning

in that remark. He never spoke to ladies in double entendres. But for some reason, he felt that he had earned it.

In response, she looked into his eyes and ran her tongue across her upper lip, as if his second meaning appetized her. And she said, "Did you do it?"

"I don't know what you're talking about."

"Do you have something for me, something to show to Frederick Douglass? Words from a presidential diary, perhaps?"

"Until I read Douglass, I have nothing for Douglass."

That last response made her flop back in her chair and screw up her lips. "If you tell me you *have* nothing, I'll believe you. But if you tell me you *know* nothing, I won't. Is Lincoln planning a general emancipation?"

"He hasn't told his lieutenants. He's the president. He has his plans. He will tell the world what he wants them to know when he wants them to know it."

And she smiled, one conspirator to another. "Would you think me terrible if I said I find it quite exciting to be in the presence of a man who can kill three antagonists so skillfully with—what was it?" She found the paragraph in the paper and read. "'Four shots, three heads and a heart, all as if the shootist were on a target range'?"

He had managed to reveal nothing to her. He had tamped down his guilt at killing three thugs. He was ignoring his guilt over losing the day-book and dissembling with the president. All perhaps because he now felt something very much like . . . lust. Whatever he had done and failed to do in the last few days, this young woman had been his only constant. He had not thought of her constantly. But when he did think of her, he saw her conspiratorial smile, heard her honeyed voice, smelled her intoxicating aroma, and for a few moments forgot his descent into darkness.

It seemed that she felt the same something, because she stood suddenly and said, "The *Megatherium* awaits."

. . .

Soon, they were in the West Range, beneath the high, arched ceiling, beside one of the Gothic pillars. It was quiet but for the distant voices echoing from the library.

She looked at the face of an Indian and said, "As black as a Negro."

"Another problem to solve," said Halsey, "once we settle the question of slavery."

Then there was silence between them.

Somewhere outside, the drums were thrumming. His heart pounded. So did her breathing. He could see it as her breasts rose and fell beneath her dress.

He slipped a hand around her waist and turned her into the shadow. She let him press her against the pillar, and before she kissed him, she reached up and took the sides of his face in her hands. The feel of her fingertips on his cheeks was as electric as if she had touched his manhood.

He brought his mouth onto hers. And she met his hard kiss with an open mouth, soft, moist, pliable.

Then she whispered, "It *was* Lincoln's diary, wasn't it?"

That was a question to cause a man to lose his manly momentum. He pulled back and looked at her. A shaft of sunlight fell through the arched windows, highlighting her strawberry blond hair. And he asked himself if she was simply using him.

But before he could ask her, or kiss her, or tell her the truth about the daybook and the death of McDillon, he saw the face of Detective Joseph Albert McNealy.

It appeared from behind the pillar. Then a pistol came straight at Halsey's head.

Constance Wood screamed.

.   .   .

Halsey Hutchinson lost track of time beneath the burlap sack.

He could hear the rumble of voices, the dripping of water, the thump of shuffling feet, and the thrumming of drums, like the boiling of water in a giant steam engine.

He flexed his shoulders to uncramp his arms, which were cuffed behind him.

Then he heard footsteps. The burlap bag was pulled away.

A single lantern hung from a beam above his head. Somewhere in the distance light fell through an open door. Figures hulked in the darkness between.

He said, "I am Lieutenant Halsey Hutchinson, of the Twentieth Massachusetts Volunteer Infantry, seconded to the War Department telegraph office. I demand to—"

"Save it, Lieutenant."

Halsey could not see the man. He spoke to the darkness: "What am I doing here?"

"I ask the questions."

"Where am I?"

The answer arrived in the form of a leather gauntlet across his face. "I told you, I ask the questions. Now, then—" The man thrust his face into the light, a bushy black beard, dark eyes, black brows, a blue civilian suit. "—do you know who I am?"

Halsey took a moment to calm the ringing in his ear, then said, "Lafayette Baker."

"Very good." The man straightened, his face disappearing into the shadows. "Then you know from whom I derive my power."

"Secretary Stanton."

"From Executive Order Number One, transferring control of all political prisoners and the investigation of all suspected traitors to the War Department."

"That does not explain why I'm here," said Halsey. "Wherever I am."

Baker's shadow turned, took something from a shadow behind him, and held it in front of Halsey's face. "They say you are an expert in handguns. Can you identify this?"

"A pistol," said Halsey as mildly as he could.

"It's an Adams thirty-one-caliber pocket revolver. Note the manufacture—barrel, grip, and frame all of single piece. Note the handsome engravings. I always say that a good gun should be a thing of beauty, expressing the care that goes into making it." Baker looked over his shoulder at the other shadow. "It's like the care in a good investigation, eh, Detective?"

"Yes, sir." That was McNealy's voice.

Baker turned back to Halsey. "Note the ease of handling." With nimble fingers he popped the cylinder out of the pistol, then popped it back in, then pointed the gun at Halsey, who told himself not to flinch. Instead, he made eye contact . . . first with the barrel and then with Baker, who squeezed the trigger.

The hammer retracted and snapped down on an empty chamber.

"Double action," said Baker. "Very smooth. No wonder that British officers in the Crimea came to rely on this weapon."

"It's the main competition for the Colt Wells Fargo," said Halsey.

"Now manufactured in your own town of Boston. Is that where you bought this?"

"Yes. I was carrying it when I was arrested."

Baker gave the barrel a sniff. "Fired recently. Did you shoot anyone with it?"

"Not since Ball's Bluff."

"Good answer. I'd say 'Not since Ball's Bluff' to every question, if I had your record." Baker turned. "Don't you think it's a good answer, Detective?"

"An excellent answer. Deflects a lot of suspicion."

"But"—Baker turned back to Halsey—"why does this pistol smell of powder?"

"I shoot targets at the range on Mason's Island. It keeps me sharp."

"So, you shoot targets with an Adams thirty-one-caliber revolver, serial number 2342, which we find on your person. But we also find, at the McDillon murder scene, an Adams thirty-one-caliber revolver, serial number 2343. How do you figure that?"

Halsey said, "Coincidence?"

Baker laughed. "I've been told you have an answer for everything. 'Coincidence' can't be one of your best."

Halsey agreed. These detectives had been to the murder scene. They had gotten the pistol that Squeaker's boys had stolen from Halsey. What else had they gotten?

"Just answer this," said Baker. "Did you kill three men in McDillon's yesterday?"

"I killed no one."

"That's not what Detective McNealy thinks." Baker handed the pistol back to McNealy. "He thinks you shot the place up because they killed your cousin and stole his pistol. And Detective McNealy is a man of great insight."

"So I've heard," said Halsey.

"And I've heard that you're a lawyer."

"I was in law school when the war began." Halsey shifted in the chair and moved his arms. "I decided the law could wait with the survival of the Union at stake."

Baker said, "I came from a place where there was no law, and no lawyers, and no courts, where a man might be killed for a shovel, or a piece of beef, or a ticket home. I'm talking about San Francisco, in the Gold Rush. Some of us took the law into our own hands back then. They called us vigilantes. Now I am a vigilante for the Union."

"Then you agree. The law *can* wait when the survival of the Union is at stake." Halsey sensed that it was the answer that this Lafayette Baker wanted to hear.

"I'm not bothered by the killing of three men who needed killing. But something else bothers me, Lieutenant. There was word in certain low places that Squeaker was peddling something that belonged to the president, a daybook. And we know that he lost one on your watch in the telegraph office."

"We know that he lost it," answered Halsey. "But who can say where?" He was getting better at lying, or at least it was coming more easily to him.

Baker studied Halsey. In the distance, the voices rumbled, the water dripped, the feet shuffled. But Baker seemed to be searching for a truth in Halsey's eyes that had not revealed itself in his answers. Then he turned to McNealy. "He's yours. Lock him up. Let him go. Do what you will. I have other fish to fry." And Lafayette Baker was gone.

Now, McNealy's beard and brow appeared in the lantern light.

Halsey said, "Nice to see a friendly face."

McNealy reached into his pocket for—*what*? A sap? A pistol? Halsey prepared for pain. It would either be immediate, or the long-term pain of imprisonment, at least until he could communicate with Major Eckert or his father.

But McNealy produced a key and unlocked Halsey's cuffs. Then he handed him back his pistol and said, "Get up."

With a relief flooding him, Halsey followed McNealy up a rickety flight of stairs and out into the courtyard of the infamous Old Capitol Prison.

The sky was still light. It must have been around seven o'clock.

McNealy led him down Capitol Hill to Armory Square, then along the hospital barracks and out the other side to Seventh Street.

Halsey realized that McNealy was reversing the escape route from the day before, proving without words that he had watched every move Halsey made.

The drilling had ended on the Mall. The dust had settled. The drums were silent. Somewhere in the distance, a bugle blew.

McNealy led Halsey onto the Seventh Street bridge and stopped. He put a foot on the lower rail. And he looked up at the Capitol, which reflected the rose red light of dusk. "You don't like me very much, do you, Lieutenant?"

Halsey thought the question was rhetorical, so he didn't answer.

"But I believe in the Union," said McNealy. "I think you believe in it, too."

"I do."

"I also believe"—McNealy looked into the dirty canal—"that if I wanted to catch typhoid, I could drop into that water right now and pull out a bag containing a butcher's apron and hat and some old clothes, couldn't I?"

Halsey said, "I wouldn't know."

McNealy laughed. "You are persistent in your lies, Lieutenant. That's what I like about you. Persistent, smart, and stupid, too, because you underestimate your accusers."

"Disliking you doesn't mean underestimating you."

"Fair enough." McNealy pulled out two cigars and offered one to Halsey, who accepted, even though he seldom smoked.

McNealy struck a match and lit both cigars. After a few puffs, he said, "Do you know how the detective service recruits its people?"

"No."

"However it can. We have thousands of undercover operatives, looking for disloyalty, treason, corruption, spying . . . all over Washington and all over this busted country. We read all the newspapers. We watch all the depots. We even slip behind enemy lines. How do you think Pinkerton can give such good information to McClellan?"

"Some wish McClellan paid less mind to Pinkerton and more to his troop returns."

"McClellan is fighting to bring the South to its senses, so we can put Secession behind us. We can deal with the nigger business later."

"If that works, I'm for it," said Halsey.

"But there are enemy spies everywhere. So we must watch. And now, Lieutenant—" He took a puff of his cigar, the flame glowing in the fading light. "—you're one of my watchers."

"Watchers?"

"If I ask, you will answer. If I suspect, you will surmise. If I say to fetch me coffee from the War Department basement, you will jump. Or I'll tell Baker I agree with his suspicion that you stole the president's daybook and sold it to the highest bidder."

"Ridiculous."

"He thinks it was either Harriet Dunbar or Benjamin Wood who bought it."

Halsey was impressed by how close they had come to the answer.

"You may be able to help us find the truth," said McNealy. "So, if I want you to trail Wood, you'll do that, too. You follow?"

Halsey said nothing.

McNealy barely paused. "You may even get to keep kissing that niece of his when you spy on her."

"Spy on her?"

McNealy laughed. "You've been Frenchin' a rebel spy in the Smithsonian." Then he stopped laughing and brought his face closer to Halsey. "Now, get me straight. I don't care about dead gamblers. And I don't care about the president's daybook, if he's too sloppy to care about it himself. But from now on, I run you, Lieutenant Halsey Hutchinson of Boston, Massachusetts, son of privilege, family friend of Ralph Waldo Emerson. And if you fail me, I will give you back to that vigilante you just met, and you'll spend the rest of the war in a dark hole in the Old Capitol Prison. You follow?"

"I follow."

FIVE

Saturday Afternoon

"Some flea market." Peter slid into the cab next to Diana and slammed the door. Then he put his head back and wiped the sweat from his face. Good that the cab was air-conditioned. Good that he'd left his blazer in the hotel.

Diana said, "What did that guy mean about you skinning the little guy?"

"He was mad that he's one of skinnees. But I'm thinking I should go back and buy that book by Benjamin Wood. Dawkins said it was in the same lot as the Proclamation picture. The names on the endpaper might be important. And you ought to go back and sweet-talk Dawkins. Tell him we can make a deal. Tell him that we're on to something worth seven figures. Tell him he's in for half if he helps us."

"If I get it, I want it for the museum," said Diana, "or for my next book."

"Ever the scholar," said Peter. "There'll be plenty for everybody if Dawkins helps us." Peter glanced out the rear window to get a fix on the cars behind him; then he said, "Do you have Sorrel's address?"

She handed him the slip of paper that Dawkins had given her. "He lives in a neighborhood in Arlington, across the river."

"We'll stop for a minute at the hotel, then head over there."

"But Peter . . . the seminar."

"Skip it."

"The Saturday Seminars were my idea. GWU doesn't have a football team, so we need weekend activities. Besides, I moderate the panel. And maybe Sorrel will show up."

"Show up?"

"That's where I met him. It's open to the public and draws a good crowd," she said. "People like the subject: 'From Uncle Tom to the Thirteenth Amendment: the Role of Race in the Civil War.'"

"Maybe the guy in the Bonnie Blue Flag ball cap will show up, too."

Diana cocked her head and snapped a finger. "I *knew* I recognized him."

"You recognized him enough to scare the hell out of him."

"But Peter—"

"I wanted to sidle up to him at the cheese counter and start chatting."

"But Peter—"

"Instead, you lit out after him like he just stole your purse."

"But Peter! He was at the seminar last week. When Sorrel came up to me, he took our picture."

Peter thought for a moment. "That means he's been following you for a while. Maybe he hacked you."

She shrugged and looked out the window, as if she was feeling pretty stupid about that. "It could have been a lot of people. I'm in academe, don't forget."

"Where the fights are so vicious because the stakes are so small."

Diana glared at him. "They're not small if you're fighting them."

He remembered. She didn't like to be needled. He backed off and gave another glance out the back window. No one was following them. "So do you have any ideas?"

"It could have been him, or a departmental rival, or an angry student—"

"—or a lover?"

"Not me." Diana laughed. "I'm the latter-day Condi Rice—a hard-climbin' sistah who got no time for doin' the nasty with potbellied white professors."

"Very wise. A girl can hurt her reputation sleeping her way to the top."

"Hurt it by saying no, too."

"Saying no?"

"Saying no on Saturday night in somebody's apartment means that on Monday morning, when the tenure committee meets, you get the black-ball."

Peter looked at her a moment and said, "You didn't let somebody on your tenure committee take you home after dinner and drinks, did you?"

She looked out the window.

"Anyone we know?" asked Peter.

She shook her head. "You might meet him. But—"

"You think he's the hacker?"

She shook her head again.

He wasn't sure if she meant "No, he wasn't," or "No, she didn't know."

So he said, "What makes you think you've *been* hacked?"

"I got an e-mail from the National Press Club. Invited me to a discussion on slavery with Henry Louis Gates on Monday night. When I registered, I put in my password and got the 'incorrect password' prompt. And—"

"Let me guess . . . it kept prompting you, and you kept trying different passwords."

"Right."

"The ones you use for your e-mail, your Gmail, your GWU.edu account, along with your bank account, your library card and—"

"I figured out it was a dummy site when I went on this morning to get a ticket for you, once I knew you were coming to town."

"Please tell me that you sent the Lincoln letter to me on a protected account."

She looked out the window again.

So, thought Peter, the hacker knew. He may have known before he hacked her. He may even have been looking for the letter, too.

. . .

Evangeline got out of the cab in front of Ford's Theatre. She had done her eyes and put on a light face of Mac Studio Fix 5. She wore a blue silk blouse, darker blue slacks, and a dark gray silk-and-wool-blend sport coat.

Abigail Simon was standing in front of the theater, waiting for her. "Nice outfit."

"Thanks," said Evangeline.

"Subtle. You got the blue and the gray both goin' on."

Evangeline laughed. "I hadn't even thought of that."

"The museum is still open, so we'll shoot with visitors. It'll be good background. Let's go." Abigail went in the museum entrance, a wall of plate glass next to the old theater.

But Evangeline stopped for a look around.

The replica streetlamps stood guard like those that lit that long-ago night. The high-fronted brick façade rose like a ghost over the narrow street. And the arched doorways were like a proscenium awaiting another performance of the passion play that had been running in the national imagination for 150 years: the "giant sufferer," as the papers called him, borne from the theater across to a little row house, there to breathe his last, there to inspire the epitaph of Secretary Stanton, "Now he belongs to the ages." Or was it "angels"?

Evangeline had thought about calling this theater "the nation's Golgotha," the place where the savior had been put to death. But she didn't want the show to be a downer, so . . . she just stood there, feeling the chill of history.

She didn't even notice the black Chevy Tahoe pulling up at the opposite curb. Out of the Tahoe stepped a young man, tall, slender, dark gray suit, dark blue tie, dark glasses. He called to her by name.

Her first thought: *What does the FBI want with me?*

As he came toward her, he smiled. "My name is William Dougherty. I'm chief of staff to Congressman Milbury. He's excited that you're preparing a program about the modern landscapes of the Civil War."

How did Milbury know where she would be shooting? How did so many people seem to know her business in Washington?

Dougherty handed her a business card. "May I watch the filming?"

Mary Knapik, the PA, poked her head out the door, "Ms. Carrington—"

Evangeline looked into Dougherty's eyes, which meant looking at her own reflection in his sunglasses. "The tickets to the museum are free."

"I'll take that as a yes," said Dougherty. "And the congressman would like to invite you to a reception at the Smithsonian tonight, in honor of the Emancipation Proclamation. It'll be a real Washington event for you and Peter Fallon."

There it was again. She said, "How did you—?"

Dougherty handed her a printed invitation.

"Ms. Carrington," said Mary, "we're ready for your close-up!"

. . .

Peter had hoped to catch Evangeline at the hotel.

When he found the room empty, he called her. She didn't answer. So he texted her:

Be careful. Just chased suspicious character through Eastern Market.

In a few moments, she texted back:

You would.

Diana laughed out loud when he showed her that. "She's still a smart-ass."

"That's why we still get along."

"Even if you decided not to get married."

"Another reason we still get along . . . I guess."

Then Evangeline added this to her text:

Suspicious characters everywhere . . .

Diana said, "Does she mean me?"

"No. She likes you." He waited for more, but that was it, so he clicked off the phone. "At least she liked you until you dragged me down here."

"I had no one else I could turn to . . . that I could trust."

"Any Lincoln letter is worth a lot. And whenever there's something out there worth a lot, a lot of people go after it. And some of them do not play by the rules." Peter grabbed an apple from the fruit basket.

"But you do?" she said.

"I do *what?*"

"Play by the rules."

"Rules?" He bit into the apple. "No rules in a treasure hunt."

. . .

The George Washington University was only a few blocks west, so Peter and Diana walked up Fifteenth, to the corner where Pennsylvania made a sharp left and ran straight past the Treasury, the White House, and the Old Executive Office Building.

"We are now in the aortic artery of American political democracy," said Peter.

The street here was all brick, like a mall. Rows of steel bollards blocked the ends at Fifteenth and Seventeenth. Pedestrians could walk through them, and the bollards could be lowered into the ground to allow vehicles to pass at the checkpoints.

"Before the days of high security," said Diana, "this was just a regular street, cars, trucks, buses . . . anybody could drive right by."

"And in the Civil War"—Peter gestured toward the White House—"you could walk up to the door and ask for the president. Now we're watched by cameras, radiation sensors, guys on the roof with sniper rifles. Makes you yearn for a simpler time."

"Except for the racism," she said. "It's more subtle today. Back then it was more . . . in-your-face."

"No iPhones back then, either." Peter pulled his from his pocket and glanced at it. "Now we can stay in touch with our assistants anywhere."

"You mean Antoine? That African American kid?"

"More than a kid. Getting a Ph.D. in History and a law degree, too."

"Not many people do that," said Diana, "white or black."

"I told him to go for history first. You need a past, even if it's ugly, before you can build a future." The iPhone vibrated in his hand. "There's my boy now."

"Boy?" Diana raised an eyebrow.

"Come on, sistah. Don't you know we's livin' in a postracial society?"

"You don't do that very well."

"I don't rap, either."

"Thank God," said Diana. "Now, what does your *boy* have to say?"

Peter read from the phone: "'This just scratches the surface, boss.'"

"*Boss?* He calls you boss? You two sound like Jack Benny and Rochester."

"A significant pairing in the history of race relations," said Peter.

"Oh, yeah? How?"

"The white guy was the straight man. The black guy got all the jokes."

Diana pointed to the iPhone. "Just read."

"Antoine says, 'Went to National Archives Web site for troop lists from Compiled Military and Service Records. Checked Mass. regiments first and . . . bingo! Lieutenant Halsey Hutchinson, Twentieth Mass. Volunteer Infantry. Corporal Jeremiah Murphy, ditto. Heading to MHS'— that's the Massachusetts Historical Society—'to read regimental history and muster rolls.'"

"That's all?" said Diana.

"We've only been on this a few hours. The National Archives Web site is the database for every Union soldier, but it only gives name and regiment. To get more, you need to read the biographies in the Compiled Military and Service Records. The government created them to determine who deserved pensions. The actual CMSRs aren't online. We'll have to go to the National Archives to read them."

"The Archives don't open till Monday."

"And by Monday, this thing could be over. We're competing with the camera-guy at the market. And he probably has friends. And there may be others. So Antoine will learn what he can from the muster rolls. But we need to get more on the War Department telegraph office."

"The War Department building was right there." Diana pointed at the Old Executive Office Building, a huge confection of French Empire flourishes, hundreds of plate glass windows and pillars, holding thousands of bureaucrats . . . a complex design for a complex world. "Of course, the Lincoln-era building was much smaller. More like a dorm in Harvard Yard. But when Lieutenant Hutchinson looked out the windows, he would have seen what we see across the street . . . Blair House, the other high-toned row houses, the Renwick Gallery."

The Renwick had been designed by the same man who designed the Smithsonian Castle, another romantic Victorian vision of the Gothic past, another strong fortress protecting knowledge and art. In 1862, the Union quartermaster had liked the construction of the Renwick so much that he made it a supply depot.

"Not much else left of Lincoln-era Washington," said Diana. "It was all chewed up by the modern world."

"Lincoln was the first modern president," said Peter. "He traveled faster than any president before, on steamboats and trains. He read by reliable gas light. He communicated electrically through thousands of miles of telegraph wires—"

"But he still lived in a city with one paved street and a stinky canal where Constitution Avenue is today."

"And even *free* blacks had to tip their hats to whites," added Peter.

"Hard to imagine," said Diana.

"But that's what I do," said Peter. "With documents and photos, I can imagine my way into the past, and maybe into a few heads, too. If I can see what they saw and think what they thought, I can find the treasures they left."

"Do you think you can think like this Lieutenant Halsey Hutchinson?"

"We'll find out, once Antoine finds out more."

.   .   .

At the Ford's Theatre Museum, Evangeline was discovering a new skill. She could ad-lib in front of a camera, even when creepy Congressional aides were watching.

The basement museum—small but packed with information—was arranged so that the visitor traveled through the war with Lincoln, following him from his ignominious 1861 arrival in Washington to his final visit to the theater.

"Ignominious," she explained, "because to avoid a threatened assassination in Baltimore, he put on a disguise and sneaked into the city at night. The papers depicted him wearing a long gray cape and Scottish tam-o'-shanter, under the protection of a Scottish detective named Pinkerton." She said this in front of a six-foot-four dummy in a long gray cape and tam-o'-shanter.

And she noticed Dougherty watching and listening from behind the camera.

The next setup was at the video screens in the middle of the floor, in front of a huge model of the half-finished Capitol dome.

Lots of visitors here, moving about, reading the cards, looking at the exhibits.

"Good production value," said Abigail Simon. "Be casual."

Casual . . . right, thought Evangeline. She looked into the lens, pretended that the key light wasn't blinding her, and said, "When you come here, you'll see remarkable multimedia exhibits."

The video screen showed photographs of the era, including a famous shot of Lincoln's first inaugural. And each image was animated by pans and tilts, slow zooms and the latest in three-dimensionalizing tricks.

Evangeline explained: "By March of 1861, seven Southern states had seceded. But Lincoln still hoped to hold the country together. He said, 'Though passion may have strained, it must not break our bonds of affection. The mystic chords of memory, stretching from every battlefield and patriot grave, to every living heart and hearthstone, all over this broad land, will yet swell the chorus of Union when again touched, as surely they will be, by the better angels of our nature.'"

A dozen people applauded her.

The PA handed her a water bottle. "Fabulous. All without a teleprompter."

Abigail said something to the cameraman, then whispered to Evangeline, "Too many words."

"Too many words?"

"This is TV. We'll do some cutting," said Abigail. "The next setup is over in the corner, by the Lincoln suit, the one he wore to the theater." And she headed in that direction.

Evangeline pulled out her script. Then she sensed William Dougherty beside her. Then she heard him say one word: "tariffs."

"What?"

He had taken off his sunglasses. His eyes were the same color as his suit. "You've been talking about the beginning of the war and never mentioned tariffs."

Evangeline held up the script. "It isn't in here. Is that bad?"

"No. That's good. So many anti-tax people try to tell you that the Civil War was about the extension of federal power through tariffs, the only federal revenue at the time. They try to say our tax system is as inequitable as the tariff system that supposedly oppressed the South."

"Politics then, politics now," said Evangeline. "Is that why the congressman is interested in our film?"

"Perhaps. He sits on the House Committee on Natural Resources. They have oversight over the National Park Service, which has oversight over a lot of the places you're shooting. And he sits on Ways and Means, which has oversight on tax policy. And he hates to see history twisted for political purposes."

Was he threatening her? Was he suggesting that she tell the story their way or she might not get permits to shoot on federal land? Was that why he was here? Did politics color everything in this town?

She decided not to lose her temper, so she gave him the kind of smile that Kathi Morganti had given the congressman on the train. "I agree with Oliver Wendell Holmes, the Supreme Court Justice. He said, 'I like paying taxes. With them I buy civilization.'"

Dougherty raised a finger. "Supreme Court Justice *and* Civil War hero."

. . .

Across town, Peter Fallon was taking a seat in an auditorium at GWU.

His first thought: good air-conditioning. His second: nice room, paneled walls, padded seats. His third: quite a crowd for a Saturday afternoon in September.

Maybe it was the air-conditioning.

Then he read the program and decided it was the speakers, a talking head from the right wing and an academic egghead who likely leaned left, a perfect pairing for a little historical grudge match. Their bios:

Terenzia "Terry" Volpicelli is an independent scholar and defender of "the Constitution as it is." He is the author of four books on Lincoln. He has lectured extensively, appeared on numerous television talk shows, on Fox News, CNN, and as a regular on LNN, the Liberty News Network. Of his new book, *Lincoln's Gestapo: The Secret Police That Terrorized America*, *Publishers Weekly* said, "guaranteed to make you think." He will be speaking about it today for the first time.

Professor Colin Conlon of George Washington University is the author of *Lincoln at Law: The Legal Education and Political Birth of Abraham Lincoln*. He received his B.A. from Princeton, his Ph.D. from Columbia. He is best known for his works on the eighteenth century, including the Pulitzer Prize winner, *Ideals and Economies: The Roots of the American Revolution*. His commentary has appeared in numerous periodicals, and he is a regular contributor to *The New York Review of Books*. He is also director of the Conlon Center for Studies in American History at GWU.

Peter pulled out a notebook and pen. This was going to be good.

The auditorium held about two hundred, and every seat was taken. People were standing along the side aisles, too. It was another of those "crossroads of D.C." crowds: white and black, rich and poor, young and old, student and professional, lobbyist and welfare mom, tourist and local.

At three o'clock, Diana led the speakers onto the dais. She had changed into a yellow sundress that looked dazzling against her coffee-colored skin.

Peter started taking notes.

No one in audience looks "off". . . . No Sorrel. No Bonnie Blue Flag ball-caps.

Volpicelli—olive complexion, black hair, seersucker suit over pink Izod shirt w/collar up. Nervous smile. Eyes shift . . . expecting attack . . . verbal? Physical? Knows hostile audience when he sees one.

Colin Conlon. Acts like Pulitzer-winner. Cool . . . condescending? Guys from Princeton always act like that, even without Pulitzers.

Diana opens: "Our question today: How did a man who, by our lights, harbored racial beliefs more in line with the KKK than the NAACP, come to sign DC Emancipation Act, Emancipation Proclamation, and insist, even when he thought it would bring defeat in the 1864 election, that the Republican Party make the Thirteenth Amendment a plank in its platform, and—?"

Conlon interrupts: "He did it because he was a political visionary!"

Volpicelli counters: "He did it because he was a political cynic!"

Fifteen minutes for each speaker . . . lines drawn in opening statements.

V. speaks fast, facts in hand, even if interprets wrong . . . sounds like Midwesterner, despite Italian name.

C. is typical prof, all "ums and ahs and on the one hand, on the other hand." Not a sound bite kind of guy. Good reason only TV gigs are on PBS docs. Too boring even for C-SPAN. But always ready to jump on Diana when she makes a point. Is he the potbellied white prof on her tenure committee, even though he has no pot?

Closing statements:

C.: Lincoln a product of his times yet a man out of time. Nice but bland.

V.: Lincoln, the railroad lawyer, a tool of the special interests: of big business investors who wanted him to sign transcontinental RR bill; of greenback guys who were happy to run up nat'l debt and take country off gold standard; of New England Repubs who wanted to tell everyone else how to live their lives. Preserving Union a euphemism for extending Federal power. Eradicating slavery a smoke screen. Juicy revisionism.

Diana walks middle road.

Now Q&A.

Peter just listened. Some good questions. Some stupid ones. And throughout, he heard echoes of the modern debate: how much power to concentrate here, in the imperial city, and how much to leave in the hands of the people who live in the places where the issues live. It had been the debate over the Constitution in 1787, it had been part of the irrepressible conflict that led to the Civil War, and it never ended.

Diana declared, "Last question!" and pointed to a guy with a bushy beard, jeans, T-shirt, ball cap, standing along the far side of the auditorium.

Like half the people in the room, Peter was pulling out his iPhone. The event was all but over. Time to make sure he hadn't missed anything important in the last hour. But as he scrolled through his e-mails, he heard this from the far side of the room:

"Professor Volpicelli, in your book you mention a Lincoln diary."

Peter looked up. A *diary*? Wow. Forget the Lincoln letter. Then he looked at the guy and saw that his ball cap had a white star, just like the guy in the flea market.

Professor Conlon sniffed into the microphone. "Let's get two things straight: First, my debate partner is not a professor. Second, while more books have been written about Lincoln than about any human being except Jesus Christ, none of them talk seriously about a diary."

"Wrong again," said Volpicelli, "at least about the diary, though it's not exactly a diary, and it may *not* exactly be Lincoln's, but—"

"You see?" said Conlon. "I said, 'talk seriously,' and this is what you get."

Volpicelli just laughed. "I'll bet you haven't even read my book."

"I have no interest in reading politically motivated claptrap."

"Spoken like one of the Lincoln flame-keepers."

"I don't even know what that is," said Conlon.

"Let me explain."

"Please don't," said Conlon.

Volpicelli kept smiling. "Diana Wilmington admits that Lincoln was a racist. She bases her whole thesis on it. So she doesn't light a candle and genuflect before the Lincoln altar. She's no flame-keeper."

"Just the author of inflammatory rhetoric designed to sell books," said Conlon.

"But," said Volpicelli, "you're one of those academic historians who refuse to see Lincoln from a fresh perspective."

"The perspective of John Wilkes Booth, you mean?" Conlon began to shuffle papers.

Volpicelli said, "I'll ignore that."

"And you should be ignored. I don't even know why you're here. You're just a guy with a word processor and some right-wing money behind you. You have no training and no degrees. I have tenure at a major university. And Assistant Professor Wilmington defended her positions among her peers"—then Conlon gave her a pointed look—"even if she has the kind of extreme ideas better aimed at the television networks than the community of scholars."

Yes, thought Peter, Conlon was the spurned suitor.

"Extreme ideas," said Volpicelli, "and pretty, too."

Then someone spoke from the far side of the room: deep voice, Midwest accent. "Mr. Volpicelli, this business about a Lincoln diary . . . what's your primary source?"

The smile fell from Volpicelli's face like a sheet of glass hit with a hammer.

Peter turned and scanned the crowd behind him.

A guy in a Hawaiian shirt and jeans was staring intently at Volpicelli. He had a skinny face, a mustache and chin strap, a sort of elongated soul patch popular in the Civil War. He looked like he could have stepped right out of the nineteenth century, but for the giant orchids on the shirt.

Volpicelli's voice lost all its cocky conviction. He fell back on authorspeak. "Buy the book and find out."

A few people hissed; a few more laughed.

As if she sensed that things were breaking down, Diana stood. "Now, folks, we'll be signing our books in the lobby. You'll know me because I'll be sitting in the middle."

That brought more laughter, then applause, then people were standing, buzzing, pushing forward to talk to the speakers, because they didn't want to wait in line or didn't want to be embarrassed into buying a book in order to get some face time.

Peter caught Diana's eye and made a gesture—*I'll see you outside*—then he turned up the aisle with lots of *excuse me*s and looked across the auditorium for the Hawaiian shirt. He had to find that guy or the one with the star on his hat.

But neither of them was in the foyer or hanging in the hallway.

So Peter decided to look outside.

He stepped from the air-conditioning into the hot little plaza dominated by the sculpted head of George Washington. He looked up and down the street. Then he saw the shirt.

The guy was standing by the statue, studying his iPhone.

Peter said, "Excuse me."

The guy looked at Peter, then at his phone, then said, "Are you the big-deal book man from Boston?"

"My fame precedes me. So . . . who are you?"

"No one you need to know. Just stay out of our way."

"I don't know what you're talking about."

"You knew enough to go snooping at the flea market." The man held his phone up.

Peter saw a picture of himself, perusing *The Killer Angels*. He said, "That's my bad side. I should have had him take another one."

The guy looked to be in his forties. His face was long and sallow from forehead to chin, sunburned on the sides . . .

Peter said, "Someone just mentioned a Lincoln diary in there, which prompted a question from you."

"That was bait, to see who'd rise. And here you are, a few hours after your girlfriend rides the train with two of the other players." He swiped his thumb across the screen and brought up a picture of Evangeline and two people on the Acela Club Car.

Peter said, "I don't know who those people are."

"The congressman and the lobbyist? You don't know who they are? Then why are you here?"

"I came for the seminar. Lifelong learning."

"It can be a short life if you don't learn the right lessons."

A black Chrysler 200 pulled up, and Mr. Civil War Soul Patch headed for it.

"Wait." Peter took a step. "Are you the hackers?"

And the barrel of a pistol popped out the back window. The guy with the bushy beard, the one who had asked the first question, was holding it. And it looked like the camera guy from the Eastern Market was driving.

"That's a Navy Colt," said the man. "A repro, but it works. Forty-four-caliber ball. Tear you to pieces."

Peter looked at the gun, then at the guy, and decided, as he usually did, that discretion was the better course. "You have a nice day."

The car sped away, but not before Peter pulled out his phone and got a shot of the plate. Then he turned to go back inside and bumped into Diana.

"What was that?" she asked.

"A player. A big player. And a Civil War reenactor, I think."

"How can you tell?"

"The sides of his face were sunburned, but not the front, as if he had been wearing a brimmed cap, like a Bonnie Blue Flag ball cap or a kepi."

"Kepi?"

"A Civil War cap," said Peter. "He also wore that mustache and chin strap. And he threatened me with a reproduction Civil War pistol."

She said, "Did he say anything more about a Lincoln diary?"

"He said I should stay out of it."

"The wrong thing to say to you."

"And a violation of the rules," he said.

"I thought you said there weren't any rules."

"Unless I'm making them up as I go along." Peter typed an e-mail address onto his phone and attached the picture of the license plate. Then he clicked SEND.

Diana looked over his shoulder. "Where's that going?"

"To a friend of mine in New York, a private detective. He'll run that plate."

Two or three students approached and told Diana how much they had enjoyed the panel. An older black woman came up and asked her to sign a copy of her book, which Diana did with a smile and some friendly chit-chat. Diana's student assistant brought a bottle of water out to her and said that the department head wanted to talk to her.

"Tell him I'll be right along." Diana turned to Peter. "I'd better see to this."

Peter asked her, "Where's Volpicelli?"

"He didn't stay. I think he wanted to split before someone took a poke at him."

"And Professor Conlon?" asked Peter.

"I asked him to have a drink with us, but he was more blunt than Volpicelli."

"Blunt?"

"He said he didn't want to drink with a scholar who had prostituted herself to popularity. He envies my book sales and notoriety."

"He's on your tenure committee, isn't he?"

She just gave him a long look.

That was enough. Diana and Professor Conlon.

She said, "The only way I'll get tenure is to do something really original, something from a primary source that no one's ever seen."

"Like a Lincoln letter?"

"Or a diary." Then she looked at her watch. "This should only take a few minutes. My department head is an ally. I need him on my side."

As she went off, Peter made a decision. He might be less conspicuous if he went to see Sorrel alone.

Diana would be angry at him, but she'd have to take a number.

.   .   .

The cabbie took M Street through Georgetown, the oldest and the youngest part of D.C. Georgetown had been there in the eighteenth century, before they decided to build the nation's capital on the marshes and hillsides to the south. Now M Street was lined with restaurants, bars, bookstores, and fancy shops. The famous Jesuit college sat on top of the hill. The best people, or the wealthiest, lived on the leafy slopes around it.

And the worst bottleneck in the city, which was saying a lot in a city of bottlenecks, may have been the left from M Street onto the Key Bridge. The meter must have clicked up a dozen times while they waited.

So Peter took the time to text Douglas Bryant, the bookseller with the ponytail:

Set aside the book by Benjamin Wood. We will discuss it tomorrow.
10 A.M.

A moment later he received this answer:

Five hundred and you got a deal.

On the Virginia side, the cabbie caught the Lee Highway and found his way out to a neighborhood of single-family homes on one of the hills that rolled back to the river. Sorrel's address put him directly across the street from Fort C. F. Smith Park.

Peter Googled Fort C. F. Smith: "built during the Civil War, one of seventy earthworks that ringed the city and protected the roads, railroads, and bridges." A few of the forts still remained. A few had been restored with plaques and plugged cannon. But where once they had been surrounded by cleared fields of fire, these ramparts now looked out on sweet suburbia, middle-class colonials and fifties ranches.

Peter got out, flipped open his notebook, looked around, and pretended to jot a few things down. If anyone was watching, they'd think he
was just another Civil War buff come to visit that old relic of an earthwork.

He stopped to read the Army Corps plaque at the entrance:

THE REMAINS OF FORT C. F. SMITH,
A LUNETTE BUILT TO COMMAND THE HIGH GROUND NORTH OF
SPOUT RUN AND DEFEND THE PERIMETER OF
THE ARLINGTON LINE . . .

He walked into an enclosure of grass-covered mounds, a few cannon,
and an old limber. Neat walkways twined across a landscape sloping gently to a collar of woods that blocked the view of the Potomac.

Peter did not know what was waiting for him at Sorrel's house, but if
he had to make a quick escape, this huge, quiet stretch of parkland would
be perfect.

Now he turned back to observe the house, but he tried not to be too
obvious. He found another plaque and read:

. . . CONSTRUCTED IN 1863 ON LAND APPROPRIATED
FROM WILLIAM C. JEWELL . . .

Look up briefly. The house was mid-Atlantic cottage style on a corner
lot, with a detached garage on the right, a big sycamore on the left. *Look
down again.*

. . . PART OF THE OUTER PERIMETER DEFENSES THAT PROTECTED
THE AQUEDUCT BRIDGE . . .

Second-story dormers, a big front porch, half screened. *Look down again.*

. . . CONTAINED TWENTY-TWO GUN EMPLACEMENTS,
EIGHT OF WHICH ARE PRESERVED . . .

Pull out a handkerchief and blow your nose. Most of the shades were drawn,
the front door was closed, and the air conditioner made no telltale hum.

THE ACCESS ROAD TO THE FORT CROSSED SPOUT'S RUN NEAR
MASON'S MILL AND PROCEEDED UP THE HILL . . .

Was anybody home? And . . . was that somebody watching him?

. . . BUILDINGS IN WHICH THE GARRISON ATE AND SLEPT
WERE LOCATED TO THE EAST . . .

In that car . . . about twenty yards down the hill, Nissan Versa, Maryland plate. Somebody was sitting in the driver's seat.

Look down at the plaque. Think. Had the car been there when the cab dropped him?

. . . PERIOD PHOTOGRAPHS SHOW ARLINGTON'S LANDSCAPE
DENUDED OF TREES . . .

Plenty of shade now, big limbs hanging over the quiet street, a gentle rustle of sound as a breeze puffed up from the Potomac.

Peter crossed the street and stepped onto the porch. He listened for the sounds of a television or radio or voices inside the house: nothing.

Then he heard a sudden, explosive roar.

He almost jumped, but it was just the guy next door, starting his lawn mower.

As the noise filled his head, Peter rang the bell. Then he waited . . . and counted.

Ten seconds, twenty, thirty.

The lawn mower sputtered to a stop. The man cursed. Then he pulled the starter cord again and the mower kicked over. He gave Peter a glance and went back to work.

Peter looked down the hill at the Nissan Versa. Still there. Guy still in it.

He rang the bell again.

Then he pulled out an Antiquaria business card (RARE BOOKS, DOCUMENTS, AND EPHEMERA, BOUGHT, SOLD, AND APPRAISED), and he wrote on the back. *Whatever your plan, I can help w/the Lincoln letter. Please call. Peter Fallon.*

The lawn mower sputtered and stopped. The man cursed.

Peter shoved the card into the mail slot. Then he turned and saw the lawn mower man standing at the bottom step, looking up. "He's not here."

Peter took the guy in quickly: about sixty; blue T-shirt, baggy shorts, sweat glistening through his comb-over, which was dyed a sickly red orange. And from the way that his potbelly was heaving up and down with each breath, he was worn out by a few minutes of work.

"Did he tell you where he was going?" said Peter.

"Who's askin'?"

Peter smiled his best book-scouting smile and introduced himself.

The guy raised a brow and wiped away a bead of sweat.

Peter watched the eyes. Did the lawn mower man recognize him? Was the name of a Boston bookseller an item in Mr. Sorrel's neighborhood, too?

"What do you want?"

"I want to talk Mr. Sorrel." Peter kept his tone calm, professional. "It's business."

"If I see him, I'll tell him you were here."

Just then, a car crested the hill, a little blue Ford Fiesta. At the same moment, an engine started somewhere down the street.

Peter saw the brake lights of the Nissan Versa flash into gear.

The lawn mower man looked from one car to the other and muttered something like "Shift change . . . son of a bitches." He watched the Fiesta rolling slowly past, then he looked at the Versa, which was pulling out to make a U-turn. And he muttered, "Shift change, *and* a U-turn. I got 'em now . . . son of a bitches."

And he pounded right up the stairs onto the porch, pushed Peter out of the way, and jammed a key into the lock.

The door banged open, and the lawn mower man banged into the house.

Before Peter could say more than "What the—?" the man burst out again with a double-barreled shotgun.

"Whoa!" cried Peter. "Hold on a minute."

And the barrels looked right into his eyes. "Out of my way, or you're first."

Peter jumped back.

"I got 'em now. Stupid Versa makin' a U-turn right in front of the Fiesta."

"That's not a shooting offense," said Peter. "It's just a U-turn."

"Two little rent-a-car shitboxes, one or the other always watchin' me. I've had it."

The Fiesta had to stop as the Versa swung out.

The lawn mower man raised the gun.

Instinctively, Peter swept a hand down, knocking the barrel toward the floor.

The Versa finished the turn and headed up the hill, past Sorrel's house. The driver did not even glance at the porch.

The lawn mower man rammed a shoulder into Peter and knocked him back. He was stronger than Peter had expected. And once Peter was off him, he swung the gun again, first at the Versa, which was disappearing over the crest of the hill, then back at the Fiesta, which was pulling into the vacated parking space. And he muttered, "I'm sick of all this damn surveillance."

Then the doors of the Fiesta started popping open, and for a second time, Peter grabbed the gun and drove the barrel down. He was close enough now that he could smell whiskey radiating from the guy, who growled and scowled and tried to pull the gun away, but now that he was ready, Peter was a lot stronger and held the gun.

Then came the sound of . . . kids. Boys. Three boys, maybe eight or nine. They tumbled out of the back of the Fiesta. Then the parents got out of the front. Dad shouted for the kids to be careful. Mom shouted for them to slow down.

And the lawn mower man relaxed the grip on the gun. He watched the kids go scampering across the road, shouting about a fort and real cannon and how cool it all was. Then he dropped into the rocking chair on the porch.

Still clutching the shotgun, Peter crouched down next to the chair.

"Thanks." The man took a couple of deep breaths. His face was covered with sweat. "I could have shot those kids."

Peter said, "So, Mr. Jefferson Sorrel—"

The man looked Peter in the eye, as if trying to decide whether to trust him or not.

Peter made it easier. He said, "About this Lincoln letter . . ."

Sorrel drew his face closer to Peter's and bathed him in a fine mist of whiskey. "I sold it."

"You sold it? Already? Why?"

"I got my price. And I'm on to something bigger, much bigger."

"What?"

"Lincoln's diary. That's why I'm so scared."

Six

June 1862

Halsey Hutchinson now understood what Lincoln meant by "gloom and torment."

They came in painful stabs of conscience whenever he thought of that daybook.

They came in the mingling of wounded pride and fear that burned in his belly whenever he received another summons from Detective McNealy.

They came in a telegram from Samantha Simpson of Wellesley, Massachusetts:

> DEAR HALSEY, I HAVE SECURED A POSITION AT THE UNION
> HOTEL HOSPITAL IN GEORGETOWN. I SHALL TRAVEL AS
> SOON AS FATHER PERMITS.

What would he tell her? That he had spent his afternoons with Constance Wood, but only because she was a rebel spy, and it had all been in the line of duty when he kissed her and caressed her and stroked her most intimate parts while she did the same for him? And what would he tell Constance? He had concluded that she was no spy. And he had already lied to her about his arrest in the Smithsonian: a case of mistaken identity.

But these were the problems of a young man facing the consequences of his own actions.

For everyone in Washington, gloom and torment came with the heat that felt like clear, sticky syrup poured into every corner and every crevice of the city.

And for everyone in the War Department, gloom and torment weighed more heavily with every dispatch from the Peninsula, because after three months of hesitating, slogging, hunkering, and posturing, McClellan was finally in motion. He was retreating.

Robert E. Lee had taken command of the Confederate forces and seemed determined to drive McClellan back from the outskirts of Richmond, back down the Peninsula, all the way back to Hampton Roads if he could. He had launched his first attack on Thursday the 26th, at a place called Mechanicsville. But Federal forces had held. So he had turned on McClellan's left at Gaines's Mill, and after a day of fighting, he had driven the Yankees across the Chickahominy River.

As night fell on Friday the 27th, Secretary Stanton left to be with his son, who had developed a full-blown case of smallpox after an inoculation. Major Eckert stayed until eleven thirty. President Lincoln, exhausted after two sleepless nights on the sofa in Stanton's office, went home to a real bed.

So, at 1:30 A.M. on Saturday the 28th, Halsey was senior telegraph officer. And he was lost in his work, with orders to write, papers to file, forms to fill. It was a good place to be. Even desk work was a good antidote for gloom and torment.

Bates finished a dispatch and put it on Halsey's desk. "McClellan's at it again."

And what Halsey read astonished him.

The general described the day's action. Then he turned to the reports of Detective Pinkerton, who had been warning for weeks that Lee commanded two hundred thousand men, almost double the size of the Army of the Potomac. And now the rebel hordes were in motion, but the government refused to reinforce McClellan, or so he charged:

A FEW THOUSAND MEN MORE WOULD HAVE CHANGED THIS BATTLE FROM DEFEAT TO VICTORY. THE GOVERNMENT MUST NOT AND CANNOT HOLD ME RESPONSIBLE. I HAVE SEEN TOO MANY DEAD AND WOUNDED COMRADES

TO FEEL OTHERWISE THAN THAT THE GOVERNMENT HAS
NOT SUSTAINED THIS ARMY. IF YOU DO NOT DO SO NOW,
THE GAME IS LOST.

Bates was smiling like a boy who had just shown his mate a dirty book and was waiting for him to get to the best pictures.

So Halsey read to the end:

IF I SAVE THIS ARMY NOW I TELL YOU PLAINLY THAT I
OWE NO THANKS TO YOU OR ANY OTHER PERSONS IN
WASHINGTON—YOU HAVE DONE YOUR BEST TO SACRIFICE
THIS ARMY.

Halsey sat back and said, "Good God."

"Insubordination," said Bates.

"Treason." Halsey thought a moment. Then he folded the sheet of thin, yellow paper and put it in his pocket.

"What are you doing?" asked Bates, eyes wide and voice shocked, as if Halsey had touched a match to the telegram.

"Making a decision."

The eastern sky was just brightening when Major Eckert arrived. He said that he couldn't sleep, so he might as well work.

Halsey handed over McClellan's dispatch.

As Eckert scanned it, his jaw muscles flexed and his fist balled.

Halsey said, "We kept it out of the pile. We wanted you to see it first."

"What do you mean, *we?*" said Homer Bates.

Eckert said, "Does anyone else know of this?"

They both shook their heads, so Eckert swore them to secrecy. . . .

An hour later, Lincoln appeared in the telegraph office, hatless but wearing his black frock like dead weight in the humidity. He went over to Eckert's desk and flipped through the pile of overnight telegrams. He read McClellan's message and said, "That's one hard raisin. Sounds like the general could use some encouragement."

The general, thought Halsey, could use some firing. But sacking an insubordinate general was not something a president should have to consider in the midst of a fighting retreat. Better for president and general both that Lincoln had not seen McClellan's final cry of anger.

Major Eckert and his superior, the supervisor of military telegrams, had deleted the last two lines . . . for the good of the president and the general, too.

Now Lincoln wrote a measured response and handed it to Bates.

Halsey went to the cipher desk, put down a few papers, and read over Bates's shoulder:

Save your Army at all events. Will send reinforcements as fast as we can. I feel any misfortune to you and your army quite as keenly as you feel it yourself. It is the nature of the case, and neither you nor the government is to blame.

Right then, Halsey was glad that he had passed the telegram up the chain of command. But his concerns about McClellan were not allayed.

What was the general's game? Why had he been so hard to move? Why had he chosen such a roundabout attack, transporting a hundred thousand men down the Potomac, then up the Peninsula between the York and James rivers, instead of driving overland and hard against Richmond? And why had he seen every opportunity for attack as another opportunity to complain?

On his walks back to the White House, Lincoln had asked these questions, too.

But there seemed to be something else on the president's mind that morning. He said to Eckert, "Major, I'd bother you for a quire of paper and the use of a desk. I'd like to write something special."

Eckert fetched him a quarter ream of foolscap-length writing paper and a Gillott barrel pen, standard issue in the telegraph office.

And as the rising sun brightened the room, a new hierarchy of desks fell into order. The president took the major's desk between the windows. The major took the lieutenant's desk in the far corner. The lieutenant was relegated to the all-purpose worktable in the middle of the room.

From there, he watched Lincoln scratching down words, scratching them out, staring out the window, studying the spiderweb stretched across an upper pane, scratching down more words, scratching them out, and after a half an hour, replacing the elaborate eagle-shaped lid on Eckert's inkstand, then pushing back from the desk and handing the sheets to Eckert. "Lock these in a drawer, if you please, Major. There'll be no more losing the notes I make in the telegraph office."

Without looking at the papers—he was a good soldier—Eckert did as he was told.

Then Lincoln asked that Halsey escort him back to the White House.

.   .   .

They walked silently through the still morning. They always walked silently until the president spoke. They walked with heads down, offering the backs of their necks to the voracious morning mosquitoes.

Halsey did a lot of slapping.

Lincoln did not seem to notice. Finally, he said, "I saw you reading over Homer's shoulder."

"I read most everything that goes out and comes in," said Halsey. "And may I say, you've been very . . . judicious . . . with General McClellan, sir."

"I suppose." Lincoln glanced toward the White House carriage drive. The crowd of office seekers was small. It was still early.

Halsey kept talking. "But Robert E. Lee seems very determined."

"The whole South seems very determined," answered Lincoln, "more determined than some people ever anticipated."

"Do you think their determination will grow stronger, now that you've signed a bill forbidding slavery in the western territories?"

"They will do what they do. *I* determined a long time ago that slavery would not reach beyond the slave states. It's what brought me back into politics."

Their footfalls crunched on the gravel path. The canopy of leaves was thick above them. The shade, even at that early hour, was most welcome.

Then Lincoln added, "Amazing what you can get done in Congress when the opposition secedes."

"But the Peace Democrats like Benjamin Wood are still there. And they fear every step you take toward general emancipation."

"Are you thinking ahead of me, Lieutenant?"

"In what way, sir?"

"You're thinking that I'm thinking about a general emancipation." Lincoln glanced at Halsey. "Or were you reading over *my* shoulder?"

"I don't know what you're talking about, sir."

"That's probably best."

They walked a bit more. Then Lincoln stopped and turned to Halsey.

On some days the president looked as if he might just collapse from the weight he carried. A film of perspiration covered his forehead, his skin appeared more yellow than sun-browned, and his eyes seemed to be sinking into circles of bruised purple flesh.

But his voice was firm: "My hope has always been for emancipation that's voluntary, gradual, and compensated. Those are my thoughts, until I compose new ones."

"Yes, sir."

"But this time I'll be more careful with the thoughts I compose because Halsey—"

"Sir?"

"I sure wish I hadn't lost that daybook." Lincoln shook his head. "Hard to believe it never turned up. But . . . we have work to do, so good day."

· · ·

On the walk home, Halsey passed Mr. Shovel and Mr. Mule Harness, as always, and almost forgot to tip his hat he was so deep in thought, wondering how much of the presidential conversation he would report to McNealy. Nothing, if he could help it.

But when he got to his room, he found a note under the door: *Seventh Street wharf. Noon.* So he would have to come up with something.

Every few mornings since the shooting at Squeaker's, a message had been waiting for him when got home: *Meet by first applecart in Center Market, 10 A.M.* Or *Star Saloon, 7 P.M.* Or some other place and time. McNealy said he liked plain-sight meetings because people in a city didn't see things right in front of them.

And his questions were always the same:

What movement on emancipation? Halsey would say none, despite what the president was hinting.

What opinions about McClellan? Halsey would offer information that was public knowledge: Secretary Stanton thought McClellan was paying too much attention to Pinkerton. Lincoln was growing impatient.

What about Benjamin Wood? Halsey would answer, "Defiant." Wood had been accused of using a *Daily News* reporter to pass secrets to the South. He proclaimed his innocence and welcomed the chance to defend himself before the House Judiciary Committee. He said he only wished that other Americans whose loyalty had been questioned and who had been thrown into jail without trial could have the same opportunity.

.   .   .

If working Washington had a heart, it beat strongest at the City Wharves between Sixth and Seventh. In better times, the wharves landed goods and food, products of the region and the world. A fleet of side- and stern-wheelers still filled the air with smoke and the screech of their whistles, but now they delivered a human cargo.

Halsey found a spot under a tree and watched a steamer named *Anacostia* unloading men, bow and stern . . . men on stretchers and men on crutches, men in pain and men in agony, men groaning with every movement, men suffering in silence, and men crying out when they could bear their silence no longer.

A hundred ambulance wagons awaited them, bound for a dozen makeshift hospitals. A hundred doctors and assistants shouted orders to a thousand black stretcher-bearers, while a hundred thousand flies filled the air and lit on the horses and their turds and the suffering men, too.

And as each wagon rumbled off, a cloud of flies followed, a great buzzing cumulus of maggot mothers, finding sustenance in the suppurating flesh of gunshot limbs and gutshot bellies, and . . .

God but he hated this war.

"Some people say this is just the beginning." McNealy materialized from somewhere behind him.

"Why are we meeting here?" Halsey had abandoned any pretense of cordiality.

"What's the matter? The heat too much for you?" McNealy squinted up at the sunburned sky. "Nobody bother with us here. Folks don't like to see such sufferin'."

Halsey watched two black men carrying a torso on a stretcher, just a torso. Four stumps wrapped in bandages marked the places where its limbs had been. Its head was turned away.

He said to McNealy, "Ask your questions."

McNealy took a cigar stub from his vest pocket, flicked off the gray ash, and jammed it into his mouth. "The usual . . . emancipation? Hearin' anything?"

Halsey said what the president had said: "Voluntary, gradual, compensated."

McNealy chewed on the cigar. "No more chance of that than of these darkie stretcher-boys doctorin' the poor bastards they're carryin'."

"So why do you need me to tell you about it? Go to the War Department and—"

"I try to avoid the War Department. You know that," said McNealy. "Eckert doesn't like me, and Stanton doesn't like anyone. But a good secret service needs to know the plans of the people they work for, so they can find out the plans of the people they work against. Makes it easier to know what to look for . . . and where."

"Look for spies, traitors, and disloyal newspaper editors."

Nearby, a man screamed. Two stretcher bearers were sliding him onto the top tier of a waiting ambulance.

Halsey saw an emotion cross McNealy's face that did not fit under the general heading of "suspicion." It looked almost like . . . empathy.

McNealy said, "This Potomac is now a river of blood, Lieutenant. I mean to stop it from reachin' the sea."

"You sure have a strange way of doing it."

"You let me worry about the 'how.'" McNealy lit his cigar. "You just worry about the 'who' and the 'what.' You follow?"

Halsey had grown to hate that question. It was always uttered as a threat. But he was trapped. He had to take it. And when McNealy paused, he knew that he was supposed to answer: "I follow."

"So what are they saying about McClellan, now that Bobby Lee's slamming him with a two-by-four, just like Pinkerton said would happen?"

"They're saying what they've said from the start. He listens too much to Pinkerton. They believe McClellan outnumbers Lee, not the other way round." Halsey paused, then decided to add a bit more, to make it appear that he was actually doing the job that McNealy expected. "Today, the president promised to send what help he can."

"Presidential promises." McNealy took out his cigar and gave a juicy spit.

Halsey tried to read meaning into McNealy's grunts and spits, a tricky game with a man who played things close. Nothing was necessarily as it seemed. But it was odd . . . the positive comments about Pinkerton . . . the negative comments about Lincoln . . . the questions about emancipation. . . .

What was *his* game?

Then McNealy asked about Benjamin Wood.

Halsey said, "When Wood last spoke in Congress, Stanton had a telegraph line run from the Capitol so that he could get instant reports and arrest Wood if he didn't like what Wood was saying. He thinks Wood's a traitor."

"Wood will be acquitted." McNealy said it as though it were a fact rather than speculation. "What else?"

Halsey hesitated before offering the next bit of intelligence, but it was the sort of thing that McNealy might know about anyway: Constance had heard her uncle musing over a candidate to run against Lincoln in the next election, and he had mentioned General McClellan.

McNealy took the cigar from his mouth. "She told you that?"

Halsey nodded.

McNealy's eyes shifted left, then right, but they were not looking at wounded soldiers or stretcher bearers or the steam rising from the riverboats. They seemed to have turned inward, into some deep cabinet of suspicions.

Halsey sensed that he had said too much.

"We should keep an eye on your Miss Constance," said McNealy.

"She went back to New York. She couldn't take the heat."

McNealy puffed his cigar. "Then we should keep an eye on her in New York."

Suddenly, a whistle screamed. Two maneuvering vessels, their decks covered with stretchers, had drifted close to each other in the current.

One gave a burst of steam and kicked forward, sending up a wave that washed over the bow of the other vessel and washed half a dozen wounded men off the deck. One of them cried out as he sank.

Halsey turned to McNealy, but McNealy was gone.

God, but he hated this war. And he hated the way he was fighting it.

II.

Washingtonians said there had never been such a Fourth of July . . .

. . . not because of the celebrations, for there were none. Not because of the heat, for July heat in Washington was like the roar of artillery. Beyond a certain point, it was not distinguishable by gradation. It was simply unbearable. But not since 1776 had the future of the republic seemed more in doubt, because McClellan had been beaten.

In a single week, Robert E. Lee had taken back all the ground that McClellan spent three months securing. Federal troops had now fallen into defensive positions at a place called Harrison's Landing, on the James River. They had surrendered the field. They had lost the advantage.

Whatever gloom and torment had lain over Washington in June seemed now like a happy memory. Bands would play, because bands were always playing somewhere in Washington. But there would be no illuminations, no fireworks, no frivolity.

For Samantha Simpson of Wellesley, Massachusetts, however, it was the most glorious Fourth of her life, because Halsey was taking her to the White House.

She had arrived on the night train from Baltimore and following Halsey's instructions, had taken a barouche from the B&O station to the Metropolitan Hotel on Pennsylvania. A bouquet of roses awaited her in her room, along with a note:

Welcome to your nation's capital. Sleep well. Tomorrow you shall meet the president. HH

For the occasion, she wore a powder blue dress with matching hat and parasol. Halsey went in uniform.

McManus met them at the White House door. "Good afternoon, Lieutenant."

"A quiet day," said Halsey. "Where's the line?"

"Most folks reckon the president's takin' a holiday. But he's in his office. And he's always happy to see Lieutenant Halsey and a lovely lady."

The moment Halsey and Samantha stepped into the vestibule, she whispered, "They know you by your *first name* at the president's house?"

Halsey did not tell her that McManus could probably not remember his last name. Some things were better left unsaid when trying to impress a lady.

But impressing her was easy enough on the red carpet in the central corridor.

Halsey watched her eyes widen as she looked into the rooms, each decorated in a predominant color. Mrs. Lincoln had spent a fortune on new draperies, carpeting, and furniture, so Halsey did not think that Samantha noticed the underlying shabbiness of the old place. The baseboards had been kicked and scuffed by the hundreds of people who came each day to see the president. The red carpet showed the wear of muddy boots and the scars of souvenir hunters who had cut swatches to take home. And a few souls had even carved initials in the wainscoting.

But as they ascended the staircase at the west end, Samantha whispered, "I am a long way from Wellesley, Massachusetts."

Lincoln's secretary, John Hay, young and sleek in a linen suit, greeted them in the vestibule at the east end and directed them to the president's reception room.

Halsey didn't much like Hay, a typical gatekeeper who looked at guests as if wondering how to keep them from his boss. The president, said Hay, would be with them shortly.

That afternoon, Halsey and Samantha were the only people in the reception room. They took the settee by the door, and Halsey heard voices and footfalls in the corridor, as if Lincoln was seeing a visitor out of his office.

"For the last time, Mr. President, I urge you. Give the nation a gift on Independence Day. Announce a general emancipation. It'll be galvanizing."

The sound of the footfalls stopped outside the reception room door.

Lincoln's voice cut through the quiet: "Senator, general emancipation may not find the kind of fertile ground in the rest of the country that it does in Massachusetts."

Halsey looked at Samantha, who at that moment looked like a little girl, with a little downturned doll's mouth, ringlets of brown hair framing a round face, and round blue eyes growing rounder as she overheard this exalted conversation.

"More's the pity," said the other voice. "But you know, sir, that you may free the slaves as part of your Constitutional mandate in wartime."

"So you've told me many times, Senator Sumner."

Samantha whispered, "Sumner? *Our* Sumner?"

Halsey nodded. He liked the feel of her warm breath in his ear.

Charles Sumner, Republican from Massachusetts and one of the sharpest Abolitionist thorns in the presidential side, said sadly, "So you will not reconsider?"

"I consider everything," said Lincoln. "I reconsider *almost* everything. And I tell you straight up, Senator, I would do it if I were not afraid that half the officers would fling down their arms and three more states would rise."

"Then there's no more to offer, sir, except my best wishes to you and Mrs. Lincoln for a happy Independence Day."

From where he sat, Halsey could see Sumner turning to take the president's hand:

"But, Mr. President," said Sumner, "you've called for three hundred thousand more volunteers. The only way to guarantee that they'll come forward without direct conscription is to tell them what this war is *really* about."

"Wait, Senator," said Lincoln. "Just wait. As I've told you before, emancipation is a thunderbolt that will keep. So be patient. Time is essential."

"Another defeat like the Peninsula, sir, and I fear that we may start to run out of time while our citizens run out of patience." Then Sumner noticed the young people.

Halsey stood. "Senator."

Sumner was burly and big-headed, with a shock of graying hair and voluminous muttonchops, quite unlike the skinny, thin-lipped Abolitionist of Southern caricature. He looked at Halsey, wrinkled his brow, and said, "Hutchinson, isn't it?"

"Yes, sir." Halsey extended his hand.

"One of our Democratic families"—Sumner took Halsey's hand and turned to Lincoln—"yet a family of proud tradition and excellent heritage."

Halsey glanced at Lincoln, about whose family none of that could be said, and saw the "faintly bemused" version of the benevolent smile.

"Good bloodlines are a good thing," said Lincoln, "in a horse or a man. But the lieutenant has proved himself . . . on the battlefield, and in the telegraph office."

"Thank you, sir," said Halsey.

The attention of the gentlemen now turned to Samantha, who was standing and fidgeting with the handle of her parasol.

"And here is a young lady I also recognize," said Sumner, "the daughter of a fine Abolitionist preacher, the Reverend Mr. Simpson of Wellesley, Massachusetts."

Lincoln took her hand. "I hope you'll ask him to compose a prayer for me."

Samantha curtsied, so that the bottom hoop of her skirt brushed on the floor.

"Tell me, Miss Simpson," said the president, "what brings you to Washington in the height of summer?"

"I'm to be a volunteer nurse at the Union Hotel Hospital, sir."

"Do you know about nursing?" asked Lincoln.

"No, but I have always been interested in the . . . nursely arts, sir, and what I don't know I'll learn."

Lincoln's smile widened into a genuine grin. He turned to Sumner and said, "I don't see how we can lose, Senator, not with spirit like that in our ladies, too."

After a few more pleasantries, Sumner bustled off.

Then Lincoln invited the young couple into his office. And he gave Halsey a wink, as if to say that he knew how to help a young man impress a young lady.

Masculine colors and a mess of papers dominated the room. The wallpaper was green with a pattern of gold stars. The wall-to-wall carpet was green with a pattern of crimson flowers, and it was covered in papers. A heavy-legged walnut table occupied the middle of the room and was also covered in papers. A stand-up postmaster's desk fit into a corner, and was not only covered in papers, but its pigeonholes were stuffed with papers. A Winthrop desk, closed and locked, top and bottom, filled the space between the windows and appeared to be the only thing *not* covered in papers. There were even papers on the wall: maps dotted with red and blue pins to show the movement of troops.

Lincoln told them to push aside the papers on the sofa and sit.

Then he took to his black horsehair swivel chair, and Halsey observed the presidential act of sitting, which never ceased to fascinate him. It was like watching the movement of a great long-legged bird. Lincoln folded himself first at the waist, then at the knees, lowering his body in two distinct motions, a slow, steady journey of descent. And once he was altogether seated, his knees came to rest just south of his beard. No man had ever looked more ungainly in a chair.

But his conversation was easy and relaxed. In the midst of gloom and torment, he seemed to welcome the chance for a bit of distracting chatter with young people.

He hooked a long leg over one of the arms of the chair and told a few funny stories. He expounded on the view of the Washington Monument out his windows. And he gave the Abolitionist's daughter all the encouragement she would need.

When she said that she had brought little gifts for the men, like books, candy, socks, and soap, he said one word: "Tobacco?"

"Tobacco, sir?" She smiled. "My father prohibited me from bringing tobacco, but I must admit that I brought it anyway. Two cases of cut plug."

Lincoln chuckled. "This young gal's a prize catch, Lieutenant."

Halsey could feel a sidelong glance from Samantha, anticipating . . . what? *Choose your words carefully,* he told himself. "Yes, sir. A prize altogether, sir."

"Tobacco's never held much interest for me, but our men need comfort, and I'm told it comforts many a man." Lincoln stood, signaling the end of the meeting.

Halsey and Samantha stood also, and she said, "I will tell my father that my president approves of tobacco, sir—"

"Don't tell him till he's written that prayer. I don't want any preachers thinking I'm encouraging their daughters to rebel. I don't encourage rebellions."

"No, sir. You just put them down," she said.

And Lincoln's smile faded. A sudden seriousness came into his voice. "If my Maker so wills it, Miss Simpson, then yes."

That was the first time, in all their conversations, that Halsey could recall the president framing an issue in terms of a higher power.

Something in him was changing. Halsey was convinced.

Samantha left off smiling and said, "A strong notion, sir."

"To which end, I'm going down to Harrison's Landing to see the army for myself. I'll be bringing a few civilians and a few military men. I'll want my own telegraph man, too." Lincoln turned to Halsey. "So wear your uniform." Then Lincoln winked again. Mission accomplished. Young lady properly impressed.

. . .

As Samantha did not have to report to the hospital until six o'clock, Halsey took her to dinner in the quiet dining room of the National Hotel.

All through the meal, she talked while Halsey listened. She talked of her Boston meetings with the dashing John Wilkes Booth, of the graciousness of President Lincoln, of the audaciousness of Senator Sumner, of the heat, of the hotels, of her pride in Halsey, "the president's very own telegraph man," and of the adventures that awaited them both. From the brightness in her eyes, she seemed to believe that these would be wondrous adventures altogether.

Halsey did not tell her of the hard realities that underlay most wartime adventure. She would find out soon enough on her own.

She kept talking after dinner and during the carriage ride to Georgetown.

It was not until they pulled up in front of the hospital near the corner of M Street and Wisconsin that she stopped her chatter. She fell silent. Then she whispered, "Oh, my."

A dozen men were lounging on the stoop of the four-story brick building. Almost anywhere else, that number of men would have accounted for forty-eight arms and legs. But not here. Were there forty? Thirty? Halsey could not tell.

He felt her hand shaking as he helped her down. He realized that her incessant talk had been a manifestation of her nervousness. Her silence now declared it as well.

As Halsey and Samantha climbed the stoop, a few of the men who had arms offered halfhearted, almost disrespectful salutes.

At the lobby entrance, the young couple stopped and peered in. Once, this had been a fine hotel, favored by senators and congressmen. But now . . .

A man was rushing past carrying a tray covered in a cloth. Something stuck out from under the cloth. A hand? A *human* hand? Yes.

Halsey saw Samantha's color fade.

She gripped his arm, stepped into the lobby, and looked into the hotel dining room, which was now a ward with thirty beds. She took in all the suffering that expressed itself there in sounds and smells, and said it again, even more softly: "Oh, my."

Halsey decided that she wouldn't last a week.

Then a woman in a brown dress and white apron called out from behind the hotel desk: "Are you Miss Samantha Simpson of Wellesley, Massachusetts?"

Samantha nodded, as if she couldn't find her voice.

The woman came out from behind the desk. She neither smiled nor scowled. She just looked severe. "I'm Miss Dean. You're younger than they said you'd be. Prettier, too. We're lookin' for plain women, over thirty, and you're neither."

Samantha stammered, "I'm . . . I'm . . ."

"Don't be sorry." Miss Dean looked her up and down. "We need hands, so we'll take you. But remember, girlie, pretty don't count here. Work does."

Halsey did not think that Samantha would even be able to speak, but she said, "Oh, yes, ma'am. I can work."

"Good, 'cause we just got a new ambulance in, so there's men to bathe, wounds to dress, fevers to wet down." Miss Dean noticed Samantha's two trunks on the shoulders of two Negroes who had carried them in. "What's in those?"

"Clothes in one, and I've brought sundries for the men . . . books, soap, candy—"

"Tobacco?"

"Yes, two cases of cut plug."

"Then they'll like you, all right. A woman brings tobacco, the men like her even if she's as ugly as a full chamber pot. And you'll be seein' plenty of those, so come along. Need to get you out of that hooped skirt. No hoops and dark dresses, that's the rule around here. And we got other rules, too, all written down. You need to read 'em."

Samantha gave Halsey a little wave and followed Miss Dean up the stairs. The expression on her face was one that he had seen only on men . . . just before they went into battle, when they realized that they were about to do something they could never have imagined themselves doing but were going to do, because it had to be done and the Lord had put them in the place to do it.

Halsey decided that she *would* last a week.

III.

Three days later, the armed steamer *Ariel* brought the presidential party up the James from Hampton Roads, a ten-hour trip past fertile green plantations and dark wooded swamps, deep into the heart of Virginia.

Halsey found a spot on the bow, where he could catch a breeze in the hundred-degree heat and watch the downstream steamers passing with their cargoes of wounded.

The Seven Days, as it was now called, had killed two thousand federal soldiers and wounded eight thousand more, but whenever a boat passed and wounded men caught sight of Lincoln in his shirtsleeves on the afterdeck, they cheered and shouted: "Hey, Mr. President! We'll be back!" "Hey, Abe! Turn us around and we'll follow *you* to Richmond!" "Hey, Lincoln, them Rebs said you was uglier 'n Jeff Davis, but you ain't nowhere near as ugly as him!"

Lincoln spent most of the day laughing and waving to them.

Halsey spent most of the day anticipating a reunion with the Twentieth . . . with men like Sergeant Thomas Moran, who had pulled him out of the mud and thrown him into a rowboat at Ball's Bluff, and with officer friends like the Revere brothers or Oliver Wendell Holmes, who had also been wounded at Ball's Bluff but had returned to service while Halsey languished at a desk, filling forms and passing information to War Department detectives. Halsey envied Holmes. He envied them all.

. . .

Around five o'clock, word ran along the decks that they were getting close.

Halsey was glad that the heat had abated some, and it was for certain that Lincoln was glad, too, as he put on his black coat and stovepipe.

Up ahead, Halsey could see something gray and metallic sitting in the water. It looked like a huge cheesebox on a raft: the famed ironclad *Monitor.*

As the *Ariel* passed the ugly little warcraft and rounded the bend, the captain fired three quick blasts on his whistle. And the air was crushed by a booming explosion, then another and another—twenty-one in all— delivered by the broadside guns of the big-bellied ironclad *Galena.*

And once the smoke from the salute had cleared, Halsey Hutchinson was filled with awe, with a sense, for the first time in his life, of war as the most manly of spectacles, of war as the greatest endeavor of human organization . . .

. . . because before him spread the military might of the Union, a vision of power such as few men had ever seen before.

For a distance of five miles along the bank and three miles inland, the Army of the Potomac covered the earth within an impregnable semicircle of high ground. Half a dozen warships armed with Dahlgren cannon and hundred-pound Parrott rifles defended the flanks, while transports of every size steamed back and forth, delivering supplies and taking off the wounded. No man could fail to be impressed, especially when a band began to play, "Hail to the Chief."

Harrison's Landing was named for Benjamin Harrison, a signer of the Declaration of Independence and builder of a plantation house that floated now in a sea of Yankee blue and white canvas tents. It was the oldest brick mansion in Virginia and the birthplace of William Henry Harrison, ninth president of the United States. And no one who had occupied it could ever have imagined what had come to pass on that ground.

As the *Ariel* tied up, Lincoln walked to the bow and waved his hat at the cheering troops, while General McClellan and his staff paraded down the dock to meet him.

At least the Young Napoléon looked like a general, thought Halsey. He had a pouter-pigeon chest puffed up with a double row of brass buttons. He strutted when he walked, as if riding a proud mount that was doing the strutting for him. And when he stopped at the edge of the dock to wait for the gangplank, he stood with perfectly erect posture, one foot slightly ahead of the other, like a Michelangelo statue.

Halsey watched them exchange greetings—a salute from McClellan, a doffing of the hat from Lincoln—and he wondered what the president was thinking.

He suspected that Lincoln had pegged McClellan long before the June 28 telegram and had repented of ever choosing him. But what a fine pedigree McClellan had presented: second in his class at West Point, honorable service in the Mexican War, a meteoric rise from field engineer to president of the Illinois Central Railroad, then the early victories in western Virginia, which brought him riding to the rescue after Bull Run. And none could say that he had failed to mold the Army of the Potomac into a disciplined, well-organized fighting force.

But like a man who had fashioned a beautiful silver hammer, McClellan seemed afraid to drive nails with it for fear of scratching it. Instead, he had offered hesitance, petulance, and bald condescension toward his civilian superiors.

Lincoln seemed able to put all that behind him for the good of the country. But when he and McClellan shook hands, Halsey felt a blast of cold winter right there in July. Then, as drums beat and bands played and troops paraded into positions on the trampled wheat fields, president and general retreated to the afterdeck to sit, face-to-face, knee-to-knee, and confer on the predicament of the great army arrayed before them.

From a lower deck, Halsey watched, as if he were in a theater observing a pantomime.

The men talked for a time. Then McClellan reached into his pocket and produced a letter.

Lincoln looked at it quizzically.

McClellan gestured for him to open it.

The president put on his spectacles and read. Then he gave McClellan a polite nod, folded the letter, and put it into his pocket.

McClellan seemed to wait, expecting something more from the president. Instead Lincoln stood, put on his stovepipe, and said in a loud voice, "Let us review the troops, General."

McClellan's face reddened. His saber rattled as he rose. He seemed displeased.

. . .

For the next two hours, as the bloodred sun set and a big yellow moon came up, the riverbank shook with the roar of men and drums and bursts of music.

McClellan led. Lincoln rode at his right. The general appeared masterful, as well postured on horseback as on foot. The president looked like a very tall man whose legs were as long as his horse's and whose trousers were too short for his legs.

Halsey suspected that McClellan had planned it that way. Later, he heard that McClellan claimed to have ordered the troops to cheer. But Halsey saw with his own eyes how much those men loved the president.

As Lincoln rode up and down the columns, in and out of the regiments, the cheers of each unit burst forth like a rolling barrage. And each time a new band struck up a new tune, Lincoln's horse reared and shied, and the president had all he could do to stay in the saddle, clutching the reins in one hand while trying to wave his stovepipe with the other. But the more he struggled with horse and hat, the more those men cheered.

Morale, anyone would have to conclude, was far better than expected.

Meanwhile, Halsey was delivering new codes to the telegraph office in an outbuilding near the mansion. No one seemed impressed that an officer from the War Department had come to visit. So he had an operator sign for the materials. Then he went up to the main house to find an adjutant who might direct him to the Twentieth.

Instead, he found another military hospital.

That gracious old mansion had become a charnel house. Those not lucky enough, or sick enough, or well enough to have been shipped out or died filled every room and poured the last of themselves out onto the Turkish carpets that once had been beautiful but now were covered in a red-mud mix of Virginia dirt and Yankee blood.

Halsey glanced into the room on his right, the dining room. All the lanterns on the oil chandelier were glowing, yellow and greasy in the gathering dusk.

Over in a corner, by the china cabinet, two men in bloody aprons were leaning over a body. One of them got up and carried a bowl of red muslin bandages toward the door. He looked at Halsey and said, "Help out or step out, Lieutenant."

Then Halsey heard a weak voice. "Lieutenant? Lieutenant Hutchinson?" The voice came from the other corner, by the pantry.

"Sergeant Moran." Halsey picked his way over to a cot and a familiar face.

"I never thought I'd see you again," said the sergeant with a thick brogue.

"How are you?" Halsey knelt.

"Takin' a long time to die." Moran's face was waxy, as if he were dead already.

Halsey took his hand. "Maybe you won't . . . die."

The sergeant managed a laugh. "I'm gut shot. I'll die. They already told me. Got it at Glendale. Your friend Jimmy Lowell, too. Died like a . . . like an officer should."

"So I heard."

"I have to say ye look the same, Lieutenant, darlin', but ye don't sound the same. That charmin' voice of yours, it's . . . it's—"

"I lost it," said Halsey.

"We've lost a lot, sir. Good voices . . . good men . . . and for what?"

"For Union," said Halsey, even though it sounded rather hollow just then.

The sergeant's eyes seemed to search the ceiling for something. Then he said, "I come from Spiddal, you know."

Halsey patted his hand. "Yes. Spiddal in County Galway."

"A fine fishin' village it is, filled with fine men, fine men."

"I know," said Halsey. "You told me many a tale of Spiddal."

"But I never told you what I thought when I joined the regiment."

"What was that?"

"I never thought you Harvard officers could equal Spiddal men for courage. I thought you was all toffs and nancy-boys, tin soldiers and nothin' more. But . . . but, I have to say, ye done good, the lot of ye's." He struggled through a wave of pain. Then he whispered something else that Halsey could not hear. Then his grip let go.

Was he dead? Halsey could not tell. He stood and looked down dumbly.

One of the surgeons came over. "A tough old Mick. Shot right through the liver. Just bleedin' out slow and steady. Nothin' to do for him. Friend of yours?"

"He saved my life at Ball's Bluff."

Halsey suddenly felt an overwhelming burst of emotion. And before his façade cracked, he hurried from the house, out to the veranda that overlooked the river and the glorious scene still unfolding on its banks.

A band was now playing "Yankee Doodle" for the president.

Halsey took off his kepi and put it over his face.

So much, he thought, for the manly spectacle of war.

Then a voice came from behind, low and soft. "I'm told you're one of our men."

Halsey composed himself, put his kepi back on, and turned to another bearded civilian. This one wore a loose linen duster over a checkered shirt.

"Who are you?"

"I'm known as Major Allan to most. But to you, I'm Pinkerton, Chief of the Secret Service, Army of the Potomac. McNealy says you work for us."

"I work for the president," answered Halsey.

"You work for us till we say otherwise." Pinkerton spoke with a slight Scots burr. "Now, General McClellan just gave the president a letter."

"Yes," said Halsey. "I saw it."

"It's a frank letter," said Pinkerton. "If the president acts upon it, the country will be saved. The general wants to know what's said about it in the War Department, so that he can fight this war the way it should be fought."

Halsey gave Pinkerton a long look, as if to show that he would not be intimidated. "The way it should be fought is by fighting to win."

"Military advice from lieutenants." Pinkerton made a noise, as if he were clearing his throat, though it was meant to be a laugh. "As bad as military advice from presidents."

Down below, Lincoln was climbing onto a split rail fence to give a speech. He began by shouting, "All is well."

Halsey wished it were so.

Pinkerton said, "Report what you hear to McNealy."

"I thought McNealy worked for Colonel Baker. Isn't Baker your rival?"

"Baker works for Stanton. I work for McClellan. McNealy works for me."

"And we all work for the president," said Halsey.

"We all work for the Union, and you work for us." Pinkerton turned and headed toward the command tent. "If you doubt that, remember the evidence."

"Evidence? What evidence?"

Pinkerton did not answer. He simply kept walking.

Down below, Lincoln was saying, "You have acted like heroes and endured and conquered." And even if it wasn't so, the men were cheering.

Lincoln could tell small lies in the name of high spirit, thought Halsey. Small lies could be told to men who had endured hard fighting, because fighting washed the lies away. Fighting was clean and simple. This game he was caught in was not.

. . .

As he stepped off the porch, he spied a familiar figure coming toward him: tall, gangling Oliver Wendell Holmes, newly minted captain.

Halsey put himself directly into Holmes's path.

Holmes looked up, looked surprised, then said, "Why, Lieutenant, you're rather pasty after four months behind a desk."

And both men burst out laughing.

Holmes said that he was visiting his favorite old Irish sergeant before the regiment marched out for picket duty.

"Then there'll be no chance to eat with the officers tonight?" asked Halsey.

"I'm afraid not, but—" Holmes pulled a sausage and some cheese from his knapsack. "—mail call today. Boston sends victuals. I've brought a bit for Sergeant Moran. Perhaps there'll be some left for us."

"Moran's asleep," said Halsey. "At least I think it's just sleep."

"In that case"—Holmes pointed to a nearby tree—"dine with me before I rejoin my men."

And while the president's voice echoed up to them and the western sky burned red, Halsey enjoyed the camaraderie he had hoped for.

Holmes cut pieces of sausage and cheese for each of them. Then he gave Halsey a sip from the canteen he was carrying.

Halsey coughed back the taste of powerful liquor.

Holmes laughed. "The Irish boys call it poteen. They make it themselves. They wanted Moran to have a last taste. I promised I'd deliver it."

Then Holmes took the canteen and raised it in toast to their departed comrades.

For a few minutes, they passed canteen, sausage, and cheese—a sip and a bite, a bite and a sip, a sip and a sip—like comrades out of Homer. And they talked . . . about the bravery of the men, about their sweethearts, about their homes in cool, sweet New England.

Holmes also talked of the Negroes they had liberated as the army marched. "What poor dumb beasts they appear. For generations they've been whipped and cowed, and now this great cataclysm swirls around them, and they come to us crying, 'We's free! We's free!' Free to what? I wonder. What awaits them?"

"Whatever it is, it will be better than two centuries of bondage."

Holmes cocked an eyebrow. "Why, Halz, are you becoming an Abolitionist?"

"No, but right is right. And to uphold the right, I'd rejoin the regiment tonight."

"You're at the center of everything, Halz. Stay there. You see what we can only speculate on. And think of the book you'll be able to write when this is over."

If you only knew, Halsey thought.

"Besides, you can serve honorably but still sleep in a bed and eat decent food."

Halsey answered with a few bromides about standing up to enemy fire rather than sitting at a desk. Then he agreed that soft beds and steak had their benefits.

Then they went back into the big house and put a bit of poteen on the lips of the dying sergeant. They were glad when he opened his eyes briefly and ran his tongue around his mouth. It looked as if he smiled.

. . .

Early the next morning, the *Ariel* left Harrison's Landing. She stopped for the afternoon at Fortress Monroe, where Lincoln conferred with General Burnside. Then she turned up the Potomac for the night run to Washington.

And Halsey found that he could not sleep. His consternation over the encounter with Pinkerton had started to prey on him. *Evidence?* What evidence? And the living sound of that big side-wheel steamer—the slow and steady dip and thump, dip and thump, dip and thump—could not soothe him as the company of Holmes had. So he found himself wandering the deck and in the wandering found a fellow wanderer:

Lincoln was standing in shirtsleeves near the port bow, staring off into the night.

"A fine trip, sir," said Halsey. "I think you raised the men's morale."

"They raised mine."

"I'm sure General McClellan appreciated it."

"I was not there to inspire McClellan. I wanted information. I now know the status of every division."

"Was that what he wrote in the letter he gave you?"

"No. I interviewed his generals and wrote down their comments." Lincoln patted a paper in his pocket. "You could say I deposed them."

Halsey liked it when Lincoln spoke to him as an equal, lawyer to lawyer.

"McClellan's letter," Lincoln continued, "advised me on how to conduct the war, but not just militarily. Politically, too."

Halsey hesitated before asking the next question, unsure that he wanted the burden of an answer with McNealy—and now Pinkerton—expecting him to surrender whatever he gathered. But he had to ask: "Was it good advice?"

"Political advice from a general?" Lincoln chuckled. "It reminds me of the man whose horse kicked up and stuck his foot through the stirrup. The man said to the horse, 'If you are going to get on, I'd just as soon get off.'"

"Do you think McClellan is trying to 'get on,' as you say, sir?"

"He warned me that this cannot be a war against populations or property. He's for fighting a limited war, army against army, and he's dead against a war to free the Negro."

"But it isn't, is it?"

"It did not begin that way, but before we're done . . ." Lincoln's voice trailed off.

The wheels dipped and thumped, dipped and thumped, dipped and thumped.

And Lincoln said, "The general wrote, 'A declaration of radical views, especially upon slavery, will rapidly deteriorate our present armies.' Sounds like a threat to me."

"I don't think it's true, sir."

"I hope not. Senator Sumner and the Abolitionists believe not. They want to enlist coloreds. Might not be a bad idea if my call for three hundred thousand more men falls short. But the Democrats fear arming the Negroes as much as the slaveholders do." Lincoln stared for a time into the night. "I have to say, Halsey, it tears a man."

"It tears the whole country, sir."

Dip and thump. Dip and thump. Dip and thump.

"I do wish the border states would accept my plan for compensated emancipation." Lincoln drew a deep sigh. "Then you and I would not have lived in vain."

Halsey knew now that he was hearing too much. But Lincoln seemed intent on talking, as if these words, spoken into the steamer's headwind and blown off into the Potomac darkness, were part of some presidential soliloquy rather than a conversation with a young man who had left off studying the law in order to fight for the Union.

Dip and thump. Dip and thump. Dip and thump.

Lincoln listened to the sound for a time, then said, "I remember a steamboat trip when I was a young man. I was traveling to St. Louis. And riding near the bow were ten or twelve Negroes, shackled in irons, deprived for no reason but their color of the freedom that we so loudly proclaim is the ideal of our nation. That sight tormented me then, and I have to say that it torments me still."

"Slavery is a cruel institution, sir."

"If slavery is not wrong, then nothing is wrong. But my job is to preserve the Union." Lincoln looked Halsey in the eye. "If I can do it and free all of the slaves, I will. If I can do it and free none of the slaves, I will. And if I have to do it by freeing some of the slaves while others remain in bondage, that'll be my course."

Dip and thump. Dip and thump. Dip and thump.

"But I will do what military necessity requires. I will give those boys back there every chance for victory. I won't give up the government without playing my last card, and I may yet win the trick."

With those words, Halsey Hutchinson felt a burden lift. Lincoln was wrestling with it, but emancipation was coming. Once Lincoln reached the decision, the process by which he came to it would not matter. The daybook that Halsey had lost would no longer hold intelligence to damage the president.

The question, as a lawyer might say, would be moot.

. . .

Whatever Lincoln had said must have unburdened him, too, because by the next morning, he seemed as chipper as Halsey had ever seen him.

They were almost home, about a mile south of the City Wharves, when the *Ariel* struck the Kettle Shoals and stopped dead.

The captain announced that it would be two hours before the tide could lift them off. Groans of frustration echoed through the vessel. The men in Lincoln's party had expected to be back by noon and at their desks by one. All of them had said they were returning rejuvenated after seeing the enthusiasm of the troops.

But then Lincoln's voice cut through the humid air: "Two hours, you say, Captain?"

"Yes, sir."

A moment later, Lincoln appeared on the lower deck and said, to no one in particular. "Water sure looks good on a hot day."

"It sure does, sir," said one of the military staffers.

Lincoln sat on an upturned hogshead and pulled off a boot. The white sock came with it, revealing a long bony white foot. "Did I ever tell you boys about my days runnin' flatboats down to New Orleans?"

By now, half a dozen men had gathered to watch Lincoln pull off his other boot.

He said, "At the end of a hot day, we'd take a nice dunk in the river."

The boot hit the deck; then Lincoln stood and pulled off his vest and shirt, revealing an undershirt soaked with new sweat and etched with salt stains from the old sweat of a three-day journey. Then he unbuttoned his trousers and dropped them to the deck. "I hereby issue a presidential dis-position to every man aboard to go for a dunk."

Two sailors immediately began to strip. After a moment, so did the civilians.

Lincoln looked at Halsey, "Get out of those soldier blues, son. That's an order."

Within minutes, the deck of the *Ariel* was littered with shoes, shirts, trousers, and smallclothes, and a dozen bare white bodies were slithering through the brown river.

Halsey dunked and dived and did not taste blood, real or metaphorical.

Lincoln rolled onto his back and spit a long stream of water into the air, then gave out with a high, cackling laugh.

A couple of the soldiers had grabbed bars of soap and were standing on the sandy shoal, lathering themselves front and back.

Lincoln rolled over again and swam. The muscles of his shoulders and bare white buttocks tightened like cables as he stroked and kicked.

And Halsey knew he would never forget this scene.

The unfinished Capitol and the stunted Washington Monument shimmered in the heat haze ahead. A steamer filled with yet more wounded was rounding a downstream bend. But for a few moments, Abraham Lincoln seemed to forget it all in that river. He became a boy again, naked and carefree.

. . .

There was a note under Halsey's door in the National:

Meet near lock keeper's house, 17th Street at the canal. 3 P.M.

He balled it up and threw it in the wastebasket. McNealy could wait. He had promised Samantha that he would pay her a visit as soon as he returned from Virginia.

When he walked up the steps of the Union Hotel Hospital, there were ten soldiers on the stoop. Some were chewing tobacco. Others were sucking on hard candies. They all saluted except for a man who had no arms.

In the lobby, Miss Dean came up to him. "She's sleepin'."

Halsey glanced at the clock. It was only three.

"Worked a double shift yesterday." Then Miss Dean smiled, or at least tried to. Her face never quite lit up. "Let me see if she's awake."

A few minutes later, Samantha came down from her top-floor garret. She was pinching her cheeks and blinking puffy eyes. Her hoopless gingham dress was wrinkled, as if she had not bothered to take it off before she flopped onto her bed.

Halsey took her hand. "You look—"

She laughed, "Tired?"

"You've been working hard?"

Miss Dean said, "She works hard, all right, but she better learn to work better."

"I do what I'm asked." Samantha brushed her hair back from her face.

"You do, indeed, dearie," said Miss Dean. "I'm not sayin' you don't, because you do. I'll give you that. And you're gettin' better at what you do every day."

Halsey realized how much he was growing to admire Samantha. He said to her, "Can you walk with me?"

Samantha looked at Miss Dean, who nodded.

Samantha took off her apron and soon they were walking down Wisconsin, toward the stone bridge that crossed the Chesapeake and Ohio Canal.

Unlike the Washington Canal, the C&O was still a going concern. It ran beside the Potomac from Rock Creek in Georgetown far into the heartland. And the war had been good for business.

They stood in the middle of the bridge and looked along the stone-walled canal, toward the locks rising from Rock Creek. Trees shaded the tow path and the brick row houses that lined it.

"It's cooler here, over the water," said Samantha.

"It's why I thought you'd like it."

And she asked of the trip.

He described the troop review, the meeting with Holmes, and then turned to skinny-dipping with the president, which Samantha found hilarious. And the more she laughed, the more he told: "After his boots, he took off his trousers"—laughter—"stripped naked and leapt into the water"—more laughter—"swam like a big sturgeon with his hair plastered to his head"—louder laughter—"and his white behind sticking out of the water"—laughter through a covering hand—"and then he rolled over and floated on his back."

"Oh, Halsey, I cannot imagine what that must have looked like."

"Let's just say I can vouch for his manhood."

Suddenly, she stopped laughing and brought both hands to her face.

"What?" He put a hand on her shoulder. "What is it?"

"I am tending a poor boy whose manhood is . . . gone." And she began to cry.

He threw his arms around her and held her.

A canal boat was coming upstream, pulled by a mule team on the towpath. As the men went past, they whistled at what appeared to be young lovers stealing an embrace.

Halsey pulled her back so that they could not see her, and whispered, "You do not have to stay. There are others to take your place."

"What?" She raised her face to him. Those round blue eyes were red with exhaustion and tears. "You want me to go back to Wellesley?"

"There will be no shame in it."

"If I were a man and showed cowardice, there would be shame on me and my children and my children's children."

"Perhaps not—"

"But I'm a woman, and I'd be a coward if I left that hospital with so much to do."

He said, "I've seen it on the battlefield and in life, Samantha. One person's cowardice is another's good sense."

"Oh, Halsey, I don't believe that and neither—" Suddenly she stopped speaking.

"What?"

"That man."

Halsey turned but he saw nothing unusual and no one familiar.

"There was a man by a tree. He just dropped down under the bridge."

Halsey looked over the stone parapet but saw nothing on the towpath.

She said, "I've seen him before. He wears a blue suit and a blue kepi and red neckerchief. He looks like a ferret. He's even come to the hospital."

Halsey took the stone staircase and jumped down to the towpath.

But he saw nothing. Could the man have disappeared that quickly? Or had he ducked into one of the houses along the route?

He walked under the bridge and came out on the other side. He looked in both directions, then looked up at Samantha and shrugged.

She appeared tiny and vulnerable up there, with her head and shoulders peeping over the stone parapet. But she had spine. That was for certain.

He would not let her be drawn into this.

. . .

"You ignored my note." McNealy was sitting on one of the shoeshine chairs.

Halsey stopped and looked around. "Where's Noah? He works till eight."

"I gave him a dollar and sent him home." McNealy lit a cigar and gave a jerk of his head. "Climb up here and chat."

Halsey took the other chair.

A new regiment was marching by. Their band was playing "Hail, Columbia," and the men were moving with a nice, easy step.

McNealy said, "I hear you met Pinkerton."

"Do you work for him or Lafayette Baker?"

"I ask the questions, Lieutenant. You answer. You follow?"

Halsey asked again.

McNealy took his cigar from his mouth. "I'll tell you my business this once. I came from Chicago with Pinkerton when the war started. I helped him track spies in the city. When he headed for the Peninsula with McClellan, he asked me to stay and transfer to the War Department. I may work for Baker, but I feed Pinkerton. You could say I'm his eyes in the War Department."

"And I'm yours?"

"You wanted the job so much, you shot your way into it."

Halsey ignored the joke. "Pinkerton spoke of evidence against me. What is it?"

"Beyond the gun? What else is there? A daybook, maybe?"

Instead of answering, Halsey revealed his own suspicion. "Do you have it?"

"The daybook?" McNealy laughed. "If I had it, I wouldn't need you. I'd give you back to Baker and be done with you."

"And what would you do with the book?"

"Use it for good." McNealy kept his eyes on the soldiers tramping past.

"For good?"

"I told you I didn't care about it, but I do. I'd bet it has more than addresses and dates. I'd bet Lincoln was usin' it to sort things out in his own mind."

"What makes you think that?"

"He was so bothered to lose it. A man says things to himself he might never say to the world, especially a man in Lincoln's position." McNealy puffed on the cigar. "Imagine . . . Lincoln writin' down his real opinions about generals or congressmen or niggers. If I had such a thing, I'd have every politician in this town jumpin' like a circus dog. I could get them to end the war tomorrow."

"End it or win it?" asked Halsey.

"There'll be no winnin', Lieutenant. We've lost already, all of us. The country's lost its amity. You've lost your voice. I've lost a brother."

"A brother?" This surprised Halsey.

"At Shiloh, Second Ohio, under Captain Linus Rawlins. Went off to war when the first bugle blew. Left a wife and two little babies."

"I'm sorry," said Halsey, and for the first time, he felt something other than fear or contempt for Joseph Albert McNealy. He said, "So . . . what can I tell you?"

"Lincoln's gettin' closer to emancipation. What do you know?"

Halsey said, "No more than that."

McNealy gestured to the troops marching past. "Be a damn shame if all these boys were goin' to their deaths in a war to free the niggers."

"Now you're sounding like Benjamin Wood."

"Or McClellan. He knows his men will throw down their arms rather than fight for the nigger. I hear he told the president as much in a letter. Did Lincoln say anything about it? About the letter, I mean."

Halsey described what he'd seen on the *Ariel*. "Lincoln read the letter and put it in his pocket. McClellan wanted to talk about it. But it seems that Lincoln has decided *he's* the commander-in-chief, not McClellan."

"Which makes McClellan's as mad as a nigger with his hand caught in a beehive."

After a moment Halsey said, "I have nothing more on the letter."

"Nothing on the letter. Nothing on the daybook. And nothing on a that ledger that disappeared from Squeaker's." McNealy took another puff of the cigar. "I've asked you about the ledger, haven't I?"

"You know you've asked half a dozen times," said Halsey, "and you know what I've answered." He had decided to lie about the ledger, which might prove useful some day. "I have nothing for you."

"I'm beginning to think you have nothing at all." McNealy twitched around so that his face was close to Halsey. "Just remember, if I think you're holding out on me, you'll be in the Old Cap tomorrow."

Halsey said, "I know what I'm up against."

"No, you don't." McNealy settled back in the chair. "You're in Washington. You're in the country's political bowels, where every man is out for himself first and his party second, even if the country gets the shit. It's all politics."

"It's war," said Halsey. "Not politics."

"And what's war but politics with bullets instead of words? Frontstabbin' instead of backstabbin'. Everyone's playin' political games. Lincoln, Wood, Pinkerton, Baker, me . . . even you. Though I think you're playin' games with your prick, too, eh? The pretty nursie-girl from Boston?"

"Leave her out of this, and tell your people to stop following her."

"My people?" McNealy laughed. "If my people are following her, she won't even know."

"Then who was spying on us this afternoon, on the bridge in Georgetown?"

McNealy thought a moment, as if he might know. Then he said, "I have no idea. But if that Constance finds out about your nursie-girl, she might stop pullin' your prick in the Smithsonian."

"Leave Constance out of it, too."

"How can I? She's a rebel spy."

"She's no spy," said Halsey.

McNealy smiled. "I know."

"You know?"

"She's an Abolitionist. She's gone to New York to hear Frederick

Douglass. An Abolitionist with an uncle who hates niggers." McNealy chuckled, got up, brushed cigar ash off his jacket. "It's like Pinkerton and me. He's an Abolitionist who's loyal to a Union Democrat named McClellan. And I'm just a commonsense white American who wants the bloodshed to end. But remember—"

"What?"

"Until it ends, I *run* you."

As Halsey watched McNealy head down the Avenue, he wondered again, what *was* his game? Halsey meant to find out. He would not be run much longer.

.   .   .

The next morning, he stopped for a shoeshine.

While Noah Bone cleaned the Virginia mud off his boots, Halsey asked about the detective dressed in brown. "Do you know where he lives?"

"Detective Greenback? That's what I call him since he pay me a greenback to go home last night."

"His name's McNealy," said Halsey. "And I'll pay you a lot more to find out where he lives, where he eats, who he talks to . . ."

"Why you think I can do that?"

"I think you know more than you let on, Noah. I'll give you fifty dollars."

"Fifty? That's a powerful lot of money, sir. This must be dangerous."

"Not particularly."

"I don't like doin' dangerous things, and I don't like my boys doin' 'em either."

"There are men marching into walls of bullets right now," said Halsey. "They're fighting and dying for the freedom of your race. That's dangerous."

Noah's hands stopped. He looked up. He stood up. He stepped back. Then he unbuttoned the top three buttons of his shirt and turned. "I show you this once, Mr. Halsey, since you seem a decent man." And right there in the sunshine on Pennsylvania Avenue, Noah dropped his shirt, revealing his shoulders and upper back.

In an instant, Halsey repented of whatever he had just said to offend Noah Bone. The scars layered Noah's back and ran in long raised ridges of discolored flesh, some black, some purple, and some a sort of greasy white, like tallow.

Noah quickly pulled the shirt up and buttoned it. "I don't show them too much. Most folks see them when I sweat through my shirt and don't know what they's looking at. But—" Noah gestured to his back. "—that there's what you call dangerous. That there's a life of gettin' caught and runnin' away."

"From where?"

"A plantation down Fredericksburg way and a massa who whip his slaves worse than he whip his dogs." Noah spread polish on Halsey's shoes. "From the time I'se a boy, he whip me. Then one day, I run away. Well, he come and get me and whip me some more. When I can, I run agin, and he catch me agin. I run agin and agin, and he whip me agin and agin till finally, he jess give up. One day, I run and he don't chase me."

"And you came to Washington?"

"And I worry about the slave catcher till I meet a white woman who know a man who write papers sayin' I'se his freed slave. Then I go to work for myself."

"You've done well," said Halsey, "in the shadow of the Capitol."

Noah looked up at the rising dome and gave a laugh. "When I got here, they had a slave pen over behind the Center Market, with a fine view of that fine buildin' up there and a nothin' but a little lean-to so them poor colored folks could get in out the weather. A reg'lar pen like a pig-pen, where slaves was bought and sold and whipped, and families was broke up, and papa slaves was sent off to make baby slaves in other states, jess like they was animals."

As he listened, Halsey began to think that perhaps the Abolitionists had been right all along, and he had simply not been paying attention. He was now.

"You never heard such wailin'. But I think, safest place for a runaway is right across from that slave pen, 'cause what runaway gonna put hisself in a spot like that? He must be a freedman, that colored bootblack. That's how I want them slave catchers to think."

"Well, you're safe now."

"But I never rest. Why you think I watch my world like I do? 'Cause up till a few months ago, them slave catchers could grab me and haul me off on nothing but their say-so, and no piece of paper gonna stop 'em. Now, I don't have to fear that, thanks to Mr. Lincoln and District Emancipation. No more, no more." He started buffing in rhythm to the words. "No more, no more."

Halsey said, "Would it make a difference if I told you that I need help so that I can help the president?"

Noah looked up. "It might."

"It's true."

"Well, sir, I used to have one rule, but now I has two. I shine any man's shoes who pay my price. And I help any man who's helpin' Mr. Lincoln."

SEVEN

Saturday Afternoon

"Is Halsey Hutchinson talking yet?" asked Peter Fallon.

"He's whispering," said Antoine. "So am I, because I'm in the reading room at the MHS. They hate it when somebody's cell phone goes off."

"You still have that gangsta rap ringtone?"

"You mean Ice-T doin' 'High Rollers'? I save that for Saturday night. My phone beeped once. I thought Fitzpatrick would throw me out."

"Put it on vibrate, and go out under the stairs."

"Hold on."

Peter imagined Antoine in the staid old Boston library.

It was Peter's favorite place to do his research, with librarian James Fitzpatrick bringing out mountains of material, no matter the subject. And hidden under the circular stairway in the foyer were restrooms, coatracks, and a courtesy phone.

"Okay," said Antoine. "I can talk now. But couldn't you wait?"

Peter supposed he could have.

Or he could have called and apologized to Diana, who had already left an annoyed phone message about going off without telling her.

Or he could have called Evangeline. She had left him a message telling him to buy a dress shirt and tie, because they had been invited to a reception at the Smithsonian.

Those calls could wait.

This couldn't, because Peter Fallon was now in full Civil War mode. . . .

·   ·   ·

Even after Peter had saved him from shooting up a family of Civil War enthusiasts, Jefferson Sorrel had not been very friendly.

He had explained, almost as a way to get Peter to leave, that he was a dealer himself, with his own Civil War sales site on the Web. He had bought often from Dawkins but had never expected to find a Lincoln letter in the backing of an engraving. After offering it to Diana Wilmington, he had put out word, "just to test the waters." And a preemptory offer of three and a half million had come from a regular customer.

Sorrel had taken it. Now he was watching his back and wondering about the mysterious "something" referenced in the letter, with its "potential to alter opinions regarding the difficulties just ended and those that lie ahead."

"You think it's a diary?" Peter had asked. "What makes you think so?"

Sorrel had made a wave of his hand, as if to chase Peter away. "I've told you too much already. Maybe I don't think it's anything. Maybe I think I'll just take the money and go off to Florida. Maybe that's what I'll do."

But Peter had proposed a partnership rather than a vacation. He had pointed out that finding a Lincoln diary would make everyone rich, "and two heads are better than one, especially when they belong to a pair of smart guys like us."

Sorrel had said that he would look for it himself. But now that the secret was out, he expected competition. "A lot of guys have been watching me."

"Like the ones in the Nissan Versa?" Peter had asked.

"They work for the guy I sold it to. They're in it for politics. Others are in it for the money."

"As always," Peter had said. "Who are they?"

"You'd know some of them. And some of them, I don't even know." Sorrel had wiped the sweat from his forehead, and some of the hair dye came with it. "Florida's lookin' awful nice."

Then he had asked Peter to apologize to Diana Wilmington, explaining that he wasn't very good with, "male-female stuff," and even worse with "white-black stuff."

Then he had said, "Okay. We're done. Get lost. And stay lost. . . ."

. . .

Now Antoine was telling Peter, "I need some time, especially if I'm dig-ging through the records of the Twentieth Massachusetts. What is it we're looking for?"

"I can't really say." Peter glanced at the cabbie, who did not seem to be listening, but you could never tell.

"It's something from Lincoln, right?" said Antoine. "It has to be some-thing from Lincoln. Otherwise Hutchinson and Murphy wouldn't mean a damn. What is it?"

"His diary."

"Lincoln's diary? Lincoln's personal diary? No fuckin' way."

"Watch your language in the MHS, and don't say that out loud again."

"I'm in the men's room. No one can hear me."

"Well, I'm in a cab stuck in traffic."

They were inching their way across the Key Bridge, trying to get back into Georgetown. The walkers and bicycles were going faster. If there had been crawlers, they would have been going faster, too. For fifteen minutes, Peter had been looking down at the old Chesapeake and Ohio Canal. It ran next to the river, from Georgetown all the way to Cumberland, Maryland. Once it had been a highway. Now it was no more than a his-torical curiosity . . . and a nice place to stroll.

"So," said Peter, "what have you found?"

"I went through the Descriptive Roll of the Twentieth, hundreds of pages of folio sheets bound together. The adjutant or the sergeant-major would keep the records, long columns, perfect handwriting. On one side you'd get the physical description of the guy and on the other, his per-sonal service record."

"What about this Halsey Hutchinson?"

"He lived on Beacon Hill and belonged to First Parish. He was twenty-five when the war began, in his first year at Harvard Law. He'd graduated from the college in 1858 and worked for a while at American Telegraph. There was an asterisk next to that, as though it was impor-tant."

"It was," said Peter. "Anyone who had telegraph experience, officer or enlisted man, eventually got tapped for the military telegraph service."

The cabbie cursed. The light had cycled, and the traffic on the bridge had barely budged. Peter knew what the guy was thinking: Before long, this fare might pay him for distance traveled, then hop out and leave him to deadhead home through the Saturday snarl.

Peter said to Antoine, "Any other particulars? What did he look like?"

"The chart tells us he was five-eleven, one-seventy."

"Tall for the time," said Peter. "Wiry."

"He also had blue eyes, black hair. Offered to serve July 1861, sustained throat wound, Ball's Bluff. The last entry says, 'Transferred to the War Department telegraph office, March 1, 1862.'"

"Yes!" Peter almost clapped his hands. He loved to find a connection that good, that quickly. This kind of work was like putting a puzzle together, a giant three-dimensional jigsaw puzzle, and they had just found a corner piece.

Peter said, "He's working in the telegraph office, and every night, Lincoln comes over to read the news. That's how they know each other. You deserve a bonus."

"Someday deserving a bonus will mean getting one."

"Watch the pay envelope. What about Jeremiah Murphy?"

"He was from the fishing village of Spiddal, in County Galway, emigrated to America in 1862. Enlisted in East Boston, July 31, 1862."

"Sounds like one of those off-the-boat boys. When they walked down the gangplank, the recruiting agents were waiting with a bounty and a pen. After the disaster on the Peninsula, Lincoln issued the call for another three hundred thousand, but they were having a hell of a time filling it with volunteer recruits. Anything else about him?"

"Vital stats and this: wounded at the Second Hatcher's Run, February 1865. Discharged to hospital."

"One of the last engagements of the war. Send me the rest," said Peter, "but let's focus on Hutchinson, figure out what he was doing between Ball's Bluff and Lincoln's assassination."

"According to Fitzpatrick, the best account of the telegraph office was written by the cipher man, David Homer Bates. A lot of the famous stories come from him. You ever heard the one about the 'down to the raisins'?"

"Raisins?" said Peter. "No. What about them?"

"Never mind. It's in Bates's book. So is the one about Lincoln writing the Emancipation Proclamation in the telegraph office. Bates published it around 1900."

"He must have known Hutchinson." Peter watched the bicycles speeding by on the sidewalk. "Find his book in Project Gutenberg and skim it. Then go to the newspapers."

Antoine groaned. "Come on, boss. I can't be reading newspapers—"

"The Washington *Daily Republican* is on the Library of Congress Web site. You read 1862 and '63. I'll go through the rest, then—"

"That's heavy liftin'. And this all could be a fool's errand. I've read every book there is about Lincoln, and I've never read a word about a real diary. He scribbled notes all the time, wrote things, put them into desk drawers and whatnot, pulled them out later, rewrote them. His personal valet, a black man named Slade, wrote about burning lots of Lincoln pen-scratchings over the years, but—"

Just then the cabbie growled, "What the fuck?" He was looking in his rearview.

Peter said to Antoine. "Something's up. I'll get back to you."

The cab door opened and a guy jumped in. Jeans, black sport jacket, black T-shirt, the kind of outfit that looked good only on a guy who was fit, very fit. On this guy, it looked so good that he didn't bother to pull the gun that Peter saw under his jacket. He just said, "Get out."

"Hey, man." The cabbie turned around.

Mr. Fit threw a fifty on the front seat. "That's for you. This guy fucked my wife."

Peter's door popped open and a black guy in a Redskins hat, who looked fitter than Mr. Fit, reached in and yanked him out.

Mr. Fit slid across the seat and said to the cabbie, "The light's green. Get goin'."

Redskins said to Peter, "We can do this the easy way or the hard way."

"I'll take easy," said Peter. "Easy sounds nicer."

Mr. Fit began to lead Peter—or drag him—along the sidewalk, toward a big black SUV about five cars back.

Peter glanced at the cabbie, who was folding the fifty. *Thanks a lot.*

He thought about vaulting the fence and jumping down onto the towpath. He could run all day down there, and he was in shape enough to run all day anywhere. But it was a hell of a drop.

"How about a little hint?" he asked. "Where are we going?"

"Not far," said Fit. "We got tired of waiting in traffic, so we decided to save everybody some time."

"Yeah," said Redskins. "And the SUV is a better ride than that little Nissan Versa. You don't want to miss the party."

"Party?" said Peter.

"Big reception at the Smithsonian. VIP stuff."

"You guys know more than I do. What are you, FBI or something?"

They didn't answer that. But they seemed as confident as FBI. They'd snatched him in broad daylight, right on the Key Bridge, and they were acting as if they *expected* him to go with them.

That, Peter decided, would be their mistake, because he wasn't getting into a strange SUV with anybody.

A bicycle went by and they all jumped out of the way.

Another bicyclist whizzed toward them, ringing his bell.

No bike path on the Key Bridge. So the bicyclists drove along the sidewalk beside you or came up behind you, bleating, "On your left, on your left" or "On your right, on your right," while ringing their little bike bells like sanctimonious acolytes to the Church of All Things Green and Self-Propelled . . . also Self-Absorbed.

Peter saw two more bikes coming along the sidewalk, already annoying out loud:

"On your left, on your left." *Ring ring. Ring ring.*

This would take some coordination, but it was worth a try. At the very least, he'd make a scene. So he let Mr. Fit and Redskins lead him a bit farther until . . .

"On your left, on your left." *Ring ring. Ring ring.*

Fit, who held Peter by the elbow, grabbed the door of the SUV.

Peter pulled away and said, "Wait a minute, I left my iPad in the cab. It has—"

Redskins said, "Fuck the iPad."

Fit said, "I didn't see any iPad."

"On your left, on your left." *Ring ring. Ring ring.*

Redskins was standing in the path of the bikes.

A third bike was coming right behind the first two.

"Behind you! *Behind you!*"

Ring ring. Ring ring. Ring ring.

Redskins turned to the sound.

Peter didn't have to do anything but hold him in place . . . if he could.

Ring ring. Ring RING! RING RING!

With both hands and a hip, Peter leaned on Redskins and let the bike plow into the middle of him, wheel first, right . . . between . . . the . . . legs.

Redskins let out a groan and crumpled in pain.

The skinny male rider—weren't they all skinny?—went flying by in a flash of yellow and blue biking spandex.

And here came the second bike. A girl was riding it. More spandex, better fitted, blue and black, soon to be black and blue. *Ring ring. Ring RING! RING RING!*

She just slammed into the collision.

The third bike couldn't stop, and the rider didn't know what do to—jump or stop or—*Ring ring. Ring ring*—yell some more:

"On your right! No. No. Your *right*! *Your right!* No No! Behind you. *Behind you!*"

Redskins was rolling on the ground and howling in pain. Not too professional, but in the leg breaker's union, a speeding bike to the balls counted as hazardous duty.

Mr. Fit was trying to untangle himself from the second bike, but he was stumbling on the skinny biker and the girl and . . .

Everybody just stay jumbled another second, thought Peter, *another second, and . . . Yes!*

The third bike hit. Another skinny male vaulted over another set of handlebars.

Not very nice, but sometimes . . . Peter threw the third bike at Mr. Fit, snatched the first bike from the pile, jumped on, and pumped.

A hand grabbed at him.

He pumped again. Then another hand grabbed.

Then. *Pump. Pump. Pump.* He was rolling.

And right away, he started shouting, "On your left! On your left!"

Mr. Fit finally pulled free and came after Peter.

The pedestrians ahead were stopping, turning, looking.

Pump. Pump. Pump.

Peter heard Mr. Fit getting closer.

But suddenly, the door of the taxi swung open and knocked Mr. Fit into a pair of joggers.

"Hey, man, you forgot your change!" cried the cabbie.

This time Peter meant it: *Thanks a lot.*

He pulled away, sped to the end of the bridge in a few pumps, and looked down M Street: Saturday crowds choked the sidewalks, working from bar to bar and boutique to boutique. Saturday traffic was stopping, then starting, then stopping, then inching, then stopping, then sitting.

Peter didn't see a bit of running room.

But if he followed the nice brick sidewalk to his right, past the park benches that looked out at the bridge, he would find a flight of stairs leading down to the canal towpath. So he took it and cruised quickly down, then came to a little staircase.

He pounded step-over-step-over-step-over-step, standing up so that the seat didn't bang his balls, with Mr. Fit coming again, and a skinny bicyclist right behind him.

When he reached the towpath, he skidded. He almost went into the water. In this spot, the towpath was just a narrow dirt walkway next to the canal.

So he jumped off the bike to avoid hitting two people strolling toward him, turned, and as Fit burst around the corner, he threw the bike.

Fit stumbled back, stumbled into the bicyclist who was also flying down the stairs, tripped, and went right over the old retaining wall into the canal. When he hit, he sent up a huge splash of algae green water, and the sound echoed up and down the granite channel.

Peter ran a block along the towpath; then he cut up and ran along a wide alley between two rows of buildings. Just before the Wisconsin Avenue Bridge, he grabbed a cab heading south, away from the M Street traffic, and was gone.

. . .

"I can see why you didn't marry him."

"Pick another topic," said Evangeline into the phone.

"Sorry," said Diana, "but I'm totally pissed. I told him to wait and he just left."

"*Men*. Can't live with 'em. Can't live with 'em."

Diana laughed. "You got that right."

"Well, he's not here yet."

"And he's not answering his cell."

"He does that when he's avoiding a conversation."

Evangeline heard the door open, and Peter entered. She waved him to a chair. Then she said into the phone, "Yeah. That's how he rolls. That's one way of putting it."

Peter gestured. *Who is it?*

She mouthed the word, *Diana.*

He shook his head. He didn't want to talk with her just yet.

So Evangeline said, "Listen, I'm sure he's sorry for leaving you. But cut him some slack. Will we see you tonight? Good. Yes. A big night."

Evangeline hung up and turned to Peter. "She's pissed. What did you do?"

"I went off on my own."

"And from the look in your eye, you got into some trouble."

"You know me too well."

"I can always tell when you've had a jolt of adrenaline or testosterone."

"Just adrenaline. With testosterone, you fight. Adrenaline is all flight."

"So you've been . . . flighting . . . er . . . fleeing? Running?"

"Running like hell." He dropped onto the sofa and kicked off his shoes.

"I suppose this means you didn't get the suit I asked you to buy."

Peter shrugged. "I brought two clean shirts and a tie in my overnight."

She looked at his trousers. "And those? You can't wear those tonight. Dockers look like a brown paper bag on your butt once you've been sitting in them. And if you've been running in them—"

"Actually, I was riding a bicycle."

"The only thing worse would be hand-to-hand combat."

"I gave that up a long time ago."

"Let's hope so." She handed him a small shopping bag. "A present."

In the bag: a white shirt with French cuffs, 15/34, and a silver gray tie.

He said "Very nice, but this doesn't solve the blue blazer and Dockers problem."

She reached around the bedroom door and pulled out a garment bag.

"I promised myself when we got together again that I'd never try to change you *or* dress you. Here's the exception that proves the rule, grabbed off the rack at Joseph A. Bank after we finished filming. Forty-two regular jacket, thirty-six/thirty pants."

He got up and gave her a kiss. "Where is it we're going again?"

"A preview reception for the new Smithsonian exhibit. It's called 'Lincoln and Liberty Too.' It's a collection of documents and artifacts—"

"—relating to all things emancipating."

"How did you guess?"

"Because they tried to borrow a few things we're using in our Boston show."

"We were invited by a congressman I met on the train this morning."

"How is it you met a congressman and a lobbyist on the train, and you didn't tell me? I had to hear it from some guy who knew a guy who took a picture of you."

"Picture? Where did you see the picture?"

Just then, there was a knock at the door.

Peter's antenna went up. After the chase through Georgetown, he couldn't be too careful. As Evangeline started toward the door, he reached out and stopped her.

"Oh, Peter, I told you. I don't have time for this stuff. I'm—"

"I know, I know. You're heading in a new direction. But—"

She looked toward the door and called, "Who is it?"

"Room service."

Peter looked through the peephole: a guy in a hotel jacket, a cart. Looked like room service, could be a ruse. Peter asked, "What do you have?"

"A bottle of wine, sir."

"What kind?"

"White, sir."

"Read the label—"

Evangeline said, "Oh, Peter, stop it."

"If it's expensive wine, we'll know it's not a trick."

She rolled her eyes, cracked the door, and said over the safety bar, "Let me see the card, please."

The server passed it through the opening.

Evangeline glanced at it: Kathi Morganti, Hamill and Associates. Then she said to Peter, "It's safe, Mr. Suspicious."

Peter let the server in, had him open the bottle, tipped him a ten.

"Generous," said Evangeline.

"Suspicious but generous." Peter handed her a glass and took a sip. "Puligny-Montrachet. Very nice."

Evangeline picked up the card. "This is from the woman I met on the train this morning, the lobbyist. And a guy took our picture. How did you know?"

"The guy was no guy. He was part of some kind of gang that's gotten into this Lincoln letter business."

She said, "You never know who you'll meet on the Northeast power corridor, but I didn't think that meeting the congressman and the lobbyist was a coincidence."

"Neither did the guy who took your picture. What's in the note?"

She read: "'It seems that a client of ours dispatched two overaggressive members of his security staff to bring your boyfriend over for a chat.'"

"That would be me," said Peter.

"The client would like to apologize in person. He will have a limo waiting at six, to take you to his condo for cocktails. Kathi Morganti."

"She's the lobbyist?"

"Works for a big K Street firm. And she knew who you were. The truth is, she was more interested in you than in me."

"Does she say who the client is?"

Evangeline turned the paper over. "No."

"So, are we going to see him?"

"We?"

"You're the contact, and if he can order a good bottle of wine, he probably has good hors d'oeuvres."

She shook her head . . . not for *no*. More like, *Oh, no, not again.*

"Evangeline, this is heating up quickly, and it could be huge."

"No."

"But I need you." He sipped his wine. "You're my foil when I sit down with some guy who thinks that he can play me because he has more money, or more muscle, or better taste in wine—"

"No chance of that."

"—or a gun."

"Gun? Peter, not more guns."

"C'mon." He tapped his glass against hers. "Married or not, you're my better half. If I'm aggressive, you're calm. If I'm sarcastic, you're complimentary. If I'm respectful, you're insulting. You're the salt to my pepper, the wine to my cheese, the—"

"Go and shower."

"—reality check to my flights of fancy."

"Shave, too."

The suite had two bathrooms. Plenty of room for two people to get ready.

When Peter emerged in his new gray suit and silvery gray tie, she was wearing a red dress with a maillot top and a black paisley pattern, finished with a little black silk jacket and a string of pearls.

"Beautiful," he said. "Makes me wonder why I decided not to marry you."

She planted a kiss on his lips. "I decided not to marry *you*. But in that outfit—" She brushed his hair back. "—all you need is a little more gray on the sides, and you'd be my dream date. Cary Grant as Roger Thornhill, man of the world, man on the run."

"But Cary parted his hair on the right. The only man I ever saw who looked good parting his hair on the right." Peter opened the door. "After you."

She hesitated. "Whenever you open a door and say that to me, I always think, 'I am but mad north by northwest.'"

"Mad?"

"Mad to be walking out the door with you . . . right into trouble."

"You love it."

.   .   .

The limo was waiting. The driver held a discreet sign: FALLON/CARRINGTON.

"Mr. and Mrs. Bruce are looking forward to meeting you." The driver, a slender black man with gray hair, gave them a courtly bow and invited them into the limo.

They drove down Fifteenth Street, with the expanse of the President's Park and the famous Ellipse on the right. Then they turned onto tree-lined Constitution Avenue, and Peter said to Evangeline, "I defy anyone not to be impressed looking out these windows."

On the right, the White House glimmered in the distance. On the left, the Washington Monument loomed over them.

As they came up to the light on Seventeenth, four mounted horsemen, Capitol Police, clip-clopped past and rode out onto the Ellipse.

"I love the sound of them horseshoes," said the driver.

"Once, it was all you'd hear in a city," said Peter.

Evangeline asked, "What's that over there?"

"The Organization of American States." Peter was looking out the right side.

"No. *That*. What's that little thing?" Evangeline pointed out the left.

At the southwest corner, on the edge of the Mall, was a tiny one-story brick building.

The driver said, "That's the lock keeper's house, ma'am, the last remains of the Washington Canal and one of the oldest buildings in the District. Once, the canal cut up from the Anacostia and come right along here."

"The canal followed Constitution Avenue?" said Evangeline.

"Yes, ma'am. It's one of the most famous streets in America today, with fancy museums and all, but back then, just a trench full of dirty water."

"With stone sides," said Peter. He'd seen pictures.

"Sure is a nicer place today," said the driver. "But there's just as many scalawags."

"More," said Peter.

"Sir?"

"More scalawags. And a lot more government," said Peter.

The driver chuckled. "You keep talkin' like that, Mr. Bruce'll like you a lot."

"And what does Mr. Bruce do for a living?"

"Oh . . . I'm just a driver, sir. Sometimes I drive the limo, sometimes a black SUV, but I keep my job by bein' discreet."

"Discreet," said Peter. "I like that."

Then he put a hand on Evangeline's knee. When she was wearing stockings, he loved to touch the nylon. When she gave him a look, he whispered, "Discreet."

She removed his hand. "Dream on."

The limo sped past the Bureau of Indian Affairs and the Federal Reserve. Then it crossed the Theodore Roosevelt Bridge and soon was cruising down the hill into Rosslyn, a cluster of high-rises that defined prime D.C.-area real estate: skyscrapers with unobstructed views across the river to the low-rise capital city.

The limo pulled under the portico of a twenty-five-story building. To the north and south were similar buildings. To the east, there was nothing but the George Washington Parkway and the Potomac.

A big black man opened the door on Peter's side. He was wearing a dark suit and no ball cap, but it was Mr. Redskins, recovered from his afternoon impact.

"Long time, no see," said Peter.

The driver popped out, opened the door for Evangeline, and said across the roof of the limo, "You be polite to Mr. Fallon, Andre. Don't be yankin' him out of my car like you done with that cab."

"Sorry about your balls," whispered Peter.

Andre ignored them both and said into his headset, "Coming up."

The condo building had a large lobby, a concierge desk, circles of chairs, reading tables, glass doors leading to tennis courts, swimming pool, and patio.

Andre put them onto the elevator and pushed a button. On the twentieth floor, a man was waiting: Mr. Fit. He looked liked a Secret Service agent in a black suit, white shirt, black tie. He stood with his hands folded in front of him, an earpiece connected to a wire, and sunglasses, even though he was in a condominium hallway.

"Fancy meeting you here," said Peter.

Fit said nothing.

Peter introduced Evangeline, who offered her hand. "And you are?"

"People call me Jonathan Jones, when I invite them to."

Evangeline smiled. "Am I invited?"

"You're invited to see Mr. Bruce." The guy gave Peter a jerk of the head, and they followed him to the door of a corner apartment. With a courtesy knock, he opened the door, and gestured for them to step in.

Peter whispered to Jones, "I just wanted to slow you down, not dump you in a canal. I hope you've had your shots, tetanus, hepatitis, and so on."

Jones closed the door in Peter's face and stayed outside.

. . .

A large foyer, a long hallway to the left, a dining room directly ahead, a living room to the right, and roseate evening light pouring in from every direction because all the windows were floor-to-ceiling.

A woman in her early fifties came out of the galley kitchen and, it would seem, straight out of the 1950s. She reminded Peter of June Cleaver, with neat-clipped blond hair, a flowered dress, an apron over it and—yes—a petticoat under it.

She offered a hand. "I'm Jan Bruce. Welcome to our Washington abode. My husband will be right out. I told him that he just *had* to get ready if we were having guests, but he's such a USC football fan, and they played Syracuse this afternoon, so he was glued, no, he was *crazy*-glued to the TV until the final play. Came in off the tennis court—he just *loves* his tennis—that's why we bought this place—I'm sure you saw the courts above the Parkway—and after he played three sets he came up and hit the sofa and never left it till the final gun."

"Did SC win?" asked Peter.

"A last-second field goal. They beat Syracuse . . . *in* Syracuse." Jan Bruce made a delicate little fist pump. "Fight on for old SC."

"Good news," said Peter. "Wouldn't want Mr. Bruce in a bad mood. His security people are grouchy enough to begin with."

"Oh, don't mind them." Jan Bruce flounced ahead of them into the living room. "They're a bit zealous, but we need good security these days."

"Do we ever," said Evangeline.

Jan gave that remark a nervous little laugh. Then she took drink orders and gestured to the windows. "Feast your eyes. I'll be right back."

The living room offered one of the most magnificent panoramas Peter and Evangeline had ever seen. In a single sweep of the eye, they took in Georgetown, the Key Bridge, the Kennedy Center, the Watergate complex, the Capitol dome, the Washington Monument, the Lincoln and Jefferson memorials, the meandering Potomac, and the Pentagon, too.

"A city of bridges and monuments," said Evangeline.

"A city of power grabs and power brokers," said Peter.

"A city of grand dreams and greed." Their host came into the room in a golf shirt and slacks. "That's why Jan and I love the view. She likes the dreams. I'm a greed man myself." He laughed and offered his hand. "David Bruce."

He wasn't too tall or too heavy or too old or too young. He wasn't too much of anything. He was just . . . round . . . round face, round cheeks that crinkled when he grinned, round belly but nothing to get in his way on the tennis court. And there was an energy about him, like a bouncing ball, something . . . round. He shot a hand out to Peter, two quick shakes, then to Evangeline, two more . . . and he invited them to sit.

Straight off, he apologized to Peter for the scene on the bridge.

"I hired Andre and Jonathan out of an overseas security company of ours. Sometimes they still think they're in Iraq. Nothing more dangerous in Iraq than sitting in traffic, on a bridge, waiting for a car bomb to go off, when you're trying to pick someone up and bring him in for questioning."

"Is that what this is?" asked Evangeline. "An interrogation?"

"Not in the least." Mrs. Bruce brought in a tray with cocktail shrimp and some kind of hot puff pastry, two glasses of white wine, and two Scotch-on-the-rocks. "This is a just a friendly get-to-know-you."

David Bruce handed Peter and Evangeline glasses of wine. "I hope you like California chardonnay. It's Buehler. A better value than the French stuff."

"California's fine," said Peter.

Bruce leaned back. "Let me ask you, Mr. Fallon, are you political? Conservative? Liberal? What?"

"I belong to the common sense party."

"I'm not familiar with them."

"He made it up," said Evangeline.

"My liberal friends think I'm too conservative," said Peter. "And my conservative friends think I'm too liberal."

"Ha," said Evangeline.

"You sound just fine by me," said David Bruce. "I like a man who won't be pigeonholed. It means he listens to his own inner voice."

"I apply the rules of common sense," said Peter. "When some Democratic nanny-stater tries to tell me what kind of lightbulb to use or how much salt to put on my steak, I'm a conservative."

Bruce elbowed his wife. "He eats steak, honey. I like him already."

"But when some Republican tells me the only way to advance our national cause is to turn every man into his own entrepreneur, succeeding or failing on the basis of pure Social Darwinism, which means survival of the fittest, the smartest, or the kids of the most connected, then I'm a liberal."

"Not liberal enough," said Evangeline.

"More liberal than I am," said David Bruce. "I have many interests and a few strong beliefs. I believe we are crushed by taxes, paralyzed by regulations, oppressed by a federal government that seeks to control us at every turn. And it all began with Lincoln. He birthed the monster."

"Monster?" asked Evangeline.

"He was the first president to spend huge amounts on internal improvement like the transcontinental railroads. He printed paper money and deficit-financed a massive war. Before that, he put such heavy tariffs on the South that they decided to secede."

"He didn't do that," said Peter. "Northern politicians did, before he was president."

But Bruce kept to his talking points. "*And* Lincoln authorized our first income tax to pay for his war. I bet you won't put that in your travel shows, Miss Evangeline."

Peter had heard the tariff stuff before. The South had more ports than the North, so they paid a disproportionate amount in import and export duties, up to 80 percent of the national tariffs with only 20 percent of the population. Peter didn't doubt the statistic, but he questioned whether Americans would really have slaughtered 620,000 fellow Americans . . . over tariffs.

David Bruce bounced up and began moving about. "The South wanted to secede, and nowhere in the Constitution does it say that you can't. Lincoln knew that. So, when he realized that he was going to lose his war of federal dominance because he was fighting from a dishonest premise—"

"The Constitutionality of a *compulsory* Union," Mrs. Bruce interrupted.

"Thank you, dear," said Bruce, and he turned back to Peter and Evangeline. "When he realized he was going to lose, he decided to change the mission and free the slaves, even though slavery was headed for doom in a few decades anyway."

Evangeline said, "Did anyone tell the slaves that?"

Bruce ignored her. "The Emancipation Proclamation was an act of desperation. He didn't care about blacks or he would have freed them all in 1862."

Evangeline whistled softly. "I heard that there were people who believed this stuff. I never thought I'd meet one."

"You've lived a sheltered life," said David Bruce.

"She's from the Upper West Side," said Peter, "by way of Cambridge. She may not be sheltered but she's a bit . . . insulated."

"Thanks a lot," said Evangeline.

Bruce laughed. "I'm from Pasadena by way of Nebraska."

Peter said, "Pasadena or Manhattan, you know you're putting a lot on Lincoln without any evidence."

"Precisely why I buy every Lincoln document I can," said David Bruce. "If we know what he thought and why he acted, we may learn to hold him in less awe and perhaps hold his greatest accomplishment—the extension of federal power—up to a bit more scrutiny. Then we can chip away at it."

Evangeline looked at Peter, as if to say, *Aren't you going to argue with him?*

Peter just smiled. *Let the guy keep talking.*

Bruce went over to the window and this time, he stopped bouncing. The sun was setting. The white buildings reflected the glow. Purple night was rising in the east. "Consider the design of that city over there. First, they took a grid and laid it over the landscape. Elegant and beautiful in its simplicity. East-to-west streets lettered, north-to-south streets numbered. Something everyone could understand."

"Like a flat tax," said Mrs. Bruce.

"Then they complicated it by laying all sorts of diagonals and circles on the grid. What appears simple at first is actually quite complex . . . needlessly complex."

"Like most federal laws," added Mrs. Bruce.

Peter agreed. "It's the perfect metaphor for the opposing visions of national government, and how they have to work together."

"But it's hell to navigate," said Jan Bruce. "So we never come without a driver—"

"—or a lobbyist." David Bruce gestured again to the view. "All those monuments make you feel proud. But when you go back to the Willard, look at the buildings across Pennsylvania. They call it the Federal Triangle. But in the Civil War, they called it Murder Bay. It was crawling with prostitutes, gamblers, drunkards." He looked at Evangeline. "Which name do you think I prefer?"

"Wait, wait, don't tell me," she said with a flat deadpan.

"Just a lot of bureaucrats justifying their existence," Bruce continued. "They exist . . . to exist, and to murder individual freedom."

"So," said Peter, "why did you want to talk to me?"

"Because you know that history is not an abstraction."

Peter said. "That's the theme of my whole career."

"And the reason I wanted to talk to you, even before you were seen visiting Jefferson Sorrel."

"*Before?*" That caught Peter off guard.

"As soon as Sorrel put out the word that he had a Lincoln letter, our friends at the Suzanne Hamill Agency picked up on it, and our security people started investigating."

Evangeline said to Peter, "He's admitting that he was the guy who hacked us. So he probably sent that lobbyist onto Amtrak this morning, just to follow me."

"Actually, she was there on business," said Bruce. "So it worked out. And you weren't the only ones hacked. When Sorrel said he'd shown the letter to the Museum of Emancipation, we hacked all their trustees."

"Isn't that a crime?" asked Evangeline.

"Well, golly, I don't know. I should ask my lawyers."

Evangeline glanced at Peter. They both thought it: He actually said "golly" without a trace of irony.

Bruce sat again. "We've surrendered too much power to a government that bears no resemblance to what the framers imagined. And it all began with Lincoln."

Evangeline sipped her wine. "And you're not even from the South."

"This is not a North-South thing. The South understood that the threat of secession is an important tool in preserving freedom. So did plenty of Northerners called Copperheads. And Lincoln waged an un-constitutional war against all of them."

"And to prove that, you want to find the 'something' in the Lincoln letter?" asked Peter.

"It's why I *bought* the letter." David Bruce flipped open a folder on his coffee table and there it was in a Mylar sleeve: the "Executive Mansion" header, the familiar handwriting, and beside it, the envelope, addressed to Corporal Jeremiah Murphy.

David Bruce held it up. "What a mystery is here. A certain 'something,' a lieutenant in need of a presidential pardon, a president on the last day of his life."

Peter wiped his hands on a cocktail napkin, took the Mylar, and read the letter again. Then he handed it to Evangeline.

She said to him, "Now I know why you couldn't wait to come to Washington."

David Bruce sat on the edge of the coffee table so that he was face-to-face with Peter Fallon. "I've heard that this 'something' is a diary of some sort."

Peter nodded. "There's a scholar who's written about it. Not sure it's true."

"But if it is, imagine what it might contain. I think Lincoln knew all along that he didn't have a constitutional leg to stand on when it came to enforcing the federal will on a rebellious Confederacy. And as long as that was his goal, the North was going to lose. Did he talk about that in his diary? Did he talk about shifting gears, about turning it into a war to free the slaves? I'd love to know."

"You mean like George Bush," said Evangeline, "when he couldn't find weapons of mass destruction in Iraq, turning his fight into a war for Iraqi liberation?"

Bruce jerked a thumb at Evangeline and said to Peter, "She's tough."

Peter said, "You're thinking, if the father of federal power, the secular god of the republic, reveals his inner struggles with these issues, it would prove that he wasn't so paternal or godlike?"

Bruce nodded and whispered, like the disciple of a different god, "Then we could question Lincoln about everything that has flowed from his vision of an all-powerful federal government."

Evangeline processed all that, then whispered to Peter, "I think it's time to get back to the real world."

Bruce grinned at Evangeline. "Yes, she's tough, Mr. Fallon, maybe too tough."

And Jan Bruce's voice cut through the sudden tension. "You should know that my husband has people looking for this 'something,' looking hard."

"But we don't need to be rivals," added David Bruce. "I paid Sorrel a good price for the letter, right in line with the auction price for the 'Little People's Petition' letter. If this 'something' is what we think it is, I'll pay almost anything for it."

"And," said Jan Bruce, "we *have* almost anything."

"Yes, dear," said Bruce, "we've done well."

Jan Bruce said, "David took my father's mail-order business for seed-buying Nebraska farmers and turned it into one of the largest online retailers in America. LibertyTreeSales.com."

"That's where I heard the name," said Evangeline. "Fifty billion in annual revenues. Stock up steadily every year, four percent dividend."

Bruce jerked his thumb at Evangeline again. "Tough and astute."

"I bought a thousand shares," said Evangeline, "with my divorce settlement."

"Very, *very* astute. So she must know that I'm good at what I do," said David Bruce. "And I've been in retailing long enough to know that you get what you pay for. So, Mr. Fallon, I'd like to buy the right of first refusal on whatever you find." He took a check from the leather folder.

Peter looked at the check, then at Bruce, then back at the check.

Evangeline took a sip of wine and almost spit it out when Peter said, "Half a million dollars?"

"And if my people find it before you, you'll still get the money."

"What if Sorrel finds it?" asked Peter.

"He won't," said Jan Bruce with sudden coldness.

Peter looked at the check.

Evangeline looked at Peter. "Take the money and run?"

Peter said. "I'll have to report it as income."

"Ouch," said Bruce. "I hate to think how much the Feds will take out of this."

"David hates the tax man," said Jan Bruce. Then she stood, once again all June Cleaver calm. "And as we have theater tickets, we'd like to thank you for coming and look forward to seeing you again soon."

. . .

In the elevator, Evangeline said, "We just met the Warren Buffett of Internet sales and marketing."

"Good description." Peter was tapping the envelope on his fingertips. "He feels Midwestern. You might not agree with him, but you can take him at his word."

"His word that he'll use you? He just tried to buy you off."

"He can afford it." Peter slipped the check into his jacket pocket.

"But Peter, what if you find this diary and he uses it to—?"

"What? To shut down the federal government?" Peter laughed.

"He's looking for Lincoln's smoking gun," she said.

"Lincoln's smoking gun is on display at Ford's Theatre. It belonged to Booth."

"I mean a smoking gun to use in the spin wars."

They popped out in the lobby.

Peter gave Andre a little wave. Andre did not move a muscle.

Evangeline kept talking as they headed for the door. "This town is all about the spin wars, about how you make your own truth out of anybody's facts. A politician's finances, his family, his wife, his girlfriends—"

"—his *boy*friends."

"Or history itself," said Evangeline. "It's all up for grabs. And somehow, Mr. David Bruce sees this lost 'something' as a weapon, and he expects you to put it into his hands."

"He nearly owns the Internet now. What else does he want? World domination?"

"I think he'll settle for America, and—call it my incisive instinctive intelligence—but if my train ride with his lobbyist is any indication, he's aiming at Capitol Hill, and his first target is a certain congressman from Upstate New York."

"Then we'd better get on to the Smithsonian and talk to him."

They came out under the portico.

The shadows were long and deep now. It was still warm but the fading

September light warned that the season was changing, even here on the banks of the Potomac.

As they waited for the limo to roll up, Peter checked e-mails on his iPhone.

"It's from Antoine. 'I read Bates book: many mentions of Hutchinson. He's there for 'down to the raisins,' story, often escorts Lincoln back to the White House at night, passes McClellan's June 28 telegram up the chain of command, watches Lincoln contemplating spiderwebs as he writes the Emancipation Proclamation, and, get this—'"

Peter slowed down as he read the rest.

"'—was a boon office companion until he got into personal difficulties that brought the Provost Guard to arrest him at the War Department one rainy night in the summer of 1862. . . .'"

EIGHT

July 1862

Almost every day since returning from the Peninsula, Abraham Lincoln had spent time at Eckert's desk in the telegraph office. He said it was easier to concentrate there, away from the many distractions of the White House.

He wrote and scratched, thought and wrote, and gazed sometimes for ten minutes or more at that spiderweb outside the window.

It was as if he knew that he, too, had been caught in a web woven by Abolitionists, radical Republicans, Union Democrats, and antiwar Peace Democrats, to say nothing of the eleven seceded states, and he meant to break out of it with the words he was writing.

He sometimes appeared determined, sometimes depressed, occasionally cheerful, but usually as expressionless as the safe under Eckert's desk.

On the afternoon of July 11, he stalked angrily into the office and took the sheets away in a folder. That was the day, Eckert explained, that he had met with congressmen from the border states and urged them toward compensated emancipation, "not emancipation *at once*, but a decision at once to emancipate *gradually*."

From the president's demeanor, it appeared that compensated emancipation had not gone over. Lincoln would not be buying his way to Negro freedom, even in the four loyal slave states—Missouri, Kentucky, Maryland, and Delaware. He would have to spend human capital instead.

A few days later, he brought the sheets back and continued to work on them from time to time until the morning of July 21.

Overnight, a violent storm had blasted the city with nerve-shattering claps of thunder and lightning strikes as close as Lafayette Park. Behind it had come cool air on a breeze that was now blowing gently in the open windows of the office.

When Lincoln entered, Halsey was finishing his paperwork, and Major Eckert was starting his day. Eckert unlocked the drawer, removed the sheets, gave them a brief glance, and handed them to the president.

Lincoln offered that benevolent smile. "Curious, Major?"

"You said it was something special," answered Eckert, "so I suppose I am, sir."

Lincoln gestured for Halsey to step closer. "This document gives freedom to the slaves in the rebellious states, for the purpose of ending the war."

And there it was: the Emancipation Proclamation, just a few paragraphs, written and rewritten across several pages and several weeks, right under Halsey's nose.

"I intend to issue it as an executive order, using my war-making powers. We deprive the rebels of field hands and teamsters and all the other supports that four million unpaid laborers give them. We do what's right and what the Constitution allows."

At that moment, Halsey Hutchinson was not sure what he felt. He had seen the war. He had suffered in it. He wanted it to end. And yet, how much more blood would be spilled to make this proclamation a reality?

In committing to free the slaves, even if he was freeing them only in the states where he had no authority, he was changing the meaning of the war, or to use a metaphor better suited to the son of a Massachusetts textile manufacturer, he was not trying to mend a tear in the fabric. He was ripping it all the way through in order to make of it something entirely new.

Lincoln swore them both to secrecy "until this is made public." Then he left. He did not ask for an escort, as if he knew that he was now on his own.

. . .

When Halsey saw Mr. Shovel and Mr. Mule Harness that morning, they tipped their hats, as always, and he tipped his.

Mr. Shovel said, "Glorious mornin', sir."

If you only knew, thought Halsey, *how glorious it was for your race.*

He expected the Emancipation Proclamation to shake the world that day or the next. But no news issued forth from the Executive Mansion. So Halsey resolved to carry the president's secret for as long as necessary, even if McNealy, Pinkerton, and Benjamin Wood together held him down and tried to beat it out of him.

Besides, he had other things to occupy him . . .

. . . starting with his speculations on that daybook. It might not hurt the president, once emancipation had become the policy, but it still worried Halsey.

Had Squeaker managed to sell it?

A sale to Benjamin Wood or his Copperhead allies would by now have led to some public revelation regarding Lincoln's ruminations on a general emancipation.

A sale to Harriet Dunbar—if she really was a Confederate agent— might have led to angry cries from Richmond editorialists, exhortations to fight ever harder against the Yankee aggressor coming to change the Southern way of life.

And if Squeaker had not sold it, where was it?

Halsey still suspected McNealy.

. . .

All was not gloom and torment, however.

Samantha had filled the void left by Constance, and she seemed to be growing by the week.

She worked days and he worked nights. But Miss Dean had given her a day of rest on Tuesdays, so it had become their day together.

They had gone to Nixon's Cremorne Garden Circus to see acrobats and tumblers and horse tricks. They had visited Brady's studio to have their portraits made for cartes de visite, cardboard-backed images suitable as calling cards. Halsey had worn his uniform and held his kepi on his lap. Samantha had worn her hoopless gingham nursing dress and apron, so that her family could see how confident she appeared.

And on that Tuesday, Halsey took her to lunch at the Gosling on Pennsylvania Avenue, a restaurant that advertised daily in the Washington *Republican*: "The very best that the market affords of all that the appetite can crave either to eat or drink." It was, thought Halsey, truthful advertising in a city where lies abounded.

The girlish roundness was already gone from her cheeks. The happy chatter had given way to calmer tones and quieter talk. Scraping lint and cataloging medicines in Boston were no training for what she had seen at the Union Hotel Hospital. But as she said over a bowl of steaming she-crab soup, how much worse was it for suffering men?

She was, however, still girlish in some things. That afternoon, Halsey took her to the Smithsonian, to the West Range, to his favorite pillar. When he stopped to kiss her, she responded nervously and chastely, a quick embrace, a quick collision of lips, and even quicker disentanglement at the approach of footfalls in the gallery.

But it was enough for Halsey.

.   .   .

He returned to the hotel around five that afternoon.

Noah said, "I think you need a shine, sir." Then he winked.

So Halsey climbed into the chair.

Noah grabbed the brushes and went to work.

Halsey could almost see Noah's eyes roll across his head from left to right as a man crossed Sixth Street, passed the shoeshine stand, and went into the hotel.

"Can't be too careful," said Noah. "Even I don't know all the watchers."

"What do you have for me?"

"My boys done the job, once I told 'em they was doin' it for Mr. Lincoln."

Perhaps they were doing it for Lincoln. But Halsey was doing it for Halsey . . . who did not need a law degree to know that if a man held something over you, you should find something to hold over him. Perhaps McNealy had a taste for talkative whores . . . or for rigged card games . . . or for extorting money from frightened rebel sympathizers.

As Halsey paid, Noah slipped him a few sheets of paper.

In his room, Halsey propped his pillow against the headboard, stretched out, and was impressed by the quality of the notes. The Bone brothers had followed McNealy across Washington for two weeks and set down everything: where he went, what he did, whom he talked to.

Teaching Negroes to read, thought Halsey, might have its advantages.

He studied the names, the times, the addresses, and looked for patterns.

McNealy lived in Ryan's Boarding House near Third and East Capitol. Each day, he visited the Old Capitol Prison, no doubt to confer with Lafayette Baker. Then he went by the Pinkerton office on I Street. Playing both ends against the middle, thought Halsey . . . or both detective services.

And every morning, at eleven fifteen, he sat on the same bench in Lafayette Park and opened a newspaper. He read for ten minutes, then he left, unless another man sat at the other end and opened a newspaper. Then they talked from behind the papers.

The notebook also listed private addresses that McNealy visited. Two caught Halsey's attention: 1150 Sixteenth Street, at the corner of K, three blocks north of the White House, and 1912 Pennsylvania, west of the White House, near Washington Circle.

McNealy went past the Sixteenth Street address every day and often went inside.

He had visited 1912 Pennsylvania three times around ten o'clock at night. Each time, he had gone to the barn at the rear, to a meeting of a dozen men "and one strong-voiced woman." And there was a pattern: If McNealy met the man in Lafayette Park on a Monday morning, he would go to number 1912 on Tuesday night.

Whatever his game was, it grew only more puzzling.

Halsey had seen these addresses. But where? He could not cross-reference them until the middle of the night, when the telegraph office was deserted for a time.

Then he opened the bottom drawer of his desk and removed his papers and codebooks. Beneath was a false bottom he had fashioned from an old piece of furniture. After McNealy had rifled his room, he decided he needed a hiding place for items like Squeaker's ledger book, an envelope containing a hundred dollars in emergency cash, and spare ammunition for his pistol. Where safer than the telegraph office?

He took out Squeaker's ledger, flipped through it, and there it was: the address of the house on Sixteenth at K. Next to it was the name "Dunbar." *Harriet Dunbar.*

Joseph Albert McNealy was spending time with a Southern sympathizer.

As for 1912 Pennsylvania Avenue, there was no name written next to it, nothing but a little sketch that looked like a trunk and overhanging branches. A tree? A *tree*?

Harriet Dunbar . . . and a tree?

In the morning, he went home by way of K Street, so that he could get a look at Dunbar's house. It was one of eight joined façades on the northwest corner, white-painted brick, black shutters, four stories in one of the city's better neighborhoods. Here the aroma of brewing coffee and fresh bread almost covered the smell of horseflesh and turds, like a layer of cologne on an unwashed body.

What had McNealy been doing with Mrs. Dunbar? Were they conspiring? Were they lovers? What high-toned lady would have any interest in a slouchy snoop like Joseph Albert McNealy?

Halsey wanted to watch the house, but he knew that a young man in Brooks Brothers would begin to look suspicious if he loitered too long.

So he turned and noticed two black men coming in the opposite direction. One carried a pick, the other a six-pound sledge. He crossed I Street and glanced over his shoulder. Now they were following him. But the streets were busy, so they kept their distance. When he crossed New York Avenue at Thirteenth, they crossed. When he turned east on F Street, they turned, and again when he turned south on Seventh.

In the block after D Street, there was little foot traffic. The stores were not yet open. So Halsey stopped and looked into the window of Shephard and Riley's Bookstore. Displayed in a handsome pyramid were nine leather-bound volumes and a sign: JUST ARRIVED! *GREAT EXPECTATIONS*, BY CHARLES DICKENS. ENTIRE SERIAL IN A SINGLE VOLUME.

The two young black men came by.

The taller, whom he now recognized as Noah's son Daniel said, "Stay away from Miz Dunbar's house. They're watchin' it."

"Who?" asked Halsey.

"Don't know, but they're watchin'," he answered without breaking stride.

"Yeah," added the other, Noah's son Jacob, "and stay away from Lafayette Park, too. We'll go there. We'll tell you what we see."

Then Daniel said, "And that *Expectation* book ain't a patch on *Tale of Two Cities*."

. . .

Halsey decided to let the young black men do the watching while he stayed in his room and wrote a letter to his sister. Sitting down with pen and paper to converse with Karen, two years younger and already a mother, gave him a sense of normalcy, a feeling that somewhere, life was proceeding in an orderly way. He imagined her reading his words in her Beacon Street parlor, in the evening, after her husband, a young doctor, had returned from work at the Massachusetts General Hospital.

> *Thank you for your letter of the 21st instant. This week I do not have anything as exciting to tell as skinny-dipping with the president, only that the heat continues unbearable and the war grinds on. But the feeling is very strong that we are moving toward a new phase. Last week, Lincoln signed the Second Confiscation Act, which clarifies the Negro issue for military commanders. Slaves who reach Federal lines in battlefield states will be free. I also think he intends to move against slavery in some larger way, which may have some impact on Father's business. Miss Samantha has proven herself a fine nurse and, if I may say so, a fine companion when we can steal a bit of time. Don't read "between the lines" here, and don't go telling Father, though he would love to hear that I have taken a wife and given him an heir. First, we must rescue this Union and, as I am coming to believe, free the slaves, too. Love, H.*

He posted the letter and went to sleep. He must have been exhausted because he slept until three in the afternoon, despite the heat and the noise of the day.

When he awoke, two notes had been slipped under his door.

The first, from McNealy:

Meet at lock keeper's house, Washington Canal and 17th, 4 P.M.

The other came from Jacob Bone:

McNealy met man with newspaper today. This means that tomorrow, he will go to meeting at 1912 Penn.

On his way out, Halsey said to Noah, "Tell your son, I want to get close to the meeting tomorrow. See if he can find a way. He'll know what I mean."

Noah nodded and touched the side of his nose.

.   .   .

The President's Park was a green expanse south of the White House, bounded on the east by Fifteenth Street, the west by Seventeenth, and on the south by the Washington Canal. The white canvas tents of an army encampment occupied the higher areas. An elliptical horse track circled below it.

Officers were exercising their mounts in the late afternoon light. Drums were thrumming. Troops were marching. No one paid attention to the man in the brown suit who stood at the low canal wall and tossed stones into the filthy water.

Nearby, the lock keeper, an old man in a straw hat, sat in front of his little stone house and swatted flies. There wasn't much for him to do, not since the canal and its traffic had slowed to a trickle.

Without turning, McNealy said to Halsey, "What's your game?"

"What's yours?"

"I told you, I ask the questions. You answer. You follow?"

Halsey did not respond.

So McNealy turned and repeated it: "You *follow?*"

Halsey nodded.

"All right, then. Why were you outside Harriet Dunbar's house this morning?"

"Was I there?"

"We're watching the house. We saw you. Why were you there?"

Halsey tried a half truth. "The morning after the president lost his daybook, I saw Squeaker pass something to Mrs. Dunbar in the Willard. I thought—"

"You thought you'd do my job? Three months later?" McNealy studied Halsey and said, "You're worried, aren't you?"

"Worried?"

"Don't try to fool me. I get up at four o'clock every morning, no matter when I go to bed. If you can't get up earlier than that—"

"I'm not fooling you."

"You've heard something, so you're worried. Emancipation is coming and you're worried about what's in that daybook you stole."

"I didn't steal it."

"But you lost it. Now you're worried what's in it could queer Lincoln's plans."

Halsey looked across the canal, toward the cattle grazing around the half-finished Washington Monument. "All I know about his plans is that he signed the Second Confiscation Act when Congress sent it to him."

"A Republican president and his Congress—" McNealy gave a spit. "—there's a pair that's hard to fight."

"I thought our job was to fight the enemy."

"The enemy is everywhere." McNealy gestured toward the President's Park—the horse track, the tents, the cavalry corral over by Fifteenth. "Everywhere. And I think there's more emancipation news. But if you don't, we're done."

"For good?"

"For now." McNealy snapped the cigar butt into the canal. "You can't be shed of me that easy."

Halsey said, "If I can't tell you anything new about emancipation, and we know what the president thinks of McClellan, and I have nothing worthwhile on Congressman Wood, because his niece is my source and she's in New York—"

"She's back."

"Back?"

"Surprised?" McNealy pulled out a telegram. "From our people in New York. Back four days ago, along with the uncle called Fernando. Start diddlin' her again. Get her to talk about what she sees and hears. That shouldn't be too hard . . . or . . . maybe something might *get* hard. The rest will be easy."

"You're a crude bastard, McNealy."

"No," said McNealy. "Just a bastard. And from what I saw in the Smithsonian, she liked it. So did you."

Halsey didn't say it, but he thought it: *You son of a bitch, you watched us.* He resolved that soon, he would have something to use against McNealy.

. . .

But McNealy was right. Constance had come back to Washington.

She was waiting for Halsey in his room.

At first, he did not even notice her. Instead, he saw his uniform on a hanger in the corner. It looked as if it had been sponged and pressed. The gilt thread on the shoulder straps glittered in the backlight from the window.

Then he heard her voice. "That's for later."

"Constance?"

She lay propped against a pillow, with the sheet drawn up to her neck.

He stood there, trying to decide if he was pleasantly surprised or simply shocked.

He had tried not to think about her since she left. But he had missed her. She had more passion than Samantha, and she had given him more gifts . . . the softness of her breasts when he slid his hand under her chemise, the softness of her sighs when he slid his fingers down the front of her skirt . . .

She said, "I had the hotel clean your uniform. We're dining with my uncles at the Willard. They want to talk to you."

He closed and locked the door.

She said, "I guess I missed the Washington heat . . . and you."

For Halsey, "shocked" was fading, "pleasantly surprised" rising.

"I told my uncles I would have to bribe you to be in their presence." Then she threw back the sheet. "I did not tell them with what."

"Pleasantly surprised" now grew into "thrilled beyond measure."

Constance was wearing only her underclothes—silk chemise, drawers with lace trim around the waist and the thighs, light blue stockings held up by dark blue garters.

She reached out. "It's wartime, Halsey. Things are different. And I've thought of this every day we've been apart."

He let her draw him to the edge of the bed. He sat and looked her up and down, as if she were a work of art. Where would he start?

As if she could read his mind, she whispered, "You can start by taking off some of those clothes."

So he did. He took off his jacket and tie. Then he leaned forward and kissed her more gently than he ever had in the Smithsonian.

And with his lips on hers, he touched one of her breasts. She sighed. So he slid his hand under the fabric; then he pushed up the loose silk and brought his mouth down to one of the sweet, salty nipples. She sighed again and arched her back.

Halsey had always believed in the order of things. Until the day that he slipped the president's diary into his pocket, he had done everything as it should be done, step by step, systematically, predictably, even in battle. But there was no order to this.

The touches, the kisses, the sighs and strokes and sensations, all embraced and mingled and withdrew suddenly, only to mingle again.

He slid her stockings down and thrilled to the feel of cool flesh as the fabric peeled away. She pulled his shirt up over his head. He ran his hands along her calves and milk white thighs. She caressed his chest and shoulders. He hesitated a moment, and then, through the silk of her drawers, he touched her and felt how ready she was.

He had never traveled this far with any women—unless he paid—and even then he had been reluctant.

But when she raised her legs and slipped those silk drawers down and off, all reluctance and all thought were gone, all surrendered to sensation.

Everything happened quickly after that.

When they were done, she said, "Now, let's go see what my uncles want."

As he put on his uniform, he thought only briefly of Samantha, and only to remind himself that in wartime, a young man had to take his pleasures where he could.

. . .

When they came down to the lobby, Halsey sensed a quiet excitement in the air. The setting sun reddened the scene beyond the tall windows. Noah's son, Daniel, was going about lighting gas lamps. Jacob was polishing the brass andirons in the fireplace. A bottle of brandy and a snifter had been set out on the low table in the corner, beside a certain chair. John Wilkes Booth was due back in town, and all would soon be in readiness for the famous guest.

Halsey was glad that Booth was not sitting in the corner already, offering fresh remarks from behind his newspaper.

Harvey, the desk clerk, looked up from his ledger and smiled. "Good evening, Lieutenant . . . and Miss Hutchinson."

Constance had probably presented herself again as his *sister* . . . Miss Hutchinson.

A moment later, Halsey wished that Booth had been there, or his *real* sister, because sitting by the empty fireplace, in a cool blue dress and hat, hands fidgeting with a yellow telegram, was Samantha Simpson of Wellesley, Massachusetts.

She stood and said his name.

Constance looked at the young woman in the corner, then at Halsey.

Samantha looked at the young woman on Halsey's arm, then at Halsey.

And Halsey felt as if he had been shot. . . .

A young man who has spent an hour absorbed in the wonders of a woman, especially for the first time, often feels a physical exhilaration that infuses his whole being. It starts in his loins, a sensation not unlike the tingling in the gums after a glass of good brandy. It radiates warmly upward into the rest of his being, like brandy, giving him a sense of satisfaction, of pleasure, of continuing desire . . . all at once.

But a young man who has betrayed a young woman for whom he has deep feelings may experience an equal and opposite sensation when he looks into her eyes. His insides wither. His stomach turns to acid.

For Halsey both sensations met, absolute joy and the desire to crawl into a hole. Worse, he thought, than being shot.

Three sets of eyes shifted, four if Halsey included the amused desk clerk.

Outside, another regiment was marching past to the simple *rat-tat, rat-tat, rat-tat-tat-tat* of a drum.

And Halsey wondered who would blink first. Who would speak first?

Constance. She said, "Is this your *other* sister?"

"*Other* sister?" Samantha looked Constance over from her expensive shoes to her fine peltote jacket and said, "If I had a sister, she would not be visiting a man in his hotel in the afternoon."

"It's evening," said Constance. "And it's wartime, Miss—"

"—Simpson, and I know well what wartime is, Miss," and then she added, "or is it Mrs.?"

Halsey wanted to apologize to Samantha, but how could he in front of Constance, after what they had just done?

The drums suddenly sounded louder. The front door was swinging open.

And John Wilkes Booth was dropping his bags in the middle of the lobby, making a fine thespian entrance for himself. "The wandering bard has returned."

"Welcome back, Mr. Booth." Harvey rang the bell for a boy.

In an instant, a young Negro in a red jacket, whom Halsey recognized as Noah's third son, Ezekiel, appeared.

Then Booth's eye fell on the little trio by the fireplace. "And what have we here?"

Halsey had never been so happy to see anyone.

Booth sauntered over, doffed his hat, and bowed. "The beautiful *sister* of my favorite Massachusetts Democrat, and"—Booth's eyes turned to Samantha—"a young lady whose kindness to me in Boston keeps me forever in her debt."

"Then perhaps," said Samantha, "you would repay me by seeing me to the train."

"The train?" said Halsey. "You're leaving?"

"My father has been taken ill." She held up the telegram. "He may not survive."

Halsey reached out and touched her hand and now he said it: "I'm so sorry."

She pulled her hand back. "I'm sure that your *sister* will ease your pain."

Samantha offered her arm to Booth, who took it, tipped his hat to the others, and led her to the door, saying, "We will take a barouche. A lovely lady should not have to walk up the hill to the depot. . . . Harvey, see to my bags."

Constance watched them leave. Then she said to Halsey. "Just one question. Is she a Republican or a Democrat?" Then she slipped her arm into Halsey's, and he let her lead him out onto the Avenue. What else could he do?

. . .

As Congress was now in recess, the Willard dining room was only half-full. So the talk and the harp-strumming echoed harshly off the high ceilings.

Halsey had regained his composure on the walk.

And Constance had said the right thing: "I expected that there would be other women drawn to you. It's why I came back. I intend to fight for your affections, Lieutenant Halsey Hutchinson. So prepare for battle."

And he had to admit that she used weapons he could not resist. So he offered his arm and they walked together across the dining room.

Benjamin Wood sat alone, staring out at the twilight.

His skin had tightened across his forehead. His black beard appeared blacker, his complexion whiter, his face even more like a skull waiting for crossbones. A Congressional hearing could wear on a man, even if the committee had dissolved with no finding. Wood was not a traitor. He would not be thrown in the Old Cap. But he would be watched.

As the young people sat, Wood greeted Halsey with this: "You, sir, are not an honorable man."

"Not honorable?" said Constance.

"Before you say that again," answered Halsey, "remember that I'm armed."

Wood said, "You could have warned me, and you didn't. The Confiscation Act . . . compensated emancipation to the border states . . . these are things I should know about."

"As a Congressman," said Halsey, "you should know about them before I do."

"Our agreement was that you'd tell me what you know and hear, not pass judgment on it. If you had, I might know about the latest rumor."

"What rumor?" asked Constance.

"That two days ago, Lincoln told his cabinet he wants to emancipate the slaves in the rebellious states, and only there . . . as a military measure."

So, thought Halsey, Lincoln had presented his proclamation to the cabinet, at least. He said, "I can't tell you what I don't know."

"Fortunately"—the skeleton smiled—"you are not my only source. A secretary in Postmaster Blair's office overheard him discussing it. They've decided to win a battle before they announce it. Otherwise, it appears as an act of desperation. But when it happens—if it happens—it will appear as what it is, an act of outright political cynicism."

"It's an act of nobility," said Constance suddenly.

Benjamin looked at his niece. "What?"

Another secret out, thought Halsey.

"You heard me," said Constance, "an act of nobility."

Just then, another man approached the table.

This, Halsey surmised, was Uncle Fernando. He was almost as tall as his brother but appeared far less severe. He wore clothes that were well cut with nary a bit of black, a wardrobe designed to make men like him on sight rather than put them in mind of an undertaker: brown claw-hammer coat, burgundy satin waistcoat, yellow cravat. Fernando was a dandy. And despite the pockmarks that spread from chin to cheekbone, he went clean-shaven, so that his face appeared open and honest. It was all for show.

In January of '61, Mayor Fernando Wood had proposed that New York secede from the Union and declare itself a "free" city. This would have guaranteed that trade with the South continued, which would have guaranteed that Mayor Wood continued to control the patronage power of a bustling port. Fortunately for the nation and the reputation of New York, thought Halsey, the City Council rejected the proposal, and the voters turned Wood from office in the next election.

Fernando said, "So this is the young man who has captivated our Constance."

"Our Constance is an Abolitionist." Benjamin almost spat the words.

Fernando sat and looked at her. "Then it's true that you went to New York to see that highfalutin' coon, Frederick Douglass?"

She sat back, surprised. "Who told you that?"

"I may be out of office, but I have my spies." Fernando turned to Halsey. "Is this your doing? Turning this girl into an Abolitionist?"

"No," answered Halsey. "But s*he* may turn *me* into one."

Constance gave Halsey a raised eyebrow, a look of surprise, a little smile.

"Has that been her pillow talk?" Fernando asked Halsey. "Read Frederick Douglass, dear Lieutenant, and hear the whip whistle? Then I will kiss you again?"

"How dare you, Uncle?" said Constance.

Benjamin said, "Did you think, Lieutenant, that you could have this girl for nothing?"

"Have me?" said Constance angrily. "*Have* me?"

Benjamin ignored her. "Tell us everything you hear about this emancipation business, Lieutenant. Let us make the judgment on what's important."

"Meanwhile, we'll count on our armies to keep losing," said Fernando. "But even if McClellan finds a way to win a battle, the proclamation works to our benefit."

Halsey was now confused, but politics could be confusing. "Benefit? How?"

"By giving us a club to beat the Republicans in the next election," said Fernando.

"There are plenty of people in the North," added Benjamin, "who will rebel if Lincoln turns this into a war of nigger insurrection."

"And they will elect me to Congress," said Fernando, "so that I can help my brother stop Lincoln from ruining the country."

Benjamin kept his eyes on Halsey. "If we take the House, we can force a negotiated peace and bring the South back into the Union on the old standing. Help us, and we'll let you see Constance again."

"Again?" she said. "Again?" She stood.

"Where do you think you're going?" said Benjamin.

"It's not where I'm going, Uncles. It's where you've *been,* and who you've seen, and why." She looked at Halsey. "Ask them where. Ask them who. Hear them lie."

Halsey noticed the Woods exchange glances.

"In the meanwhile," she said, "I will take a bit of air." She stepped away from the table and stalked toward the door.

Heads turned to watch her. Heads always turned to watch her.

Halsey pushed back from the table and rose.

Benjamin Wood said, "Stay, Lieutenant. Order your supper. I'm buying."

Fernando stood and took Halsey's hand. There was rock-strength in the grip of this New York ward boss. "We'll be forever in your debt if you help us take the House."

"Excuse, me," said Halsey, "but the young lady needs an escort."

"Whether she has an escort," said Fernando, "is less important than whether we have an understanding."

"Understanding?" said Halsey. "Understanding where you've been, perhaps?"

"I've been to the hearings to support my brother. And I've been to Harrison's Landing to see for myself the condition of our armies."

Benjamin rose and put a hand on Halsey's arm. "Remember, we are the true Sons of Liberty. I live in hope that we can restore this Union, but I am not so unnatural a worshipper of it that I'll build it upon the dead bodies of my countrymen."

Fernando winked at Halsey. "He's quoting himself now . . . his last speech before Congress. He speaks like that for the eavesdroppers."

As if he liked that idea, Benjamin stepped back, looked around, and proclaimed, "Whatever this president may be planning about emancipation, I will resist it. When the Executive hand, for the first time in our history, was interposed between the citizen and his rights, the germ was planted of a danger far mightier than rebellion. Now he's calling for three hundred thousand more troops, he's drafting out of the state militias, and Stanton threatens to arrest any who question this recruitment plan."

"As the Wood brothers do so question," said Fernando.

Benjamin continued to fulminate. "Tyrannical encroachment by an executive is rebellion against the only sovereignty I acknowledge—that of the people. I will not let this executive step on the necks of free men to mount his throne."

A few in the dining room applauded. A few more hissed. The rest kept eating.

There was, thought Halsey, no man less inclined toward mounting a throne than Lincoln . . . and no greater windbag than this cadaverous congressman, unless it was his fast-talking brother. He broke away and went after Constance.

. . .

He did not see her in the rambling lobby.

He thought about going upstairs to knock on her door, but . . . *air.* She had said she needed air. So he went out onto Pennsylvania Avenue.

Streetlamps were glowing. Carriages were clattering by. People were hurrying east toward the Capitol and west toward the White House, or they were crossing to the "bad" side of the street, where business boomed when the sun went down.

And there she was, heading toward the pillared bulk of the Treasury Building. He called her name and caught up to her as she crossed Fifteenth.

"They're as bad as rebels, Halsey. I had to get away from them."

"You can't get away from them. Men like that are everywhere."

They walked south, so the President's Park came into view on their right. The canvas tents shimmered in the gloaming. The overhanging branches gave pattern to the glow of the streetlamps.

She said, "Did you ask them where they went?"

"Harrison's Landing."

"That's all they said? That's all you know?" She started walking more quickly.

He grabbed her and turned her. "I have to get to work. And I can't let you walk farther alone. That way's not safe."

She tried to pull away. "I can see my way back myself."

He held her arm and said, "Tell me what else I should know."

"Halsey, let me go."

That caused two men across the street to call out, "Hey! Hey, mister!" One had an eye patch; the other wore a Union kepi, a red tie, a blue suit, a neat Vandyke.

Halsey released her and reached for his pistol, because little good ever happened south of Pennsylvania, even when two men appeared ready to help a lady in distress.

The one in the kepi asked Constance, "Is this Halsey feller botherin' you, miss?"

"No, gentlemen. But thank you."

"Well, you be good, Mr. Halsey," said the one with the eye patch. Then they retreated into the shadows.

"Everybody's a hero," Halsey muttered. Then he turned back to Constance. "Now . . . what more should I know?"

"It's what the president should know." She paused, as if for dramatic effect.

Halsey realized that the whole night, from her appearance in his bed to that dinner with the two-headed Wood snake to this scene beneath the streetlamp had *all* been for effect.

She said, "My uncles went to Harrison's Landing to see McClellan."

"A congressman and a candidate, going to see a general . . . it seems reasonable."

"Unless you know why."

"Why?"

"They went to ask McClellan to run for president against Lincoln in two years."

"Ask him directly? How do you know?"

She raised her chin and set her jaw, as if to say that she had returned to the fight, and she expected Halsey to join her. "They thought I was coming back to Washington simply because I missed you. But I came to spy on them . . . and I missed you."

A barouche went past with a colonel and two giddy women sharing a champagne bottle. Three soldiers sauntered by. Piano playing and laughter came from a saloon across the street. "Oh! Susanna" was the tune. Men leaned against trees, lurking, lounging. Halsey noticed all these things. But his mind had turned to McClellan. A general is supposed to carry the fight to the enemy, not entertain the politicians who want to carry the fight to the president.

So *that* was his game.

Constance said, "You see the president every night. You must tell him. You must tell him what McClellan told my uncles."

"What was that?"

She pulled from her purse a sheet of paper. "I slipped Uncle Benjamin's notes from his briefcase and copied them." She held the sheet up under the streetlamp and read, "'McClellan wonders what would happen if he took his rather large military family up to Washington to bring some order.'" She looked at Halsey.

"That's military insurrection," he said.

She read more. "'. . . calls emancipation an abomination . . . sees God's wise purpose in his loss on the Peninsula, says if he had taken Richmond, the fanatics of the North might have gained the political upper hand, making reunion impossible . . . knows that turning this into a war of slave insurrection will mean total war, rather than limited war he has tried to fight.'"

Halsey Hutchinson was shocked. All he could say was, "Good God."

"He promises a response soon." She folded the notes and put them into the pocket of her peltote. "That is what the president needs to know. My uncles have to be stopped. The Copperheads have to be stopped, or Lincoln will lose Congress in November and the White House in two years . . . if he hasn't lost the war by then."

. . .

Constance was right.

But would Lincoln accept information that Halsey claimed a young woman had copied from notes she had taken from the briefcase of a congressman who had heard the conversation and then written it down? That, the lawyer-president might suggest, was hearsay of the highest order.

But Halsey had something else that might indict McClellan.

Around ten o'clock, he opened the drawer in his desk, pried up the false bottom, and took out the original of McClellan's June 28 telegram. He put it into his pocket and waited for the familiar footfalls, but the president never appeared that night.

At 6 A.M., however, Secretary Stanton looked into the cipher room and scowled. He always scowled, but lately he had reason, as his son had died of the failed inoculation. He scowled at Homer Bates, who was deciphering a telegram. Then he scowled at Halsey and pulled a sheaf of papers from under his arm. "An errand, Lieutenant. Deliver these to the president so that he can peruse them before our morning meeting."

It was the perfect assignment.

Soon, Halsey was riding a borrowed horse north of the city. He had forgotten how peaceful these green fields and woodlots could appear. Even the new Harewood Military Hospital, a dozen whitewashed barracks rising from a confiscated farm, had the quaint look of a country retreat.

After about three miles, he turned up a graveled drive lined with fir trees. It led to a plateau atop which sat the Old Soldiers' Home, a great stone castle where war veterans could live out their days in dignity amidst trees and gardens. And when they passed, they could go into the ground in the peaceful cemetery across the road, though both the home and the cemetery appeared to be at full capacity.

Flanking the castle were two stucco cottages. The larger, perched on the ridge best situated to catch the cooling breeze, was the president's summer retreat, his escape from the bugs and miasmic heat near the river.

Lincoln's valet, a light-skinned Negro named William Slade, answered the door. "The president is having breakfast with his family, sir."

"I have important papers," said Halsey. "I've been ordered to deliver them to his hand." That was a lie, but Halsey had to see the president.

So Slade ushered him through the house to a porch where Lincoln was sitting in the sunlight with his son Tad.

As Halsey stepped out, he caught sight of a tiny woman in a long white robe disappearing through another door. He said, "I'm sorry to interrupt, sir."

"Mrs. Lincoln's sensitive about young men seeing her in her nightclothes," answered Lincoln. Then he told Tad, "Say hello to the lieutenant."

The boy looked up at Halsey with eyes that seemed sad but filled with hopeful curiosity, the eyes of a lonely boy who had lost his brother and playmate and seemed to be wondering if this newcomer might bring some fun. He said hello.

Halsey smiled. "Hello, Tad. You have quite a spot to enjoy breakfast."

The view was to the south, across the rolling farmland, toward two distant shapes: the unfinished Capitol dome and the unfinished Washington obelisk.

Tad's response, lisped through a cleft palate: "What's wrong with your voice?"

The president said, "Now, Tad, you know not to ask questions like that."

"I was in a battle," said Halsey. And as if to offer a bit of brotherhood to a boy with his own deformity, he pulled back his collar and showed Tad his scar. "I was shot."

"Oh," said the boy. "Did it hurt?"

"For a long time," said Halsey. "But not now."

Lincoln said, "What can I do for you, Lieutenant?"

Halsey put the papers on the table. "Secretary Stanton wanted you to see these."

Tad grabbed a piece of toast and went running off.

Lincoln glanced at the papers. "These could have waited."

Halsey heard a door slamming and from the house, a woman grumbling about "business at all hours . . . not a moment's peace," and a male voice placating her.

Lincoln glanced toward the sound, then back. "You'll forgive me for not inviting you to breakfast, Lieutenant, but—"

Halsey said, "Sir, I think it's my duty to tell you that I dined last night with the Wood brothers of New York, the Copperheads."

Lincoln took a sip of coffee and smiled. "I forgive you."

"Thank you, sir, but—"

"Strange name, Fernando. I hear that his mother gave it to him because she liked a character with that name in a novel. I wonder if the fictional Fernando is a conniver, too."

"Hard to say, sir. But . . . do you know where he's just been?"

"Harrison's Landing," said Lincoln.

Halsey was not surprised. The War Department detective service knew which connivers to watch. He said, "Do you know *why* they went?"

"I imagine they went to congratulate McClellan on his conduct of the war." Lincoln picked up his spoon and dipped it into the soft-boiled egg on its little stand.

Halsey watched the long fingers work around the shell. "'Congratulate,' sir?"

"McClellan says that with more men, he can take Richmond. But if I give him a hundred thousand, he'll send a telegram of thanks, then tell me that Pinkerton determines the enemy has been reinforced by a hundred and *one* thousand, and therefore, he cannot attack. This is the kind of war-making that Peace Democrats congratulate." The eggshell cracked beneath Lincoln's fingers.

"I think, sir, that these two Peace Democrats went to do more than congratulate him," said Halsey. "I think they went to persuade him."

"To do what?"

"To run against you in the next election."

Lincoln sat back, looked out toward the city, and said, "Well . . . if McClellan wants the job that badly, he can have it."

"I thought you should know, sir."

"I can't say I'm surprised." Lincoln went back to the egg.

"And I thought you should know that in fighting as he does, sir—"

"Or doesn't," said Lincoln.

"—General McClellan may not be working in your best interests."

"His hopes for a limited war will be dashed when we announce emancipation." Lincoln took his napkin and wiped the egg from the corners of his mouth.

"If you're waiting for a victory before you announce it, sir, you should know that McClellan sees a Godly purpose in defeat."

"In defeat?"

"In his defeat before Richmond. He thinks his loss on the Peninsula means the Lord doesn't want the Radicals and Abolitionists to gain the political upper hand and drive through to emancipation."

If a man's face could suddenly go gray, as brown leather goes gray when splashed with water, it was Lincoln's. His voice went gray, too. "Where did you hear this?"

"From Wood's niece. She made notes from the notes that her uncle made of conversations with McClellan." As he said it, Halsey knew how convoluted it sounded.

Lincoln said, "I'll need something more concrete than that before—"

Halsey was already putting the June 28 telegram on the table.

Lincoln looked at the yellow sheet, picked it up, and read it all, even the words at the end that accused him and Secretary Stanton of treason.

Out on the lawn, little Tad had begun an imaginary battle with a Confederate regiment. He was wielding a carved wooden musket and making the sounds of gunfire.

Lincoln asked Halsey, "Where did this come from?"

Halsey told the story of deleting the last lines the night the message came in.

Lincoln said, "I'm most appreciative, Lieutenant, but in the future, I need every bit of information. However—" And as usual when he chided someone, Lincoln softened. "—it's the role of a man's friends to protect him now and then."

"McClellan's not my friend, sir."

"No, but I am. You were protecting me from bad news . . . or from my own anger at words that this general shouldn't have said."

"Yes, sir."

"Men sometimes say things in writing that they shouldn't . . . sometimes in a telegram to their superiors, sometimes in a daybook to themselves."

And there it was again. That daybook was still on Lincoln's mind, even after he had come to his conclusions about emancipation. What else was in it? What else kept him thinking about it?

But the conversation was over. A young man was appearing in shirtsleeves on the back porch: Lincoln's son Robert, on his summer break from Harvard. His below-average height and round face, thought Halsey, favored his mother's side of the family. His friendly but phlegmatic personality favored his father's.

As they exchanged pleasantries, a tiny woman in a prim black dress now joined them. She seemed to have calmed her anger. She smiled and said to her husband, "Father, have you not even invited this young man for a cup of coffee?"

"I was just leaving, ma'am," said Halsey.

Lincoln picked up the yellow telegram and put it into his pocket.

. . .

"You've been to see the president?" McNealy was leaning against a tree at the corner of Fifteenth and Pennsylvania, in front of the State Department.

Halsey had left the horse at the War Department stable and was walking home. "I went on an errand for Stanton, if it's any business of yours."

"It's *all* my business. What else?"

Halsey decided to test him with another jolt of truth. "I went to warn the president."

"Warn him?" McNealy fell in beside Halsey. "Of what?"

"The Wood brothers asked McClellan directly to run for president."

"Who told you that?"

"Why do you care?"

"You keep forgetting," said McNealy, "I ask. You answer. You follow?"

"No. *You* follow." Halsey picked up his pace and legged around the corner onto Pennsylvania, forcing McNealy to quick-step behind him.

"Don't be smart with me. Who told you that the Woods went to see McClellan?"

"It doesn't matter," answered Halsey. "The president already knew."

McNealy said, "It was the girl, wasn't it?"

Halsey kept walking, past the Willard and across Fourteenth.

"You told me three weeks ago, Lieutenant. And your silence tells me now. It was the girl. Did she tell you while she was pullin' your prick?"

"Whoever told me," said Halsey, "it has nothing to do with my prick. It's treason. Tell Lafayette Baker to arrest the Woods."

"We don't arrest congressmen. It makes the president look bad."

"Then tell Pinkerton to arrest McClellan."

"Maybe I'll tell one of them to arrest you."

"You can't arrest me." Halsey stopped at the corner of Thirteenth. "I'm your eyes in the War Department. You said it. You need me. Now, I have a telegram to send. Then I'm going to bed. It's been a long night."

He left McNealy standing there and hurried on to the National. He never looked over his shoulder to see if McNealy was following. He went into the hotel telegraph office and wrote out the message for his sister, Mrs. Karen Hemmick of Boston.

PLEASE GO TO WELLESLEY AND VISIT REVEREND SIMP-
SON. HE IS GRAVELY ILL. BRING MY BEST WISHES TO HIM
AND EXPRESSLY TO SAMANTHA.

When Halsey came out, McNealy was sitting in the shoeshine chair.

Noah was buffing his boots and sweating like a field hand. He said to Halsey, "Shine, sir? I really think you need a shine."

McNealy puffed up his cigar and said, "Forget him. You just finish my boots, boy. And tell me again what your sons do here at the hotel."

. . .

Halsey did not sleep well.

And when he awoke, there was a note under the door, in Constance's handwriting:

> Do not visit today. My uncles remain angry with me. I shall calm them. Meet me in the ladies' parlor tomorrow at noon.

Outside, Noah Bone did not offer his usual greeting. He just gestured to the chair, and Halsey sat. The rays of the sun, long and low, were slanting now from the west.

Noah began to brush. "That McNealy feller done his damnedest to scare me."

"And did he?"

"Scared the piss right out of me, sir. And give me a colic in the belly, too, sayin' he could throw anyone in the Old Cap, includin' me and my boys if we knew somethin' bad was happenin' and didn't tell."

"He can't do that." Halsey lied to offer a bit of assurance.

Noah looked up. "I'm a hardworkin', God fearin' man. I have a good wife. We have good boys. We live right by the Baptist church. We go every Sunday and sing and pray and praise the Lord. And I want to keep doin' it. So you got to tell me . . . are we really helpin' Mr. Lincoln, like you say?"

"I can tell you with certainty that Lincoln's helping your race. And I'm helping Lincoln. So . . ." Somehow, Halsey thought that if he phrased it with the logic of a syllogism, it would all sound more believable.

Noah looked down again and began to brush.

Halsey watched the black hands working. He could feel the tension radiating like the sweat from Noah's whip-scarred shoulders. He was sorry that he had dragged Noah and his sons into this. But they had all been dragged into it, a whole nation had been dragged into it, from Lincoln to this Negro who shined shoes and watched his place in the world. And there was no telling where it would end.

Finally, Noah looked up. "My son says for you to see the maid at 1910 Pennsylvania, named Miz Stetson. Go there tonight. He wrote some stuff down to tell you. And he needs one of them cartes, if you got one, so's she can know what you look like."

Halsey climbed down, pulled a carte from his breast pocket, and gave it to Noah, who gripped his hand with fingers that felt like steel cables. "You better be doin' right by my boys . . . and Mr. Lincoln."

Halsey did not know if he was doing right by anyone anymore.

.   .   .

But he had to see Constance again, no matter her note, so he stopped at the Willard before walking on to the War Department.

He did not see her or her uncles in the dining room, but he could feel eyes turning toward him, as always. And he sensed that the new hotel detective, hired after the murder of John Charles Robey, was watching.

So he crossed the lobby as if he owned it. His father had always said that was the way to go into any room. Those who bid you well would respect you, those who did not would grow wary, and those who suspected you would drop their suspicions.

As he climbed the stairs, a man passed on the way down. He wore a Union kepi, a red tie, a blue suit, a neat Vandyke. Halsey stopped and turned. Familiar?

Then he hurried on and knocked on Constance's door. No answer. He put his hand on the doorknob to test it.

"You lookin' for someone, mister?" The house detective, a burly man in a bowler hat and stained cravat, jammed his face close to Halsey's. His breath smelled of onions.

"I'm looking for Miss Constance Wood," said Halsey. "We had an appointment."

The detective raised bushy caterpillar brows. "I've heard it called a lot of things. That's the genteelest yet. *Appointment.* But she's not home, is she?"

"Apparently not."

The detective stepped aside and made a sweep of his arm toward the top of the staircase, politely telling Halsey to get the hell out.

Halsey brushed past him and bounded down to the ladies' parlor.

He stopped in the doorway and scanned the room. A woman was sitting in a chair, her back to the door. She was reading at the library table beside an oil lamp. She seemed to be about the size of Constance, and her hair was . . . he could not quite tell the color.

So he removed his hat, stepped into the room, and approached. "Excuse me."

The woman looked up. Her hair was not strawberry blond but brown going gray. And her face was tight, severe. . . . Harriet Dunbar.

She smiled. "Yes, young man."

"Forgive me, ma'am. I've—"

Her eyes shifted to the house detective, who was standing in the doorway.

"Is this feller botherin' you, Miss Dunbar?"

She stood. "Lieutenant Hutchinson has mistaken me for a much younger woman."

"You remember me?" said Halsey.

Harriet Dunbar batted her eyes, as if she were flirting in some Tidewater parlor. "Why, Lieutenant, I remember all the young men who visit my salon."

"Well," said the house detective, "maybe it's time for this young man to be movin' on. I don't like fellers wanderin' about my hotel, botherin' the ladies."

Halsey had questions for Harriet Dunbar, but not with another detective listening. So he gave her a bow and left. As he passed the detective, he put on his bowler, touched the brim, and said, "If you're plannin' to stay, I'd take off the hat. It's the *ladies'* parlor."

. . .

Around nine o'clock, Halsey told David Homer Bates that there was a lovely young woman at the Willard, the niece of a congressman, and he just had to see her once more before they sent her back to New York. It seemed a good excuse for leaving the office in the middle of his shift.

Bates agreed to cover for a few hours.

Halsey told the sergeant at the duty desk on the landing that he was going to the privy. The sergeant logged him out. Logging back in would be difficult, but Halsey would find a way.

Though the night was sultry hot, the western sky was flickering with light, and the low rumble of thunder rode the east-running clouds.

Halsey pulled his hat down and headed northwest on Pennsylvania.

Carriages clattered by. A man and his wife pushed a baby pram with two crying children. A pair of Metropolitan Police came toward him in their square hats, navy blue coats, and copper badges. They gave him the eye, so he tipped his hat.

Private dwellings lined the south side of the street, brick row houses with high stoops and tall windows, interrupted here and there by an empty lot that looked like a missing tooth in a row. At Twentieth Street, the Western Market occupied the odd-shaped block on the north side. And freestanding houses broke the pattern, too, relics from an earlier time, with fences and barns in the backyards and fruit trees on the little front lawns.

Number 1912 was a separate house on the south side, just a few hundred yards from the circle named for the Father of His Country. Number 1910, where Halsey was to find help, was the last house in a joined row of six, all brick fronts with handsome wrought iron balusters and tall windows.

Following the instructions of the Bone brothers, he cut through to an alley that ran behind the row houses to number 1910 and knocked twice on the back door.

A black woman peered out, then looked down at a carte de visite in her hand, then at him again, then opened the door.

He smiled and said, "Mrs. Stetson?"

She was small and wizened but well preserved and well dressed in a maid's gray dress and apron. Wire-rimmed spectacles gave her an air of erudition, as did her diction: "Step inside, and wipe your feet. You have until ten-oh-five exactly. That's when Master Bigsby and his wife come home from the theater."

"Thank you, ma'am."

"I wouldn't help you at all, but Jacob Bone says you're helping Mr. Lincoln. And if helping the president means you need to see what goes on in Doc Wiggins's house, well, you'll see all his guests from the bay window."

"So that's their name? Wiggins?"

"It's the house of Dr. Joshua Wiggins." Mrs. Stetson took an oil lamp and led him up the back stairs to the main hallway, then into the darkened parlor, with its pianoforte and fancy furniture. She pointed to the bay window. "Watch from there."

Halsey promised that he would be quiet and invisible.

She appeared nervous, eyes shifting, ears cocking to every neighborhood noise. She said, "Don't light any lanterns. And if you see a carriage pull up and a lady get out in a yellow dress, you run for the back door, because that's Mistress Bigsby. She gets the vapors if a play is too frightening and leaves early."

So he crouched down beside a marble-topped table. And he watched.

· · ·

A short time later, two men walked along Pennsylvania Avenue, turned at the tall fence that separated 1910 from 1912, and went down the alley between them.

In the next half hour, Halsey counted at least a dozen men going in. He tried to collect details—features, faces, sizes—and record them in his little red diary. One man stopped under the streetlamp and lit a cigar. He was wearing a gray suit and an eye patch. He seemed familiar, but men with eye patches were a common sight in Washington.

Around nine forty-five, a woman scurried along the sidewalk and went down the alley. The mysterious "strong-voiced woman," thought Halsey.

Ten minutes later, he recognized the slope-shouldered lope of Joseph Albert McNealy, who came from across the street and went straight down the alley.

The distant thunder now rumbled like a running battle moving toward Washington.

A horseman trotted along. A produce wagon rolled in from somewhere. The Metropolitan Police came back and walked on toward Washington Circle. The young parents rolled by with the baby pram and two children peacefully asleep.

Then Halsey heard a voice in his ear. He almost jumped.

Mrs. Stetson said, "Time to go, mister. Time to light the lamp."

As he stood, a carriage clip-clopped up to number 1912. And Haley saw what he could not believe: the Wood brothers climbing out and going into the house. He had to see more.

At the back door, he took the maid's hand, "The president appreciates what you've done."

"I don't believe you, sonny. I don't believe you ever laid eyes on the president. I let you in here because of the Bone boys. Now, you just run along."

He stepped out into the yard, heard the door close and lock behind him. He went down the alley, as if he were leaving, then doubled back.

He knew that if he had to, he could easily lose himself in the maze of fences, grass patches, barns, privies, and sheds back there. As he passed one hedgerow, he heard a dog growl, but he kept moving until he reached the six-foot board fence that separated the Wiggins property from Bigsby's. He slinked along until he was close to the Wiggins barn, so close that he could smell the hay.

He peered through a space between two twelve-inch boards and tried to find an angle that would allow him to see in the barn window. He could hear muffled voices and words like "Knights of the Golden Circle . . ." and "We are not Knights . . ." A dispute? "In Illinois, men are arrested on suspicion of being Knights . . ." Or agreement? ". . . a thing that violates every man's rights."

Halsey pressed his ear against the fence, but the words were drowned out by another rumble of thunder, louder, closer. The flicker of lightning appeared higher in the sky. A puff of wind rustled the leaves in the big sycamore that shaded both properties.

Halsey looked up into the tree and wondered if he could climb onto a low-hanging branch and shinny out over the Wiggins property.

Then he heard the back door of the barn open and through the cracks in the fence, he saw lantern light. Was someone walking the perimeter, just to make sure there was no one like him hiding in the shadows? He put his hand on his pistol and waited.

A door creaked and shut, a sound followed by a groan and a thundering of . . . another kind. Someone was using the privy.

So Halsey moved along the fence, searching for a better listening post.

What he heard was a growl. Then a fence board moved, and a dog's head appeared just a few feet away. It was some kind of terrier. It growled in Halsey's direction. Then it yipped, as if it didn't know whether to be aggressive or back away, as if whatever was crouching in the darkness might leap up and eat him.

When the outhouse door opened, the dog pulled out of the fence and yipped from the other side.

A man's voice said, "What're you barkin' at?"

Halsey saw the light of the lantern moving along the fence. He wanted to run. But any movement now would be worse than none. So he held his breath.

The fence board popped open, then fell back, then popped open, then fell back. The man on the other side was kicking it. He said, "So that's how you been gettin' out. Goddamn cur." Then came a thump and the dog yelped.

The lantern light went away. The barn door banged shut.

Halsey released his breath.

They were having an argument now over the future of "the Copperhead cause" and "the Knights" and "the Sons."

Halsey thought of the tree that Squeaker had drawn in his ledger book. A Liberty Tree. The Sons of Liberty? And he remembered the words of Benjamin Wood: "We are the true Sons of Liberty today." During the Revolution, the Sons of Liberty had gathered around Liberty Trees and rebelled against a tyrant king.

Then, amidst the muffled talk, Halsey heard something that almost made him vault the fence: "daybook." Someone said something that began, "Lincoln doesn't know . . . ," but it went all muffled in another rumble from the cosmos.

The distant thunder was no longer very distant.

Halsey crawled to the loose fence board and lifted, opening a twelve-inch space.

He took off his hat and stuck his head through the fence. He looked up the alley and down, first toward the Avenue and the streetlamp, a hundred feet to his right, then toward the outhouse, twenty feet to his left. He saw nothing, not even the dog.

He pulled his head back. He tried to raise a bit of saliva. All he could raise was nervous bile. So he swallowed and stuck his right leg through the space, then his shoulder, then his head. Then a flash of lighting lit the sky and the alley for just an instant.

He waited a moment. Then he pulled the rest of himself through, but his belt buckle caught on the fence board and made a loud pop. He stopped again, stock-still, waiting, listening, halfway through the fence, his right arm on one side, his pistol on the other.

But all he could hear was the wind rustling the trees and the low rumble of voices. Nothing was coming . . . except the rain.

So he pulled himself all the way through the fence and dropped into the alley. Then he scuttled to the window, stopping where he could finally hear and see inside.

The men were sitting in a circle. There was a banner tacked to the side of a stall. It was yellow and showed a golden crown and the letters KGC.

The man in the eye patch was standing beside it. His beard was neatly trimmed. His gray suit fit like a gentleman's armor. His accent proclaimed Virginia aristocracy. "I'm a Knight of the Golden Circle. I will do what I can to help the South win. And every person in this room should know that."

The Wood brothers sat opposite the man and his little pennant, forming a New York delegation of disloyalty, thought Halsey.

The man with the eye patch went on, "Our goal is to secede, take over Mexico, and create a golden circle of slave states around the Gulf."

"The Golden Circle is fantasy, Hunter," said Benjamin Wood. "We care about the country we have. We care about stopping the war and saving the Union."

"*We* care about liberty for the South," said the man in the eye patch, named Hunter.

"But," said the woman, whose strong voice sounded very much like Harriet Dunbar's, "we can all work together toward two goals: the preservation of Southern rights and the defeat of Lincoln."

"I agree," said Fernando Wood. "We are all Copperheads. Whether we want to see cotton and manufacture flowing again through the portals of New York Harbor or see slavery extended west and south, we all agree that deposing King Lincoln is paramount."

McNealy turned to the potbellied man sitting next to the woman. "What do you say, Dr. Wiggins?"

"King Lincoln has put out the call for three hundred thousand more troops. It's our job to discourage recruits, encourage desertions, and damage the war effort however we can. We can do it best by making common cause."

The woman now shifted in her seat, and Halsey could see her face: Harriet Dunbar, having a busy night. She said, "The goal should be to defeat the Republicans in November and Lincoln in two years. We fight on the battlefield and the ballot box."

The others agreed. Most of them looked prosperous, well dressed, well bearded, well fed. This was not some gathering of rapscallions but a council of war between factions seeking an alliance.

Halsey thought of Shakespeare's conspirators, plotting to kill Caesar. *So are they all, all honorable men . . . and women.*

As the first raindrops began to splatter down, Fernando Wood rose and said, "At election time, we'll need every tool we can get."

"Including secrecy," said Hunter.

"If secrecy is the thing," said Benjamin Wood, "we are all for it."

"So why," demanded Harriet Dunbar, "is your niece telling people that you went to Harrison's Landing to see McClellan?"

Constance? These people knew about Constance? That—and not the electricity in the storm-charged air—made the hair stand on the back of Halsey's neck.

"She's not really our niece," said Fernando. "She's our cousin's daughter."

"And an Abolitionist." That was McNealy, accusing.

"True," said Benjamin. "We failed her in that."

"And she's failed all of us," said Harriet Dunbar, "because she's putting it about that you want McClellan to run against King Lincoln."

"Come now, Mrs. Dunbar," Benjamin scoffed. "A politician as smart as Lincoln already knows the names of the men who want to unseat him."

"And what does she tell her Boston gentleman?" asked Dunbar. "He's been seen lurking in front of my house. He rode to see the president this morning. He was looking for her in the Willard tonight."

"And last night," said Hunter, "she read notes to him, aloud, right on the street."

That was where Halsey had seen Hunter and his eye patch. He was one of the "heroes" who had offered to help Constance the night before. He had been following her . . . or Halsey.

"What kind of notes?" asked Benjamin Wood.

Hunter turned to the Wood brothers. "Damning notes about things McClellan said in private to you. Notes she copied from your briefcase."

For a moment, there was a strange sound from the Wood brothers—silence. Both were apparently struck speechless.

Fernando recovered first, countering with a question, a good defensive tactic. "How did you hear that?"

"Skeeter and I heard it. We were hiding in the shadows across the street."

"You heard it over the traffic?" said Benjamin.

"Lose an eye to a Yankee bayonet," said Hunter, "and see how much your hearing improves."

"That girl needs to know that there are some in this room who do not take kindly to spying for Abolition," said Doc Wiggins. "She could get us all in trouble."

"She could get herself in trouble, too," said McNealy.

"True," said Uncle Benjamin, "but I wouldn't say she's spying."

"That's a strong word," said Fernando. "A misled girl, but—"

"She needs a good talking to," said Doc Wiggins.

Talking to? Halsey did not like the sound of that.

But Fernando was changing the subject: "Now, seeing as I'm just down from New York, I need more of a filling in on this so-called daybook."

"It could have value," said McNealy. "Now . . . or later. But remember, it's not a gun you can reload. Once it's used, it's used for good."

At that moment, the dog found Halsey. He came snuffling around the corner, stopped, and growled at the figure crouched by the barn.

As a crack of thunder spawned a brilliant flash, the dog began to bark.

And Halsey heard, "Get up, mister. Get up real slow." Then a pistol pressed against his head.

Halsey turned far enough to see the man's blue kepi, red satin tie, and trimmed Vandyke. He realized that this one had been spying on him and Samantha that afternoon at the canal, and he had been the other "hero" on the street the night before, the one called Skeeter. And just a few hours ago, he had run past Halsey on the stairs in the Willard.

Now McNealy was appearing from the back of the barn. He was carrying a lantern that obscured his face, but Halsey could tell that lope.

The voice behind Halsey said, "Is this your boy? What's he doin' spyin' on us?"

Then came another explosion of thunder, like the bursting of an artillery shell directly above them, and before a thought had fully formed for Halsey, the world exploded in a flash that was cold blue and blinding.

All in an instant, he felt the current blow through him and knock him backwards. The man with the gun went flying. McNealy dropped the lantern, which shattered against the side of the barn. The dog started yelping. And the big sycamore fell in three directions at once, split from crown to ground.

The fence collapsed under the weight of the tree.

Flames flickered to life around the shattered oil lantern.

McNealy recovered his wits, grabbed Halsey, and growled, "You damn fool."

Inside the barn, people were scrambling and shouting. They could not get out the back because the door was blocked by the tree, so they were coming from the front.

McNealy said, "Run. Punch me and run, but not to the War Department. Head for the C&O Canal, the towpath. Wait for me near the first lock."

Halsey just stared at him. Was McNealy helping or setting him up?

McNealy said it again. "Punch me and run."

So Halsey hit him in the face, kicked the dog off his cuff, and scrambled up and over the smoking tree. He glanced behind him and saw the flames rising. Then he heard Harriet Dunbar cry, "Find that son of a bitch and kill him!"

Halsey dropped from the tree. Then he leaped over a hedgerow into another yard, where a big dog on a chain lunged for him. He sidestepped the dog and ran down an alley and out on the south side of the block, at I Street.

He could go west toward Rock Creek and get to the C&O Canal in a few minutes. Or he could turn in the other direction. To make the decision, he asked himself a simple question: Did he trust McNealy? He answered by turning east.

. . .

Thunder and lightning were blasting a barrage of rain onto the dark Washington streets, turning the dust to mud and driving everyone inside.

If Halsey could get back to the War Department and time it, he could sneak up the stairs past the duty desk, even if he was soaking wet. But he was wondering instead if he should go straight to the Willard and warn Constance.

The words "a good talking to" had sounded more than ominous.

In rain so heavy that he could not see from one end of the block to the other, he ran south on Twenty-second to F, then east to the intersection of Seventeenth. When he got there, he pulled himself up against the side of the Winder Building and peered across the street. He could see the south and west entrances of the War Department. And even in the rain, he could see soldiers at each door. *Soldiers?* Provost Guard?

Was this why McNealy had told him not to go in? What was happening?

He turned back on F and went around the block to the corner of G and Seventeenth for a clear look at the front of the War Department: four more Provost Guard.

It would not be a good moment to try to sneak by, so he would go to Constance instead. Best take a roundabout route, out of sight of the Provost Guards at the War Department and the half dozen more watching the corner of Seventeenth, in front of the art museum turned supply depot. The Guard seemed to be setting up a perimeter around the whole Executive Area, and Halsey did not want to get caught in it.

So he turned west and started walking. The storm was blowing quickly away to the east now. But he was soaked through and his shoes squished with every step. He planned to take Eighteenth north to H, then skirt Lafayette Park and get on to the Willard.

He had not gone far when he saw two dark figures coming toward him through the slackening rain. He reached for his pistol. Then he recognized them and relaxed.

He usually saw them in the morning, but they were coming now in the opposite direction, moving more slowly, as if they were tired. One carried a shovel, the other a mule harness. One was tall, the other fat. Both were as black as the night. The rain dripped from their hat brims, but they tipped them just the same.

As Halsey tipped his hat in return, they recognized him.

One of them said, "Damn wet night, sir."

"Seems to be stopping, though," said Halsey.

"Y'all be careful, sir," said the other.

Halsey gave a wave over his shoulder and said, "You, too. It's past curfew."

"We got passes, sir. Negro night passes. We work late."

"Well, good night to you, then."

Halsey squished on and noticed another man coming along the block, coming fast with his head down.

McNealy? No. This was a lone stranger. He did not appear threatening, so Halsey kept walking but went only a few steps more when the man angled toward him, never breaking stride, and jammed a pistol into Halsey's ribs.

It was the one in the red tie and Vandyke, the one called Skeeter. He had changed his hat. "We been all over this neighborhood lookin' for you." He whistled, and Hunter came bounding from the shadows on the other side of the street.

Hunter turned his eye patch to Halsey and said, "You are now fucked, Mr. Lieutenant—"

At that moment, Hunter made a strange sound . . . or more accurately, his head did. In truth, it was a combination of sounds, a thump and a twang at the same time, the sound of a head hit by a shovel and the sound of the shovel vibrating from the impact.

Before Skeeter could react, a mule harness smashed into his face, knocking him back. The shovel followed right after it.

Halsey looked down at the two bodies, both as unconscious as horseshoes.

Mr. Shovel said, "We done tol' you to be careful, sir."

Halsey Hutchinson tipped his hat.

. . .

Twenty minutes later, Mr. Mule Harness, whose name was Jim-Boy Williams, went down an alley off Fourteenth Street and into the service entrance of the Willard Hotel. He had a message for Miss Constance Wood, to be passed through one of the Negro bellmen. He would not have done it except that Halsey had paid him a dollar, which was twice what he made for a day's work digging fortifications.

Halsey would have gone in himself, but as they approached the hotel on the Pennsylvania side, he had noticed four Metropolitan Police standing next to a wagon with bars on its windows. And after seeing all the Provost Guards around the War Department, he was beginning to feel uneasy. Who were they looking for?

So he and his new friends had doubled back around the block. Now, Halsey and Mr. Shovel, who called himself Jubilo Freedom, waited in an alley on Fourteenth, about fifty feet up the street from the east entrance of the hotel.

Down the street and across, a group of men stood under a streetlamp, smoking, talking, spitting, laughing: reporters, in their element, and in their own neighborhood. That side of Fourteenth was Newspaper Row, where the *Washington Evening Star,* the *Chronicle,* the *Daily Republican,* and half a dozen other papers kept offices.

The door of the hotel swung open and a tall man in a police uniform stepped out: William Webb, Superintendent of the Washington Metropolitans. He stuck his thumbs into his belt and cried out. "All right, boys, gather round!"

The reporters scrambled over and began shouting questions. He threw up his hands and told them all to be quiet. Then he said, "It's official. She's dead."

"Can you spell her name."

"C-O-N-S-T-A-N-C-E W-O-O-D."

Halsey suddenly felt sick. He wanted to vomit, to retch right there in the street.

"Is she related to the congressman?" shouted one of the reporters.

"She's the daughter of his cousin."

"Do we know who did it?"

"We have solid evidence that it was the man who's been seein' her, by the name Halsey Hutchinson. He works in the War Department."

In the shadows, Jubilo Freedom looked at Halsey and whispered, "Ain't that what your name is?"

Halsey could not speak. He was holding down a dry heave.

Webb shouted, "The suspect was seen accosting her in the street last night, and according to the Willard house detective, he was lurking about her room this evening. And one of our men at the National Hotel just talked to Mr. John Wilkes Booth himself, who says he believes these two were involved in flagrante delicto last night."

"In what?" shouted one of the reporters.

"It's Latin," said Webb.

"What's it mean?" shouted another.

"It means fuckin'," said another.

"That's what I thought."

"Did Booth see them doin' it?"

Webb waved his hands. "That's not important, boys."

"What else did Booth see?"

"He saw the lady in this Hutchinson's room a while back. And he said that on the day of the shooting at McDillon's, Hutchinson asked him for the layout of the place."

Halsey felt a rope tightening now. There were three killings he *had* committed.

"Is this feller dangerous?" asked one of the reporters.

"Armed and," answered Webb. "But the Metropolitan Police have jurisdiction here. The Provost Marshal claims control at the War Department."

"So the fugitive is military?"

Fugitive? They were calling him that already?

"He's a soldier in a civilian department. So he's wearin' a brown suit and bowler hat. He checked out of his office at nine thirty. He told his partner that he was planning to see—here's the quote, boys—'the daughter of a certain congressman who was going back to New York.' That's like a confession. So the military is after him, and the War Department has detectives. But the Metropolitans are on the case, too, boys. Bet on us."

Jubilo Freedom whispered, "Shit on a shingle and feed it to Mama."

"What?" Halsey could finally speak.

"You's in a powerful lot of trouble, mister."

One of the reporters shouted, "How was she killed?"

"He cut her throat. She's dead in the bed."

"Was it bloody?" cried another.

"Who found her?" cried another at the same time.

Webb, a tall man with a bushy mustache and eyebrows to match, took a deep breath. "A maid found her, after a guest in the room below complained of the blood comin' through the ceilin'. So, yeah, it was bloody."

Ugly, scandalous, bloody . . . nothing better to sell papers. The reporters all began to shout at once.

Halsey wanted to jump out and say that he was innocent. But he didn't think he had the strength, and he knew that he was being set up by . . . someone.

Webb said, "He can't cross the bridges without a pass, and we're watching the depot. If he tries to ride north on the Seventh Street Pike, we have a patrol up at the tollgate, too. He can't hide, and I tell you, boys, he has to swing for what he did."

Just then, Jim-Boy came back along the alley. He looked down the street at the cluster of men: then he said to Halsey, "I ask you this once, mister, is you a murderer?"

Halsey shook his head.

Jim-Boy said to Jubilo, "Do we believe him?"

"Don't know," said Jubilo. "Don't many white men tip their hats to us ever' day."

Halsey managed to get out the words, "I need a place to hide. Just for tonight."

"Don't know 'bout that, neither," said Jubilo.

Halsey pulled out a fistful of paper money. "I'll give you all I have. Fifty fresh new Yankee greenbacks."

Jim-Boy and Jubilo looked at each other, and Jubilo said, "That's more than we make in a month diggin' forts." Then he snatched the bills. "Just for tonight."

"You's on your own for the next four blocks," said Jim-Boy. "Jess keep back, till we get to our meet-up. Then you be in the clear."

"Yeah," added Jubilo, "so long's you got a strong nose."

Halsey had no idea what they were talking about, but he did as they said. He waited until they had reached the corner of F Street, made sure that all eyes were still on the police superintendent, then slipped out of the alley.

If the police were watching the Willard and the National, if the Provost Guard was looking for him at the War Department, if agents for something called the Knights of the Golden Circle were after him, too, he needed to hide, at least until he could find his way to McNealy, who had saved him once already that night. And he realized that McNealy might still be waiting for him in Georgetown, at the C&O Canal, by the first lock. So Halsey stopped at Eleventh.

Jim-Boy looked back from the other side of the street. The corner was deserted, so he called out, "Don't be laggin' on us, mister. Our ride won't wait."

Halsey hurried across the street, splattering through mud and puddles, and said, "I'm going back. I think I can find help in Georgetown."

"Georgetown?" said Jubilo. "That's a long walk."

"I have a friend. He wanted me to meet him by the canal, by the first lock."

Jubilo and Jim-Boy looked at each other, and Jim-Boy said, "By the first lock?"

"Can't be much of a friend," said Jubilo. "That's how we come home. We cross the Akka-duck Bridge, then take the towpath, and—"

Jim-Boy said, "They's Provost Guards all over that canal tonight, like they's lookin' for someone."

So there it was, thought Halsey. His earlier instincts about McNealy had been true. He said, "Let's keep goin'."

They went a few more blocks, when Halsey noticed a powerful stink and realized what they meant about a strong nose.

"There's our ride," said Jim-Boy.

"Yeah. Men makin' money," said Jubilo. "Good honest labor."

It was a wagon drawn by two horses, and it was filled to the brim with . . . shit.

There were two Negro men on the seat. Jubilo introduced them as his brothers, Hallelujah and Zion.

"Call me Hal for short," said Hallelujah. "Our mama cry hallelujah and give praise every day that we's free colored folk with our own jobs in our own city of Zion."

"That's right," said Jubilo. "We also pray every day for the year of Jubilo, when all our people cross the River Jordan and git on to Zion, the land of milk and honey."

Zion said, "Yeah, milk and honey . . . and the leavin's of the white man's bowels."

Hallelujah and Zion drove a night soil wagon. They worked between ten at night and six in the morning, emptying necessaries and hauling the contents away. Business was always dirty, but always good.

Hal said that if their brother vouched for a man, they were glad to help him.

Zion just chewed on a toothpick. "Is he in trouble?"

"He's in trouble, but he seem a righteous man to me," said Jubilo.

"And he give us fifty dollars," added Jim-Boy.

"Fifty dollars?" said Hal. "Then sit on the rail, sir, and mind the splatters."

The wagon rolled east through the quiet city, east toward the places where freedmen and contrabands had taken up residence on their long journey to Zion, and Halsey wondered what his father would think.

Then the shock settled on him like an embracing fog, as it had when he was shot at Ball's Bluff. It protected him from his grief at the death of Constance, and from the pain of realizing his own predicament, and from the stink of the night soil wagon.

NINE

Saturday Night

No American city was more beautiful than Washington, D.C., at night. Los Angeles appeared to float on a sea of luminescence. New York pierced the sky with eighty-story spears of light. But Washington's white monuments seemed at once more monumental and more accessible at night, like beacons in the darkness.

So Peter had the limo driver take them by the Lincoln Memorial, just for a look at the temple of America's most cherished myth: in a democracy, a boy born into backwoods poverty could rise to the pinnacle of national power. But while the hero immortalized in that temple did not seem to suffer from what the Greeks called hubris—pride before an implacable fate—he had paid the ultimate price for his striving.

The limo didn't stop. It was enough to admire the memorial from a distance. Then they swung around the Mall and pulled up at the south entrance to the National Museum of American History.

Peter and Evangeline showed picture IDs, passed through the metal detectors—even at big Washington parties, there were metal detectors—and heard music.

Peter recognized the Ninety-seventh Regimental String Band, three guys in Civil War uniforms who played bass, mandolin, guitar, banjo, fiddle and sang familiar tunes like "Kingdom Coming" and "The Bonnie Blue Flag," along with obscure artifacts of a forgotten time, like "Just Before the Battle, Mother" and "He's Coming to Us Dead." They were the soundtrack for an era and for the evening. And just then, they were singing the campaign song that gave the exhibit its title: "Lincoln and Liberty, Too."

"Hurrah for the choice of the nation, our chieftain so brave and so true."

Peter and Evangeline walked across the white stone floor and into the three-story glass-and-steel atrium. Rising in front of them was a wall with the impressionistic silver-spangled American flag. In the gallery beyond was the original Star-Spangled Banner.

The Ninety-seventh was performing on a raised platform: *"We'll go for the great reformation, for Lincoln and Liberty, too."*

Abraham Lincoln and his wife were greeting visitors, flanked by an honor guard of Union soldiers in crisp blue uniforms.

Showbiz at the Smithsonian.

While there were enough Lincoln impersonators in America that they had their own national convention, this guy was one of the best. Six-foot-four, gaunt, well bearded . . . he even had the raised nodule on his right cheek.

And the woman next to him was appropriately short and round faced.

Peter took a brochure from Mrs. Lincoln, who gestured to the huge atrium as if it were the family library in the White House. "Please avail yourselves of some refreshment, sir. The new exhibit is in the Albert Small Documents Gallery beyond the escalator."

"Thank you, ma'am," said Peter. "And you look marvelous tonight."

She curtsied.

"But remember," said Mr. Lincoln. "No food or drink in the exhibit rooms."

"I wouldn't dream of it, sir," said Peter. "And knowing that you don't drink strong spirits yourself, I may abstain in your honor."

Lincoln bowed. "Enjoy the night."

As they walked away, Evangeline whispered, "Peter, they're actors. Let *them* play the roles."

"Look around you," he said. "Everyone in this room is playing a role."

Hundreds of people filled the grand atrium, crowding around the stand-up tables, the bars, and the huge hors d'oeuvres array in the middle of the floor. It was business attire for the men, but on a Saturday night, the ladies were wearing a few more sparkles, a little more silk, and lots more color than on a workday.

Peter and Evangeline had been in crowds like this before, parties where they had stumbled into a "company town," where everyone knew

everyone else, or seemed to, and nobody paid them much attention because nobody thought they were, well . . . anybody.

*"We'll go for the son of Kentucky, the Hero of Hoosierdom, too, the pride of
those 'Suckers' so lucky, for Lincoln and Liberty, too."*

The music echoed up to the skylight three stories above. So did the
roar of conversation from an atrium full of insiders.

Peter and Evangeline heard snippets about this committee and that
hearing, this bill and that rider and all the earmarks, too. They also picked
up on talk about the challenges faced by modern retailing in the world of
cybercommerce because, as the program announced, "This exhibit was
sponsored by the American Retail Sales Association."

"Our David's good sling is unerring. The Slave-o-crat giant he slew . . ."

Peter noticed Senator Kerry from Massachusetts. Chuck Schumer was
there, too, attracting a crowd of New Yorkers. Most of the congressmen
they saw were running unopposed. The rest were back in their districts
campaigning.

"Then shout for the freedom-preferring, for Lincoln and Liberty, too."

A few heads were finally turning their way. A good-looking couple
always made heads turn, even an anonymous couple in Power Town,
USA. Who were they? Worth a bit of conversation? A little schmooze?

"We'll go for the son of Kentucky . . ."

"You get the wine," said Evangeline. "I'll get us some hors d'oeuvres."

"Can't work the room on an empty stomach."

"Can't work it without somebody to introduce you, either." She
scanned the room. "So where's Diana? She said she'd be here."

"Maybe she's over at the bar." Peter headed in that direction.

Evangeline loaded plates with California rolls, ginger, and soy. She
wondered what Old Abe would think of people eating raw fish cut up by
smiling Japanese chefs all in his honor. She popped one into her mouth
and looked around for Congressman Milbury.

"They'll find what by felling and mauling, our railmaker statesman can do."

Instead, the congressman's chief of staff, William Dougherty, found
her.

"I wish they'd shut up," said Dougherty. "I can barely hear myself
think."

"The People are everywhere calling, for Lincoln and Liberty, too."

"It's a pleasure to see you, too," said Evangeline. "Is the congressman here?"

"Upstairs, at the permanent Lincoln exhibit. There's a TV crew up there. He could find a TV crew in the middle of the ocean. Is your boy-friend here?"

"We'll go for the son of Kentucky . . ."

"I take it you're more interested in meeting him than me."

"I'm interested in a certain 'something' referenced in a certain letter."

"I thought the letter was secret," said Evangeline.

Dougherty looked around at all those people seeing and being seen, looking without seeming to, and he said, "In this town, nothing is secret . . . for long."

"The hero of Hoosierdom, too . . ."

Peter excused his way back through the crowd with two glasses of wine.

Evangeline took one and introduced Dougherty, "who knows about the letter."

"The pride of those 'suckers' so lucky, for Lincoln and Liberty, too."

Peter toasted with his glass, popped a piece of sushi into his mouth, and said to Dougherty, "So, which side are you on?"

"I work for Congressman Milbury. We're trying to get him reelected in a very difficult race."

"And what did you say his reelection had to do with the Lincoln let-ter?" asked Peter.

"I didn't," answered Dougherty. "But the congressman says that if you found it, or the mysterious 'something' referenced in it, and donated it to the Smithsonian, he'd be indebted. And what a remarkable legacy for the nation's most prominent treasure hunter."

Peter hated being called a treasure hunter almost as much as he hated being called "Pete." He said, "I'm a dealer in rare books and documents, not a treasure hunter."

"So up with our banner so glorious, the star-spangled red, white, and blue."

Evangeline glanced at Peter's breast pocket, as if to ask, *Want to tell him that an hour ago, you took a half-million-dollar retainer to hand over this "something"?*

But she knew what he was thinking: nothing worse than politicians sticking their noses into his business. Invariably, they were looking for something . . . publicity, a contribution, or outright surrender to their city, state, or district. When politicians came in the front door, Peter usually headed for the back.

"We'll fight till that banner's victorious, for Lincoln and Liberty, too."

William Dougherty said, "We wanted you to come tonight because this institution is near to the congressman's heart."

"Staying in business is near to my heart," said Peter. "So before I think about donating things, I have to find them. Then I have to think about their value."

"I'm sure you would agree that there's a difference between the *cost* of something," said Dougherty, "and its *value*."

Peter's wineglass stopped in midair.

Evangeline knew that he was now officially pissed. First Dougherty called him a treasure hunter. Then he came with the cost/value speech.

She slipped a hand into Peter's arm and said, "The Lincoln letter is worth more than three million dollars. I can't imagine what a certain 'something' would be worth."

"Nor can I," said Dougherty, over the final resounding chorus. "But I've asked one of our advisors to guide you through the exhibit. And since the speeches are about to start, it's a good time to sneak off to the gallery."

As the sound of applause for the Ninety-seventh echoed, Dougherty led Peter and Evangeline through the crowd, past the escalator, to the Albert H. Small Documents Gallery.

Two uniformed reenactors stood at the door, Union soldiers holding their muskets at parade rest. Beside them was a table for people to leave their glasses.

Dougherty made a little wave to a tall, well-dressed gentleman who smoothly broke away from another conversation and came over: Professor Colin Conlon.

Every town was a small town, thought Peter, no matter how big it was.

"Professor Conlon is our expert in all things historical," said Dougherty.

"So you're the document hunter," said Conlon, with a tone that made "hunter" sound like "thief."

Peter disliked him even more than he had at the seminar, which he decided not to mention. He also decided not to mention his friendship with Diana Wilmington.

Then Conlon turned to Evangeline. "And you're the TV person, making a film about the Civil War without contacting the author of the newest work on Lincoln."

"Would that be you?" said Evangeline.

"Yes, dear," said Peter, all phony sweetness. "*Lincoln at Law*. It sounds interesting. It's on my bedside." It did sound interesting. It was not on his bedside.

But with another writer flattered, another attitude was adjusted. Conlon gave Peter a small bow of the head.

Then Evangeline suggested that she should have her producer contact him.

Conlon beamed. "If I had people—as you media people say—I'd tell them to get in touch with your people, but since I don't"—he dipped in his pocket—"my card."

A cheap date, thought Peter.

Dougherty excused himself. "I must warn the congressman that he'll be on in ten minutes. You're in good hands."

"Follow me," said Conlon.

Peter and Evangeline put their wineglasses on the tray and entered the gallery, a small space in a big museum, soundproofed so that people could concentrate on the documents, low-lit to protect them. And for the moment, it was almost empty. Most everyone else was out in the atrium enjoying the wine and the music and the shoptalk.

But Peter felt a chill, because this was a true sanctum sanctorum.

He knew there was a reason for all this. Someone wanted something from him. But until he found out exactly what, he would just enjoy this moment.

Evangeline felt a chill, too. She'd been in the presence of a lot of amazing documents and always tried to keep calm, on the principle that one of them had to.

But what they were seeing was truly amazing.

Directly in front of them, exhibited in a tall glass obelisk, lit from above with low light and laser alarm, was a small leather-bound book. It had been opened to the endpaper, where was written, in pencil, the words,

The following extracts were taken from speeches of mine delivered at various times and places. And I believe they contain the substance of all that I have ever said on Negro equality. A. Lincoln.

Peter wondered, could this be the "something" in the letter? Could this be the diary that everyone was rumoring about?

But Conlon explained that Lincoln had cut out and pasted his 1858 campaign speeches into this little book, adding annotations here and there. He gave it to one of his supporters after he lost the senatorial election to Stephen Douglas. It now resided in the Library of Congress.

Conlon said, "Some of his speeches were off the cuff, so the newspaper versions were the only record."

An interactive screen allowed the viewer to turn the "pages" of the little book, see the articles reprinted from the *Chicago Press & Tribune,* a Republican paper, and the *Chicago Times,* which supported Douglas.

"In the extreme partisanship of the time," Conlon explained, "Lincoln knew that the Republican paper would do a better job of recording his words, and the Democratic paper would be more careful with Douglas."

"There was spin, even then," said Evangeline.

"It makes today's vitriolic opinionating sound like chamber music."

The side walls were lined with documents, letters, and images showing the run-up to the Proclamation and its immediate impact. But the heart of the exhibit was displayed at the end wall, in a long case, with exit doors on either side, guards in Civil War garb at each one, and a huge blowup of the painting, *First Reading of the Emancipation Proclamation,* on the wall behind. Lincoln sat at the center of the painting, holding a sheet of paper, and surrounded by his cabinet on that historic day in July 1862.

Directly beneath were the four Lincoln-signed versions of the Proclamation, gathered from the National Archives, the New York State Library, and the Abraham Lincoln Presidential Museum. Two sheets, four sheets, four sheets, and one: dated July 22, 1862; September 22, 1862; January 1, 1863; and June 10, 1864. As for the case itself: fifteen feet long, low light, double-chamber glass, and filled, Peter assumed, with nitrogen gas to stabilize temperature and humidity in a closed environment.

He decided that even if the "something" referenced in the Lincoln letter turned out to be no more than a list of office supplies for the White

House, his Washington trip had led to a high point in his career right here, right now.

"This is the first time that these four drafts have been displayed in one place at one time," said Conlon, "ever."

The July 22 version came from the Robert Todd Lincoln papers in the National Archives, a page and a half, written on two long sheets.

Evangeline read the last words, just above the signature, almost to herself, "then, thenceforward, and forever free."

Conlon said, "Lincoln had been toying with the idea of a proclamation. After seeing how badly things were going militarily that summer, he knew that he had to do something to change the odds of the war. This is the version he read to his cabinet."

Peter said, "The one he wrote at Major Eckert's desk in the telegraph office?"

Conlon sniffed. He was good at sniffing to express professorial condescension. "Lincoln was thinking and writing in many places—the telegraph office, his summer cottage, the White House—and he made notes of all sorts. As you can see, this was the final version. There's hardly a change or a deletion in it."

"He could have thrown the other notes away," said Peter.

"I suppose. But Eckert isn't very reliable. He told his story many years later and claimed that Lincoln had actually told him what he was writing. I don't think Lincoln would bother telling a mere major."

Peter didn't argue. He was still trying to figure out why Conlon was giving this little tour. And there were three other versions to look at.

Evangeline pointed to the September 22 version. It had somehow become the property of a New Yorker who had contributed it to his state library.

She said, "How much do you think *that's* worth?"

"A crass question," said Conlon.

"I run with a crass crowd." She shot a glance at Peter.

"It's priceless," said Conlon. "It's the second Declaration of Independence."

A good description, thought Peter, and the right price.

He studied the handwriting, the heavy paper with the light-brown lines to guide the writer, the brown ink, and at the very top, the words written in pencil, *By the President of the United States of America, a Procla-mation.* This was the version that would be read to the troops and distrib-uted across America in September of 1862. It gave rebellious states a hundred days to return to the Union or forfeit control of the greatest part of their wealth, the single largest financial asset in America: the four mil-lion men and women held in bondage.

Suddenly, the lights in the case faded to black. The documents disap-peared.

It was so startling that Evangeline almost jumped.

Conlon explained, "Conservators recommend these documents be on exhibit for limited periods, even in low light, to prevent cumulative dam-age. The New York folks want their edition be visible for no more than eighty hours in a year."

"Why all the worry?" asked Evangeline.

"Iron gall ink on acid paper," said Peter, "as sensitive to light as a baby's bottom on a sunny beach."

"Let's hope that the 'something' referenced in the Lincoln letter hasn't been left in the sun," said Conlon.

"The 'something' could be nothing," said Peter.

"That's not why you're here, Mr. Fallon. But let me say this, right in front of this cabinet of wonders: Whatever is out there belongs to the American people . . . not to Diana Wilmington and her failed museum, simply because she's black, and not to a certain client of Suzanne Hamill and Associates who'll pay anything to sully the Lincoln legacy."

Peter and Evangeline looked at each other. Conlon knew about David Bruce?

"And not"—Conlon stepped closer to Peter—"to men like yourself."

"Are you speaking for everyone," said Evangeline, "or just the histo-rians."

"Historians respect history," said Conlon. "We don't plunder it for profit."

Peter had heard this before. It was the 2.1 version of "treasure hunters and cost/value." But he had never heard it in a room that was, for the mo-ment, the second most important national reliquary in America. The *most* important was a block away, the National Archives, where they kept the Declaration of Independence and Constitution.

"Is this why the congressman invited us?" asked Peter. "So that you could give me a speech?"

"The congressman agrees. And he's asked me to draft a preliminary bill that allows the federal government to seize any article that meets the standards of a national treasure."

"Then I'd better find this 'something,'" said Peter, "before the law takes effect."

"I am planning to convene a panel—"

"You would," Peter said. "When in doubt, call a panel out."

"—to determine what in fact is a national treasure."

The lights came on again in the main display case.

Evangeline said, "I think we're looking at a few."

Peter turned to the January 1, 1863, version of the Proclamation. It had been handwritten by a professional "engrosser," bore Lincoln's signature, and was stamped with the seal of United States, which was festooned with the red, white, and blue ribbons. The ribbons had faded. So had the ink.

"A perfect example," said Professor Conlon, "of what I'm talking about."

Peter ignored Conlon and studied the signature:

Lincoln had spent New Year's morning receiving the public at his traditional reception in the East Room. Then he went up to his office and took up the pen, but put it down again, explaining that he had shaken so many hands, his own felt paralyzed. And he wanted his signature to appear firm; otherwise, people would think he hesitated. But he had no hesitation. He said, "If I ever go into the history books, it will be for this act. My whole heart and soul is in it." Then he flexed his hand a few times, took the pen, and signed. Behind every document, thought Peter, there was a story.

But Conlon was still distracting them with talk: "We're drawing on several sources for our standards. A national treasure should have extraordinary intrinsic and monetary value, unique and irreplaceable to the nation—"

"Check," said Peter out of the corner of his mouth.

"—be the work of human hands, of great cultural value, of historical significance, and of inherent aesthetic value."

"Check, check, check, and check again," said Peter; then he directed Evangeline to the fourth document. "A signed Leland-Boker printing."

"Another example of what I'm talking about," said Conlon. "Lincoln signed forty-eight copies for auction at the Philadelphia Sanitary Ball in June 1864. Counting the Robert F. Kennedy copy sold recently, only twenty-four are known to exist."

Peter glanced at Evangeline, giving her the honors.

She said, "Twenty-five."

That stopped Conlon in his pedantic tracks. "Twenty-*five*?"

Evangeline rolled her eyes to Peter.

Conlon whispered, "You own a Leland-Boker?"

Peter nodded.

"Signed?" said Conlon.

"A national treasure," said Peter.

After a pause, Conlon said, "Well, there may come a time when we decide that such a thing belongs in a museum."

Peter said, "Who's we? The government? Democrats? Republicans?"

"A panel. When in doubt, call a panel out." Conlon headed for the exit. The sound of distant applause signaled the end of one speech, the beginning of another.

Peter turned to Evangeline and said, "*Now* do you see why I made up my own political party?"

. . .

They stayed a few minutes more with those magnificent documents, and as they left, the reenactor standing "guard" at the exit said, "Good evening, Mr. Fallon."

Peter stopped and looked at the face under the kepi.

The man said, "We have a deal, right? Five hundred dollars, cash or check."

"Bryant?"

The flea market bookseller had taken his hair out of its ponytail and put on the uniform of a Union soldier, but not the uniform that Peter would have expected, given the Lee and Stonewall T-shirt he had been wearing that afternoon.

"I thought I might see you here," said Douglas Bryant. "Big Boston honcho like you, he doesn't come to D.C. just for the monuments. Hell, you're a monument yourself."

"Apparently this guy knows you," said Evangeline.

"Just not very well," said Peter.

She pointed to the dark blue insignia on Bryant's uniform. It looked like a Star of David. "Are you supposed to be Jewish?"

"That's the patch of the Union Eighth Corps. I'm from West Virginia, so I march as a private in the Tenth Regiment, West Virginia Infantry. And since my wife is from Fairfax, sometimes I go over to the other side and march with Longstreet's Corps."

Peter said to Evangeline, "The Civil War lives."

"So if you have five hundred Yankee greenbacks, I can sell you the book right after this shindig is over."

"I have four hundred," said Peter.

Bryant shook his head. "No way, Mr. Boston. Five hundred or nothing. From what I just heard, you can afford a lot more than that, so your friendly weekend bookseller and Civil War reenactor will get his price."

Evangeline said, "What are we talking about here?"

"A book called *Fort Lafayette*," said Peter. "No dust jacket. No signature. Piss-poor nineteenth-century wood-pulp paper. But my curiosity is piqued."

"It's more than piqued." Bryant grinned, flashing those yellow teeth that added a bit of authenticity to his 1862 aspect. "You're as hot as a teenager seein' a pretty girl in a bathing suit. Otherwise you wouldn't have texted me an hour after you left."

Peter cut to the chase. "I have the cash. When can I get the book?"

"Tonight. I'm scheduled to stand here for another half hour. Meet me out on the plaza afterwards. My van is parked on the Mall."

. . .

Up on the podium, Congressman Max Milbury was rambling about the importance of Lincoln, liberty, freedom, equality. "There's a reason why I have a bust of Lincoln in my office on Capitol Hill, and you see it here tonight. . . ."

Peter grabbed a second glass of wine, leaned close to Evangeline, and whispered, "Blah, blah, blah."

She said, "If you're planning on negotiating with that rube in the soldier's suit, I wouldn't drink any more wine."

"I'm not negotiating. I'm paying his price. And he's not a rube."

The congressman was saying, "I want to thank the American Retail Sales Association for recognizing the importance of bringing all these majestic documents together in one place. You know how much I appreciate you all."

Then Evangeline heard a voice behind her.

"The congressman is about to make a political statement"—it was Kathi Morganti—"in an apolitical atmosphere."

"Is there such a thing in Washington?" asked Evangeline.

"In town for less than a day and already you're cynical." Kathi turned to Peter. "So this is the famous document sleuth?"

Evangeline said, "At least she didn't call you a treasure hunter."

"Much appreciated," he said.

"Why are you here?" asked Evangeline. "Your clients want to unseat Milbury."

"The Smithsonian's neutral territory," said Kathi.

"Like the gym in *West Side Story*," said Peter.

Kathi said, "Handsome, successful, and quick with his cultural references . . . If I was single, I don't think I would have left this guy in Boston."

Evangeline said to Peter, "For some reason, this woman thinks that she's been invited to talk about our—"

"Wedding that wasn't?" said Peter.

"Nothing out of you, either," said Evangeline.

Peter nodded. He knew enough not to push. He said to Kathi, "We met your client this evening. What's his war on Milbury all about?"

Kathi said, "Look around you. This place is loaded with representatives from brick-and-mortar retailers. They're here to support the Smithsonian's great show, because you can't run a political event in any of these museums. But if you make an unrestricted gift, you can run a party, and you get to invite a percentage of the guest list."

"I take it you're not part of the percentage?"

"I represent one of American's major online retailers," said Kathi. "The gasbag at the microphone introduces a bill every session to force online retailers to pay sales taxes in every state, even if they don't have a physical presence in them."

"The classic clash," said Peter. "Big government liberal versus avatar of unfettered capitalism."

"I prefer to call it the public good against private greed," said Evangeline.

"We call it billable hours," said Kathi. "And whatever you call it, you're in the middle of it. My client takes it very seriously when he hires someone. Very seriously."

Peter looked at Evangeline. "That sounds like a threat."

"More like a warning," said Kathi. "Bruce has the resources to win . . . here and in Upstate New York, where Milbury is fighting a Republican lawyer who's campaigning as we speak, while Milbury sucks up to this group." She finished her wine. "Now, if you'll excuse me, I see a Democratic staffer I need to schmooze."

"You just told me this was an apolitical night," said Evangeline.

"I lied." Kathi Morganti smiled that rictus smile. "Nothing's apolitical in this town . . . unless it's dead."

. . .

They never got to talk to the congressman. He was surrounded by too many admirers and contributors. They never got to talk to Dougherty again because he was herding contributors toward the congressman and spending schmooze time with Kathi Morganti. They never got to talk to Diana Wilmington, either. She had promised to be there but never showed up.

Peter didn't like that.

As soon as they were outside, he called her, but got her voice mail.

"Maybe we should go up to Georgetown and see if she's home," said Evangeline.

"Buy the book first," said Peter.

Private Bryant was waiting on the plaza, with his musket at parade rest. He said, "It's a bit of a walk. Finding a parking spot along here's like finding gold, or a rare book, eh, Mr. Fallon?"

"How far?" said Evangeline.

"A couple of blocks. It's on Constitution, near Seventeenth."

"These are long goddamn blocks," said Evangeline.

"And every cab is called for, so forward march," said Peter.

"Glad I wore half-heels. I wish I wore sneakers."

They walked along the edge of the Mall, with the Washington Monument above them, so brilliantly illuminated by a circle of floodlights that you could see history written right into the stone. The construction had been suspended in 1858. By the time they got back to finishing it in the 1880s, they couldn't find the same color granite. So it went from white to a bit . . . *off* white.

Douglas Bryant chitchatted for most of the way about the joys of being a hard-core reenactor. None of that farbing stuff for him. "Farbing," he explained, was a term for reenactors who didn't embrace the whole experience, guys who stayed in motels and ate at McDonald's after they'd done their Civil War thing.

Bryant said that farbs never found out what it was like to go four or five days without bathing, or to feel the chafe of the wool trousers in the heat, or to eat sloosh, a mixture of cornmeal soaked in hot bacon fat then wrapped around a musket ramrod and cooked in the campfire, or to sleep on the damp ground and slap at the bugs all night after marching and "fighting" all day.

"Why do you it?" asked Evangeline.

"So I can know what it felt like."

"When I want to know what felt like to be miserable a hundred and fifty years ago," she said, "I read a book."

"Hey, Mr. Boston, your girlfriend's no fun."

"Yeah," said Peter. "Way too serious."

Bryant's blue van was parked under a tree on the north side of Constitution Avenue, between Fifteenth and Seventeenth. On the grass a short distance away stood the memorial to the U.S. Army Second Division: a giant hand holding a huge golden sword, low parapet walls extending on either side. In the distance beyond the monument, the White House reflected its floodlights.

The traffic on Constitution was light, and the sidewalk on that side was deserted. But it was a warm Saturday night in September, so there were plenty of strollers and school groups and tourists across the avenue, wandering the graceful paths around the Washington Monument.

Bryant went to the back of the van, looked around to make sure that no one was watching, and opened the doors.

Of course, on that stretch, thought Peter, someone was always watching. A panel truck parked between the White House and the Washington Monument had probably been inspected by the U.S. Park Police, X-rayed by some FBI roving radiation van, and visited by bomb-sniffing dogs, too. And once Bryant opened the back, Peter expected all the *food*-sniffing dogs in the District to come running. Was it old cheese? New garbage? Something alive? Or something dead?

The back of the van was piled with boxes, books, a couple of folding chairs, a table, and a laundry basket of dirty of clothes, including the gray jacket and butternut trousers of his Confederate uniform, a cooler, a shopping bag full of cereals and fruits, a pile of banana and orange peels, and an old drum.

"Do you live in this thing?" asked Evangeline.

"Only on weekends. I'm driving up to Antietam tonight. Giving demonstrations tomorrow. My wife will meet me up there. She plays Clara Barton. Hundred and fiftieth anniversary of the bloodiest day in American history. Lots of activities, lots of fun."

"Fun," said Evangeline. "Yeah."

He reached into his box of jumbled books and produced *Fort Lafayette*.

Peter pulled five C-notes from his wallet.

They made the exchange.

"Nothin' like the Yankee Greenback dollar to make a foot soldier feel rich," said Bryant. "Legal tender throughout the Union, first issued in July of 1862, shortly after the first income tax. Three percent on all incomes over six hundred dollars. Some of my friends in gray uniforms call Lincoln's income tax the beginning of the end."

"A history lesson with every transaction," said Evangeline.

Peter said, "What about a receipt?"

"Oh, a stickler, hunh?"

"We like to establish the chain of ownership," said Peter. "If this book turns out to be worth a lot, it's always good to know that I obtained it legally."

"If it turns out to be worth a lot," said Bryant. "I'll shoot myself . . . or you."

"No," said Evangeline. "You'll sue him, unless he has a receipt."

"This lady is a real product of the twenty-first century. Sue. Sue. Sue." Bryant went around to the driver's side and pulled out a clipboard. "I'll write you a receipt."

Peter asked, "Can you also give me a copy of your receipt from Dawkins?"

"Dawkins doesn't give up much. You found that out this afternoon. Go to Antietam and ask him tomorrow. There's a big street fair in the town of Sharpsburg to commemorate the anniversary. He said he might go. But he's a mysterious old African American."

"I like a long chain of ownership," said Peter.

Evangeline said, "Hey, boys, I'm getting a little tired of standing here while you two talk about provenance."

"Provenance?" said Bryant. "I've never been to France."

She didn't know if he was joking. She stepped up onto the sidewalk and looked out at the traffic buzzing by and the Washington Monument rising above the trees. Then she turned and looked back toward the White House. And she saw . . . horses.

Yes, four horses and their riders—U.S. Park Police in blue helmets— were cantering across the wide Ellipse. Every so often, they would stop and practice some maneuver or other. In the bright ambient light of the city, they looked just . . . beautiful.

The beauty of them took Evangeline out of herself for a moment, so she didn't hear the cars rushing past or the three motorcycles roaring up and pulling into a single spot about a hundred feet away.

Peter was saying, "Any idea where he got this book and the engraving of the Emancipation Proclamation?"

"I'm afraid not," said Bryant.

"Did he offer you anything else?"

"He had some old engravings of Jesus and Frederick Douglass, from 1860s editions of *Harper's Weekly*. Not worth much but nicely framed . . . and some letters."

"About what?"

"They came from brothers who had enlisted in the Colored Regiments. Their name was Freedom, of all things. And— Oh, shit."

Peter looked over his shoulder, past Evangeline, who said, "I do not like the sound of that." She turned and saw three bulky men getting off motorcycles and coming toward them on the sidewalk.

Peter said, "Unh . . . why, the 'Oh shit'?"

"Those guys want the book you're holding," said Bryant.

"How do you know?" asked Peter.

"They came around the stalls after you left today. They offered me a thousand for it."

"A thousand," said Peter, "and you didn't sell it?"

"I made a deal with you," said Bryant, as if the question insulted him. "A deal is a deal."

"That means these guys are on to something," said Peter.

"You're damn right we are." That was a familiar voice, much closer. It was the guy in the Civil War soul patch, appearing from behind the Second Division Monument. He must have been watching the van all night, waiting to call in his boys: Burke, the beard who had been on the train with Evangeline; the big one from the Eastern Market; and a smaller guy, who just hung back. Two of them were wearing the Bonnie Blue Flag ball caps. And the leader, the one with the soul patch, had changed his Hawaiian shirt to a blue T-shirt with the same insignia on the breast.

Douglas Bryant, Private, West Virginia Volunteers, snatched up his Springfield musket, pulled back the hammer, took a percussion cap from the leather pouch on his belt and put it onto the nipple. Then he shouted, "You boys don't come any closer!"

"That thing ain't loaded," said the one with the bushy beard.

"But this is," said another, and he pulled a big pistol from his belt. It looked like the Navy Colt that Peter had seen earlier that day.

Bryant whispered to Peter, "Reach into the laundry basket. There's a handgun. It ain't loaded. Just point it."

The four guys kept coming. The traffic roared along. Nobody seemed to be watching.

Douglas Bryant said, "I buy my minie balls online at Track of the Wolf, fifty-eight-caliber, sixty-grain service load. And I *am* loaded. So one of you is going down."

The four slowed at that, then stopped about fifty feet away.

Peter pulled the pistol out. It was small, engraved, all of one piece.

Bryant said in a very loud voice, "No need to cock it. It's an Adams pocket revolver, double action. These jokers do anything funny, just point and shoot."

Peter said, "Okay," then he told Evangeline to get in the van.

"Oh, Peter," she said, "I told you this was crazy, and I didn't want any part of it." She turned and started to walk toward the four guys. "You, in the beard, you stalked me on the train. Now you stalk me on the Mall. Who in the hell do you think you are?"

Mr. Soul Patch said, "We're the guys who think that you're in the way. We warned your boyfriend this afternoon and now we're telling you, whatever you just bought from this guy, we want it."

"Well," she said, "you can't have it!" And before anyone could react, she'd pulled a whistle from her purse and blew into it, shrill and loud.

"Hey, stop that," said the one called Burke.

She did it again.

In the distance, a horse screamed, and then came the sound that infantry had feared since men first marched: the pounding of hooves on hard ground, horses coming at the flank.

The Park Police were galloping across the elliptical road that gave the Ellipse its name.

The four guys gave a look toward the horses, then they jumped on the three bikes, with Mr. Soul Patch riding piggyback, and sped off in three directions. One bike went east, two went west, with one of them peeling off onto Seventeenth, right in front of the little lock keeper's house.

"Hide the pistol," said Bryant. "I don't have a permit. I just bought it from Dawkins. I don't even know if it works."

"Good evening, Officers," said Evangeline.

"Howdy, gents. My name is Private Douglas Bryant of the West Virginia Volunteers, I just came from guarding the Smithsonian."

"What was that whistling all about?" asked one of the cops.

"The lady here thought those bikers were coming to bother us."

"Bikers scare me." Evangeline smiled sweetly. "But I like horses."

One of the big mounts snorted and banged his iron shoe on the sidewalk.

Bryant said, "It turns out those boys were just stopping for directions."

A cop watched the three bikes going in three directions and said, "Either they don't listen too good or you don't direct too good."

"Don't know about that, sir, " said Bryant, "but I know the way to Sharpsburg in the dark. I'm headin' there now."

"Oh, yeah?" said one of the officers. "For the big show tomorrow? What unit?"

"Well, tonight at the Smithsonian, I wore Yankee blue, but tomorrow—" He reached into the back and pulled out a gray kepi. "—I may play one of Longstreet's boys. They held the Confederate right that afternoon."

"Reinforced by John Bell Hood at the critical moment," said the officer. "Have a good trip. And ma'am, don't be so quick on that whistle."

When they were gone, Bryant said, "It was the accent. That cop was from down Virginia way. His ancestors might have marched with ol' Longstreet."

"If they'd asked me my unit," said Peter, "I'd have said Twentieth Massachusetts."

Bryant laughed. "That would have gotten us all arrested."

. . .

Bryant dropped them at the hotel. As they crossed the sidewalk, Peter got a text from Diana Wilmington:

Missed you at opening. Left before speeches. Can't stand Milbury. And you know about Conlon. Also, getting up early for drive to Antietam. I'm signing books up there for Dawkins. May be on to something with him. And I'm shooting on battlefield with Evangeline.

Peter texted back:

Stay safe. Many factors in play.

Then he said to Evangeline, "Antietam? Did you know you're shooting at Antietam tomorrow?"

"I just found out." She waved her iPhone at him. "Schedule change:

Lincoln Memorial Monday, Antietam tomorrow to capture local color and shoot an interview with Diana. We're supposed to leave first thing."

"Perfect," said Peter. "We'll all go and have another talk with Dawkins."

As they entered the lobby, a big black man rose from a chair in Peacock Alley. At first, his silhouette seemed nothing but threatening. Instinctively, Peter put Evangeline behind him. Then a deep bass voice filled the lobby the way his bulk filled the doorway: "Well, if it ain't my old friends."

Evangeline said, "Now I *know* we're in trouble."

Peter said, "Henry Baxter, what brings you to the Capitol City?"

"I'm hungry for half truths, partial to malarkey, and suffer from a surfeit of cynicism, so I thought I'd come to the city where such things are always in fashion." Henry executed a bow, which wasn't easy with the big belly that hung over his belt.

He was wearing a blue blazer and blue turtleneck, jeans, running shoes. And as he always said, his vital stats were all about fours and forties: sixty-four going on forty-four, six-four, two-forty plus forty, .44 Magnum, licensed as a private detective in four states and the District of Columbia. Fours wild, and Peter was very glad to see him.

Henry straightened, buttoned his blazer over his belly, and said, "I also looked into those boys in that Chrysler 200."

"They were on motorcycles tonight," said Peter.

"In cars or on bikes, they're still trouble. So I decided to drive down and lend a little muscle to No-Pete and the E-Ticket." He used the nicknames he'd given them when they first met in New York. "No-Pete" because Peter hated to be called Pete. "E-Ticket" because that was the best ride at Disneyland, and Henry said that for all her attitude, Evangeline always made it a fun ride, too.

She told the front desk that she would be having another guest sleeping on the pull-down sofa, so they should send up linens and towels.

. . .

Room service from the Willard: twenty-dollar Black Angus burgers all around, along with bottles of Yuengling, steak fries, and at Henry's request, chocolate sundaes.

"Gots to lay off de sundaes, boss"—he slapped his belly—"but jess dis one time mo'."

Evangeline joined him. She did not admit that she had been eating more sundaes of late, especially since the wedding that wasn't.

Peter liked savory. So his dessert was a second beer and a bag of potato chips.

Henry kicked off his shoes and put his feet on the coffee table. "I found a parking spot right on F Street, and tomorrow's Sunday. So I can leave the car all day. But we may be movin' around."

"I am not going on the run," said Evangeline. "I am not going to ground. I am going to Antietam to film tomorrow, then I'm coming back to finish at the Lincoln Memorial on Monday."

Henry said, "I swear, No-Pete, you'd think this gal didn't enjoy your company."

"Yeah," said Peter. "She's giving me a complex."

"Well, after she sees this, she'll think about stickin' close." Henry pulled out his iPad. "That Chrysler 200 was a rental, so the plate didn't give me a lot. But I have some friends who have some face recognition software."

He tapped a few commands, and up popped Mr. Civil War Soul Patch, in a grainy cell phone photo. On the other side of the screen, a database of pictures quickly scrolled through to the same face, without soul patch.

"Harrison M. Keeler," said Henry. "Born, Cincinnati, Ohio, 1960. Educated at Ohio State and Case Western Reserve Law School. Worked in Ohio Attorney General's Office for two years, prosecuting tax fraud, then ran for state rep as a Republican. Lost. Hung a shingle, went into tax law, three years later, ran for state senator as a Democrat. Lost. But he paid his dues and went to Washington with the congressman from his district. Worked as a staffer, more tax policy. When the congressman jumped over to a big K Street lobbying firm, he brought Keeler along."

"So he's another Washington insider?" said Peter.

"He was," said Henry. "But he ain't no mo'."

"At least he's no biker," said Evangeline.

Henry went back to the computer. "He was indicted for mail fraud and obstruction of justice in 2003. A big lobbying scandal."

"What did he do?"

"He was pumping out all kinds of goodies, fancy trips, Redskins tickets and so on, in exchange for political favors."

"That's standard, isn't it?" asked Evangeline.

"Up to a point. But he did a lot more of it and did it better. Never any bribery, but he bought off congressmen and senators with charitable contributions that somehow found their way into political PACs. Made sure congressmen got jobs for nephews on K Street. Did the tit-for-tat dance all across the district. It was money for the pols and fees for the lobbyists and good news for all the clients who come to Washington looking for a government hand."

"Or handout," said Evangeline.

"They don't call lobbyists the fourth branch of the government for nothing," said Peter.

"Pedal to the political metal, baby. That was Keeler. His big rig was just barrelin' down the D.C. highway till it hit a pothole called the House Ethics Committee. He ended up in the middle of a nasty old bipartisan scandal. Two congressmen went down, and so did he. Ended up doing eighteen months in the federal pen. His wife divorced him while he was in. When he got out, he went off the grid. Didn't write a book or try to rehabilitate himself like that other lobbyist, Jack Abramoff. Just disappeared instead."

"But he's back."

"From what my boy in the New York FBI tells me, Harrison M. Keeler made some friends on the inside, bad actors who appreciated his expertise in the tax laws they'd been violatin'. They also liked his general attitude toward the governing structures of our fair republic. When he popped up again, he was running a Web site called KnightsofLiberty.com."

"We should check that out," said Evangeline.

"Yeah, well, they're into survivalist shit, anti-federal stuff, anti-tax, but anti-big-business, too. They use a star on a blue field as their symbol."

"The Bonnie Blue Flag," said Peter, "one of the earliest symbols of Southern resistance. A good song, too."

"Appropriate," said Henry. "He's a rebel, through and through."

"A real RW," said Evangeline.

"What's that?" asked Henry.

"Rightie wacko."

"Honey, when you get that far out, there ain't no right and no left, just a big circle. A man can go so far on the right, he ends up comin' back on the left, or the other way around. Keeler's last bit on his Web site is all about how we should start shootin' bankers who've been sittin' on the bailout money from 2008 and won't lend it. Now, is that a rightie or a lefty or just one pissed-off motherfucker?"

"Is he in trouble now?" asked Peter

"Not now. But he's looked at a few indictments . . . drug traffickin', haulin' guns across state lines. And somebody got killed on his property out in Ohio, and—get this—it was land that some folks say was once owned by the Knights of the Golden Circle."

"Who were they?" asked Evangeline.

"A group of Confederate sympathizers," said Peter. "Founded in 1858. Had big dreams of making the South the power in an empire that included Mexico and the Caribbean. There were cells in all the border states, where they helped Union deserters and committed sabotage. There's even a myth that John Wilkes Booth belonged."

"So I don't like 'em on general principles," said Henry. "Supposedly they buried gold all over the South. Some say they did it so they could keep fighting after Lee surrendered. You can see these treasure maps on all kinds of Web sites. But no one ever found any of this gold. Point is, if you're in touch with these boys, and in competition with them, you need Henry and his big-ass gun."

Evangeline gave Henry a long look, shook her head, and said, "Shit. Just plain shit."

"Ain't it the truth," said Henry. Then he pointed to her sundae. "If you ain't gonna finish that, can I?"

"No." She picked up the plate and scooped the ice cream into her mouth.

Peter's iPhone bonged.

There were two e-mails. The first came from a generic Gmail account.

He read it, then read it aloud: "'It's been said many times in Washington: Follow the money. If you want to know more, meet me tomorrow, alone, 7 A.M., Overland Garage, Nash Street, Rosslyn, spot D32.'"

Evangeline said, "That sounds fishy."

"But interesting." Peter took a sip of beer. "That's the Watergate mantra, 'Follow the money.' And the sender wants to meet in the garage where Woodward and Bernstein met Deep Throat."

Henry clapped his hands together. "Intrigue. I love intrigue."

Evangeline said, "What's the other e-mail?"

It came from Antoine. Peter read it to them: "'*Daily Republican*, 1862: Halsey Hutchinson was accused of murder in August. Allegedly killed niece of NY Congressman Wood, a big Copperhead. Halsey disappeared. I am attaching the news stories. Will keep reading.'"

Peter clicked on the links. While he drank another Yuengling, he read of the bloody scene in the Willard Hotel, of the charges of John Wilkes Booth, and so on.

"Amazing," said Evangeline. "He knew Lincoln *and* Booth."

"It may be a small town today," said Peter. "It was even smaller back then."

There was a note above the next link: "'Here is the last reference to Halsey. It describes a shoot-out on the Aqueduct Bridge, near the site of Key Bridge today: 'The shootist, heavily bearded, wore a brown suit and derby. Detective Joseph Albert McNealy of the War Department detective service, says that the man was dressed just as Halsey Hutchinson had been dressed on the night that he murdered Constance Wood, and he used the same kind of pistol, an Adams pocket revolver.'"

Henry said, "Hey, wait a minute."

"What?"

He looked at his computer again. "Harrison M. Keeler. Middle name, McNealy."

"And Peter," said Evangeline, "that pistol you were holding tonight. Bryant called it an Adams. He bought it from Dawkins."

"That boy back in Boston is a real history detective," said Henry.

Ten

August 1862

Halsey Hutchinson needed a friend.

He was thankful for those he had and for the help they had given, but he needed a friend with power.

It had been four weeks since the murder of Constance Wood.

Her uncles had taken her body home to New York. Benjamin had told the newspapers that he blamed her death on the immorality of a war that would cause even upstanding young men like Halsey Hutchinson to commit murder. Then he and Fernando had gotten on to the business of campaigning for Congress.

Even as Halsey mourned for Constance, he could not imagine how the news had affected his father and sister. He was happy at least that his mother was no longer alive to hear the lies . . . or the truths.

In normal times, he would have turned himself in, hired the best lawyer in the capital, and called on his father to help him clear his name . . . of the Wood murder, at least. The shootings at McDillon's would require a more complicated explanation. But Halsey feared that if he surrendered himself in wartime Washington, he would be dragged to the Old Capitol and forgotten.

He had also read the words "shot while escaping" in the papers. Before District emancipation, it had been the fate of more than one fugitive slave. It had also happened to deserters and to a whoremaster who had been taken as a spy and never even made it to the Old Cap.

So Halsey doubted that a man accused of four murders, also "armed and dangerous," would have much chance.

His carte de visite had quickly appeared on wanted posters across the city. Clerks in every telegraph office had surely been ordered to watch for anyone sending messages to the Hutchinsons of Boston. And a detective had probably been dispatched to intercept all mail arriving at the homes of Halsey's father and sister.

So, he had decided to disappear, at least for the time being.

But to where? As he had joked grimly to himself, when the Lord dropped a man into shit, perhaps he should stay there.

Jubilo's brothers needed help on the wagon, since Jubilo and Jim-Boy had taken better jobs digging fortifications. Hauling night soil was hard work, done best with at least three sets of hands: a hole man, a rope man, and a tub man.

The Freedoms were planning to look for help at the contraband camp on Q Street, where runaways had been gathering ever since the District emancipation.

But on Halsey's first morning with them, the family matriarch, who called herself Mother Freedom, had brought her face close to his, studied, and said, "I do not see a guilty man before me. I see the blue eyes of one who tips his hat to colored men, which he don't have to do, which means he must show respect to all of God's humans, which he don't have to do, which means he's a Godly man, which most men is not. And I am on the side of God. So, the Freedom family will give this Godly man safe lodgin' in the shed out back, which he ain't to leave till dark, and if he do, he ain't to come back till dark. He will repay us by workin' on the wagon."

"Do that mean we don't have to pay him?" Zion—the youngest, tallest, and scrawniest of the brothers—had asked.

"A man does a honest night's work," Mother had answered, "he gets a honest night's pay. We are not slave drivers. But we'll charge him half his pay for lodgin' and food."

Zion had looked Halsey from head to foot. "How do we know we can trust him? How do we know he won't get us all in trouble?"

"We can trust him because I have looked in his eyes," Mother had said. "He won't get us in trouble because he's in too deep himself."

Hallelujah, the oldest brother, nearly as big as Jubilo and more practical than Zion, had said, "This man ain't workin' with us, 'less he work the hole."

"He'll work the hole." Mother Freedom had raised her chin as regally as a queen giving a decree. "He'll be the new 'prentice hole man . . . if that meet with his approval."

"It does," Halsey had answered.

After a short time in the presence of that small but formidable woman, in her little freestanding house on the east edge of the city, with Jesus and Frederick Douglass looking down from engravings above the fireplace, Halsey would have approved no matter what she had asked him to do, even if it meant climbing into the waste hole of a privy and shoveling shit into a bucket so that a man at the top of the hole could lift the bucket and hand it to another man who dumped it into a tub and carried it to a wagon . . . for that is exactly the job she had given him.

But there would be advantages to hiding here.

The Freedoms discouraged visitors with two barking dogs . . . and a powerful stink. They called the lot next to their house the compostin' yard. They dumped the waste there each morning and dutifully covered it with a layer of dirt. Then, while the boys slept through the day, Mother Freedom sold the compost to farmers who hauled it out to Maryland to fertilize their fields. And the neighbors didn't complain, because the Freedoms saw to it that their gardens and corn patches were fertilized for free.

The brothers had Negro night passes, of course, but no one ever checked them, because the police never bothered the soil wagon. It wasn't worth the smell.

So it would be safe work for Halsey, especially if he could somehow pass for a Negro. So he put on gloves, buttoned his collar high, kept his hat pulled low, and let his beard grow. Within a week, it covered most of his face with thick black hair. And to cover the white parts, Mother Freedom gave him a piece of burnt cork.

The first time he blackened his face, she chuckled and said, "Don't you go singin' 'Camptown Races' on us, boy, or we have to put you in the coon show."

"I don't sing . . . anymore."

"No, not with that there croakin' voice you got."

And he had ridden the wagon, worked the hole, and done as he was told. Hallelujah needed to remind him only once to tip his hat to the few white people that passed in the middle of the night.

. . .

But he could not live like this for long. So he waited until his beard was so bushy that only those who had looked into his eyes would recognize him, while those who had glanced at his wanted poster would walk blithely by. Then he tested the day-lit streets.

As the Freedom wagon was rolling toward home one morning, he got off and told the brothers that he would see them at nightfall. He wiped the burnt cork from his face, put a shovel over his shoulder, and walked. He walked with the knowledge that the smell he absorbed at night would keep most people at a distance, including detectives and Provost Guard. He walked all day, as if familiarizing himself again with the city that he had come to know and hate. He even walked to Lafayette Park, sat on a bench, read a newspaper, and watched for McNealy.

But McNealy never came.

As for the news in the paper . . . there was none of emancipation, as yet, perhaps because there had been no Union victories, as yet. And because there had been no news of emancipation, the Abolitionists had continued to hammer at Lincoln.

For a week, Halsey had been following the exchanges between the president and Horace Greeley of the *New York Tribune*.

Greeley had written an open letter to the president called "The Prayer of Twenty Millions." It was the prayer of emancipation.

Lincoln had responded with an open letter of his own, in which he said, "If I could save the Union without freeing *any* slave I would do it, and if I could save it by freeing *all* the slaves I would do it; and if I could save it by freeing some and leaving others alone I would also do that."

Halsey had heard echoes of his conversation with Lincoln on the *Ariel*. And he had wondered what the Abolitionists would say if they knew that as far back as the Seven Days, Lincoln had been composing a document that would change everything.

Halsey had begun the war as a Unionist without much commitment one way or the other to Abolition. In Boston, he had known few freedmen and did not mix with the Abolitionist crowd. In the regiment, he had run with officers who worried less about the Negro than about the social standing of the other officers.

But in Washington, he had met Negroes of character, industry, faith, and goodness of heart, people who wanted no more for their families than any white man did for his. And he had come to understand that the white man's greatest sin was in seeing these people at best as inferiors and at worst as a species of property.

This war, Mother Freedom had told him, was to be the expiation of that sin.

Expiation. A three-dollar word, thought Halsey. But Mother Freedom used such words and used them well.

She had learned to read in a Quaker school. Now she read widely and kept a collection of books in a little case beside the fireplace: the Bible, Frederick Douglass's *Autobiography of a Slave, Uncle Tom's Cabin, Oliver Twist,* which she read to her sons to show them that "not only colored folks had hard lives," and *Fort Lafayette* by "Ben Wood, the congress-man, a book to tell us what the other side thinks of us."

She even subscribed to the *Liberator,* "that fine Abolition paper by that up-north Boston man, Mr. Garrison." And when the August 22 edition arrived in the mail, she sat Halsey down to discuss it, because it contained reports on Lincoln's open letter and on another controversy:

Two weeks earlier, Lincoln had invited a delegation of freed slaves to the White House. Mother had proclaimed it her proudest moment, "the first time that Negroes ever went into the White House by the front door without holding it first for the white folk."

But the *Liberator* now reported what Lincoln had said to those freed slaves: He had begun by admitting that slavery was the greatest wrong ever inflicted on a people. Then he had added, "But when you cease to be slaves, you are yet far removed from being placed on an equality with the white race. On this broad continent, not a single man of your race is made the equal of a single man of ours. Would it not be better if we separated?" Then he had asked those freed slaves, men raised up in American bondage who had since tasted American liberty, if they would consider leading a Negro migration to Africa or Central America.

Mother Freedom read this story aloud to Halsey, took off her reading glasses, and shook the paper at him. "This is the first time I am angry with Mr. Lincoln."

So were the Abolitionists. In the *Liberator,* William Lloyd Garrison took Lincoln sternly to task, saying that the nation's four million slaves were "as much the natives of this country as any of their oppressors." And they were entitled to live here and "die in the course of nature."

"Your Mr. Garrison speaks truth," Mother said.

"I agree," Halsey answered. "Lincoln's wrong. And that's not a thing that I say often."

But Halsey was left wondering later, in his little shit-smelling shed, what *Lincoln's* game was.

Did he believe his own words? Or was he simply trying to soften the blow of emancipation, which would anger many Northerners and hurt the party in the fall elections? Was he preparing Americans, before revealing in his proclamation the cold military logic and sure moral rectitude of freeing the slaves? Or was he simply the man he had described to Halsey months before, nervously walking a rail fence between two fields, one filled with furious Abolitionists and the other with rabid Negro-haters of every political stripe from Secessionist to Copperhead.

Halsey did not know, but he decided that if he needed a friend, he should go straight to the most powerful man he knew.

Being "armed and dangerous," he wouldn't be able to stroll into the White House. And if he attempted to sneak into the president's cottage at night, he might be shot by some insomniac veteran who was armed and dangerous, too. So one morning, he cleaned the cork off his face, jumped off the wagon, and headed for Vermont Avenue.

. . .

Each day, the president rode down the Seventh Street Turnpike from the Soldiers' Home, took Rhode Island Avenue to Iowa Circle, picked up Vermont and rode on to the White House, a journey of three miles that he usually made on horseback, alone. Sometimes young Tad rode along on a pony that went with tiny mincing steps to keep up. And sometimes, Lincoln rode in his carriage with his secretary, John Hay.

But he would always pass between seven and nine, so Halsey got there early on the Thursday morning of August 28. He picked a quiet spot in the block between N and M Streets. Then he leaned on a lamppost and opened a newspaper.

The day was clear and hot. August offered no more mercy than July.

And according to the paper, Robert E. Lee was offering no mercy, either.

As Halsey read, he read his own understanding of events into the story:

Annoyed with McClellan's perpetual "slows" and perhaps growing more distrustful of the general since Halsey's last report, Lincoln had created another army out of troops that McClellan had expected to reinforce him. It was called the Army of Virginia, General Pope commanding.

And like a man who knows that some barking dogs will never bite, Robert E. Lee knew that McClellan would never attack his flank if he turned on Pope. So he did.

After weeks of maneuvering and skirmishing, the Army of Virginia was now facing a second battle in the railhead town of Manassas, along the banks of Bull Run.

McClellan, ordered to pull out of Harrison's Landing and bring his army north in support of Pope, had obeyed . . . but slowly.

Meanwhile, Stonewall Jackson's "foot cavalry," the fastest-moving infantry on earth, had slipped around Pope and gotten into the Federal supplies at Manassas. They had eaten all they could gobble, taken as much as they could carry, and burned the rest.

As the breeze carried the smoke of their fires thirty miles to Washington, the paper proclaimed with rare understatement that tension was building in the capital.

Tension was building in Halsey, too, as he looked up and saw a cloud of dust. People on the street turned their heads. Somebody waved. And there, rounding Iowa Circle, came the tall man in the tall stovepipe hat.

In an instant, Halsey's hopes rose, then sank.

Little Tad was not riding with the president. A detachment of cavalry was. Lincoln's advisors had been urging him to accept protection on his commute, and with the rebel army so close, he had.

Lincoln glanced at Halsey as he passed, but no recognition registered on the president's face. He simply rode on and the cavalry thundered after, their huge mounts kicking up stones and causing the ground to shake.

Halsey knew right then that he would never get closer than that to the president.

But he wondered, as he watched Lincoln canter down the avenue, how much the president knew about the Copperheads and the Sons of

Liberty and the Knights of the Golden Circle, all dreaming of Northern defeat, all hoping to put McClellan in the White House, all trying to fuel the "fire in the rear."

And what of his musings in the daybook? Could they still hurt Lincoln?

There had been talk of the daybook in the barn, but still it had not surfaced.

If the looming battle produced a victory that led to an emancipation decree, it would be better if the daybook was in the hands of a friend, no matter what it said.

Halsey decided that he still had to find that daybook. With it, he might clear his name of the McDillon killings at least . . . or transform the shooting of three gambling-hell thugs into the act of political and personal loyalty it was, rather than the cold-blooded act of vengeance depicted in the press.

Finding it would be *his* expiation.

. . .

But he still needed a friend, perhaps one more accessible than the president, perhaps Major Eckert, who walked from the National Hotel to the War Department at ten minutes to seven each morning. So the next day, Halsey leaned against a storefront on Pennsylvania Avenue, picked up another paper from the street, waited, and read:

MOVEMENT TOWARD MANASSAS was the headline.

Details were wanting, of course. Battlefield details were always wanting, even after the battles were over. And rebel cavalry units were good at cutting telegraph lines. But this much the city knew: General Pope and his army were preparing to engage.

Meanwhile, "McClellan chafes in Alexandria. Of his five corps, roughly twenty thousand men in each, two remain on the Peninsula. Fifth Corps has gone to reinforce Pope. Sixth has been ordered to march. And Second, currently spread around the District forts, may also be summoned."

Halsey's Twentieth was in Second Corps. That was where he truly wished to be, marching with friends against an enemy he could see. Instead, he waited till seven thirty. Then he wondered if Eckert would be coming at all. With a battle looming, Lincoln had probably spent the night at the War Department, so Eckert would have done the same.

Halsey could imagine the tension in the telegraph office as the messages clattered back and forth, as the president paced, as the secretary scowled, as Homer Bates nervously decoded and the president read word by word over his shoulder.

If Halsey could not be with the Twentieth, he wished that he were back in that office. But here he stood like a beggar, hoping to clear his name, and if he lacked powerful friends, he still needed observant friends. So he folded the paper and walked toward the National.

. . .

"Yes, sir, these is some dirty boots, mister. What you been doin'? Muckin' a stable or somethin'?" Noah Bone pulled out two heavy-duty brushes and went to work.

Halsey said, "I don't have the money to pay you."

Noah's hands stopped.

Halsey waited. Did Noah recognize the voice or was he simply angry? If it was one, he would go right back to polishing. If the other, he might throw Halsey off the chair.

Noah's hands started moving again, and he whispered, "You got no right to come back here. That detective come and ask about you every day for two damn weeks."

"What did he ask?"

"Who your friends are . . . all your friends . . . white and black."

"What did you say?"

"I say I don't know many Harvard-goin' white men who needs colored friends—and I don't—and that's all I know."

Halsey looked out at Pennsylvania, at a jangle of wagons and barouches and horses. If there was tension in the air, he could not feel it in the street, but he could feel it in Noah Bone. He said, "You shine Major Eckert's shoes, don't you?"

"I shine any man's shoes who pay my price. I shine yours. I shine your boss's."

"He's not my boss. He's my superior officer . . . and my friend."

"Well, maybe he's your superior officer, but he ain't your friend no more."

Halsey slumped a bit in the chair. "What has he said?"

"The mornin' after it all happen, whilst I'se shinin' his shoes, he's sighin' over what he's readin' in the paper, and then he just come out with it, 'cause he know I shine your shoes, too. He come out with how bad he feel, how be . . . be . . . be-*trayed*."

"What did you say?"

"Nothin'. 'Cause Mr. Booth come up and sit next to him and they start talkin'."

"What did Booth say?"

"What he say in the paper, 'bout you wantin' a map of Squeaker's . . . 'bout you and Miss Constance in the hotel the day 'fore you—" He caught himself. "—the day 'fore she was killed . . .'bout all kinds of things I don't rightly want to hear 'bout, knowin' that me and my boys has helped you."

Halsey said, "Noah . . . I didn't kill her."

Noah looked up. "I don't care. Do you know what they do to me if they think I'se talkin' to you?"

"I need time to make this right. If you can't help me, don't turn on me."

Noah spit on Halsey boots and said, "I ain't a fool, but I ain't a snitch, neither."

"Then . . . can I call on you or your sons if I need your help?"

Noah said nothing. He just buffed until Halsey's shit-shoveling boots were shiny and clean. Then he threw the buffing rag over his shoulder and stepped back.

Halsey climbed down and pretended to put a coin into Noah's hand. He said, "I won't bother you again."

And Noah said, "Are you still for Mr. Lincoln and agin' those agin' him?"

"More than ever."

"Then I'se for you, even if they's a reward on you. My boys, too."

"Thank you." Halsey turned and almost bumped into John Wilkes Booth, just coming out of the hotel.

Booth jumped aside, then looked into Halsey's face.

Would the bushy beard and laborer's rags deceive a man who made his living in disguise, playing other people? Halsey tugged at the brim of his hat and grunted.

Booth pulled out a handkerchief, brought it to his nose, and stepped around Halsey.

As Halsey took to the sidewalk, he heard Booth, say. "Which chair did that fellow sit in, boy? I'll have the other. Wearin' rags and spit-shined boots . . . takes all kinds, boy."

Noah said, "I shine any man's shoes who pay my price, sir, Abolitionist, Union Democrat, or outright Secesh . . . no matter how bad they smell."

Booth said, "A wise philosophy, especially for a darkie."

.   .   .

Now that the encounter with Booth had proved how truly invisible he was, Halsey relaxed and just walked. He liked the steady step, the rhythm of movement, the awareness off the world around him as if he were, to quote Emerson, the transparent eye, looking, experiencing, absorbing.

He visited all the places where he had met in plain sight with Mc-Nealy: the City Wharves, the Star Saloon, the Center Market. He even went along B Street, between the south edge of the President's Park and the Washington Canal. Looking toward the White House, he saw the familiar black-frocked figure on the south lawn, peering through a brass telescope at the distant smoke of battle.

But Halsey saw McNealy nowhere.

And nowhere could the transparent eye find an answer to his hardest question: How had a young man so careful, so judicious, so responsible, ended up as a fugitive sneaking around a city by day and shoveling shit by night?

Toward suppertime, he worked his way back to Ryan's in the East Capitol neighborhood where congressmen and senators boarded in session, where office seekers, contractors, and confidence men stayed year-round. Here the privies filled fast, literally and figuratively.

Halsey guessed that if McNealy came home, it would be around now, for a hot meal. So he waited two hours in the shadow of an old elm. The aroma of a boarding house stew wafted into the street and made Halsey's mouth water.

But McNealy never went in or came out. And in a way Halsey was glad, because like a dog that stalked a bull, he did not know what he would do if he caught his quarry.

Instead he made mental notes of everything about the house and grounds. The privies stood next to the stable, opposite the chicken coop. They had windows on the sides for ventilation and exterior latches. And Halsey remembered something McNealy had said, about getting up every morning at four. He also remembered that the Freedoms would be working three blocks away that very night.

II.

By 3:30 A.M., they had emptied two privies on Seventh near East Capitol. The wagon was so full, said Hallelujah, they'd have to dump it before the last job.

Halsey asked how long that would take.

"Home and back," said Hallelujah, "'bout a hour."

That was what Halsey was hoping to hear. He told them that he would see them at four thirty at the last job, another address on East Capitol.

"Y'all stay out of trouble," said Zion, "or you be gettin' us in it."

Halsey watched the wagon roll north and wondered again if he could trust Zion. He kept looking for signs of treachery from the youngest brother.

How easy it would be to catch Halsey in an outhouse hole with nowhere to run. And why not? The Freedoms owed him nothing. He owed them everything. But they must have known that harboring a fugitive was a crime, so perhaps he was safe.

He followed East Capitol until he came to the little alley beside Ryan's boardinghouse. He carried his shovel over his shoulder and his Adams .31 in his belt.

He held a slip of paper to the streetlamp so that if someone happened to peer out, they would think he was simply checking the address of his next job. Then he went up the alley and around to the back. There came a flutter of clucking in the henhouse, which meant that the rooster would start making a racket soon. A horse snorted in the stable.

Halsey noticed a lantern flickering to life in a room at the rear of the house. Then the back door opened. He ducked behind the privies as a slender woman with a single long braid of hair came out. She wore a white robe and carried a chamberpot. She opened the door of the privy, splashed something down the hole, and went back inside.

The hens fussed a bit more. He knew he could not stay long, because once the rooster began crowing, people would be awake in the houses all around.

Then the back door of the boardinghouse opened again.

Halsey saw the silhouette he had been waiting for: McNealy, almost true to his word, rising at ten past four, visiting the privy.

Halsey came around to the side, peered in, saw McNealy, sitting in his shirtsleeves, head down, chin on hands. He pushed his pistol through the window and pressed it to the side of McNealy's neck. "Don't move a muscle, not even your asshole."

McNealy said, "Hutchinson?"

Halsey stayed back so that McNealy could not see his face. "If you raise your voice, I'll blow your brains out. And you know that this gun doesn't make much noise in a closed space."

"How would I know that?"

"You heard it at Squeaker's, when you followed me and found the day-book."

"I didn't find it."

"I don't believe you."

"I don't have it."

"Then who does?"

Something scurried along the path in front of the outhouse: a rat. It glanced up at Halsey, then shot across the yard toward the chicken coop.

Halsey said to McNealy. "Who has it?"

"Harriet Dunbar, or Doc Wiggins, or Eye Patch Hunter and that weasel Skeeter."

"I don't believe you," said Halsey.

"I don't care. And I've been wondering . . . how did you ever find us that night?"

Halsey pressed the gun harder. "I ask the questions, Detective. I ask and you answer. You follow?"

McNealy laughed but said nothing.

Halsey repeated, "You follow?"

"I follow."

There was a small victory, but Halsey told himself not to relax. His hand and the gun were inside the little window, and he was outside. He was holding the pistol tight around the grip, finger twitching on the trigger. It was no way to win a shooting contest. But he couldn't miss, even if he jerked the trigger like a woman. So he gripped tight and said, "That night . . . you set me up."

"When I told you to meet me at the C&O Canal?"

"You told the Provost Guard to go there, too."

"They went to break up an underground railway, but not for darkies. For deserters. Wiggins owns a string of canal boats. Puts the deserters on them at night, sends them off. Nobody ever sees them again. I learned about it at their meetings. I ordered the raid on a night when we were meeting, so they wouldn't suspect me."

"I don't believe you."

"I just told you, Lieutenant. I don't care."

"Who killed her?"

"It's your face on the wanted posters."

Halsey jammed the gun harder against McNealy's neck.

"Whoever killed her didn't want her spreading what she knew about McClellan's deepest thoughts, I'd bet."

"You'd *bet*? You don't know?"

McNealy said, "It could have been her uncles. It could have been Doc Wiggins."

"What about these Knights of the Golden Circle? What's their game?"

"That's what I'm trying to find out."

"Do they know you work for the War Department?"

"They think I'm a double agent."

"How did you convince them of that?"

"I didn't. *You* did."

"*Me?*" Halsey almost lowered the gun.

"Why do you think we always met in plain sight?"

Halsey answered, "Because people don't see what's right in front of them."

"Because it was easier for them to see us. I told them you were my source in the War Department. But you damn near blew it, sneakin' around outside, peepin' in the window like some slave catcher lookin' for runaways."

Halsey had been taught in law school never to ask a question to which he did not already know the answer. But this witness kept shocking him. He said, "Why was Mrs. Dunbar in the ladies' parlor at the Willard the night that Constance was murdered? And why was that Skeeter on the stairs?"

"Skeeter went up to snatch the McClellan notes from Constance's room while Mrs. Dunbar kept her busy. They didn't want the world to know their favorite general thinks God smiles on his defeats."

The rat scuttled back with something in its mouth. An egg?

"In a little while," said McNealy, "you'll smell bacon, when Mrs. Ryan starts cookin' my breakfast. I need to go. So let me ask you a question. . . . What's *your* game?"

"I want that daybook."

"I can help you get it." McNealy turned his head, as if he was sure that Halsey would not shoot now. "Or *you* can help *me*."

"*I* help *you*? How?"

.   .   .

McNealy predicted that whether the Federal troops won or lost the battle thirty miles away, there would come a moment when chaos would wash over the city and its bridges.

The army controlled travel on all the bridges. The Long Bridge spanned a mile from Maryland Avenue to Alexandria. The flat Aqueduct Bridge crossed at Georgetown. It had once been an actual aqueduct, allowing canal boats to pass, but the army had drained it and planked it so that troops could use it. And the Chain Bridge went over the thin, rocky water a mile upstream.

Artillery covered the Virginia approaches to each bridge. And the Provost Guard checked passes. Everyone needed a pass, from Jubilo and Jim-Boy to General McClellan himself.

But in a crisis, the flow of people became too great, and the need to move them superseded the need for security. And McNealy expected that by afternoon, there would be a crisis.

At worst, it would be the panicked flood of soldiers and civilians fleeing into the city ahead of the victorious rebels.

At best, it would be a surge of wagons and people rushing out to bring the wounded home, because the ambulances of the Medical Corps were scattered from the Peninsula to Washington, and most of the medical supplies that should have been with General Pope's army were sitting in the District quartermaster depot.

"Either way, they'll throw the bridges open, and spies and traitors and contraband niggers'll cross like it was market day in peacetime. A Copperhead holding a valuable daybook just might see a chance to get to the other side in all that confusion."

"Why?" asked Halsey.

"Because the sound of artillery gets everyone nerved up . . . Knights of the Golden Circle, female spies, even Peace Democrats. They've watched Lincoln strip McClellan down to a sergeant's guard and a tent. So they called a meeting last night to do what they can to help him, or they won't have anyone to beat Lincoln."

"Do *you* want to make McClellan president?"

"I told you . . . I just want this damn war to end. No more dead brothers, no more widowed wives and cryin' babies sufferin' through the winter on some Ohio dirt farm."

"What do you want from me?"

"Watch the Aqueduct Bridge. I'll watch the Long Bridge. If you see any of them cross—Hunter, Mrs. Dunbar, fat Wiggins—see where they go. They may try to bring the daybook to McClellan's camp. He has officers on his staff who have Copperhead instincts. And if you can get your hands on the daybook along the way . . ."

"Don't you have other spies?"

"I do, but you're here, and you have a motive. Bring the daybook back, we'll talk you out of the McDillon murders and find a way to pin the Constance Wood killing on Skeeter. I expect he's the one who did it anyway."

"And what if you find it?"

"You swap me Squeaker's ledger for it. I know you have the ledger, even if you say you don't. A book of gambling debts, liquor bills, girl bills, boy bills. That could have some value."

"It could," said Halsey. He did not add that there was no way he could get to the ledger because it was hidden in his desk in the telegraph office. Instead he asked, "How do I know I can trust you?"

"You don't. But like I told you, I may be your only friend."

.   .   .

Later, on the back of the night soil wagon, Halsey decided to take Mc-Nealy's bait, but he would not swallow the hook. He would nibble, have a meal, and move on. He would trust nothing that McNealy said.

And if he could not get his hands on the president's daybook, he would try to get out of the District altogether. He might cross into Virginia, or move north through Georgetown, steal a horse, and start riding. If he could slip through the ring of forts, he would find easy going toward Baltimore, then perhaps the train to New York.

So he slept until the late-afternoon meal that Mother always cooked on Saturdays.

Jubilo and Jim-Boy had ended work early and told of what they had seen on their walk home: Secretary Stanton had put out a call for volunteer nurses and doctors, and Washingtonians had answered. Stanton had also asked them to bring medical supplies, including painkillers.

"They's all reportin' to the Surgeon General," said Jubilo. "Right there at Fifteenth and F. So they's mobs just millin' and pushin' and shoutin', all the way down to Pennsylvania and all the way over to Fourteenth. And plenty of 'em brung the kind of painkillers that make a man drunk to make him painless."

"They all got a sniff of winnin' in their snoots," said Jim-Boy. "So they all wants to be in on the back-slappin' and boozin'."

"A colored man could go plumb crazy gettin' through a crowd like that, tippin' his hat ever' which way," added Jubilo.

Jim-Boy looked at Halsey. "And not a one of 'em tip back."

Bad manners, thought Halsey . . . and chaos. Time for him to go.

So he finished Mother Freedom's pig's-foot stew. Then he went to the shed and put on the trousers of his brown suit. They had shrunk some after their soaking in that thunderstorm, but they would do. He combed his beard but did not trim it. He put brass-rimmed reading glasses on the tip of his nose for effect. He bundled his things, shouldered his holster, holstered his pistol, and put on the suit jacket.

Then he looked around the little shed, at the dirt floor, at the sunlight poking through the cracks in the barn board, at the burlap mattress stuffed with hay. And he thanked God for the simple human comfort he had known here, for a place to sleep, work to do, food to eat, and friendship.

He closed the door and went back into the little house. Jim-Boy had gone off, and the Freedom brothers were all napping with full bellies, but Mother was sitting in a shaft of late-day sunshine, darning socks.

She looked up. "You leavin'?"

"It's time." He knelt by her chair and took her hand. "I want to thank you."

"I do what the Lord commands, since the day my Maryland master heard the Quaker call and repented of his evil, repented that he beat my mama from the time she was little, cuffed her so hard round the ears, she grew up deaf, repented of all his sins, all the livelong day, and part of re-pentin' meant drivin' my mama and me into the city one mornin' and droppin' us right in front of the Center Market. I was ten, maybe. I asked my mama what this meant.

"She said, 'Freedom, Molly, honey.' That's my real name, Molly, Molly Blodgett, Blodgett bein' the name of that master."

"Freedom," said Halsey, "a fine feeling."

"Freedom? It made my mama scared is what it done. Then we met some good white Quaker folks. They helped us, and we got on. I've now lived fifty-four years and I tell you, I been slave and I been free, and I rather live right next to a smelly old compostin' yard as a free woman than slave for a king in golden palace.

"And I made me a vow that I would do what I could so's others could taste this sweet honey. Since then, that shed has hidden many a runaway dreamin' of freedom. And the mornin' when you come here, you had the same scared look and the same innocent eye. So I made you my first white runaway. You are a man set on a righteous path, and you are dreamin' of freedom, too. I hope you find it."

And Halsey gave the old black woman a hug. He did not think about it at that moment, but she was the first Negro he had ever embraced.

Then the door to one of the bedrooms opened and Zion peered out. Halsey's eyes met his. Did he look disappointed? Suspicious?

"Y'all leavin'?"

Halsey straightened up and nodded.

Zion said, "Good. I ain't never felt too com-fable with you around."

Mother said, "Now, Zion—"

Zion kept his eyes on Halsey. "And you ain't never trusted me, neither."

"That's not true," answered Halsey.

"I seen the way you look at me," said Zion. "Like you was 'fraid I'd turn y'all in for the re-ward."

Mother Freedom said to Halsey, "Were you worried about that?"

"A man in my position worries about everything," said Halsey.

"Remember the word of the Lord in Matthew," said Mother. "'Who of you by worryin' can add a single hour to his life?'"

"If you're leavin'," said Zion. "I'll give you a ride."

Halsey felt the suspicion jump. "I thank you for the favor, but—"

Zion rose up to his full height. He was as skinny as one of his own shovel handles but almost as tall as Lincoln. And he was angry. He was always angry. Halsey accounted his anger as something normal for a Negro whose station in life was in a privy, late at night, looked down upon by those who would never do such labor themselves. But that did not mean that Halsey trusted him.

"I ain't doin' you a favor," he said. "I'm doin' us a favor."

"That's right," said Mother. "We made us a rule that you never come in or go out 'cept in the dark. We done it for a reason."

"Folks see a white man in a brown suit and bowler hat walkin' out of here," said Zion, "they get suspicious."

.   .   .

Zion took him in the "clean-haulin' wagon." It was covered, and had canvas sides and padded seats, so that Halsey could ride in the back and no one would see him. Zion said he would go as far as Pennsylvania and Seventh. "But I ain't drivin' nowhere near where they's white men drinkin' too much."

Then they headed west on Maryland Avenue toward the Capitol.

Halsey did not like this fix at all. He considered sliding out the back and dropping off. But there was too much traffic.

After fifteen minutes of rocking and jostling through the ruts, Zion stopped the wagon, leaned in, and said, "We comin' up to the Capitol now. We can roll down Pennsylvania and dump you."

"Good."

Then Zion smiled at Halsey for the first time. "Course, I could make a name for myself if I turn south for half a block."

The Old Capitol was half a block south. Halsey did not think the joke was funny. He did not even think it was a joke. So he put his hand around his pistol.

Zion knew he had it, because Halsey always had it. Zion had even commented on how pretty it was, on how much he would like to have a little Adams pistol just like it. Perhaps this was the moment that Zion had arranged to get the pistol and the reward, too, because suddenly the ground began to shake.

Halsey looked out the back and saw a dozen Provost Cavalry riding up.

So, Zion was doing it here, well away from his home, with the fugitive dressed in the same clothes he had been wearing the night he was framed. Far better to deliver him to the Provost Guard right in front of the Old Cap than to bring them to the compost lot while Halsey slept . . . or to a customer's hole while Halsey shoveled.

Halsey slipped the gun from his pocket and was about to put it against Zion's spine when the Negro leaned in and said, "Hunker down. They's a big square of canvas in the corner. Pull it on up over your head. I see if I can talk us clear."

Should he trust Zion . . . or shoot him?

"Go on," whispered Zion. "There ain't no shit on it. Pull it on up over your damn head, or we both be in jail."

Halsey had no choice. The Provost Cavalry was almost on them. He covered himself, and Zion snapped at the reins.

The captain of the guard said, "Hey, boy, where do you think you're goin'?"

"Good afternoon, suh," said Zion in a tone so subservient that Halsey thought it was someone else.

"What's in that wagon, boy?"

Zion said, "Nothin', suh . . . yet. I'se jess headin' on down the market. Doin' my Saturday shoppin'. Mama cooks beans for the church supper on Sunday nights. I gots to buy the mo-lasses."

Two of the soldiers laughed and said the word as Zion had said it: "*Mo*-lasses."

"For the church supper?" said the captain skeptically.

"I got the call to be a good Baptist, suh, and the bestest part's the church supper."

"Don't be funny with me, nigger. The Provost Marshal has called for all wagons in the city to bring medical supplies to the front."

"The front?" The bottom fell out of Zion's voice.

Through a hole in the canvas, Halsey saw a mounted soldier peer into the back of the wagon. He held his breath so the canvas would not move.

The officer asked for Zion's name and for the papers to prove it. Zion said he could show a Negro night pass.

After a rustling of paper, the captain growled, "This says you're a shit man. You haul shit in this wagon?"

"We . . . ah . . . we likes to call it night soil, suh."

"Do you haul *shit* in this, nigger?"

"I clean the wagon every Sat'day mornin'. Scrub it out good, but I don't know that y'all want to be haulin' no medicine in it."

Apparently, the captain agreed, because a moment later, he shouted, "Come on!"

The sound of the hooves receded. Then the canvas was flipping off Halsey's face and Zion was looking down at him. "*Now* do you trust me?"

"I never doubted you."

"Then put away your pretty pistol."

After a short ride along Pennsylvania, Zion pulled up in front of the Center Market and jumped down. Then he stuck his head back into the wagon. "I'm goin' in to buy some *mo*-lasses. You wait five minutes, then you slip off."

"Thank you, Brother Zion." Halsey offered his hand.

Zion said, "You know all them times you look at me like you thinkin' that I was thinkin' 'bout turnin' you in?"

Halsey nodded.

"I was."

And Halsey laughed for the first time in weeks.

. . .

Chaos was the word as Halsey approached the Willard. The whole block, over to the Treasury and up to F Street, was jammed with ambulances, wagons, shouting cavalry officers, soldiers, men with satchels, men with flasks, men with women from the south side of the street, and a few women who had actually come to do some nursing.

A train of wagons and ambulances was lining up on Fourteenth. An officer was shouting that there would be another train of private conveyances lining up soon on Fifteenth. One row of ambulances had already left for the Long Bridge. Others would go by way of the Aqueduct Bridge and head south to the Columbia Turnpike, then west for Manassas.

Halsey pushed his way through the crowd, avoiding eye contact and conversation. He would trust no one. He would trust nothing that McNealy had said. He knew that McNealy might be using him. So he had made a plan and a promise to himself that he would not be caught in any man's web. He would try instead to spin one of his own. So he hurried to Lafayette Square, then went two blocks north to Harriet Dunbar's house.

He knocked on the door and when the black butler appeared, he asked if this was the home of Mr.—he made up a name—Dolan. The butler was about to speak when Mrs. Dunbar scurried to the door and said, "Who is it?"

"This gent's lookin' for a man named Dolan."

She glared at him.

He kept his hat on his head. Perhaps she would not recognize him.

She said, "No one around here by that name."

"My apologies, ma'am." Halsey spoke as Cousin John had, with a mock British accent and fake formality. As he went off the stoop, he felt her eyes boring into his back.

At least she was at home. He would watch for her on the bridge.

Then he made for the Bigsby house on Pennsylvania.

Mrs. Stetson, the colored maid, answered the door.

He tipped his hat and asked for Dr. Wiggins, once more with the

British cast to his Boston accent, which made him sound rather British to begin with.

Mrs. Stetson said, "Doc Wiggins lives next door."

"Would you know if he happens to be at home?"

"I wouldn't."

Halsey tipped his hat. "My apologies."

Mrs. Stetson looked back into the house, then said, "Hey, mister?"

Halsey stopped. Had he pushed too far?

She whispered, "Doc Wiggins is up to no good."

"I'm afraid I don't know what you mean."

"Yes, you do. And after the lightnin'-strike night, I tried listenin' to their talk in the barn. I listen from the privy. Far as I can figure, they want to keep my people slaves forever. So, no, Doc Wiggins is not at home. But you watch out for him. I seen him leave a bit ago with the eye patch–wearin' man and the one they call Skeeter."

"Did you ever hear them talk about something called a daybook?"

"Last night. I heard them and the lady argue on what to do with it."

"Thank you. And . . . how long did it take for you to recognize me?"

"Low, croakin' voice like that, it's hard to forget. You be careful."

. . .

Evening was coming on. The light was fading as Halsey came up to M Street and followed it across Rock Creek, then passed the Union Hotel Hospital.

A dozen men were lounging out front, watching a cavalry guard approach a wagon and announce that they were confiscating it by order of the Secretary of War.

The driver started to complain.

One of the soldiers on the stoop spit tobacco and shouted, "Don't you know there's a war goin', mister? Get out and walk!"

The others all laughed, and a few applauded.

And then . . . Halsey saw her. His heart leaped to his throat, which was good because it kept him from calling her name.

Samantha had come back. She stepped to the front door and rang the supper bell. Then she turned and was gone.

He stood there for five minutes, hoping that she would come out again, wondering if he should go in and know the pleasure of her company once more before he was hauled away. But he reminded himself that if he persevered this night, he would be able to send her the letter he carried in his jacket, next to her carte de visite:

Dear Samantha,

I hope that this finds you well and that the Lord in his mercy has brought comfort to your father, whether he remains among the living or has passed to his reward. I continue my efforts to clear my name. I may not be innocent of the hurt I caused you, but I am innocent of other things. I now hold a document that may absolve me of certain transgressions. Please tell my father and sister, in confidence, of this letter. Knowledge of my existence will come as a tonic to them both. I am deeply sorry for hurting you. I will not deny that my feelings for Constance were strong, but so are they for you. If the Lord gives us the opportunity to meet again, I will express them in person and hope that you will hear them.

Then he reminded himself that it had been Skeeter watching Samantha that evening on the bridge. And Skeeter—or Hunter—was probably still watching her, watching for Halsey. And those men murdered women. All the more reason to persevere.

So Halsey turned and headed for the Aqueduct Bridge.

He had not gone far before he saw Doc Wiggins stepping out of a house on the towpath, right by the first lock. The doctor was carrying his bag. Had he just seen a patient? Or was he still running his safe house for deserters, even after a raid from the Provosts?

Could that be? Or had McNealy lied about the raid? Halsey reminded himself of his resolve not to trust a word McNealy said.

The doctor climbed into his carriage and put the bag on the floor at his feet. His Negro driver called to the horse, and the carriage started to roll along the towpath.

Halsey sidestepped and dodged and hurried to keep up.

Presently, the carriage arrived at the guardhouse by the bridge. Men and women were pouring across, and guards were waving most of them along, though here and there, they would stop a Negro or a pretty girl. Not-so-random searches seemed the order of the day, and high spirits, too, because reports from the battlefield had it that the Federal troops were driving Stonewall.

This time, people were saying, Bull Run would be different.

Doc Wiggins simply held up his bag to pass.

Halsey watched it dangle ostentatiously in front of the guards, like a symbol of rank or professional honor. The guards saluted. The doctor returned it to the spot between his feet. And Halsey decided that if he were a smuggler looking to spirit a presidential daybook out of the city, he could think of no place better to hide it than a doctor's bag.

Halsey walked onto the bridge as if he owned it, tipped his hat to the guards, and kept going. And suddenly, he felt a sense of freedom. He was out from the trees, away from the buildings of the city, out under the broad darkening sky. And he was taking action.

He moved quickly, but the carriage was picking up speed.

The Negro driver was shouting ahead of him at the white people on the bridge. "Gangway! Doctor comin'! Doctor comin' to help the troops. Gangway! Gangway!"

And the hooves of the horse set up a staccato *clip-clop, clip-clop*, like a melody above the baseline scuffling and stomping of all the feet crossing the wooden bridge.

Halsey knew that if he did not move quickly, his chance would pass. So he broke into a trot, then came up on the side of the carriage and leaped aboard.

"What is this?" said Dr. Wiggins.

The driver turned. "Hey, there!"

Halsey rammed the pistol into the doctor's side. "Tell him to keep driving."

"Whoever you are, you're a dead man," said the doctor.

"Tell him."

Clip-clop, clip-clop, clip-clop.

"Keep goin'," said the doctor to his driver. "Now, what do you want?"

"You need a talking-to, Doctor."

"A talking-to?"

"Isn't that what you said about Congressman Wood's niece?"

Wiggins eyes narrowed. "Who are you?"

"You know right well."

The doctor looked over his shoulder.

Halsey said, "Don't be looking for help. Just open your bag."

"My bag?"

"Open it!"

Doc Wiggins looked over his shoulder again.

Now Halsey saw why.

Instead of trapping the doctor, Halsey had trapped himself.

Hunter and Skeeter were following the carriage on foot. Somehow, Halsey had gotten between them. Or McNealy had set him up after all.

Clip-clop, clip clop, clip-clop.

The doctor told the driver, "Stop! Stop right now!"

Hunter came up on the left, Skeeter on the right, and Hunter said, "Like I told you before, Lieutenant, you are fucked. Your nigger friends, too."

Halsey decided not fight this personal war by half measures. If he did, he would never escape, Samantha would never be safe, and the Freedoms would suffer, too.

So he stood in the carriage, raised the pistol, and shot Hunter once in the forehead. Hunter's eye opened wide, almost in shock, as if to ask, *How dare you?* He staggered for a second. Then his legs collapsed under him.

Now the Provost Guards were coming from both ends. The pounding vibration of their feet made the bridge shake.

Halsey grabbed the doctor's bag and kicked the doctor away, but Skeeter grabbed his leg. Halsey turned and put two shots into Skeeter, chest first, then forehead, and did not feel an instant's remorse.

All around, people were turning, ducking, crouching out of the line of fire.

Doc Wiggins grabbed his collar

He pulled free, pointed the pistol, and the doctor dived away as fast as a fat man could.

Halsey did not shoot the doctor. Instead, he jumped off the carriage, stumbled on Hunter's body, and as he tried to catch his balance, dropped the doctor's bag. It flopped open and spilled out bottles and pills and a few sharp instruments, but the daybook? Where was the daybook? Buried deeper, down at the bottom?

Halsey pointed his pistol at a do-gooding bystander who came up behind the carriage. Then he whirled and pointed at another coming from the front. Then he half-whirled and pointed at the Negro driver, who ducked away.

The Provost Guards were almost on him. So he shoved the pistol back into his holster, snatched the half-open bag, stepped over the railing, and dropped straight down, like a sashweight dropped from a roof. He hit the water feetfirst and felt the current suck him deeper and turn him over and pull him along.

That was good, because it protected him from the musket fire that followed him downstream. In a short time, he was a quarter mile away, riding the current toward Mason's Island in the middle of the river. And he had nothing in his hands. The bag was gone.

He fetched up on the mudflat at the upstream end, crawled up to the trees, and collapsed. It was nearly dark. He could barely see the figures on the bridge. He suspected that they could barely see him. But the mosquitoes found him quickly. And the police or the provosts would find him, too. They would post a guard at the footbridge that led from the Virginia side, and they would come for him as soon as the sky grew light.

So Hunter was right. Halsey was . . . fucked. But Hunter would not be right about anything else, and Squeaker had liquidated his debt, as well.

Like Lafayette Baker, Halsey Hutchinson had become a vigilante. He might have been a fool to trust McNealy or to start shooting on the bridge. But he would be a bigger fool to stay on that island.

So he could wait, or he could swim.

If he was lucky, he could fight the current across to Rock Creek, then move up the shallow stream on foot, hiding his trail and himself in the sliver of a ravine that separated Georgetown from Washington. If he was unlucky, he would be dragged downstream by the current and wash up on Kettle Shoals . . . dead.

He decided to swim.

III.

Three weeks later, a man who called himself Private Jeremiah Murphy crossed Antietam Creek and moved with his regiment into a grove of trees. To the west, up a gentle slope, spread a huge cornfield. At dawn, it had been covered with green stalks. Now it was soaked in blood and layered with bodies.

Captain Oliver Wendell Holmes came among the men, saying, "Cheer up, boys. It's folly to pull a long mug every time you face enemy fire. When we go in, we go in like soldiers. We hold our place in the line. And we lick 'em."

He did not inspire any wild cheering. Most men were too frightened.

But Jeremiah Murphy was at peace. Though he was as cotton-mouth scared as any man there, the enemy before him would be far easier to confront than whatever he had left behind in Washington.

He had sewn a pocket inside his private's jacket. It contained remnants of a carte de visite of Samantha Simpson of Wellesley, Massachusetts, a fresh letter to her, and a letter to Abraham Lincoln, too. He hoped that someday he would mail them, or that someone who was burying him would do it for him.

And if he died that day, he would die knowing what few other men on the field could: that victory would lead to the proclamation of emancipation.

Robert E. Lee had stopped to offer battle on the long, low ridge that ran north from Sharpsburg, Maryland. There was no doubt of his intention or of his opinion about the opposing commander, because he had put Antietam Creek before him and the snaky twists of the Potomac River less than a mile to his rear. He meant to fight, and he expected to win. After all, he had not lost a battle yet. . . .

.   .   .

On that last Saturday in August, early reports suggested a great Federal victory at Second Bull Run. But early reports had proved inaccurate. The Confederates had smashed General Pope and sent a torrent of beaten men and frightened civilians pouring back across the Washington bridges.

By Sunday morning, the Provost Guard and Metropolitan Police were too busy to be bothered searching Mason's Island for a black-bearded man in a brown suit.

It would not have mattered anyway, because Halsey Hutchinson by then was hiding in a hollow near Rock Creek. He had fresh water from the stream, firewood from the deadfall, and plenty of neighbors. Some were vagrants, some were deserters, and all lived in fear of sweeps by the Metropolitans.

For two days, he hid out, dried out, and tried to figure out what to do next. On Monday, he ventured out.

Hunger forced him, and the resolve to get clear of his troubles. He still had his pistol. He still needed a friend.

But the first familiar face he saw belonged to General McClellan, who came galloping along M Street with an entourage of officers, raising clouds of dust and cheers. The Young Napoléon was a great galloper, thought Halsey, especially when his fortunes were on the rise.

Lincoln had determined that General Pope was not the man to defend the city. So he had turned back to McClellan. The troops were happy. The people of Washington were happy. Halsey suspected that Lincoln and his cabinet felt differently.

Halsey learned of all this from a copy of the *Daily Republican* posted on the message board in front of the State Department. The paper also contained an article on the Aqueduct Bridge shooting, and it quoted Detective Joseph Albert McNealy, who linked Halsey Hutchinson to two more murders. Yes, he thought, McNealy had set him up again.

So that night, Halsey slipped down to the Washington Canal and fished a canvas bag out of the water, right at the spot where he had dropped it four months before. It contained a floppy felt hat, rough linsey-woolsey shirt, and long leather apron. He brought them back to his hideout, rinsed them in Rock Creek, and dried them by his campfire. The next day, he took to the streets in the guise of a butcher's helper.

He went first by the Union Hotel Hospital, hoping to glimpse Samantha. He lingered on the corner for half an hour or more, and then he saw her, and his heart leaped up again. Then she called the men to lunch, and the sound of her voice caused his heart to sink. In the noonday sunshine, he realized that it had never been Samantha but another young woman in a hoopless gingham dress, another who might once have been girlish but now had been toughened by hard work and war.

So he turned and headed for the National. He might have hoped to see Samantha, but he had to see McNealy. After four days of reliving the events on the bridge, he believed that the daybook had not been in the doctor's bag. Maybe McNealy had it. Maybe he'd had it all along. Maybe they could still work a deal. Or maybe he would kill McNealy on sight. He was getting good at killing.

In any event, Noah could play the go-between because Noah shined McNealy's shoes.

So Halsey watched the hotel all afternoon. But Noah was busy the whole time. Never once was there an empty chair or a chance for Halsey to approach.

Then, about four o'clock, a young man with a long, boyish face and a sprouting mustache stepped out of the hotel and climbed into one of the shining chairs. He wore the dress frock and insignia of a Union captain: Oliver Wendell Holmes.

What was he doing in the city? And where was the Twentieth?

Halsey realized that not only was he looking at one of his oldest friends but also at his best chance for a different kind of freedom.

After his shine, Holmes jumped down and started west along Pennsylvania.

Halsey came up behind him and with an Irish accent in his graveled voice, he said, "Excuse me, sir."

Holmes glanced at him. "Not interested."

"Oh, I ain't sellin' nothin'. My name's Murphy. I'm . . . I'm Irish."

"So you are." Holmes did not break stride. "And a long way from home."

"From the symbol on your hat, I'm thinkin' you're a long way yourself, sir, a long way from Massachusetts."

Holmes picked up his pace, as if he had better places to be.

Halsey was pleased that Holmes had not yet recognized him. If his closest friend in the regiment could not see past the beard and the brogue, who else would? He said, "I'm also thinkin' you'd be knowin' a friend of mine who's no longer with us."

"*I* know a friend of *yours*?" said Holmes. "Can't imagine how, but—"

"His name was Sergeant Thomas Moran."

Holmes stopped and studied the man beneath the brim of the filthy felt hat. But no glimmer of recognition lit his face. He said, "You knew Tom Moran?"

"We was from the same town, sir, a place called Spiddal in County Galway, a fine fishin' town it is, filled with fine men, fine men."

"As he often said." Holmes went back to walking.

Halsey followed. "I'm told he even rescued one of your best friends at Ball's Bluff, a man who's forever indebted to him. A fine, brave man by the name of—"

Holmes stopped again and looked into Halsey's eyes . . . and looked . . . and looked some more. "Halsey Hutchinson."

"The very one," said Halsey. "Moran always told me that he never thought you Harvard boys'd fight, till he saw ye's go into action at Ball's Bluff."

Holmes's eyes lit. Then they darkened. Then he turned and started walking again, as if he had just looked upon a friend suffering some dreadful disease and wanted to get away before he caught it.

Halsey followed, dropped the accent, and said, "I did not kill Constance Wood."

"Did you kill the others? In the gambling hell? On the bridge?"

"You could say that I've been forced to fight this war in the shadows."

"I'll take that as a yes."

"You sound like a lawyer."

"Not yet," said Holmes.

"But you've heard of attorney-client privilege."

"I can't represent you in a court-martial, if that's what you're asking."

"I'm asking you to sign me up."

"As what?"

"A private. I'd rather shoulder a musket than fight in the shadows." And across the next four blocks, Halsey Hutchinson told his story, including the part about the president's daybook. "I thought I had it in my grasp on the bridge. I was . . . misled."

"It would be a remarkable document," mused Holmes.

"But it has eluded me. The opportunity to serve has not."

"So you want to hide out in the regiment?"

"I'll be an Irishman from the same village as Sergeant Moran. I know everything about Spiddal, because he never shut up about the place. And when I was a boy, my nursemaid was from the village of Dunslea. My father had to fire her when I started speaking with a brogue."

Holmes nodded. He almost smiled, which Halsey took as a good sign.

"What's more," said Halsey, "I have a black beard, a croaking voice that no one in the regiment has heard, and a personality so blackened that I'm grim, sour, and not much at all for campfire small talk. But I can fight. And if I die, I die."

A soap salesman at a little stand in front of the Willard called out to Holmes, "Hey, soldier-boy, maybe you should buy a little lather for your dirty friend, there."

Holmes ignored him and kept walking up Fifteenth and turned onto the Pennsylvania straightaway.

As they passed the White House, Holmes looked ahead and said, "They're here."

A dozen men in blue uniforms were waiting on the corner of Seventeenth, in front of the art museum that had become a supply depot.

Holmes explained that he had gotten a twelve-hour pass to give himself a few of "the necessities of life" at the National. Then he was to collect a dozen recruits sent from Boston and march them on to the camp at Tennallytown.

"You've had a lot of replacements, then?" asked Halsey.

"We weren't at full strength to begin with. Five hundred thirty-some to start . . . never more than eight hundred. Back now to less than five hundred effectives."

"So you've sustained terrible losses. You need reliable men."

"We do, and there are some companies that have been completely reconstituted since Ball's Bluff. So there's a chance that if we put you in the right spot, no one would recognize you." And in front of the White House, Holmes stopped and looked Halsey in the eye. "If I do this, no man can ever know."

"I'll sign on as Jeremiah Murphy, from Spiddal, County Galway, recruited straight off the boat in East Boston. I got separated from my unit but found my way here."

They both knew that such military white lies were told every day.

A new recruit might decide, after signing or training, that soldiering was not for him. He might desert. Later, he might think better of his decision, and if he presented himself to the right officer at the right moment, the result might be reinstatement rather than a firing squad. It was a brutal fact, growing more brutal by the month, that every regiment needed men, however they came.

At the supply depot, Holmes drew a private's uniform for Jeremiah Murphy, explaining with a wink to the quartermaster that Murphy had joined the regiment late. Halsey put the uniform on right in the depot. He shouldered a musket and marched through the Washington streets to freedom . . . and expiation.

A few days later, he was marching north with the Twentieth.

The great pursuit had begun . . .

. . .

. . . because Robert E. Lee had not chosen to sit in Manassas consolidating his power. He saw his main chance in Maryland. A victory there might bring a border state to the side of the South and convince the European powers to recognize the Confederacy. With the Union Army in disarray and McClellan in charge, anything was possible.

So Lee had smashed into Maryland.

And McClellan had chased him to this gentle landscape of hills and valleys, of pretty stone bridges and green pastures and fertile cornfields, a place that two days before had been slumbering as peacefully in sun as it had since the birth of the republic.

McClellan had begun the battle by ordering First and Twelfth Corps to attack at dawn, north to south, against the Confederate left. For two ferocious hours, men had fought in the cornfield and around the whitewashed Dunker Church.

Meanwhile, the Twentieth, in Sedgwick's Division, Sumner's Second Corps, had awaited orders. And a few may have wondered with Halsey: Why hadn't they attacked in coordination with First and Twelfth? If they had struck from the east when the Confederates were turned north, the day might already have been theirs. And emancipation might be a forthcoming reality.

But the cornfield had fallen silent. That first ferocious clash had petered out. Confederates and Federals had fallen back. McClellan was doing what he always did: overestimating his enemy, holding too much in reserve, and coordinating his attacks with the precision of a casual picnic.

Then the bugles began to blow and the drums to beat.

Brigade front was the order, battle formation.

Five thousand men came crisply out of the woods. Amidst the shouts of officers and sergeants, they spread their lines across the eastern edge of the cornfield: three brigades, each brigade two ranks deep, each rank numbering near eight hundred men, each man shoulder to shoulder with the next, creating a front of five hundred yards.

With a wave of his hat, ancient General Sumner cried, "Forward."

Stragglers from the cornfield fight were coming toward them now. Some were helping wounded. Some were tending to wounds of their own. Some were running, their eyes fixed on nothing but the safety of the woods. Some simply walked, weaponless, eyes vacant, expressions blank.

"Pay them no mind," cried Captain Holmes.

Someone else shouted, "Fight fiercely, men! Remember your heritage. And if any one of you shows cowardice, I'll shoot you myself."

That was Lieutenant Heywood Wedge, Harvard '61. His cousin, Douglass Wedge Warren, '61, was the line closer. The regimental commander, grandfatherly Colonel Lee, MA '51, rode at the side of his men with Lieutenant Colonel Palfrey, '51. And there were Harvard brothers, Major Paul Revere, last in the class of '52, and Edward, the regimental surgeon, and Pen Hallowell, '61 and his brother Ned, and many more.

Some soldiers called this a rich man's war and a poor man's fight, but not the men of the Twentieth, not the Irish and German immigrants, not the fishermen from Nantucket and the woodsmen from the Berkshires. While the officers of the Harvard Regiment could be as class-conscious in camp as in their clubs, they never asked their men to go where they would not go themselves.

The Twentieth held the far left of the second brigade. Halsey went in the second rank, with his eyes on the back of the man in front of him, who watched the swaying shoulders and glittering bayonets and fluttering flags of the brigade in front of him.

Swaying, glittering, fluttering . . . from a distance the advance must have looked like blue fabric waving over the green rolls of farmland. But from ground level, it was the definition of war's horror, because as the fresh brigades crossed the cornfield, they stepped over all the carnage of the morning.

There were dead men, dead horses, broken wagons, broken bodies, brains, innards, and blood pooled in puddles, and blood running in rivulets along the blasted cornrows, and the wounded, in blue and butternut, waving weakly to show that they still lived, that to step on them might squash the last bit of life out of them, that to keep going might mean the last of life for those who could still step.

But the brigades did not stop.

Once across the cornfield, they would have to scramble over a split rail fence, cross the Hagerstown Turnpike, and head for a line of trees beyond.

Halsey wiped the sweat from his forehead and wondered why.

Were they hoping to seize those woods and turn the Confederate left, which had been mauled by the two Federal corps that now lay in ruins amidst the corn rubble? Or were they heading for the Confederate cannon beyond the woods?

Two things bothered Halsey.

First, the brigades were too close. It was difficult to maintain lines across a five-hundred-yard front. But they should have been keeping a distance of at least fifty yards, so that one brigade could volley over the one in front of it. These brigades were no more than fifty *feet* apart.

And second, an attentive commander would have put flanking columns at either end of the line, so that if the enemy struck from the right or left, the flankers could simply make a quarter turn and fire into them.

Then a more immediate problem arose:

Up ahead were the trees, and beyond the trees was a ridge, and on the ridge were Confederate cannon, and above the trees, forming visible arcs in the sky, were the shells and balls that the cannon were now firing at those three long brigades of Federal infantry.

The game of chance had begun.

No amount of courage could change the outcome of an artillery barrage. No amount of cowardice would help, either, unless the coward could make it off the field. Once a man went in, whether he went in smartly or as scared as a child, when exploding shot and twelve-pound balls filled the air, it was all a matter of inches and instants.

Halsey had played the game once before. He could pick out the green troops just by watching them flinch every time a shell exploded or a cannonball plowed up the ground. But flinching just wasted energy. The veterans lowered their heads and pushed forward, as if the storm of iron pouring down were no more than a burst of summer rain.

This storm took out scores of men with every thundering burst and flash. But the officers cajoled and exhorted and the line closers pushed and pulled. And once each brigade had crossed the cornfield and scrambled over the fence and quick-stepped across the pasture into the West Woods, the artillery fire slackened.

They were now moving through open woodland with tall trees and little underbrush. Exploding shot in the green canopy above could create havoc. So why had the artillery stopped? Was something else brewing? Halsey wondered what would happen if they were attacked from the rock outcroppings and underbrush on the left.

As the first brigade passed through the woods and out into the field on the far side, Confederate skirmishers opened up from behind the rock walls that divided the field, and the artillery on the heights lay down carpets of canister on the exposed Yankees.

But the second brigade could not come into action, because they were too close to the first. So they stayed at the edge of the woods, took fire in the dappled shade, watched men fall around them, and waited. Halsey leaned on his musket. A sergeant nearby pulled out his pipe and began to smoke.

Old General Sumner was out in the sunshine, out where the fight was. He had balls for certain, thought Halsey, but fewer brains because all at once, he seemed to realize something that he should have seen before he ordered the attack, something very bad coming at his flank.

He wheeled his horse toward the trees and shouted, "Back, boys! Back! For God's sake, move back, you're in a bad fix!"

But before the troops could respond, Vesuvius erupted. That's what Halsey thought. He had been to Pompeii. He had read about the pyroclastic flow that burst from the volcano and engulfed the ancient city in an explosion of superheated gas that propelled rocks like bullets before it.

That was the rebel fire: hot gas and thousands of fifty-eight-caliber lead rocks exploding from the outcroppings on the left.

The colors of the Twentieth went down. But in an instant they were up again.

Officers began to shout. Men turned toward the fire. Others turned away.

The colors went down again. But in an instant they were up again.

Halsey dropped to one knee, turned to the rear and fired. One shot, then another, then a third. Handle cartridge, tear cartridge, charge cartridge, ram home, raise, prime, fire. And all while bullets screamed around his head and men fell everywhere.

He knew that he was firing into the third brigade, which was collapsing back there in the battle smoke and sunlight. But he was hitting rebels, too. So he reached for another cartridge.

And Holmes was on him, slapping him with the flat of his saber, "Dammit, wait for orders. You're firing into your own men."

"Bejesus, sir!" cried Halsey, who had grown so used to Irish expressions that they came as second nature, even then. "But the enemy is behind us."

"Behind us? But—"

And someone else shouted it, then someone else.

The enemy was behind them . . . and beside them . . . and in front, too. The rebels had gotten them in a big bag and the only way out was to the north, to the right.

Already, all around, troops were breaking and running.

But the officers and men of the Twentieth tried to maintain discipline.

Colonel Lee shouted, "Column right, ordinary step!"

Some men heard him. Some did not.

Those who did formed columns of four, muskets shouldered.

Halsey wanted to run, but he tried to remind himself that this was what he had yearned for, the purity of combat, the simplicity of battle. And yet nothing was simple in the close-packed confusion. Bullets screamed from every direction. Confederates appeared and disappeared like spirits in the smoke. Federals kept firing into their own formations.

Holmes started to run to the head of the column now pulling itself together for a retreat. He looked as if he was running away, but he was waving his sword above his head so that the men in his company could see him.

Some rebel saw him, too, because a bullet struck him in the back of the neck and sent him pitching forward.

A sergeant cried for the company to move out with the rest of the regiment.

Colonel Lee shouted, "Don't stop! Leave the wounded. Even the officers."

But if an Irish sergeant could break ranks to help Lieutenant Wedge, Halsey would break ranks to help his friend.

He ran over to Holmes and knelt. Blood was gushing from two holes in Holmes's neck. He was shot through and through. A dead man, for certain. But his eyes opened wide and searched back and forth as if looking for something in the sky above.

And Halsey decided to stay with him, even though the Twentieth was retreating now into the curtains of smoke and sunshine.

All around, the woods were emptying of blue jackets. But one was coming toward them: the chaplain. He knelt and looked at Holmes. "You're a Christian, aren't you?"

Holmes tried to speak, but all he could do was flutter his eyes.

"Well, that's all right," said the chaplain. Then his eyes widened at a new sound.

Above the roar of battle came the yip-yip-yip of the rebel yell.

The Confederates were giving chase to the retreating remnants of Sedgwick's Division.

The chaplain jumped to his feet and ran off.

But Halsey turned to the onslaught, a hundred Confederates, a thousand, more, leaping from the rocks, exploding from the brush, charging through the trees.

If this was the end, he resolved to go down with his best weapon. So he reached under his jacket and pulled his Adams from his belt.

He told himself that they were paper targets, not men, targets in a range. Stay calm. Make your last moments count. Victory might still follow . . .

. . . and expiation.

A young Confederate in a checkered shirt stopped to fire at him. Halsey put a bullet right under the brim of his gray kepi. Another charged from the right with bayonet raised. Halsey stopped him dead with a shot in the chest; then he hit a third in the neck, an officer, and sent him spinning. He fired a fourth at a big bearded fellow charging in bare feet. He missed. His next shot hit the man in the belly, but the man kept coming.

The barefoot rebel had enough momentum to drive himself forward, smash Halsey in the face with his musket, and fall on him.

When Halsey came to, a dead body lay on top of him, stinking of sweat and tobacco, of campfire smoke and bacon grease. Halsey pushed him off and looked around.

The Confederate wave had rolled on. The roar of battle resounded now to the northeast, the direction of the retreat. Federal artillery was hammering the blue September sky and, Halsey hoped, the Confederates, too.

Then he heard someone say, "I don't have time to be spending on dead men."

"I know this man," said someone else. "He's a valuable officer. I command you to do what you can for him."

Halsey saw a doctor kneel beside Holmes and force a swallow of brandy into his mouth. Miraculously, Holmes gagged, coughed, and woke.

The other man, a captain, said, "Wendell, can you speak?"

"I think so," croaked Holmes.

"Can you walk?"

Holmes rolled onto his side and tried to stand.

"You need to get up. Those rebs'll be fallin' back soon. Most of 'em'll take the road, but some might come back through the woods, so we need to get you out. There's a farmhouse to the north, a field hospital."

Halsey stood, wobbled a bit from the blow on his head, felt over himself for a wound, but the blood on his coat belonged to the dead rebel.

The captain said, "Help me, Private. Help me get Captain Holmes to his feet."

Halsey said, "Yes, sir," without thinking of his brogue.

Holmes uttered, "Thanks, Halz. I . . . I . . . ."

"Halz?" said the other captain. "Is that your name, Private?"

"Ah, no. He must be off his head." Halsey found his brogue and hoped that Holmes remembered, too. "You look just grand there, Captain, darlin'.

Never seen a man before could take a ball through the neck and stand up not half an hour later."

"I watched you with that pistol, Private," said the other captain. "You did well, but privates aren't supposed to carry pistols."

"I see it as a little somethin' extra, sir." Halsey gave the officer a wink.

"Well, we won't tell anyone."

And with Holmes between them, they walked north, through the carnage. It looked as if half of Sedgwick's Division was down and dead in those woods. The dead rebels clustered around the place where Halsey had made his stand. It did not make him proud.

. . .

The armies fought all day, moving from north to south across a five-mile front. And no one needed to wait for the troop returns to know that this was the bloodiest day of the war, which made it the bloodiest American day since the Pilgrims signed their compact.

After leaving Holmes in that field hospital, Halsey found his way back to the regiment, which had regrouped in woods north of the cornfield. He reported on Holmes and the others he had seen: Lieutenant Norwood Hallowell and the Wedge cousins wounded in the farmhouse, Dr. Revere dead on the field, near the body of a man he had been stitching back together.

Late that afternoon, Halsey watched as a woman in a long blue dress lead two stretcher-bearers onto the field to tend a man hidden by a dip in the earth.

Someone said her name was Clara Barton, and she had driven a wagon filled with medical supplies all the way up from Washington.

As she leaned over the man to tourniquet his arm, a shot popped somewhere, and a burst of blood exploded at the man's head. Clara Barton jumped back in surprise, then looked for a moment at the fresh blood on her hands. She wiped them on her apron and gestured for the stretcher-bearers to follow her to another man.

By God, thought Halsey, but there was courage everywhere on that field.

He only hoped that McClellan did not waste it.

The next morning, they waited for orders to renew the attack. But the orders never came. Soldiers in the line speculated, but the dour Irishman with the black beard said nothing. Private Murphy spoke only when spoken to, and briefly at that. He was known in the regiment as the anti-Mick, since most of the Irish boys were such big talkers.

Halscy suspected that McClellan, with two fresh corps that he had not used, was still overestimating the rebel force, especially if Pinkerton was anywhere nearby. So the armies looked at each other all day, Lee from defensive positions around Sharpsburg, McClellan from the lawn of a beautiful farmhouse above Antietam Creek.

And that night, Lee retreated. He had not left the enemy in command of the field, but he had left. So the battle was a tactical draw, but the Union could claim a victory.

Four days later, as men moaned in makeshift hospitals, as burial details dumped bloated corpses into mass graves, as thousands of dead horses burned in huge, stinking pyres, Second Corps was ordered south to Bolivar Heights, just above Harper's Ferry.

It had been the Confederate seizure of Harper's Ferry that had given Lee the confidence to turn and face McClellan. Now the Confederates had abandoned the indefensible little town at the confluence of the Shenandoah and Potomac and had retreated deep into the safety of Virginia. The war might have ended at Antietam if McClellan had pressed his advantage. But it would go on.

. . .

Cool breezes ruffled the grass on the plateau where the Twentieth camped. The tents looked clean and bright in the September sun. The quartermaster constructed a huge brick oven so that the regiment could have soft bread. Its aroma wafted like the scent of home through the camp. They even had a mail call.

And when the men gathered to collect their letters on September 24, Captain Macy appeared before them. He was in charge because Colonel Palfrey had been struck in the shoulder by a cannonball, and Colonel Lee was "indisposed." The old man had snapped after the horror in the West Woods. He had left his command and ridden off, only to be found three days later, drunk and diarrhea-stained in a Maryland barn.

Halsey sympathized. He could have used a good drunk himself after the battle.

But whenever one of the other soldiers offered him a bit of home-brewed popskull, Halsey declined for fear that he might drink too much and drop his accent. This made him an even stranger breed of Irishman, one who didn't talk much and didn't drink at all.

Captain Macy stepped up onto a table, held up a piece of paper, and said to the regiment, "I have something from Washington. It's been sent to all the troops. But I want to read it to you myself. I want you to know what you are fighting for."

Halsey held his breath.

Macy read, "By the President of the United States, a Proclamation . . ."

Halsey looked around at the other soldiers and wondered if they had any idea of what was coming.

A series of "that" clauses got it started: "That it is my purpose, upon the next meeting of Congress . . ." was about compensated emancipation. "That the effort to colonize persons of African descent . . ." was a return to an oft-criticized plan.

The soldiers were looking at one another, wondering why they had been brought together to hear old news. And then came something entirely new, in the third clause:

"That on the first day of January, the year of our Lord one thousand eight hundred and sixty-three, all persons held as slaves within any State, or designated part of a State, the people whereof shall then be in rebellion against the United States, shall be then, thenceforward, and forever free—"

And the dour Irishman with the black beard let out a hoot.

A dozen men looked at him in shock. A hundred groaned. A hundred more cheered.

In the rest of the reading, Halsey heard little of poetry. Lincoln was issuing this document in his role as the nation's leading lawyer. And there was enough emotion in it without his eloquence to stir up more. Halsey listened closely, but with his inner ear, he was listening for something else, for the shouts of joy echoing from a shoeshine stand at the National Hotel and from a composting lot on the east side of Washington.

And he felt tears filling his eyes.

A few of the other soldiers saw and gestured, but Halsey did not care. He barely knew them. None of them were friends.

Besides, men in that army sometimes cried for no reason, even the strongest.

.   .   .

Lincoln had crossed a wide river and there would be no turning back, even if he lost the House of Representatives in November, even if a day-book emerged that showed how he had struggled with this decision for a year or more.

But what did it all mean for Halsey? What should he do now? Return to Washington and try to clear his name? Or seek expiation and personal redemption on the battlefield?

A few days later, he read the newspaper description of the Washington celebration on the night of September 22.

A happy crowd of Abolitionists, Unionists, freedmen, and former slaves paraded along Pennsylvania and up the White House carriage drive as they sang "The Battle Hymn of the Republic."

Lincoln, in his shirtsleeves, stepped to the window above the door.

And in his mind, Halsey traveled from Bolivar Heights to that familiar place and that glorious moment. . . .

Cool breezes had driven the humidity away. The gaslights around the White House glowed like footlights in a theater. The crowd was full of joy and liquor that smelled sweet in the air. And once they had finished singing, someone shouted, "Give us a speech, Abe!"

The light from the lantern directly above him made Lincoln's face appear even more shadowed and gaunt than usual. And the portico made his voice echo toward an even higher pitch. But his words were hopeful:

"I can only trust in God that I have made no mistake. It is now for the country and the world to pass judgment on this proclamation."

"We judge it all right, Abe!" shouted someone at the back of the crowd.

And everyone roared.

Lincoln raised his hands. "There's no doubt, we are environed with difficulties, but they're scarcely so great as the difficulties of the men on the battlefield, who would purchase with their blood and their lives the future happiness and prosperity of this country."

Halsey felt himself filling with tears again, as the crowd began to sing, "We Are Coming, Father Abraham."

And Lincoln cried, "Let us never forget them!"

"We are coming, coming, three hundred thousand more, from the winding Mississippi to New England's rocky shore!"

Halsey was standing in the dark outside the White House, the dark through which he had walked so many times with Father Abraham, and he began to hum that marching song, and he found that he could hit a note here and there, and so he began to sing, beside the flickering camp-fire on Bolivar Heights. "We are coming, *coming*, three hundred thousand more . . ." Then he caught himself.

Then he thought of something that Lincoln had said to him on the *Ariel*, about not having lived in vain. He thought of the wounded and the dead, from lucky Holmes to the late Revere to the lowliest private. He thought of all those who would be wounded in the battles ahead, all those who would feel the fatal shot in their belly and go tearing at their clothes to see where they had been struck. And he knew that if he and the rest of them saw this thing through, none of them would have lived—or died—in vain.

And he decided that he would buy the future with his blood. Lincoln's proclamation had made it the legal tender of the age.

. . .

The next day, he cut open the pocket inside his uniform and took out two letters. One he posted to Samantha, telling her that he lived and served anonymously. He signed it "HH." The other went to Lincoln, warning him about the Copperheads and the Knights of the Golden Circle and the fire in the rear. He did not sign it, but he hoped that the president received it and heeded it.

And on the brilliant afternoon of October 1, the president came to Bolivar Heights to review the troops.

By then, word had spread of disaffection with the Emancipation Proclamation.

While some soldiers had wept with joy, others had wept with anger. Officers had grumbled and threatened. Rumors flew that when a War Department major named Key was asked why McClellan had not destroyed Lee at Antietam, he said, "That is not his game. The object is that neither army shall get much advantage, that both shall be kept in the field until they are exhausted, when we will make a compromise and save slavery."

When Lincoln got wind of Key's remarks, he court-martialed him right in the White House, discharging him as an example to other disaffected officers . . . and perhaps to McClellan himself.

But on October 1, Lincoln and McClellan rode side by side again. It was a somber review, nothing like the raucous evening at Harrison's Landing. The soldiers presented arms. The drums beat. McClellan looked dour. Lincoln looked, as one soldier said, like he already had a foot in the grave.

Halsey wanted to break ranks and shout, "Mr. President, don't trust him!"

But Lincoln knew what he was about. He knew how much damage his proclamation had done to the party already. He was not about to do more by firing a Democratic favorite before the fall elections.

The Democrats took thirty-one new seats in November, including one for Fernando Wood, but they did not take Congress. So while the fire in the rear would grow hotter, the fire to the front would become an inferno that would consume the nation or forge it anew.

And Lincoln understood that McClellan, even after Antietam, was not a man made for the inferno. He relieved the general with the pouter pigeon chest, the massive ego, and the timid soul just a few days after the votes were counted.

A month later, the Army of the Potomac marched for Fredericksburg . . . and the expiation of blood.

ELEVEN

Sunday Morning

"Do you know what Lincoln did two days after he signed the Emancipation Proclamation?"

The voice echoed across the floor of the Rosslyn parking garage.

Peter was leaning against a pillar at space D32. He straightened, took his hands out of his pockets, and said, "I don't know. What?"

A man appeared from behind a black Lexus. He wore khaki trousers, white Lacoste shirt, and blue blazer. He said, "Honest Abe suspended habeas corpus for anyone who encouraged desertion, resisted the draft, or engaged in what he called 'any disloyal practice.' In essence, he suspended the Bill of Rights."

"Good morning, Mr. Volpicelli," said Peter.

"I heard that you wanted to talk to me yesterday. But I left after that last question from Harrison Keeler."

"Why?"

"I've made a few enemies along the way. He's one of them. I never expected him to follow me to Washington for my first appearance with my new book."

"Is that why we're meeting here?" asked Peter.

"I thought you'd appreciate it." Volpicelli looked toward a green SUV on the other side. "But I told you to come alone."

Peter had driven Henry's Ford Edge. Henry had ridden in the back, under a blanket, and was watching them now through a video tap to his computer. Peter wouldn't have come alone, but he had to admit that meeting in this garage showed a certain flair on the part of this particular Deep Throat.

Outside, the day was humid heading toward hot. But it was dark and cool in the garage.

A motorcycle roared up Wilson Boulevard and idled for a moment. Volpicelli's eyes shifted. Then the roar receded.

"Nervous?" Peter said.

"If Keeler and his Bonnie Blue Flag boys find us," said Volpicelli, "I may be glad you brought backup."

"Why are you so afraid of Keeler?"

"An angry man . . . angry at Democrats, angry at Republicans, angry at independent scholars who beat him to his own family research."

"You?"

"Have you read my book, *Lincoln's Gestapo?*"

"Provocative title."

"Unlike you, I can't count on the wisdom of the ages to sell my books. I have to be provocative. It's what gets me onto Fox News and LNN."

The SUV door swung open and Henry climbed out. "Gettin' crowded in that backseat, No-Pete. Has he said yet what he means by 'follow the money'?"

"He's getting to it."

Henry Baxter ambled over. That's how he moved, casual and relaxed, as if he *weren't* taking in everything around him, noticing details that no one else saw, and preparing to spring, sprint, or spin at the first sign of danger. That, Peter knew, was how Henry wanted it. That was probably how he'd walked point in Vietnam, too.

Peter introduced him. "Henry helped us out on a big case in New York."

"I like big cases." Henry grinned. "And when I hear that some white guy in a golf shirt is writin' books dimmin' the noble glow that falls on the Great Emancipator, without whom my granddaddy might've spent his life pickin' cotton, without whom we might only now be gettin' round to integratin' the lunch counters, well . . . it's time to inject my opinions into the conversation, along with my street smarts, my heavy weaponry, and my eloquence on issues large and small."

Volpicelli just stared, as if he had never seen such a package of a man before. Most people hadn't.

Henry folded his arms and leaned against a pillar. "As we think this has something to do with Keeler's middle name, please continue with your dissertation."

"Keeler's middle name," said Volpicelli. "You have good researchers."

Henry said, "My smart nephew is in Boston right now, combin' the libraries and floatin' through the info cloud."

"And he's only been at it for twenty-four hours," said Peter.

"Well, let me show you something I bet he hasn't found." Volpicelli pulled out two photographs and put them on the hood of the Lexus.

Peter had seen hundreds of Civil War photos like these: groups of men standing stiffly, hands folded or slipped into coats, eyes staring at the camera or off toward some far horizon. The pictures were usually taken outdoors, with backgrounds of forest, field, or campground, as if the men were off on some boyish adventure. And one of the subjects was invariably blurred because he moved at the wrong moment.

The first image showed five men in front of a tent. Two wore Union kepis and uniform trousers. Three wore civilian garb. A campfire smoldered in the foreground.

The second showed eight men in suits or linen dusters in front of a brick building with high windows and Palladian-style fanlights.

Peter studied the faces frozen in time, the tin cups on the table beside the campfire, the turds on the city street, the fading whitewash on the sides of the brick building, the bars on the windows. He said, "The past can be mysterious and mundane at the same time."

"I've been looking at pictures like this since I was a kid," said Volpicelli. "My father came as an Italian POW. He got a job as bricklayer, fell in love, never went back. He always told me to study American history, because it was a tale of men trying to do good, even when they ended up doing bad."

"My folks come against their will, too," said Henry. "They got a more *nuanced* opinion on the history."

"When I decided to write about Lincoln's secret police," said Volpicelli, "I went to all the photo databases and searched every image of the various intelligence services."

"How many services were there?" asked Peter.

"You had Pinkerton's Federal Secret Service, the War Department detective service, then the Bureau of Military Information, the Washington Metropolitan Police—"

"Like the CIA and FBI and NSA and—"

"And nobody trustin' anybody," said Henry.

Volpicelli pointed to the man sitting by the campfire in a canvas duster and porkpie hat. "It started with Pinkerton. He kept an office on I Street and spent most of 1861 tracking spies around D.C. But when McClellan headed for the Peninsula, Pinkerton went, too. So Stanton slipped his own man into power in Washington, Lafayette Baker. When Lincoln fired McClellan, Pinkerton went, too, and left the field to Baker and his boys. They arrested over three thousand Northerners during the war, locked them up, answered to no one."

"And what's worse?" said Henry with sudden anger. "Lockin' up a few newspaper editors for a few months or lockin' up ten generations of black folks forever? You come with all this Lincoln-the-tyrant bullshit, but there's only one truth for a black man, then or now. Lincoln did what he had to do, and what he did was right."

Peter cleared his throat, as much for Henry as his throat. *Let's dial this back and do the job.* Then he said, "What about McNealy?"

After a nervous look at Henry, Volpicelli pointed to a man standing behind Pinkerton in the first photo. He wore a three-piece suit, a thick beard, a brown porkpie hat. "There he is."

"Hard-lookin' little dude," said Henry, who calmed down quickly, which was part of his charm and part of his threat. You never knew when he was going to go off again.

Then Volpicelli pointed to the other picture, to a big man with a bushy black beard. "That's Lafayette Baker in front of the Old Capitol Prison." Volpicelli ran his finger to the other side of the picture. "And who do you think that is?"

Peter and Henry looked from one shot to the other, and Peter said, "Our boy."

Volpicelli said, "He's the only man you'll find in both pictures, the only man I've ever found in pictures with both men . . . Pinkerton and Baker, that is."

"So you decided to write about him?" said Henry.

"I wanted to build the book around him. But he didn't leave much of a trail."

"Detectives are supposed to *find* trails," said Henry, "not leave 'em."

"So I wrote mostly about Baker. There's plenty on him. Not only did he throw suspected traitors in prison and run the manhunt for Booth, he bribed people he was watching, held a few for ransom, and in general was the kind of corrupt SOB who thrives whenever laws are suspended."

"Hey, man," said Henry, "corrupt SOBs thrivin' every day in every way, no matter what kind of laws we got goin' on."

"Back to McNealy," said Peter, "and his connection with Keeler."

"I was almost done with my book," Volpicelli explained, "when I saw an item on eBay: 'Rare Civil War letters from two brothers—George McNealy of the Second Ohio Volunteers and Joseph Albert McNealy of the War Department detective service—all written to the same woman.'"

"How much did you pay?" asked Henry.

"Five thousand, and I would have paid a hundred thousand if I had to."

"A hundred? You must get big advances," said Peter.

"David Bruce supports my research. He agrees with me that Lincoln was the avatar of big government and an enemy of the Constitution."

Henry made a noise that sounded like a growl.

Peter said, "You and Bruce? I'm not surprised. A match made in heaven. So . . . who was selling these letters?"

"A guy who found them in the attic of a house he'd bought outside Cincinnati, the house that Keeler sold after he got out of the can for lobbying violations."

"So Keeler thinks they're his?" asked Henry.

"He didn't even know about them, but he must Google himself regularly, to see if anyone is saying anything bad about him. And he must have had the name McNealy in his searches, and they mentioned McNealy in the *Publishers Weekly* review of my book. So Keeler contacted me and asked to buy the letters, but by then, they were the property of David Bruce, and David doesn't give things up too easily."

"What's in them?" asked Peter.

Somewhere on the floor above, a door banged. Volpicelli jumped.

Henry went for his gun. "Say, man, why you so damn nervous?"

A car was moving now. Volpicelli rolled his eyes to the concrete ceiling, tracked the sound across and down a ramp, then waited until he heard the gate rise.

"I thought that if you worked for David Bruce," said Peter, "you had his security to protect you."

"David Bruce believes that in business or treasure hunts, rivalries work best. Competition on a large scale and small. He may have given you a retainer. But he's still betting on me and his boys, and he's dangled a nice big bonus, so Andre and Jonathan don't want me giving away information."

"So," said Henry, "that's why we're meetin' here instead of some fancy hotel?"

Volpicelli nodded. "I'd rather be sitting down to breakfast in the Palomar."

"And," said Henry, "if those Bruce boys came through here now and found out that you were talkin' to us, there'd be—"

"Gunplay?" said Volpicelli. "Maybe."

"In that case—" Henry pointed to his SUV with the smoked windows.

. . .

Meanwhile, in front of the Willard, Evangeline was waiting for her seven thirty ride to Antietam. She was standing under the awning, close by the doorman.

Henry had wanted to call one of his D.C. friends to provide security, but she insisted that she'd be safe.

When the production van pulled up, it was good mornings all around. No worries. No surprises. No motorcycles or Chrysler 200 drive-bys.

But then . . . as the van headed west, Evangeline glanced back at the hotel to see the definition of sleeping with the enemy: Kathi Morganti, lobbyist for David Bruce, and William Dougherty, chief of staff for the sworn enemy of David Bruce, leaving the hotel together.

Maybe it was a breakfast meeting. In power towns, people took breakfast meetings even on a Sunday. Didn't they?

So why was Dougherty's hair wet, as if he had showered? And why was Kathi still wearing the blue satin dress she'd been wearing the night before? Was Kathi getting pillow talk to feed to her client? Was Dougherty giving it because he expected his boss to lose the election and he liked the idea of a job with Hamill and Associates? Just who was using whom?

Evangeline raised her phone and took a photo. She could not tell if Kathi saw her or not.

.   .   .

Henry had settled into the front seat of his SUV. Volpicelli and Peter were in the back, behind the dark glass.

Peter said, "How many letters did you buy?"

"Two dozen. Eight from the brother killed at Shiloh, the rest from Joseph, consoling his brother's widow, sending her money, promising her that if she could just survive the war, there'd be better days ahead, that there was still a man to love her and provide for her kids."

"Hard-lookin' little dude in love with his brother' wife," said Henry.

Volpicelli opened a folder of letters and picked one up: "April 10, 1865. He tells her to calm her fears, because the war has ended, and he has a line on something, 'that I've known about since '62. It's a daybook that belongs to an important man. An associate considered selling it right after the Emancipation Proclamation, and she insisted on selling it before the '64 election, but I told her to wait. I told her it's a weapon to use once. Now's the time. It could bring a big price.'"

Peter said, "A daybook could just have addresses and appointments in it."

"And 'important' could mean anybody," said Henry. "Stanton? Seward? Grant? Hell, some folks thought Frederick Douglass was the importantest of them all."

"It's Lincoln," said Volpicelli. "Look at when they thought about selling it, always at important political moments. But McNealy doesn't want to waste it. He tells her in an earlier letter, 'the Democrats have waited too long to nominate McClellan, and Sherman has taken Atlanta, so Lincoln will win, no matter what.' But on April 10, 1865, the war is over. Lincoln's thinking about Reconstruction."

"Which he didn't live to see," said Peter.

"And a few of my grandaddies didn't live *through*," said Henry. "Now, these letters are nice, but unless this jive-ass starts tellin' us about fol-lowin' the money—"

Volpicelli raised a finger for quiet, as if he was getting used to Henry's bluster.

Peter laughed, because he knew that Henry's bluster could be plenty real, but that finger stopped Henry, and he just looked at it, quivering in midair.

Volpicelli said, "You attended the Smithsonian event last night?"

"Very nice," said Peter.

"And you met Professor Conlon. Did he give you the speech?"

"Which one?"

"About all these documents being part of America's heritage, about this daybook belonging to the nation rather than to the merchants of greed—"

"He sees an entrepreneur like me as the Prince of Darkness," said Peter.

"No," said Volpicelli. "He sees David Bruce as the Prince of Darkness. You're just one of his minions. Conlon wants to bring you back from the dark side, because he's a classic liberal supporting another classic liberal."

Henry drummed his fingers on the wheel. "Follow the money, baby."

"Professor Conlon has received huge NEH grants over the years, thanks to Milbury. The National Endowment for the Humanities is the fountain of life for a lot of academics," said Volpicelli.

"Keep talkin'."

"And the man who fills the fountain controls those who drink. The more he pours, the more power he has, which is why he waters the culture-makers, the elite liberal college professors who tell *The New York Times* that they back his crazy ideas like a Federal National Treasure Law, or—"

"—affirmative action?" said Henry. "Or food stamps? Or Social fucking Security?"

"Or," said Volpicelli, ignoring Henry, "a value added tax."

"A VAT?" said Peter.

"Milbury is planning to introduce a national VAT. It will be in lieu of state taxes. It will be applied to every purchase in America, from insurance policies to shoe lacings."

"Now, that," said Henry, "is some motherfuckin' money."

"No," said Volpicelli. "That is a revolution, the biggest grab at federal control since the Civil War. It's the reason that David Bruce will do anything to destroy Milbury. Why do you think Milbury came to Washington last night, when he should have stayed at home to campaign?"

"Because the Congressional session starts on Monday," said Peter.

"Because the American Retail Sales Association underwrote that event at the Smithsonian, and they support Milbury with big bucks every election."

Peter laughed. "A VAT will never pass."

"ARSA is paying an army of lobbyists to push it in every corridor on Capitol Hill. They talk about saving Main Street and the mom-and-pop retailers, but some of them are bigger than all the online retailers combined."

"You have your lobbyists, too," said Peter. "Like Kathi Morganti."

"Bruce is paying Hamill and Associates to fight the VAT like it was a Russian invasion." Volpicelli paused. "It may not be Russian, but it stinks of socialism."

"What's this VAT supposed to do?" asked Henry.

"Level the playing field," said Peter.

Volpicelli said, "Right now, online outfits don't have to pay state taxes in states where they're not physically located, so they can pocket the profit or undercut the brick-and-mortar retailers. Bruce's operation does fifty billion in sales every year. This VAT will be a five percent national sales tax. That's two point five billion out of Bruce's pocket."

"We followin' the money now, baby."

Peter said, "A national VAT would be hard for online retailers to fight. When it comes to sales taxes, it's the nuclear option."

"The federal government collects the VAT and redistributes it to the states," said Volpicelli. "More federal control, more federal mandates, more chances for the people who inhabit all those buildings on the other side of the river to justify their existence."

"And *that's* why you want to refight the Civil War?" said Henry.

"We want to reignite the argument over states' rights," said Volpicelli. "Not to memorialize slavery but to make Americans understand that too much federal power is a dangerous thing. It's what the South fought against."

"Tell that to my ancestors in the slave huts," said Henry, "saltin' their whip-stripes and cryin' for their lost babies."

"We'll have a new kind of slavery if we keep giving in to things like a national VAT, so—" Volpicelli put the folder of letters into Peter's hand. "—go ahead. Take them."

Peter looked at Volpicelli. "You'd give me your research?"

"I want to see this diary or daybook, no matter who finds it. I want to see what Lincoln really thought about extending federal power with his illegal proclamations."

"I may give you an argument on the illegal part," said Peter.

"May?" said Henry. "I may shoot this son of a bitch."

"Shoot me or argue with me," said Volpicelli, "but agree that a Lincoln diary will offer an interesting analogue to our modern difficulties, and it will be amazing scholarship."

"So, win or lose the tax fight, you can write a book about it, and the world will no longer think of you as David Bruce's Libertarian butt-boy?" said Peter.

"Libertarian butt-boy," said Henry. "Why didn't I think of that?"

Volpicelli ignored Henry and said to Peter, "I work with Bruce because I believe in his vision. What's your excuse?"

Fair question, thought Peter. But he still hadn't signed the check.

.   .   .

You could draw a line in any westerly direction from Washington, D.C., and somewhere between fifty and a hundred miles out, it would pass through a place where a mighty battle had been fought. In two hours or less, you could drive to Petersburg, Cold Harbor, Spotsylvania, Chancellorsville, Fredericksburg, Manassas, Harper's Ferry, Ball's Bluff, the Monocacy, Antietam, or Gettysburg.

Some of these places had shrunk from massive battlefields to a few monuments and a few famous features in the midst of suburban sprawl. But a few remained as enormous stage sets, grand outdoor theaters where it felt as if the matinee had just ended and the actors had gone out for dinner.

Antietam was one of the grandest, just seventy miles northwest of Washington.

Peter and Henry made it in an hour and a half, about an hour behind the film crew. They stopped first on the road into town, at a place called the Pry House because Douglas Bryant had sent Peter a text, telling him to pay a visit.

I have some info. But can't talk. Soldiers with cell phones are FARBS!

Farmer Pry had built a handsome brick house and a big barn on the bank of the Antietam, so well sited that the day before the battle, Mc-Clellan's staff commandeered the property, brought the family furniture out onto the side yard, and set the general up with a telescope and a fine view of the land rising gently toward the Sharpsburg Ridge.

The National Museum of Civil War Medicine ran the property, which had been restored with white picket fences, long graveled drive, and gorgeous lawns. On the Sunday of Battle Anniversary Week, the parking lot was packed. A string band was playing. Scores of visitors were climbing the stairs to the house. Kids were scampering on the grassy ridge where Lincoln's careful general had made some of his most timid decisions. And a huge canvas pavilion in front of the barn had become a demonstration field hospital where "doctors" were helping "wounded" while the tourists watched.

A big box wagon sat at the edge of the grass, and woman in Civil War dress was talking to a lot of parents and kids. "I'm Clara Barton."

Peter led Henry over to the edge of the group.

The woman had a round face and friendly smile, like the real Clara Barton. She was saying, "After the fighting ended around the Cornfield and the West Woods, I went out to help and . . . look at this." She held up her sleeve. "A bullet hole. I was reaching toward a poor fellow, and the bullet passed through my sleeve and right into him."

"Wow," said a kid. "Is that the real dress?"

"It's a real style from the period." The woman stood and showed them her apron and added, "If I was doing something other than kneeling on the battlefield, I would have worn a hoop in my skirt. Hoops were the fashion but very difficult to kneel in."

Another kid pointed to the line of stretchers. "Are all these men gonna die?"

"No," said Clara Barton. "The ambulances arrive from the battlefield a few miles away, a doctor examines each man and decides if he's mortally wounded, needs surgery, or just a bandage."

She pointed at Douglas Bryant, who lay on stretcher, moaning in pain. "He's been shot in the stomach. That's usually a mortal wound in 1862, so they may give him something for his pain and get him out of the hot sun. Those who need a little patching up will be cared for out here. And those who need surgery, which means mostly amputations, will be going into the barn for chloroform and—"

"Gettin' their legs cut off," said a wide-eyed boy.

"Maybe . . . and you know, kids, there's a display of an amputation. It starts in five minutes in the barn. You might want to go in. All but the little ones."

The kids were already rushing off, moms and dads hurrying after them.

Doug Bryant raised his head from the stretcher and said, "Are they gone?"

"Nice moaning," said Peter.

Henry said, "A fine Sunday afternoon you got goin' on here."

"What can be bad?" Doug Bryant got up. "Sunshine, rolling countryside, teaching kids about history."

"I thought you'd be playing a rebel," said Peter.

"Clara Barton served the Yankee soldiers," said Mrs. Bryant.

"And if my wife wants to play the Yankee angel," said Bryant, "I'm happy to be the Yankee wounded."

"Like two kids playin' doctor," said Henry.

His wife said, "Later we'll have him play a dead man. He does a great bloater."

"Bloater?" said Henry.

"That's when you puff up with gas after you've been dead on the field for a few days." Bryant blew up his cheeks and bulged out his eyes and his belly.

"That is *gross*," said Henry. "Man, get outta here with that."

"Pretty good, hunh?" Bryant grinned.

Henry said to Peter, "Can we find out what we come for and git on?"

Bryant gave them a jerk of his head and led them over to a quiet spot near a tree. "I got a phone call this morning, from one of the vendors at the market. He said he'd moved into Dawkins's spot for the day. It's prime real estate, with the shade and the nice corner near the gate. And about ten o'clock, four guys came over. They looked like a club of some kind. They all had blue T-shirts on. And ball caps with the white star on the blue patch."

Peter looked at Henry. "Keeler and his pals."

"They asked for Dawkins. The guy said, 'Gone to Sharpsburg for the festival.' I tried callin' Dawkins. But like I say, he's a mysterious old African American."

"Ain't we all," said Henry.

"I just figured you ought to know if they're lookin' for him." Bryant gave a nervous laugh. "Every time I hear a Harley roarin' along the road out there, I jump."

Peter asked, "Do you still have that Adams pistol?"

Bryant pulled it out of the pocket in his uniform. "It's not loaded or permitted. If anybody asks, I'm tellin' them it's a repro. But I'll point it if I have to."

"Hang on to it." Peter gave Henry a jerk of the head and they started to leave.

Bryant called after them. "Fellers. This is a hobby. It's supposed to be fun. It hasn't been fun since you come around."

"Don't you worry," said Henry. "It all be over soon."

. . .

In another two miles, Route 34, the Boonsboro Pike, led them up through the Antietam National Cemetery and down into the town itself. They grabbed the first parking spot they saw, because Main Street was closed for the Battle Anniversary Festival.

The center of Sharpsburg was no more than a clock, the library, and Nutter's Ice Cream Parlor. Main Street was barely wide enough for two cars. But it seemed a friendly place. Most of the houses had front porches that came right to the sidewalk, festooned in American flags and bunting. Some were joined façades. Some stood free. A few looked as if they had been there when Lee and Lincoln traveled back and forth on that road.

A string band in Union garb had set up at the corner of Mechanic Street, on the little bit of lawn in front of the library. Hundreds of people packed the street in cut-offs and tank tops, flip-flops and sandals, ball caps and eyeshades, and period dress, too. There were soldiers from both sides mixing and chatting, ladies in hoop skirts, kids in loose shirts and knee breeches. And the curbs were lined with stalls, selling . . . selling . . . selling . . . kettle popcorn, candles, handcrafts, quilts, hot dogs, local honey and jellies, antiques, tube rides on the Potomac, Civil War books, uniforms, figurines. Sometimes Peter thought that the Civil War had started more cottage industries than the Industrial Revolution ended.

Over the sound of the band, Henry said, "Your boy shouldn't be too hard to recognize. Ain't too many black folks here, even if we celebratin' the day that white boys died for the Emancipation Proclamation."

Donald Dawkins was sitting at his table, under a beach umbrella, with his wares displayed, including a pile of Diana Wilmington's books and a little sign, AUTOGRAPHED BY THE AUTHOR. He had his nose buried in a book, but his head snapped up when Peter cast a shadow across his table.

Peter sensed his discomfort right away. "Good morning."

Dawkins said, "What's good about it?"

Henry said, "Way to bring the happy, there, bro."

Dawkins said to Peter, "You got more black friends than I do, Black Irish."

"Speaking of which," said Peter. "Where's Diana? I thought she came up here to sign books with you."

"She's with that TV chick. They went to the battlefield to shoot some scenes."

"How's business?" asked Henry.

"Folks buyin' lots of popcorn, not many books. And that band only knows three songs. One of 'em is 'Dixie.'"

"That's a shame," said Henry, "but it's a catchy tune."

Dawkins looked down at his book, as if he was giving them the same treatment he had dished out the day before at the flea market.

"Diana told me you had some things we might want," said Peter.

"I got nothin'."

"I've brought foldin' money," said Peter, "a thousand in cash, so if Diana hasn't paid you yet, I'll buy those pictures of Jesus and Frederick Douglass, along with the collection of letters you offered Bryant."

"I told you, man, I got nothin'," said Dawkins angrily.

Henry folded his hands behind his back and started whistling "Dixie." Peter gave him a look.

Henry said, "What? This old boy's just whistlin' 'Dixie' on us. So I'll whistle right along."

Peter turned to Dawkins. "He said that, not me."

Dawkins eyes shifted. "I got nothin' 'cause I already sold it."

"To Diana?"

"To the fellers watchin' us right now."

"Who's watchin' us?" Henry looked around.

"Same fellers who come round last week lookin' for the engraving, the one Sorrel bought. They figured out I come up here today. So they come to buy everything left from that lot that Sorrel picked over. Offered me five G's and said if I didn't take it, they'd be trouble. So, I promised Diana, but I sold to them . . . the engravings of Jesus and Frederick Douglass, some letters, and—say, did you really pay five hundred for that *Fort Lafayette*?"

Just then, a black woman came up the street from Nutter's and put an ice cream soda in front of Dawkins. She was about fifty, with a little extra weight in the hips but an air of youth about her still. She gave Peter and Henry a big smile and sat at the table, right behind the bobblehead Lincolns, and opened her own ice cream soda.

Dawkins said, "This is my wife, Savannah. I brung her up here for a pleasant afternoon and that's what I'm tryin' to give her."

She said, "I haven't had a real ice cream soda from a real soda fountain since I was a girl. She dipped her spoon, then looked up. "Say, you gents aren't here to bother my husband like those others, are you?"

"No, ma'am," said Henry. "We here 'cause we heard what a beautiful wife he had, and we just had to see for ourselves."

She laughed. "I got enough sugar in my cup right here, mister."

Peter said, "Who were those guys, what did they look like?"

"I told you," said Dawkins, "they're watchin' right now, right over in the tavern."

"And they're botherin' me, too." Savannah took a long sip of soda.

Henry said, "They're botherin' you because your husband has some valuable stuff."

"And a lot of junk," she said.

"That picture of Lincoln reading the Emancipation Proclamation," said Peter, "that wasn't junk. I'd love to know where it came from."

"Don't say nothin'," said Dawkins.

"That ain't constructive," said Henry.

"No, it ain't," said Savannah. "We got that stuff from the attic of a neighbor lady who passed. Esther Molly was her name."

"Now, don't say no more," ordered Dawkins.

But Savannah ignored her husband and talked faster and faster. Maybe it was the sugar. "Funny last name, 'Molly.' But anyways, I used to bring her cake and coffee on Sunday mornin' after church. Lived alone in a big row house. And do you know, just from that human kindness, she left us . . . everything. Her row house, the furniture, everything."

"Didn't she have any children?" asked Peter.

"Lost her only boy in Vietnam."

"I was in Vietnam," said Henry.

"Me, too. Got this." Dawkins pointed to his left leg.

Peter lifted the cloth and looked under the table: a prosthetic leg.

"You got that in the Nam," said Henry, "and them boys are botherin' you?"

Dawkins nodded.

"Well that ain't right." Henry turned and started across the street.

Not good, thought Peter. He said to Dawkins, "Don't go anywhere." Then he followed Henry to the opposite sidewalk, past a stall selling quilts, into the tavern.

.   .   .

Captain Bender's was the only restaurant in Sharpsburg. And it was jumping. The bartender was pouring as fast as he could. One waitress was rushing from counter to table with burgers and fries and fish 'n' chips. All the tables at the front were full. All the pool tables at the back were racked up and rolling. There were young families, couples, tables full of reenactors in blue and gray. And the boys in the blue T-shirts were sitting at a round table right in the window, just where Dawkins said they'd be. Three of them had taken off their hats.

Peter grabbed Henry at the door. "Let me handle this. You just stand there looking—"

"Pleasant?" Henry folded his arms and leaned against the wall. Some piped-in oldie from the Rolling Stones was competing with the indoor din and the outdoor string band. Henry started to hum along.

Peter walked over, borrowed an empty chair from the table next to them, and sat. "Mind if I join the Knights of the Golden Circle?"

"It's Knights of Liberty," said the big one who had been at the Eastern Market the day before.

"And yeah," said Steve Burke, the one with the beard, the one from the train. "We do mind."

Keeler looked over his shoulder. "Who's your friend?"

Peter said, "He's the head of security for Fallon Antiquaria."

Keeler said, "Why would you need security?"

"I'm very insecure. Why are you bothering my friend Dawkins out there?"

"He's not your friend. He's your next mark. We're trying to do business with him. Then you come along. Did Kathi Morganti get you into it? Or was it Dougherty? You look like another gun for hire."

"Just like you, Harry," said Steve Burke, "just like all of us. A lawyer, an accountant, a doctor, a lobbyist. All white-collar criminals. The only difference between us and the guys still wearing the white collars is that we got caught."

Peter said, "So why do you want this diary?"

"For the money," said Keeler.

"That's a motive I can appreciate," said Peter. "It's pure."

"And simple. Unlike the usual D.C. dance. Spin brings power, power brings money, money brings more spin and more power." Keeler took a long draft of beer, then wiped the foam from his mustache. "Do you know that the thirty largest companies in the United States pay more for lobbyists than they do in taxes? The Kathi Morgantis of the world spin the truth to the Doughertys, who tell the congressmen, and the money flows. The lobbyists get big fees. The staffers get job promises from the lobbyists. The pols get contributions. And the corporations get to run the rest of us."

"And we," said Steve Burke, "won't be run."

"That's right," said the quiet one sitting beside Keeler. Peter pegged him for the accountant. "The drug companies get their price protections, the hedge funds get their interest carryovers, the oil companies get their sweetheart leases, all because they have lobbyists, and all the poor schmucks outside this window . . . don't."

Peter wondered what kinds of Medicare frauds, embezzlements, and bribes had brought them all together in federal prison. But he didn't have time to find out. He said, "I'd just like to know why you were taking pictures of me at the flea market."

The big one leaned across the table and said, "None of your fuckin' business."

"Easy, Doc." Keeler made a small gesture. "This is a family place."

So, thought Peter, there was Mr. Medicare Fraud.

Keeler turned to Peter. "You must know my story by now?"

"Congressional staffer and lobbyist, disgraced, indicted, imprisoned."

"Sent to jail for playing the game, schmoozing, talking, writing position papers, picking up tabs, running golf tournaments, selling ideas to politicians while they sold their souls for Super Bowl tickets. I did it all. But it's a corrupt system, no matter how hard they try to clean it up."

Steve Burke was wearing the hat. He pointed to the symbol. "Do you know what that is?"

"White star on a blue patch," said Peter. "You're an admiral."

"It's the Bonnie Blue Flag. Southern rights. Independence. Self-determination. Don't try to live my life and I won't try to live yours."

"Fair enough," said Peter. "So you're in this for the philosophy, too. And for playing rebels when you go reenacting on the battlefield."

"We're not playing anything," said Doc, the big one. "And they don't let you reenact on a battlefield because it's sacred turf to both sides, you damn fool."

Keeler said, "We're in it for the money. Kathi Morganti and Congressman Milbury both understand that motivation. They play the spin-power-money game as well anyone."

"And when the time came," said Burke to Keeler, "they both testified against you in front of the House Ethics Committee."

"So revenge is in play, too," said Peter.

"Maybe. But money is always in play," answered Keeler. "I'll bet you're carrying a few thousand in foldin' money right now to give to that black guy across the street, all to get your hands on something worth—what—twenty million?"

"Maybe. But you just paid five thousand for it."

"True." Keeler drained his beer and plunked it down. "That means we have what we need right now to find that diary."

"Then go and find it." Peter stood. "But the world better hear about it or I'll hound you all the way back to your Ohio compound. And if you threaten my friends—"

"Here's my threat." Keeler stood and brought his face close to Peter. "This thing belongs to me. So stay out. You and your potbellied pal over there—"

From the door came a deep voice. "Who you callin' potbellied?"

A few of the tables around them fell silent. And the silence radiated through the bar.

Keeler glanced over his shoulder and said, "You."

In a flash, Henry crossed the floor, picked Keeler up physically, slammed him against the wall, right beneath a Baltimore Ravens poster, and said, "I am what you call big-*boned*."

Peter noticed the bartender take a Louisville Slugger from under the bar.

Doc and Burke and the accountant started to stand.

"Y'all just keep your seats," said Henry. "This won't take but a second. Then all the nice folks can finish their lunches." He looked back at Keeler. "I am the biggest-boned motherfucker you ever met, and I don't like skinny rats botherin' brother veterans, like Don Dawkins out there, sellin' his books and his bobbleheads. You remember that."

Henry dropped him, stepped back, and raised his hands as if he were a weight lifter after a clean and jerk. It also told the bartender that he was done as the aggressor.

Peter looked at Keeler and his friends. "We are now in a race. That's good. I like races. I usually win."

.   .   .

" 'Pow' goes the No-Pete." Henry laughed. "I like the way you stood up to him."

"I wouldn't have done it if I didn't have you behind me."

"Well, when you gave them that speech about houndin' them back to Hicksville, they were like, damn, this bookseller got some *stones*."

"If I was just a bookseller, I wouldn't even have gone in there," said Peter. "I'm a seeker of the truth. Now, let's get Evangeline and Diana and get back to D.C."

Route 35, the Hagersburg Pike, took them past the Battleview Market and then up onto the gentle ridge where Lee had made his stand.

The visitor center was a standard piece of sixties government architecture, glass and steel, flat and square, handsome but unobtrusive.

Peter ran in and asked the young ranger at the desk where the film crew was shooting.

She opened one of those classic National Park Service brochures, all designed the same way from Mount Desert Island to Haleakala, with pictures and information on one side, features map on the other. She said, "They received permits to shoot at the Dunker Church, the Cornfield, the observation tower at Bloody Lane, and Burnside's Bridge." She circled each place on the map.

A short time later, Henry was driving the battlefield loop road, going with the flow of slow-moving tourists.

The Dunker Church, a little whitewashed replica of the building that had seen such slaughter, came up on their left. No film crew.

So they rolled along the Hagerstown Pike, past one monument after another, to the Cornfield.

"The Twentieth Massachusetts would have scrambled over the fences along this road around nine o'clock," said Peter. "They were heading for the woods, where they'd be ambushed."

Henry looked into the woods on their left. "Nasty-ass place for a fight."

"Oliver Wendell Holmes was shot through the neck and survived. He was back in the spring, got shot again, in the foot, then served in Washington for a while before his discharge."

At the corner of the Hagerstown Pike and Cornfield Avenue, they stopped. The corn was still high, as it had been at dawn on that day.

Peter said. "Hard to believe the bloodshed in this field. Men firing point-blank into each other, fighting back and forth for two hours. Then Clara Barton came across this field. It's where she was almost killed."

"You mean that bullet hole story is true? Damn. I need to stop readin' so much poetry and read some history."

But there was no film crew at the Cornfield, just lots of interpreters and rangers and crowds, driving slowly, taking the tour, following the map.

So Henry looped back toward the center of the battlefield and took Richardson Avenue, which ran along the old roadbed called Bloody Lane. The rebels had used it for protection and slaughtered the Yankees before lunch. The Yankees had flanked them and slaughtered the rebels in the afternoon.

For a better view of the lane and the whole battlefield, the NPS had put up an observation tower. And *there* was the production van.

It was a five-story stone obelisk with a hipped roof. An NPS ranger in a stiff-brimmed hat was stopping people. Peter said he was part of the crew, then took the stairs two at a time. Henry stayed with the car. When Peter reached the top, the producer brought her finger to her lips, because Evangeline was interviewing Diana on camera:

"What is the true significance of the bloodshed here?"

Diana said, "The North had yet to win a major battle in the East and wouldn't win another until ten months later at Gettysburg. If the South had won here, Lincoln would have sat on the Emancipation Proclamation. But he seized on the victory to change the moral dimension of the war. England and France would not support the South if the North was fighting for Emancipation. And a hundred thousand colored troops would help to tip the balance on the battlefield."

"So your thesis is that he issued the Proclamation to win the war, not free the slaves?" Evangeline said. "Hence your title, *The Racism and Resolve of Abraham Lincoln*. Why such a strong title?"

"You need to shout to be heard in today's noisy culture. I was taught that Lincoln was the Great Emancipator, and he was. But history is always more complicated than myth. So I come at it from a contrarian point of view to find the truth."

"And you come to the places like this, where history happened," added Evangeline.

As he listened, Peter heard motorcycles. He looked out at the ridge, the background for Evangeline and Diana. Less than a mile away, four bikes were going into the visitor center lot.

Diana was saying, "Lincoln himself toured these sites with McClellan. He rode in one of the ambulances with his legs pulled up against his chest. The papers said how undignified he looked. And as he rode, he asked a friend to sing a few songs. The friend tried to lighten the mood with a silly ditty. The newspapers killed Lincoln for failing to show respect to the dead."

"Spin even then," said Evangeline.

"I've tried to give Lincoln flesh and blood by exploring his human reactions to the world he lived in. That's how you learn to appreciate his greatness even more."

Evangeline looked at the camera. "That's what history should be all about, folks."

"And cut," said Abigail.

Everyone relaxed.

"It felt a little superficial," said Diana. "I was just warming up."

Abigail Simon said, "We're done in the boondocks. Back to D.C."

Evangeline said to Peter, "Thanks for not messing up a take."

"Diana was on a roll." Peter glanced out across the fields. The motorcycles were rolling, too, off to the north, as if they were following the loop road. He said to Evangeline. "We have to hustle. Now."

Evangeline, who could argue with the best of them, got the point.

She made quick good-byes, said she would see everyone back in Washington, and took Diana by the elbow. "Great job, come on."

. . .

At the bottom, Henry was waiting by the SUV. "I was thinkin' about yellin' up, but I didn't want to spoil your scene. Our boys are comin'."

Evangeline had told Diana that Henry would greet her with a joke and some bluster. When Evangeline heard nothing but serious, she knew this was trouble.

Within a minute or two, they all were in the Edge, driving the loop road to get out of the park. But that meant driving at the speed limit or less. On the loop road, no one got angry, no one tailgated, because everyone was there to see the sights.

"What's going on?" asked Evangeline once they were rolling into a little wooded glade where sharpshooters would have been lurking that day a century and a half before.

Peter said, "We had a run-in with our friends from last night."

"Who are we talking about?" asked Diana.

"The boys with the cameras, the questions, and the single star insignia," said Peter.

"And," said Henry, "they're on to a hot trail."

"Can you take me back to my car?" asked Diana.

Henry said, "We want to get you back to D.C."

"But—"

"No buts," said Henry.

"What about Dawkins and his wife?" she asked. "Are they in danger?"

"They be fine," said Henry. "They got no more info to give."

"Ah, shit." Peter was looking in Henry's passenger mirror, objects closer than they appeared. Four motorcycles had just popped up. "There they are."

The women in the backseat turned.

"Why don't we find a ranger and say we're being followed?" asked Evangeline.

"Everybody in this park is followin' everybody else," said Henry. "They just fuckin' with us. They couldn't do it in the restaurant so they decided to do it here."

Peter grabbed the Park Service map and opened it. "We pass under the Boonsboro Pike, then we have a choice at a stop sign. We can go straight and drive out of the park. Or we can go left and drive up to the overlook at the Burnside Bridge."

"Can we drive over the bridge?" asked Henry.

"No. It's a relic. Five hundred Georgians held off Burnside's Corps from the overlook. But—" Peter studied the map. "—there's a traffic circle up there at the parking lot. Maybe we can use it."

"I like how the No-Pete is thinkin'."

So they went left, passed another farmhouse, and rose up onto the heights from which the Confederates had fought so bravely for so long, outnumbered ten to one.

Evangeline looked down at a beautiful stone bridge reflected in the slow-moving creek, a picture postcard, except that the stones of that bridge had once been soaked in the blood of hundreds of Yankee soldiers.

The motorcycles were right behind them, menacing.

Henry said, "These boys still don't get who they fuckin' with."

Suddenly, as he came into the roundabout, Henry leaned on the horn, to warn everyone pulling in or out. Then he accelerated and Peter thought that the SUV would tip and send them all tumbling down into the creek. But Henry whipped those four wheels around the rotary and went right back down the hill, right at the motorcycles.

One bike flew off into the bushes, another swerved, went off the road, and went banging down onto the footpath that led to the bridge. Henry grazed the third bike, and the fourth lay down on the side of the road.

"Now, that is the way to get away."

"Lucky there were no NPS cops up there," said Evangeline.

"Wait till the tenure committee hears about this," said Diana.

. . .

They took the main road south toward Virginia instead of north to I-70. As they passed out of town and went by Lee's headquarters, Peter's iPhone vibrated: an e-mail from Antoine.

Boss, The Descriptive Roll says that Jeremiah Murphy has a black beard. He's five-ten, one-seventy, same as HH. He enlists four days after that news story about the shooting on the bridge, when Mc-Nealy fingers HH. Murphy's brought back to Washington in the spring of 1865, ends up in Armory Square Hospital. I think HH and Murphy are the same guy. If you read the books you sold, you'd agree.

What the hell was he talking about?

Directly below was a link to an online version of Walt Whitman's *Memoranda During the War* and the note, "Read entry for March 1865." Peter clicked the link. . . .

TWELVE

February 1865

~~~ Halsey Hutchinson looked up at the gray sky and felt the sleet splattering his face. It told him that he still survived. . . .

Then two black faces appeared above him, and their bodies blocked the sleet.

Smoke blew through the sky behind them. Battle smoke? No. The smoke of the boilers that had driven the side-wheeler up the Potomac to the City Wharf.

"His name's Murphy. Gut shot," said a medical officer holding a sheaf of papers.

"Harewood Hospital or Armory Square, sir?" said one of the black men.

Halsey tried to speak. He got out the words, "No . . . take me to the Union . . ."

The officer said, "Yes, Corporal, you're back in the Union. You're among friends."

And one of the black men sang, "The Union forever! Hurrah, boys, hurrah!"

"No . . . no," said Halsey, "I mean . . . Union Ho . . . Hotel Hos . . . Hosp . . ."

The other black man joined in, "Down with the traitor, and up with the star."

The officer waved his hand, as if annoyed at singing stretcher-bearers. "Get movin', you boys. Put him on an ambulance for Armory Square."

The two black men carried Halsey down the gangplank while they sang, "So we rally round the flag, boys, we rally once again, shoutin' the battle cry of *freeee*-dum."

Someone on the dock cried out, "Number Three. Ambulance Number Three is bound for Armory Square. Put him in Three."

The stretcher-bearers carried, lifted, and slid Halsey into the wagon. Every movement felt like a thorny stick driven into his gut and twisted. He tried to clench his teeth and hold his cry, but he had been stoical long enough, and he just let it out. No one heard him because the man in the rack below was screaming.

Then, as the ambulance rolled up Seventh Street, the opium coursed through him. He put his head back, listened to the sleet splatter on the canvas roof, and dreamed again the opium dream that brought everything back in broad scenes and tiny details. . . .

. . . the smell of bacon grease and sweat and a dead body on top of him at Antietam . . . a Confederate sharpshooter firing from a curtained window on a Fredericksburg Street in the fading December light . . . diarrhea and typhoid and death in the winter camp . . . and still he survived.

. . . the reviving warmth of May . . . more fighting in Fredericksburg . . . the brutal June march, when the Army of the Potomac chased Lee into Pennsylvania, and the Twentieth covered thirty miles in a day, and feet turned to blister, and blood caked on thighs scraped raw by wool trousers in the heat . . . Confederate cannon tearing at the sky and Pickett's Division coming out of the woods . . . the Twentieth behind their stone wall, waiting, watching, waiting, rising, firing, and firing so fiercely that they wrecked the whole rebel regiment in front of them . . . then the cry "They've breached! To the Angle!" . . . and the Twentieth turning right to charge into the rebel flank, into the belly-shooting, face-punching, balls-kicking, eyes-gouging, nose-biting blood-brawl that ended the great battle of Gettysburg . . . and still he survived.

. . . Bristoe Station and Mine Run and another camp winter, then the news of early spring, that Grant had come east to win the war with one strategy: attack, forward or by the flank, attack and flank left, attack and flank left, until Lee had stretched his line so thin around Richmond that it pulled apart like taffy. . . .

Six battles in six weeks . . . and still he survived.

. . . though he hoped never again to utter the words *cold* and *harbor* together. Hellish, hideous, horrible Cold Harbor . . . a seven-mile front, a fog at dawn, a death march into impregnable works, scythes of orange fire cutting down thousands in minutes, fire so ferocious that the men of the Twentieth simply lay down on the field and dug in like bugs . . . then the cries of the wounded, who lay dying for days on the field while Grant and Lee dickered over a truce . . . the burial details gathering up the blackened, flyblown corpses of all the fine young men. . . .

He had survived it all, until . . .

. . . a skirmish line outside Petersburg, another push by Grant to stretch Lee's line, another move to the left, ever to the left, even in winter, even in sleet . . . a fierce blow, striking him in the belly and exploding out his back.

.   .   .

He thanked God now for opium pills and big needles of morphine. . . .

Until the drugs wore off, he floated. He floated in the ambulance. He floated above the bed in the hospital. He felt warmth, saw light, heard voices:

"A conical ball entered the right side at the external edge of the rectus muscle, about four inches from the umbilicus. Its exit was in the back, about three inches from the spine. It wounded the ascending colon to a fearful extent. The patient is now passing the whole contents of his bowels through the anterior and posterior openings—"

Halsey raised his head and looked down, expecting to see shit covering his belly.

But a voice, deep and gentle, said, "Rest easy, friend. Rest your head."

"But, my bowels. The doctor said—"

"He's talking about the lad in the next bed. His assistant is taking notes."

The accent was familiar. It reminded Halsey of the way they talked in the New York Tammany Regiment.

"Am I dying?"

"You have a bit of a fever, so lie back."

Halsey dropped again onto the pillow. "Am I going to die?"

"The bullet hit you on the left side. It missed the vitals going in and clipped your kidney coming out." The man brought a cooling cloth to Halsey's forehead.

Halsey saw long hair and a full beard, graying fast. The man's upper body was beefy, his face wide and warm. He reminded Halsey of an uncle. He said the word.

"Uncle, yes. Uncle Walt. Call me Uncle Walt."

Halsey formed the word "Walt" with his lips.

"Do I remind you of an uncle, Jeremiah?"

Halsey's eyes opened wide. "Jeremiah? My name's not Jeremiah—"

"Soothe yourself, son. It's the fever talking. We'll cool the fever, then talk."

. . .

But the fever went on for days.

And the pain burned ever hotter. It throbbed. It pulsed. It grew like a living thing inside him. Even when they gave him morphine that flowed through his veins and stung his eyeballs and lifted him up off the bed, even then, he wanted to die.

He did not know that they *expected* him to.

But Uncle Walt came every day, or every other day, or every five days. Halsey did not know, because time lost meaning. Walt talked and soothed and said that he would come more often, but he had so many young men to visit. . . .

Sometimes Halsey remembered their talk, sometimes not.

Then one morning, he awoke to the surgeon's drone: "Corporal Murphy was admitted febrile and semi-conscious, with blood in the urine indicating kidney damage. A conical bullet had entered the left side and traveled diagonally, exiting five inches from the spine. There was constant discharge of fine yellow pus from both wounds. Under chloroform, on February 22—two days ago—a piece of his overcoat was excised from the posterior opening. Redness somewhat less today. Prognosis, guarded."

Halsey drifted again. He did not know how long he slept. Hours? Days? But when he awoke, he felt two things: His face was cool and his head was clear.

A soldier in a bed nearby was moaning. Halsey realized that he had been moaning for days, moaning rhythmically, almost musically with the pain of his perforated bowel.

Then Halsey turned his head on the pillow and felt its coolness. He realized that someone had shaved him. His thick beard was gone. Not even a mustache remained. If he'd had the strength, he might have panicked. Instead, he stared at the rafters and thought, fine. If this was the first step in reclaiming his identity, fine. Then he slept.

He awakened to a touch on his cheek and the New York accent: "My, but that is a handsome face under that beard. A bit gaunt, perhaps, but handsome."

"I . . . I didn't give permission. I—"

"We'll blame some ignorant orderly. But—" Uncle Walt smiled. "—it flatters you."

Halsey asked if Walt would help him to sit up.

"Lean on your right. We don't want you dragging on that wound and popping the clot. I've seen many a wounded boy pop a clot and bleed out, right in this ward." And Uncle Walt gently lifted him until he was in a sitting position.

Then Halsey pulled up his nightshirt and looked at the wound in his abdomen. It was covered with a bandage, stained yellow and red in the middle.

Walt said, "You're pale. I'm thinking this is the first time you've sat up."

"It is. It hurts like a . . . like a gunshot."

"I'll get you a little relief."

As Walt went off, Halsey took in the world around him, the hospital that he had watched them putting up three years earlier.

The ward was one of ten buildings on the Mall, each about 150 feet long and 25 wide, side-by-side, like barracks, with twenty-five beds on each wall, windows at regular intervals for good airflow, woodstoves every thirty feet, a desk and wardmaster's office near the front door, which opened onto Seventh Street, an indoor privy at the back, and a rear door that opened onto the Mall. Every bed was assigned, and every form of battlefield wound, amputation, and illness was present and accounted for.

To his right lay the moaner. To his left lay a man who had not made a sound or raised his head in all the time that Halsey had been there. From across the aisle, a man was frowning at him. The man had no reason to frown at him, unless Halsey's feverish ravings had taken the man's sleep. Then Halsey realized that the man had no legs, and he was probably frowning at whatever fate lay ahead of him.

Walt soon returned with opium pills, ministered them, chattered on a bit about his job at the Bureau of Indian Affairs, then asked if Halsey wished to write a letter to anyone.

Halsey shook his head.

"You have no one, then?"

Halsey shook his head again. Then he let Walt talk. He talked back, but he did not remember what he said because the opium worked quickly.

. . .

Over the next week, Halsey came to appreciate the morning routine of the ward. The rumble of the ambulances on Seventh Street began around six. Coffee and soft-boiled eggs arrived by seven. Men bound for the knife were carried to the central building by eight. The surgeon visited his cases by nine.

One morning, Dr. Porter, a small man with a brusque manner, a black mustache, and a blood-splattered white coat, removed Halsey's bandages and dictated to his assistant: "Signs of cicatrices at edges, granulation in center of each wound. Redness diminished. Draining reduced. Healing slow. Patient seems alert."

"I'm, alert, sir. Alert for certain." Halsey even remembered his brogue.

The surgeon did not seem to notice. "Order a regular diet and two ounces of whiskey a day for pain. Reduce his opium to morning and evening only."

"Will that be enough?" asked Halsey.

"We stopped the morphine when it looked as if you might survive. You'll get opium tablets for a time, then just whiskey." The surgeon patted him on the shoulder. "Too much opium is no good. Binds you up. Makes you jumpy. Don't want to be jumpy when you're discharged."

"When can I walk?"

"Give it time, son. A bullet the size of your fingertip went in your belly and out your back. It's a miracle you're alive. So just lie here and be patient—that's why we call you patients—and plan the rest of your life. What's your trade?"

Halsey had to think a moment. What was his trade? "I'm a soldier."

"Until your papers come through."

. . .

Some time later, Halsey awoke to the sound of a female voice, a woman reading to a soldier nearby.

He raised his head, looked toward her, and heard Walt whisper. "You like the ladies, do you?"

"I like them. I've missed them."

"Well, there's a number of young lady volunteers in the hospitals. They're a great help. But the best lady nurses are middle-aged or healthy older women, especially those who've been mothers, because you wounded boys must be handled. A hundred things must be done that a modest young lady shouldn't have to do. You boys need mothers, women who've birthed children and know how to give care."

Halsey nodded. He was still drowsy.

Walt kept talking. "There's an illiterate old red-faced Irish woman in the next ward who takes her poor naked boys so tenderly in her arms . . . I think an Irish boy like you could use an Irish mother. Perhaps I'll send her over."

"I'd like that."

"It'll be good to hear the voice of the old country, then?"

Halsey nodded.

Then Walt brought his lips close to Halsey's ear. He smelled . . . good. He smelled of soap and clean clothes, and his skin was warm and pink, as if he had bathed before visiting. He whispered, "Do you remember what I asked you the other day?"

"I can't even remember this morning, or how this afternoon got here so soon."

"Then I'll ask again: How is it a man from Ireland sometimes speaks with no brogue at all?"

"But I do." Halsey raised his voice. "Don't I?"

"Today you do. But sometimes, you sound like a Boston Yankee, which makes me think, '*There's* a lad who's truly off his head.'" Walt studied him a moment. "Do you remember what you said when I asked you about your accent?"

"What?" asked Halsey. If his wits had been sharper, he would have thought of something, but he felt no panic because with Walt, he felt safe.

"You said, 'Time and tide are strongly changed. Men and women much deranged.' You pulled it from deep in your brain. And it's a true description of what we're living through. You said the poet was a family friend. And I thought, a man from Galway? How does a man from Galway come by friendship with Ralph Waldo Emerson?"

Halsey dropped deep into his brogue. "I wouldn't know the answer, Walt, me darlin', but if you give me a few minutes, and a glass of poteen, I'll t'ink of a good lie."

"I think you already have." Walt stood. "I know Emerson, too, personally. If I write to him, should I mention your name? Your real name?"

Halsey shook his head.

"I'll be back soon." Walt leaned down and kissed him on the cheek and whispered, "Don't worry. Your secret is safe with me."

Halsey thought, *Uncle Walt . . . a friend of Emerson? Walt* Whitman? *The poet?*

. . .

The days grew longer. The doses of opium grew lighter. And as the pain grew less, so did his cravings. The doctor told him that he was fortunate in that at least.

So Halsey decided to stand, because the sooner he could stand, the sooner he could walk, and the sooner he could walk, the sooner he could leave, and the sooner he could leave, the sooner he could get to the business of rescuing his name and future.

He waited for Walt to come again before he asked for help. He liked Walt's bulk. He knew that Walt would not let him fall.

Walt borrowed a wheelchair from one of the amputees. Then he helped Halsey swing his legs out of the bed.

Halsey wobbled to his feet and stood for thirty seconds or so, until his upper thighs turned to jelly and he dropped into the wheelchair.

Walt congratulated him, then tucked a blanket around him and pushed him through the ward to the back door. It felt good to be moving. It felt good to be rolling into the sunlight, so generous and warm that late winter morning. And it felt good to look up at the Capitol dome, gleaming white against the blue sky.

Halsey said, in his brogue, "The last time I seen that, 'twas mostly a giant cast-iron skeleton."

"Well, it's done now," said Walt, "and done well."

The symbol had become reality. The Union would go on, and as Lincoln had said at Gettysburg, the nation would know "a new birth of freedom."

In the brutal summer of '64, however, when the bodies of Yankee boys were rotting in a wide arc from Spotsylvania to Petersburg, it had looked for all the world as if Lincoln would lose the presidential election. McClellan had challenged him after all. Though deposed, the general had remained the favorite of Union Democrats and the only choice for the Peace Democrats and Copperheads.

By then, Lincoln had traveled far in his feelings toward the Negroes. Colored regiments comprised more than 10 percent of the Union Army. Colored men were fighting and dying on every front. And even though he knew it might seal his political doom, Lincoln had insisted that the Republican platform call for a Thirteenth Amendment to end slavery in all states forever, not simply as a military measure but as a moral truth institutionalized in law. He called it "a King's cure for all the evils."

Then Sherman took Atlanta. And Union soldiers took absentee ballots. And as one of them said to Halsey, "Fightin' men don't generally fight to put down treason, then vote to let it live." And Lincoln took the election.

Now, with the war almost won, the finished white dome appeared to Halsey as a new and spotless symbol of a nation whose sin had been . . . expiated.

"I like looking at it," said Walt. "It comforts me somehow."

Halsey shivered, and Walt wheeled him back, saying they had done enough for one day. Halsey was glad to slip between the sheets and pull the blanket up.

The Moaner moaned beside them. The doctor droned in the distance. The Frowner simply frowned. The day went on as all of them had in Ward A.

Walt pulled up a chair, reached into the sack of goodies he always carried, and took out a tin of biscuits and a jar of raspberry preserves. He spread preserves on a biscuit and gave it to Halsey. "A man needs a little reward after such strenuous work."

Halsey relished flavor, texture, crunch. He thought of his boyhood, when such sweet pleasures were as central to life as exploring the banks of the Charles or the beach at Nahant. And in the strange way that the senses made connections in a man's mind, he was twelve again, feeling the warm sun and the sand between his toes.

And out of nowhere, Walt said, "I've seen her."

"Who?"

"Your lady friend."

"Lady friend?"

Walt reached under the bed and brought out Halsey's rucksack.

It contained the kepi that he had been wearing when he was hit, a toothbrush, a pocketknife that he had taken off a dead Confederate, some writing paper, a copy of *A Tale of Two Cities,* and a tattered carte de visite he had carried through the whole war.

"When you were raving," Walt explained, "I went through your gear, looking for clues to the identity of a young man with the two accents."

Halsey's heart was beating so hard, he feared that it might pound the clots right out. He said, "I had many things in that rucksack. Was there a pistol? When they put me on the steamer, I was carrying an Adams pocket revolver and forty Yankee greenbacks that I'd saved from my pay."

"The gun and money were gone. Someone must have lifted them between Petersburg and here. Thievery is a common human failing. But"— Walt held up the carte de visite—"when I saw this, I said, 'I know her from somewhere.' Yesterday, I saw her. She runs a ward at Harewood Hospital. Her name is— Do I need to tell you her name?"

Halsey could not speak. His voice has grown stronger over time, but he still found, in moments of tension or duress, that his damaged throat constricted and the words would not come out.

He had written to her almost every month. He had thought of her almost every day. He had prayed almost every night that she would read his words of apology and explanation, of the lost presidential daybook, and of his quest through the war's horror for expiation. And if she had not read them, at least the writing of them had helped him to live through two and a half years of hell.

"You must have very strong feelings for her, that you'd carry this for so long."

Halsey did not know what he felt. He looked down at the blanket. He looked across at the Frowner. He looked into the eyes of Walt Whitman. "She's a nurse?"

"For as long as I've been here. I came in December of '62, after Fredericksburg."

"She started at the Union Hotel Hospital. That's where I asked to go, but . . . is she . . . is she married?"

"To hundreds of suffering young men. Would you like to see her?"

Halsey shook his head. "Not yet."

"Not ever?" asked Walt.

"When I'm stronger."

.   .   .

But strength returned slowly. Sleep took most of his time.

On the first Sunday of March, he awoke from an afternoon nap to see Walt sitting there with a journal on his lap.

"What are you doing?" Halsey asked.

"I'm a writer, you know," said Walt with a little grin.

"Of poems, yes. The modern man you sing."

"Very good. You remember what I read to you. And writers keep diaries. I've even written a bit about you and your two accents. At the moment, I'm writing down my thoughts on yesterday. It was Inauguration Day."

"Did you go?"

"No, but"—Walt read—"'I saw the president return, at three o'clock, after the performance was over. He was in his plain two-horse barouche and looked very much worn and tired; the lines, indeed, of vast responsibilities, intricate questions, and demands of life and death, cut deeper than ever upon his dark brown face; yet I saw all the old goodness, tenderness, sadness, and canny shrewdness, underneath the furrows.'"

"I remember the furrows," said Halsey, "from the first time I met him."

"Met him?"

Halsey had come to trust Walt enough that he often dropped out of character. But he quickly raised the Irish curtain again: "Or should I say, seen him, when he come to Bolivar Heights, after Antietam."

Walt lowered his voice. "I told you, son, your secret's safe with me."

"Then read a bit more if ye would, sir."

Walt returned to the notebook. "'I never see that man without feeling that he is one to become personally attached to, for his combination of purest, heartiest tenderness, and a native Western—almost rude—form of manliness. By his side in the barouche sat his little boy. There were no soldiers, only civilians on horseback, with huge yellow scarves over their shoulders, riding around the carriage, much unlike the Inauguration four years ago, when he rode down and back, surrounded by a dense mass of cavalrymen, sabers shouldered, while sharpshooters were stationed at every corner.'"

"He must feel safer now," said Halsey.

"He knows the war is nearly over." Walt picked up the newspaper he had brought. "Just hear what he said: 'With malice toward none, with charity for all.' Those are words to bind a nation's wounds just as we have tried here to bind yours."

"We're lucky to have him," said Halsey.

"I wanted to tell him that very thing, so I went to the public levee last night. You never saw such a jam in front of the White House—all the grounds filled, all the way out to the sidewalks." He read, "'I was in the rush inside with the crowd. We surged along the passage-ways, the Blue and other rooms, and through the great East Room, upholstered like a stage parlor. Crowds of country people, some very funny. Fine music from the Marine Band, off in a side place. And Mr. Lincoln, dressed all in black, with white kid gloves and claw-hammer coat, as in duty bound, receiving, shaking hands, looking very disconsolate, as if he would give anything to be somewhere else.'"

"Did you shake his hand?"

"I never got close enough. But I left knowing that there are bright days ahead for this nation, thanks to him. Democracy will survive. We will do what he asked in his inaugural. We will bind up the nation's wounds. We will go forward. And you, my friend, will walk." Walt threw the blanket off Halsey's legs. "Starting now."

Halsey stood in his nightshirt and Sanitary Commission flannel robe. He felt his legs wobble, but only a bit.

Walt knelt in front of him and slid leather slippers onto his feet. Then he offered an arm, but only an arm.

And Halsey took his first step. He went with his right foot, his good side. Then he put weight on his wounded side and felt little pain. So he took another step, then another.

The Frowner frowned, perhaps envying a man who had legs to walk again.

But soon, Halsey had reached the back door. He looked up at the Capitol for a few moments, then looked behind him for a wheelchair.

"The chair is occupied." Walt smiled, as if he had played a little joke. "You'll need to get back on your own two feet."

Halsey glanced toward his bed. It looked as unassailable as the Confederate works at Cold Harbor. But Walt urged him on. So Halsey wiped the sweat from his forehead and turned. He felt something pull in his side. He hoped it was nothing serious.

A lady nurse at the far end of the ward grabbed a wheelchair and came rolling.

Walt held up a hand. "It's time for the man to walk."

"But—"

"No buts," said Walt with surprising firmness.

The woman stopped and glared. There were some lady nurses who could not abide the poet-turned-caregiver. Halsey had heard one of them gossip about "that odious Walt Whitman, here to talk evil and unbelief to my boys." Others complained, in cold tones, that he took some men home to continue his care in a more personal way.

This one said, "The corporal's going to fall."

"If he falls, I'll catch him," said Walt.

All that Halsey knew was that Walt had eased pain and offered kindness in a world where there was too much of one and not enough of the other. And Halsey did not want to disappoint his friend. So he took another step, then another, then he stopped and wobbled, but Walt urged him on until he reached his bed, exhausted and drenched in sweat.

"Walk the length the building," said Walt, "and you'll get a reward."

. . .

A week later, Halsey did, and Walt reminded him of the reward.

Sometime around midnight it arrived: a kiss on the forehead to awaken him.

At first, he thought it was Walt, who had visited late on other nights, too.

Then he smelled jasmine perfume and sweet perspiration. And in the instant before his brain made the connection between the aroma and the woman, she kissed him on the lips. She had come to him.

When the ward was wrapped in sleep, Samantha found him and kissed him and held her face against his smooth cheek. He was glad now that he had been shaved. He could remember no feeling more exquisite than her soft skin against a face that had known snow, rain, mud, hard-ground pillows, musket-butt blows, and now . . .

When he tried to speak, she simply said, "Shhhh."

The ward was dark, but for lanterns at either end and a glow from the woodstoves. Someone coughed. The Moaner moaned. The Frowner seemed to be frowning in his sleep.

"Just lie still," she whispered.

So he did. And he took a deep breath and filled his lungs with the life-affirming scent of her and felt the rest of his body fill with life as well.

She whispered, "I prayed I would see you again."

"Do you like what you see?"

She looked him up and down and her eyes fell on the wool tent rising from the covers. "I like that you are recovering . . . rather well, apparently."

He slid a hand along her side.

She twisted away with the deftness of a woman who had learned many skills in ministering to men reaching out for comfort. Then she stroked his face with the back of her hand. "I like that you shaved your beard, too."

"I like that you're here, unless I'm dreaming."

"You're not dreaming," she whispered. "This is real."

And he was awake enough that he felt the fear that had filled him whenever he wrote to her. "Did you read my letters?"

"Every one, more than once."

"Then you know my story."

"All that you've told me . . . about the diary, the death of Constance, the shootings."

"And I told you I loved you, too."

"Did you really kill those men on the bridge to protect me?"

"They were murderers. They followed Constance and killed her. They were following you, so they might have killed you, too."

She thanked him with another kiss.

And he said, "Do you love me?" He no longer had time for subtlety.

"I've waited for you," she answered. "I've nursed and mothered and sistered a thousand men, and I am plain worn out from it, but I've waited for you."

"Is that a yes?"

"That's a promise to think about it." She urged him to get well before he worried himself about his fate as an accused murderer. . . or about their fate together.

Just then, Dr. Porter came through the ward, stopped, looked at the shadow of the woman seated on the edge of Corporal Murphy's bed.

Samantha stood and said, "So, Corporal Murphy, I thank you for a report on my brother in the Twentieth."

Dr. Porter said, "Nurse, you know that consorting with the patients is more than frowned upon. It's a firing offense. Return to your ward."

But Samantha Simpson was not the wide-eyed girl who first saw Washington on a gloom-ridden Fourth of July. She held her voice to a hard whisper and told the doctor, "I am nurse-superintendent of Ward M at Harewood Hospital. I am visiting a family friend. If you don't like it, Doctor, I'll ask permission of the Surgeon General, whose son was nursed back to health in my ward. I'm sure he can accommodate any wish you have to visit Petersburg in the spring. I hear that the fighting is very lovely this time of year." Without waiting for an answer, she turned back to Halsey. "I'll visit when I can. Count on me next Tuesday. I take Tuesday as my day of rest. I have fond memories of Tuesdays." Then she stalked out.

Halsey said, "Don't walk back alone."

The surgeon looked at Halsey and said, "Not all women are made for wives, Corporal, so don't let the opium cloud your brain."

"You forget, Doctor, you've weaned me off of the opium."

. . .

Nights had been the hardest time for Halsey. The fevers had been hotter at night, the pains sharper. So most nights, he had spent time awake, suffering, wondering, praying, listening to the clank of the steam engines that crossed the city incessantly, ignoring the snores and coughs, the sleep farts and death rattles around him.

And now something else bothered his sleep: hope . . . that Samantha would come in the night and announce herself with a kiss.

That first night, he awoke around midnight and waited. And though she did not appear, anticipation of her kiss and sweet scent caused another response beneath his blanket.

After half an hour of waiting and hoping, he thought about turning his hand to the insistent business. Soldiers joked about it, but none frowned on a man for surrendering to his need in the night. Halsey was sure that somewhere in the ward, some soldier was taking care of himself right then, his mind's eye focused on an image of his sweetheart or some stage beauty, society's promise of disease or blindness notwithstanding.

But Halsey would not want Samantha to find him like that.

So he turned his mind to other things . . . things so vexing that a man would lose any urge. Across two and a half years of war, these things had not bothered him. Survival had been his only worry, expiation his only goal. But he knew that he could not live as an Irish veteran forever, any more than he could live as a hole man on a night soil crew.

How could he ever clear his name? How could he ever be Halsey Hutchinson again?

Some time around two, he heard the Frowner crying, softly but bitterly. It was the first time that Halsey had heard a sound from him.

An hour later, as he drifted, Halsey heard a familiar sound outside. He realized he had heard it before, during his fevers. It was the sound of whispered orders, scraping shovels, dumping buckets, and the snorts of a pair of horses.

A night soil wagon had rolled up to the two four-holed privies behind the barracks, and men were working, quickly and quietly.

Halsey listened and wondered if the Freedom brothers were out there.

. . .

The next night, the Moaner died.

He simply stopped moaning, and the sudden quiet woke Halsey.

When the night nurse went by, he called to her.

She was a coarse old woman from Camden, New Jersey, by the name of Mary Cannon. She checked the Moaner's pulse, pulled the blanket over him, and whispered to Halsey, "At least he won't be shittin' through a hole in his belly no more."

Halsey agreed and asked, "Do I hear the night soil wagon again tonight?"

"Well, them privies out back fill up fast when five hundred men are doin' their business, some with diarrhea so bad, they're squirtin' their own innards down the hole. So it's a two-night job. Plus we got the indoor privies to clean, too."

Halsey asked, "Most night soil wagons are run by coloreds, aren't they?"

"I don't know about that," said Mrs. Cannon, "but them boys workin' out there right now is as black as the holes they're cleanin'."

So he told her he needed to make a visit.

She said, "You sure you don't want the chair pot? I don't recollect you've set out on the four-holer yet. Don't want you passin' out on the stool and freezin' to death."

"Tonight I feel a powerful need, and I'd rather take it outside, considerin' the heavy portion of beans I et tonight."

She chuckled at that, wrapped a blanket about him, wheeled him out to a cleaned privy, and said she'd be back in a bit. "Just don't fall in."

He spent a few minutes on the seat but had no real need. He was there to talk to the night soilers. So he wobbled to his feet, came outside, sat in the wheelchair.

The stars glittered above him. The stink simmered below.

The tub man went past and dumped a load into the wagon. Then he came back and said, "Mighty smelly out here, mister. You wants me to roll y'all back inside?"

"I'd appreciate that." And once they were rolling toward the door of Ward A, Halsey asked, "Do you boys know the Freedom brothers?"

"Why you askin'?"

Halsey understood that a colored man had to be naturally suspicious. So he said, "They did some fine work for me years ago. Always liked them. Jubilo . . . Zion . . ."

That seemed explanation enough, so the man said, "We use their compostin' yard sometimes. Mother Freedom's right generous. But they ain't brothers no more."

"Why not?"

The man slowed the wheelchair. "Only one left."

"Only one?" Halsey turned and looked up at the black face. Somewhere in the distance behind the Negro, gaslight glimmered in the windows of the Capitol.

"The brother named Zion. Jubilo and Hallelujah and their cousin Jim-Boy all joined up with the Massachusetts Fifty-fourth. First colored regiment. All but Jim-Boy died at Battery Wagner, or so we heard."

And Halsey wept until dawn.

By breakfast, the Moaner's bed was empty.

And the Frowner spoke for the first time. "His sufferin' is over."

Halsey said, "God's mercy on him." And the Frowner nodded. So Halsey asked his name. "George Smith." From where? "Philadelphia." Occupation? "Gardener." Then George Smith turned his gaze to the middle distance. He had no more to say.

Healing came in different ways and different rhythms for every man, and sometimes sadness slowed it down.

.   .   .

On Tuesday afternoon, Samantha brought fresh air and the smell of spring. She told Halsey that they were going for a walk and she wouldn't take no for an answer. Then she turned to the Frowner named George Smith and said, "Would you like to sit outside, too?"

George Smith frowned and said, "Why?"

"Because the sun is warm. It'll do you good."

George Smith said no and turned his head.

So she walked to the end of the ward, found a wheelchair, brought it back, and said to him, "I need weight in this, to give Corporal Murphy something to lean on. Your torso may be just the thing."

George Smith looked at her, then at the chair, looked off again into the middle distance, as if remembering some horror or hope, then reached out.

Halsey watched Samantha put a hand under George Smith's right arm and pivot him onto the chair. He admired the way she worked, performing an act of kindness yet making it seem a manly challenge.

"There now," she said once Smith was seated. "You'll make fine ballast."

George Smith kept his frown firmly in place. But with Halsey holding one side of the chair and Samantha pushing from the other, they headed out into the sunshine. They went past the privies, the chapel, and the quarters of the lady nurses. Then they followed a path onto the Mall, to a row of benches.

The trees were making lime green buds. The forsythia glimmered yellow in the sun. A few flower beds, planted and tended by the nurses, were pushing up tulips and daffodils.

Samantha took out a newspaper and asked her patients if they'd like to read. She said, "You must be engaged in the world if you hope to have any future in it."

George Smith frowned and turned toward the National Greenhouse, near the end of the Mall.

So she handed the front page to Halsey. "Read us something."

Halsey would have preferred talking to her, alone. He had a thousand things to say. But if she believed that engaging in the news of the world mattered for their future, he would engage. He read the first story his eye fell upon: "'Intelligence reaches us that General Robert E. Lee has appealed to the rebel legislature to permit the enlistment of colored soldiers in the Confederate Army.'"

Samantha let out a laugh. "You're making that up."

Halsey held up the paper. "No, I'm not."

George Smith's frown almost cracked into a smile.

Halsey read on: "'He insisted that those who enlist should be promised their freedom. In granting his request, the legislature said, "The country will not deny General Lee *anything* he may ask for."'"

Samantha said, "Now I know that the war is almost over."

"It's only a matter of time." Halsey looked at her. "Then we can worry about what comes next, for the nation . . . and for us."

"Get stronger, first," she said.

Halsey scanned the rest of the front page. The Federal line ran for fifty miles around Petersburg. Lee's army was melting away. The president had gone south to confer with Grant and observe the operations. Sherman had continued his relentless march north. The vise was closing.

Then an article in the lower corner caught Halsey's eye, a bit of local news: A pair of Negroes had been arrested for armed robbery in a northern ward. It would have meant nothing, except that one of them "was carrying a rare Adams pocket revolver." What's more, the suspect had worked as a stretcher-bearer at the City Wharf.

Halsey knew now where his gun had gone. And he wondered, who else was reading that paper?

II.

By the last week of March, the war was rushing to its finale.

But all the news washed over Halsey, because his fever came back.

Dr. Porter admitted he was puzzled. He observed no redness around the wound. "It must be typhoid or some other thing. Men who've survived as long as you have in the camps usually don't get sick in the ward, but some men leave here sicker than when they arrived."

Walt agreed. "Sickness kills more men than bullets, I'm afraid. This damn war sometimes seems to be nine hundred and ninety-nine parts diarrhea and one part glory."

Or perhaps it was a sign of the sadness that came back when Samantha told Halsey that his father had died in the summer of '64, of a seizure at the breakfast table, as he read of the hell of Cold Harbor. She said she had withheld the news until she felt he was strong enough to handle it.

Samantha sat with Halsey through each night of fever and grief. And since the Mall was not safe after dark, she slept in the lady nurses' quarters at Armory Square. And she helped with the other men of Ward A, also. She even got George Smith to stop frowning and talk of roses.

Then, on Wednesday, the twenty-ninth, Halsey passed through a crisis, broke a sweat, and slipped into a deep, dreamless sleep. On Thursday, he awoke to a clear head and a golden shaft of sunlight slicing in the back window, as if God were telling him that the death of an elderly father was in the natural order of things.

The ward was quiet. It was not yet six.

He looked across into the eyes of George Smith, who said, "You are a lucky man, Murphy."

Halsey wanted to say that a man who had survived two amputations enjoyed a special kind of luck as well.

But George Smith kept talking. "She sat with you till two. When she left, I was cryin'. I cry in the night. Can't help it . . . Anyways, she come over and said, 'If you want to make yourself useful, stop cryin' and keep an eye on the corporal for me.'"

"Did you?"

"All the damn night."

The man who had replaced the Moaner rolled over and looked at them as if they were annoying him; then he rolled over again. He had the fever, too.

"Watchin' you took my mind off my troubles," said George Smith. "Then somethin' funny happened."

"Funny?"

"About four thirty, the sky was just gettin' light, a feller let himself in the back door and comes down the aisle, lookin' from bed to bed. He had a carte in his hand. He saw me awake, so he showed it to me and said, 'Have you ever seen this man?'"

"What did he look like?"

"Short, slope shoulders, brown beard, heavy brow. Dangerous lookin'."

Halsey swallowed the fever-bile in the back of his throat. *McNealy.* He must have read about the gun, tracked it through the serial numbers to the Negro stretcher-bearers, and frightened them into admitting the truth: They had stolen it from a wounded soldier bound for Armory Square . . . or was it Harewood?

George Smith said, "That picture surprised me more than mealy bugs in February. It showed a lieutenant, a good-lookin' man in a fine mustache and chin strap, lookin' a lot like you, though a lot younger. You've walked some hard miles. Murphy."

"What did you say?"

"I said, 'Never seen him before in my life. Then, Mrs. Cannon come

scuttlin' up, whisperin' and yellin' at the same time, 'What's the idea of
sneakin' in here at this hour?' The feller said he was a War Department
detective and showed her the carte and a badge. She give 'em a squint and
said, 'I don't care if you're Jesus Christ Almighty come down to raise
Lazarus. There's nobody in here who looks like that, just a lot of hurtin'
men who need their sleep. Now, git on the hell out of here.'"

"What did he say to that?"

"Nothin'. Then he just went through the rest of the ward with her
shooin' him along like he was a dog lookin' to lift his leg on the furniture."

"Thanks," said Halsey. "I owe you."

"I wouldn't do it just for you. But for Miz Samantha, I'd lie like a
politician."

Life's wisdom, thought Halsey, from a man with no legs.

.   .   .

That afternoon, Walt Whitman came to say good-bye. "I get three weeks
leave from the Bureau of Indian Affairs starting the first of the month.
That's Saturday. I'll be off home to Brooklyn to visit Mother."

"I'll miss you."

"Is there a last favor I can do for you"—Walt lowered his voice—
"Lieutenant Corporal Halsey Jeremiah Murphy Hutchinson?"

So Halsey asked Walt to do three things: determine if a man named
McNealy still lived in Ryan's boardinghouse on East Capitol, stop for a
shoeshine at the National Hotel and ask for Noah, and see if a woman
named Harriet Dunbar still resided on the corner of K and Sixteenth. He
even suggested a few questions to ask.

"I will cross the city seeking your truths and your friends." Walt Whitman stood. "Where the city of faithful friends stands, there the greatest city
stands."

"That's a good poem, Walt, but they're not my friends, except for the
bootblack."

"A Negro for a friend? You are a man of many surprises, Corporal."

.   .   .

Halsey realized that he would have to get better and quickly.

But Dr. Porter restricted him to bed rest until there was no sign of fever for forty-eight hours. "Whatever you've just had shows how weak you still are."

If Halsey had been stronger, he would have checked himself out and disappeared. Then he could deal with McNealy on his own, on foot, from the shadows. But the doctor was right. He had barely survived a brutal wound, infection, fever, grief. He had little strength and no stamina.

So he spent the rest of the day reading the papers, talking across the floor to George Smith, and wondering what McNealy really wanted from him.

At this point, the Emancipation Proclamation and the Thirteenth Amendment had made slavery a dead issue . . . dead though not buried, perhaps never buried.

Halsey had seen what lay ahead. He had seen it in Virginia, whenever the Army of the Potomac brought freedom to a few more of the four million uneducated, ill-prepared Negroes being loosed upon a nation. He had seen how much the nation, deep inside, simply hated them. How Lincoln confronted this problem, how he reconstructed America after its new birth of freedom, would determine his legacy.

Halsey searched his memory for the things he had read in that daybook three years earlier. Lincoln had wondered aloud about Negro voting rights, about their limited intellectual capabilities, about the evils of miscegenation, about satisfying a national desire to see them sent back to Africa. Halsey expected that Lincoln had changed many of those positions. But what other ruminations were in that book? What had Halsey missed?

He wished now that he had sat down and read it from cover to cover. But his goal that long-ago morning had been to return it safely to the president. And that should be his goal now.

                              .   .   .

On Friday night, Samantha sat beside Halsey's bed, took his hand, and whispered, "He found me."

"He?"

"McNealy, if that's his name. He came through the wards at Harewood today, showing the carte de visite from the day we went to Brady's. He said he was looking for the man in the picture, to give him a medal."

"Did he know you?"

"He appeared not to, but he had a suspicious eye."

"He may want to lock me up and throw away the key."

"Then we need to protect you. Does anyone but Walt know your real identity?"

"Not even Walt knows everything."

"Who else in Washington knows you from before?"

"Lincoln, Eckert, Homer Bates, a few Negroes, the Wood Brothers, Booth—"

"Booth." She said the name as if spitting it.

"Do you ever see him?"

"I sometimes check into the National to recover my wits. They have very nice bath facilities for ladies there. I've seen him with Lucy Hale in the lobby."

"Lucy Hale, daughter of the Abolitionist New Hampshire senator?" Halsey put his head back and remembered. "Wendell Holmes courted her in Boston years ago."

"I've heard that Lincoln's son Robert has courted her as well. But Booth courts her now. There's a rumor that they're engaged. It may be true, considering that Booth bought a lot on Commonwealth Avenue, in the new Back Bay lands in Boston."

"The city of Abolition," said Halsey. "Once, Booth wouldn't speak to you if he thought you were an Abolitionist. Has he now become one to marry one?"

"Lord, no. He's even more outspoken in his Southern sympathies. I stayed in the National on Inauguration Day. I saw him cross the lobby in a fine top hat. I asked where he'd been. He said he had just come from the ceremony. Lucy had gotten him a ticket so that he could stand on the pediment directly above Lincoln.

"I said, 'You must have had a fine view of him as he delivered his oration.'

"He said, 'I was close enough to touch him. But why would I want to?' Then he and Lucy went upstairs."

"Arm in arm?" asked Halsey.

"Outrageous, I suppose, but—" Samantha paused. "— I for one would not go behind closed doors with him. He appears dour, depressed, focused on some other world, much unlike the Booth who escorted me to the train station one unhappy day."

"Unhappy for me, too."

"Unhappy, even if you hadn't appeared with Constance Wood."

"That was many lives ago," said Halsey.

She squeezed his hand, as if she forgave but could not entirely forget.

Then they heard a bustling at the front of the ward. Walt had returned, and like Father Christmas doling gifts from his bag, he stopped at every bed to leave a little something—writing paper, clean socks, taffy candies. But at Halsey's bed, he set down the bag and said, "A scene for a poet to memorialize."

Then he lowered himself next to Samantha.

She said, "You leave in the morning?"

"Reluctantly. With the war ending and our friend here getting well, the next few weeks in Washington will be quite joyous, I think."

"What do you know, Walt, darlin'?" asked Halsey in his brogue.

Samantha smiled and lowered her head, as if to keep from laughing.

"What?" whispered Halsey. "It worked in the regiment. It works here."

Walt said, "I presented myself at Mrs. Ryan's as a prospective boarder. I asked after the character of her guests, and she was more than happy to brag on all the men of politics and business under her roof. So I asked your question—did any of them rise especially early—since I was an early riser myself. She said no. Then I asked after a man named McNealy. She looked at me suspiciously and said he no longer lived there."

Walt paused, waited for a reaction, and asked, "Does that help?"

Halsey said, "It tells me I need to talk to the Negro bootblack."

"*There* I can help." Walt settled back. "I went down to the National, sat in one of the chairs, and allowed him to go to work."

"Noah Bone?"

"Yes. I engaged him, asked him if he had children. His hands stopped moving, and he said he had two sons working in the hotel, another marching with the United States Colored Troops. Then he stood up straight and added proudly, 'My Daniel is buyin' freedom for his race.'"

"Very noble," said Samantha.

"Perhaps, but"—Walt looked around the ward—"in comparison with this misery, I don't care much for the niggers and their troubles, despite the fine nobility I felt in Mr. Bone, honest dignity born of good honest labor, and—"

"Yes, we know," said Halsey, "you sing the common man."

"I also do the bidding of my friends," answered Walt, "and do not ask why."

Halsey backed off. "Much appreciated."

Walt's good nature returned quickly. "Now, then, this Harriet Dunbar . . . I sent Pete—he's a special friend of mine, Peter Doyle—I met him on the horse car—he's a conductor—used to be a rebel soldier—I sent him to her door posing as a delivery boy, bringing flowers." Walt paused, looked from face to face.

"And?" Halsey knew Walt as a poet, but there was some actor in him, too.

"She's dead. Murdered last October. Her body was found in the stable behind her house. Her horse was saddled but not cinched, as if she was surprised in the middle of a getaway to somewhere. A knife, slipped expertly between her ribs, into her heart."

Just then, Mrs. Cannon came by. "It's almost nine. Lights go out at nine."

Samantha said, "We know. We're nurses, too."

"Just sayin'"—Mrs. Cannon glided away—"that rules is rules."

Walt Whitman chuckled and grasped both their hands at once. "I must move on. I have many more boys to see tonight. I'll look forward to seeing you upon my return at the end of the month, when perhaps the world will have been born anew."

"I'll be gone from here by then," said Halsey.

Walt's eyes filled with tears, and he gripped even harder. "Then read one of my poems, and we'll meet again."

"That's a wonderful sentiment," said Samantha.

Walt picked up his rucksack. "Bearing bandages, water and sponge, straight and swift to my wounded I go." Then he gave George Smith a little wave and announced to the whole ward, "I am faithful. I do not give out."

Samantha whispered, "He's quoting his latest, 'The Wound-Dresser.'"

III.

Soldiers said that Robert E. Lee was a great general because he could anticipate what his opponent would do before he did it. They said that Grant was a great general because he decided what he would do and then did it.

Halsey knew that if he hoped to rescue himself and his future with Samantha, he had to think like Lee and act like Grant. He had to know what McNealy wanted, then make a plan and see it through.

So he tried to remember everything that McNealy had said to him. He tried to understand what McNealy had been doing in the miserable summer when he "ran" the young lieutenant from Boston. He tried to piece together the motivations that might have led McNealy to kill Harriet Dunbar. And he warned Samantha to be careful, because if McNealy was murdering women, he might make a habit of it.

And Halsey had to get stronger.

So on Saturday morning, he walked the length of the ward and back.

That afternoon, news reached Washington that Robert E. Lee had suffered terrible losses at Five Forks.

On Sunday, Samantha told him she was giving herself a second day off, the Lord's Day. She had trained enough volunteers to do her work as well as she. Then she walked him to the little chapel on the hospital grounds, where they attended services, sang hymns, and heard readings for the Fifth Sunday in Lent.

Ninety miles away, the papers later reported, Confederate President Jefferson Davis also went to church, and during the service, he received a message from Lee: "My lines are broken in three places. Richmond must be evacuated."

That night, the men in the hospital heard shouting and bands playing in the street. Word had reached Washington of Richmond's fall, of a city in flames, of looters and riots and the last moments of the Confederacy.

On Monday, Halsey walked the length of the ward twice without a wobble.

On Tuesday, he put on uniform trousers and jacket, donated by the Sanitary Commission, his old Union kepi, and a yellow neckerchief to cover the scar at his throat. He considered dressing in cast-off civilian clothes from a bin at the back of the ward, but he had decided that a man dressed as a soldier would be a popular figure in the next few weeks, so there might be some advantage.

Then he and Samantha wheeled George Smith along the Mall to the National Greenhouse. It was warm inside, much warmer than the overcast day. The former Frowner inhaled the aroma of damp earth and exhaled a deep groan of pleasure.

Halsey and Samantha left him amongst orchids and azaleas and found a bench surrounded by Chinese bamboo. They sat in silence for a time, listening to the trickling of a little indoor fountain. Then Samantha said, "Oh, Halsey, what are we to do?"

"I can light out for the West and you can follow later. Or we can wait till your work is done here and go back to Boston. But they'll find me in Boston. I still stand accused of killing a congressman's niece and five men. There's no statute of limitations on murder, even in a country where hundreds of thousands have been murdered on the battlefield."

"Perhaps you should let McNealy find you then, and get it over with."

"Not until I'm stronger."

That afternoon, as the papers would tell, Lincoln visited Richmond with no more than a dozen sailors and little Tad as a bodyguard. Thousands of Negroes came out of their homes and hovels to greet him, reach out to him, touch him, but not a single white person appeared.

Halsey grew stronger day by day. And day by day, the electrical charge of anticipation, of impending victory, seemed to energize the Washington air.

On Palm Sunday, Halsey went to services with Samantha. Then they walked up Seventh Street to Pennsylvania. It was his longest excursion yet. He felt invigorated in the warm sunshine, and Samantha had never looked more beautiful in her ladylike hooped skirt, hat, and peltote jacket.

At the Gosling restaurant, they ordered a bottle of champagne. Though Washington was an expensive city and no drink more expensive than champagne, Samantha said that she had saved her pennies for just such an occasion. So they toasted and let the bubbles go to their heads. They ate oysters. Then they had she-crab soup, creamy and rich, with big lumps of crabmeat and roe. They finished with roasted Chesapeake rockfish, known to these New Englanders as striped bass, along with the first beans of spring, sautéed in lemon butter.

Halsey did not fear discovery in such public places. War's-end spirit was rising. People were casting off the dark shades and filling the restaurants with laughter again. A clean-shaven corporal with a pretty girl might inspire good-natured envy but not suspicion.

Halfway through the main course, Samantha's eyes brightened with champagne and a brilliant idea. She said, "We must get you a presidential pardon."

"Wonderful. But how?"

"In the next week or two, the president is certain to make many public appearances where you might tell him your story. Or I can take to the patronage line at the White House and present myself. Or—"

Halsey clinked her glass. He liked the plan. He liked her determination even more.

They walked back across the Tenth Street Footbridge, which led over the canal to the Smithsonian Park. He would have enjoyed taking her to the West Range and his favorite pillar, but the Institute had been damaged in January by fire and was now closed.

So he stopped by a tall tree, looked around to make sure that none of the park thugs were lurking about, then pivoted her into the shadow and kissed her. This time, she kissed him back. And when he ran his hands along her flanks, she did not twist away. She turned toward his touch, encouraging him to travel higher, to touch her breasts through the fabric, to feel them respond.

He yearned to feel every part of her, to caress her and possess her. And he resolved that he would do whatever it took to have a life with her.

. . .

At five thirty the next morning, as Halsey dreamed of her sweet body against his, a thundering crash of artillery awoke the men of Ward A.

The windows rattled and the floor shook. A wounded patient screamed in terror. Another started shouting orders: "Take cover! Hidden batteries!" And George Smith did not frown. He wore an expression of total terror, as if he expected another explosion of shrapnel to take his legs again.

Then someone pulled open the front door and shouted, "The war is over, boys! Lee surrendered yesterday!"

A burst of cheering and coughing greeted the news while the guns continued to boom. Halsey didn't bother to count, but it was a five-hundred-gun salute. On and on it went, until seven o'clock, when the church bells began to ring, first one bell nearby, then another, then another until it seemed that a great symphony of bells was playing all across the capital. And the bells were soon drowned out by a military band marching up Seventh, playing "Hail, Columbia."

Halsey rushed to the front of the ward and watched them go by. A light rain was falling, so the brass horns flashed like gold in the slick gray light, and the drums set up a booming echo that resonated in the chests of every man in that ward.

Some of those men were dying, but men were always dying in the bed-lined barracks, and on this day, thought Halsey, they could say for certain that they had not died—or lived—in vain.

Soon the streets filled with fire engines and work wagons and impromptu parades. A group of navy yard workers marched up from the river dragging a pair of howitzers, firing them just for joy. Then someone came through shouting that up at the White House, they were having "a party to raise the dead and make 'em cheer."

Halsey decided that he had to see those grounds, which he had crossed so often in gloomy darkness, on the happiest day in a century. So he dressed in the uniform and yellow neckerchief. Then he glanced across the aisle.

George Smith said, "I sure would love to see that sight, the dead risin' up to cheer."

And Halsey, who had lived for so long as a loner, decided to do a favor for another friend. He dragged George Smith's rucksack from under his bed, found his kepi, put it on his head at a jaunty angle. Then he grabbed the wheelchair.

Halsey told the wardmaster that he was wheeling his friend onto Seventh for a better view. But once outside, he turned the chair toward Pennsylvania and started rolling. He had not gone far when he knew that he had made a mistake. The rain was turning the streets to mud. The mud was sucking the wheelchair down. Fortunately, as he struggled over the

Seventh Street Bridge, help arrived in a wagon full of flag-waving brick-layers.

"You boys goin' to the White House?" shouted the driver, a big-bellied man in a leather apron.

"We fought to see this day," said George Smith. "We deserve it."

"Well, my name's Appleyard, and me and the members of our little Masonic Order would be proud if you boys would honor our wagon."

Soon Halsey and his friend were bumping along B Street, singing patriotic songs and passing a bottle in the gentle April rain. And the whole way, they could hear the rumble of drums and the blasting of bugles and the booming of cannon.

B Street ran along the canal, so the masons avoided most of the happy madness a few blocks north, but as they came up to Fifteenth, the driver said, "Too much traffic up there. We'll go around." They followed the south edge of the President's Park, then took Seventeenth north to Pennsylvania and pulled up right in front of the War Department.

One of the bricklayers said, "God damn but will you look at this crowd!" Thousands were gathering on the front lawn of the White House, pushing up the carriage drive, standing on the pedestal of Jefferson's statue, clambering over the wrought-iron fences, trampling the grass on the graceful ovals. From the White House to the Avenue, from the State Department on the east to the War Department on the west, people were cheering, shouting, laughing, singing, drinking.

After two joyous blasts from the navy howitzers, now set up on Lafayette Park, Appleyard said, "How we ever gonna get close enough to hear the president?"

The band near the White House portico was striking up "Rally 'Round the Flag."

George Smith shouted, "Use me, lads. I'll get you close!"

"Good idea!" Appleyard got in front of the wheelchair and began to wave his flag. "Gangway! Gangway! We got a brave man here!"

And the people parted, so that George and Halsey and their new-found friends made it halfway up the carriage drive before they could go no farther.

Men shook umbrellas to the beat of the music. Women waved handkerchiefs. And a great cheer rose when Little Tad appeared in the second-floor window above the front door.

The boy grinned, then disappeared inside. A moment later, he returned with a captured Confederate flag and began to wave it.

People went into frenzies of delight. And a chant began for the president. Then the band struck up "Hail to the Chief," as if to lure him out.

Finally, the Confederate flag was pulled in. And Little Tad, still in the window, looked up, as if someone was calling to him. And the whole crowd seemed to draw a great breath, as if every man and woman on the lawn knew what was coming and wanted air for the cheer about to burst forth.

Then Abraham Lincoln stepped into the square of light beside his son.

Halsey Hutchinson had never experienced such a roar as at that moment, not even under Lee's bombardment at Gettysburg.

Men threw their hats into the air. Women screamed. The sound echoed off buildings and shook windows, the greatest roar of joy ever heard on the continent. The day was still cloudy, but in the memory of everyone there, thought Halsey, this scene would always play in sunshine.

George Smith, no longer the Frowner, was laughing and whistling and waving his kepi.

And Halsey Hutchinson felt tears of joy streaming down his face.

Lincoln put up his hands and the crowd simply roared the louder. He did it again and only caused more cheering. Finally a third time, and the crowd settled down.

Then the reedy voice and sharp prairie accent rang out, "I'm very greatly rejoiced that an occasion has occurred so pleasurable that the people cannot restrain themselves."

"You got that right, Abe!"

And another explosion of cheers shook the windows all around.

"I suppose arrangements are being made for a celebration tonight or tomorrow night. So I shall have to respond. But, folks, I won't have anything to say then if I dribble it all out now."

That brought loud laughter.

"We waited four years, Abe," cried someone in the crowd. "Give us a dribble!"

And more cheers erupted.

"Wait, wait," Lincoln said. "I see you have a band of music with you: I propose for closing up that you have them play a tune called 'Dixie.'"

George Smith shouted, "Why in hell you want to hear that for, Abe?"

Lincoln answered: "I've always thought it was the best tune, and our adversaries over the way have appropriated it as their national air. I insisted yesterday that we had fairly and squarely captured it and are entitled to it. I even asked the attorney general his opinion and he agreed."

Another wave of laughter rippled across the crowd.

Lincoln waited for it to settle, looked at the band, and said, "So, gentlemen, play 'Dixie,' if you will."

And never before had that song, written by a man from Ohio about the beautiful land down South, sounded more rousing, more life-filled, more of an American affirmation. And when it ended, a thousand hats flew into the air, and thousands of voices roared out their joy.

Lincoln called for three cheers for General Grant and the army, then three more for the navy. Then he gave a wave and disappeared.

But the crowd was not done. They were turning to the War Department, swarming the steps, shouting, "Stanton! Bring out Stanton! We want Stanton!"

Halsey looked up at the windows and saw no sign of the secretary. But under a tree on the lawn, he noticed David Homer Bates and Major Eckert. Both of them were still soaking up the music and revelry, which meant the cipher room might be empty.

And suddenly, Halsey Hutchnson had a bold thought. Considering the ease with which people were passing in and out of the War Department, perhaps it was time to visit his old desk. The future might depend on it.

So he asked his bricklayer friends to stay with George Smith for a few minutes. Appleyard proclaimed it an honor and stuck his flag into the arm of the wheelchair, then plunked himself down with his pint and passed it to the former Frowner.

As the band marched out onto Pennsylvania Avenue playing "Yankee Doodle," Halsey went through the trees and in the east entrance of the War Department. He climbed the stairs he had climbed so often, feeling no pain, though he had climbed few stairs since his wound.

The duty desk on the landing was empty. The sergeant was out celebrating.

On the second floor, men were going up and down the hallways shaking hands and slapping backs, passing flasks, laughing, turning the War Department into the Party Department. When the navy yard boys fired their howitzers again from Lafayette Park, everyone in the long hallway stopped, looked around, then roared with laughter and got on with the celebrating.

Halsey walked down the hallway as if he belonged. He passed the sounding room then looked into the cipher room. *Deserted*. He stepped inside and heard voices from the other side of the screen door. Stanton was talking to somebody in his office.

Outside, the crowd was still roaring. And after two more blasts from the howitzers, the band launched into "Marching Through Georgia."

Halsey pulled out his pocketknife and went straight to his old desk in the corner. He opened the bottom drawer and took out the codebooks and other materials. He glanced at the door, still heard voices in Stanton's office, then dug down with his pocketknife and pivoted out the false bottom.

And there was his hiding place, untouched for three years: a hundred dollars cash, his personal diary, a box of percussion caps, .31-caliber balls and a small powder horn for his Adams, and at the bottom, Squeaker McDillon's ledger book, a compendium of the sins, debts, and foibles of dozens of famous Washingtonians.

He grabbed them all and shoved them into his pockets and replaced the false bottom, then refilled the drawer.

When he turned, Secretary of War Edwin Stanton was staring him in the face.

"What are you doing, Corporal?"

Halsey froze. What would he say? Admit who he was, or lie? He had lied for so long that it seemed the best course. And Stanton was not a man to look to for help. He said, "I'm getting these things for Major Eckert, sir."

"What things?"

"He asked for his personal diary." Halsey pulled out his own and showed it to Stanton. "He wants to record the events as he's watching them. He's down under a tree, sir, with Homer . . . er . . . *Mr.* Bates, sir. It's a grand day, a grand day, sir."

Someone else came in the front door of Stanton's office and called. Stanton looked over his shoulder, momentarily distracted. So Halsey politely excused himself.

But Stanton wasn't done. As Halsey went down the hallway, Stanton called after him through the crowd. "Corporal, what is your name?"

Halsey, unable for the moment to think of a better lie, told the lie he'd been telling for two and a half years, "Jeremiah Murphy, sir."

"And what unit were you in before you were transferred to the War Department?"

"Twentieth Massachusetts." Halsey knew he should have lied about that, too.

"Well, that yellow neckerchief is not regulation," said Stanton. "Take it off."

Halsey obeyed immediately. He did not wait for Stanton to ask another question. He saluted and hurried down the stairs, back into the roaring party.

Now he had a bargaining chip in the game that he knew Detective Joseph Albert McNealy was still playing.

THIRTEEN

Sunday Afternoon

⟡ "'A strange case,' that's the title Whitman gave to this entry," said Peter. "He wrote one and two paragraph vignettes about his hospital visits and started them with titles like 'The Burial of a Lady Nurse,' or 'Ice Cream for the Ward.'"

"Ice cream?" said Henry. "They had ice cream back then?"

"The white folks did," said Diana. "No ice cream for the slaves."

They had crossed into Virginia and were headed east for Washington. Once they were sure that the National Park Police or the Virginia Highway Patrol weren't on their tails, they had relaxed and gone to work. Peter read Whitman. Evangeline and Diana studied the copies of the McNealy letters that Volpicelli had given them. Henry drove and offered opinions.

Peter read the Whitman aloud off his iPad, "'An Irish corporal from one of the Massachusetts regiments, initials JM—'"

"Jeremiah Murphy?" said Evangeline.

"'—suffering a serious abdominal wound, sometimes speaks with a brogue that's as Irish as Paddy's Pig. But when he raves from pain or fever, he sounds like an educated Boston man. And always he speaks in a voice resembling rough gravel sluicing down a stream. This war has produced many mysteries, large and small, in my personal experience. This is surely one of the strangest.'"

"Is he telling us that Halsey Hutchinson and Jeremiah Murphy were one in the same?" asked Evangeline.

"It sounds that way," said Peter. "If Halsey Hutchinson ran because of the murder of Constance Wood, he might have hidden out in his old regiment, where he had friends. He survives to Second Hatcher's Run, is wounded, brought back, then tries to peddle the daybook for a presidential pardon."

"I wonder if he ever got it," said Evangeline.

"The pardon?" said Peter. "Lincoln's offer came on the day Booth shot him, so probably not."

"Did this Halsey carry the daybook through the war?" asked Diana. "Would it have survived in his rucksack through two and a half years of fighting?"

"He didn't have it," said Evangeline. "Not according to the McNealy letters."

"So McNealy had it?" asked Diana.

"He seems to know where it is," said Evangeline. "He never comes out and says he has it, though, not even in the last letter." She read: "'Dear Jane, I am getting close to doing something that will guarantee the future for us all. I have played the game for four years. I have done what I had to. I see a way out. Watch your papers for the name of Benjamin Wood in a week or two, then watch for me a week later. I hope you will have me in place of my brother. We both loved you.'"

Diana said, "He sounds like a good soul."

"A lost soul," said Evangeline.

"It also sounds like he's planning to blackmail the congressman who wrote *Fort Lafayette*," said Peter.

"But after that," said Evangeline, "there's nothing more from him."

"So maybe he got back to that little dirt farm and lived happily ever after," said Henry, "screwin' his brother's wife and raisin' his brother's boys with the bucks he made in the big city in the big war."

"So much of this is about speculating," said Peter, "and there are big spaces that we never fill. That's what makes the Lincoln letter so tantalizing."

"Maybe we can track McNealy in the newspapers," said Evangeline.

"That can be your job tonight," said Peter.

"My job?" Evangeline looked at Diana. "When you wonder why I didn't want to get married, it's under the heading: 'Likes to Give Out Little Jobs.'"

"You brought it up," said Peter.

"Add," she said, "'Tries to make it sound like your fault.' But in this case, he's right."

Henry chuckled. "Hey, No-Pete, when a lady says, 'He's right.' A man should get out his pen and write down the good news."

Peter said to Evangeline, "Tell me again, how am I right?"

"If McNealy had the diary at the end, he's the one we should be studying, because he's what you always call the bridge."

"Bridge?" asked Diana.

"The bridge between the past and the present," said Peter, "the one that lets us walk across the years, over the big knowledge gaps, directly back to what we're searching for."

"Bridges is damn hard to miss," said Henry.

"I think it's a metaphor," said Diana.

"Well, ma'am, I don't know nothin' 'bout no metaphors"—Henry winked at Peter—"but you folks ought to be able to find a bridge with all your Ph.D.'s and BAs and MFAs and whatnot."

"I don't think any of us have an MFA," said Evangeline.

"I do," said Henry. "MFA, Motherfuckin' All-American."

"That should be MFAA," said Evangeline.

Henry looked at Peter. "No-Pete, sometimes I think I ought to call the E-Ticket the Nit Ticket."

"It's Nit Picker," said Evangeline.

"Nit Ticket sounds better," said Henry. "Assonance along with back-end alliteration, where those two *t*'s match. Nit . . . Ticket. And we need a nickname for Miss Diana back there."

As if she had no time for nonsense, Diana said, "Call me Professor Wilmington."

"Not yet, we can't. You ain't Professor Nothin' till you get tenure." Henry almost always had time for nonsense. It was his way of clearing the air, or fogging it. "Your mama might've named you for Diana Ross, or Lady D, as I like to call her, and you nice and skinny like her, and you carry yourself like her, too, all sure of yourself."

Peter glanced into the backseat. Diana's coffee skin had started to take on a blush. She had many fine qualities, but a sense of humor about herself, especially when she was under pressure, was not one of them.

Henry kept talking. "Callin' you Assistant Professor Wilmington may be truthful but it's a mouthful, so we call you what you'll be when we get done with this weekend."

"What's that?" she said.

"Lady T. That's *T* for 'tenure.'"

Peter also knew that Diana could laugh as well as anyone. And it took a few seconds, but the laugh finally came out, deep, throaty, sexy. She liked her nickname.

. . .

By the time they pulled up in front of the Willard around five o'clock, backup had arrived.

Henry had called, and Peter had promised to pay.

A large black man in a well-cut black suit and black shirt was waiting on the sidewalk.

"J-Man made it all the way to the NBA," whispered Henry. "Could stick the jumper from the baseline . . . the other baseline."

"Hence the nickname," said Peter.

"But just a nano too slow playin' D on his own baseline."

"Hence the job as D.C. muscle. Am I paying for his Armani suit?" said Peter.

"He's workin' at a professional discount," said Henry. "Him and me done business before. He also has a feller named Ricky the Rican, a little PR dude who's usually watchin' from somewhere we can't see. They make a good team."

Henry introduced James "J-Man" Johnson. "You'll be watchin' the ladies, J. They be in the suite, doin' book work while me and No-Pete do the fieldwork."

J-Man gave the ladies an eyeball over his sunglasses, a nod, just enough to say he was cool and all would be well.

Peter could see Diana's eyes light up. She liked the looks of J-Man.

Henry said, "Ricky makin' himself hard to see?"

J-Man said, "I don't know no Ricky."

Henry winked, as if he got the ruse. No Ricky. Yeah, right.

J-Man then extended his hand toward the hotel door, "Ladies, allow me to escort you up to your suite."

Evangeline and Diana went into the hotel.

J-Man turned to Peter and said, "The suit is Zegna, not Armani."

Peter looked at Henry. "Good hearing, too."

.   .   .

Half an hour later, Henry pulled up in front of Jefferson Sorrel's house. "Time to eyeball this old boy. He knows more than he's lettin' on."

They didn't bother to reconnoiter from the park across the street. Sorrel had said that his neighbors were on vacation. And he lived on a corner lot, so nobody was watching from either side.

They went up onto the porch and rang the bell. No answer.

They rang again. Nothing.

Peter took out his cell phone and called Sorrel's number. He heard the phone ringing. Once, twice.

"Maybe he went to Florida, after all," said Henry.

"I'm calling his cell."

Henry furrowed his brow and cocked his ear.

Ring. Ring.

Then Henry walked to the end of the porch and looked toward the back, where a one-car garage faced the side street.

Ring. Ring. Ring.

They came off the porch, followed the sound to the garage, and peered in the side window.

Ring. Ring. Ring.

There was no car, just a lawn mower, a ringing telephone, and a body: Jefferson Sorrel.

Peter saw him first. "Oh, shit."

Henry grabbed Peter by the arm. "Go slow."

"But—"

"No need to go fast." Henry took out a pair of thin leather driving gloves and put them on. Then he opened the side door and they stepped in. "That old boy's dead."

Henry went closer, crouched, looked.

"Should we take his pulse?" asked Peter.

"He ain't breathin', and from the looks of the lividity—" Henry craned his neck to study the face pressed against an oil stain on the garage floor. "—the way the blood's poolin' on the right side of his face, he been dead about ten or twelve hours. Somebody wants us to think he died pullin' on his lawn mower string."

"But the overhead door is closed."

"If they injected him with something to make it look like a heart attack, they didn't want anybody to see it go down."

"Well," said Peter, "that lawn mower was kind of balky. He cursed it a few times. And he didn't look too good yesterday. Maybe a heart attack is really what happened."

"Yeah, and maybe if I get up real slow, my knees won't creak." Henry stood . . . real slow. "Nope. They creaked."

"Shouldn't we call somebody?"

"No-Pete, you are not thinkin'. Do you really want to spend three hours with the police from Arlington, Virginia, when they show up and start playin' *CSI*?"

Peter knew that Henry was right.

"If the guy who found the Lincoln letter is dead because he knew that 'something' was a diary, anyone who's lookin' for the diary could be next. So—"

"Do we just leave him?"

"No. We take care of him anonymous-like, once we're gone."

They stepped out again, onto the pathway beside the house. No one was walking by on the sidewalk out front, so they started toward the street.

Then Peter said, "Wait."

"What?"

He pointed to the side door of the house, which led into the cellar.

"You sure?" said Henry. "The longer we hang around, the more dangerous it gets."

Peter gave a jerk of the head. "If he still has the engraving, I want to see it."

"Which engraving?"

"*First Reading of the Emancipation Proclamation*. The one that had the letter hidden in the backing."

Henry grumbled, then turned the knob. The door opened. "Unlocked. Maybe they really did just catch him in the garage while he was doin' his chores, just like any old fat white guy on a Sunday morning, and they figured that was as good a place as any to whack him."

. . .

As soon as they stepped onto a little landing halfway down the cellar stairs, Henry closed the door and pulled out the Magnum.

They stood for a moment in the semi-dark and listened.

The refrigerator was humming in the kitchen at the top of the stairs. There was no other sound.

Peter pointed down. Just a hunch. So down they went.

They stopped, waited, listened some more. Then Henry flipped on the lights. They were in what had been called a rumpus room back in the fifties: knotty pine paneling, stone fireplace, sofa, TV. But this was also a showroom for Jefferson Sorrel's collection, displayed in glass cases and frames, away from the sun, away from the prying eyes of neighbors and deliverymen, the kind of collection a man kept just for himself.

Peter looked around and whispered, "Wow."

"'Wow,' what?"

"Look at all this."

One case held muskets: Springfields and Enfields, along with a breech-loading cavalry carbine. The others held books, from Bruce Catton's three-volume *Army of the Potomac* to David Herbert Donald's *Lincoln,* or marvelous engravings of the major players, Lincoln, Lee, Grant, framed wet-plates from Mathew Brady and Alexander Gardner, a whole tray of carefully arranged cartes de visite. And on the walls hung pennants, framed under glass: a Confederate naval ensign above the fireplace, a Union National flag with thirty-five stars arrayed in a circle above the sofa.

"If I owned all this, I'd protect it," said Peter.

Henry pointed to wires running from the back of each frame and case, up to the dropped ceiling. "I guess he liked to look like he had nothin'. Doin' the collector's rope-a-dope, pretendin' this is just a little bungalow in the 'burbs. But the room's hot. You touch anything, alarms go off. Probably wired right to the police station."

"Wow."

"I swear, No-Pete, we don't have time for any more 'wows.' Quit your 'wowin and tell me what we lookin' for."

"That." Peter pointed to the far corner, near a worktable. On an easel, beneath a canvas covering, was a picture frame, about two feet by three feet. "I hope."

They went over to it. Henry inspected for wires, electric eyes, lasers. Then he carefully took one edge of the canvas and lifted to reveal the famous engraving: *First Reading of the Emancipation Proclamation.*

"Do we have Bingo?" said Henry.

"Bingo," said Peter. "Or wow. Take your pick."

Henry flipped on the light over the worktable and aimed it at the engraving.

Peter glanced at the table: scissors, matte knives, rulers, various sizes of glass, large sheets of matte board, lengths of frame, some mahogany, some stainless. "It looks like Sorrel did his own conservation work. He was replacing the old materials with acid-free paper and matting."

"And UV-filtering glass?"

"This is black and white, so it's less susceptible to sunlight, but a good conservator always uses UV." Peter looked closer. "A steel engraving, and there's a little legend, 'New York Independent, 1866.' They were a publisher. This is the version that was given out with the book, *Six Months in the White House*, by Francis Carpenter. He was the painter. The engravings were made from his work by a guy named Ritchie."

"What's it worth?"

"Fifteen hundred, maybe. You can get an artist's proof engraving signed by Carpenter himself, 1866, for twenty-five hundred on eBay. So—"

"Old Sorrel made a good deal. Worth ten times what he paid for it."

"Maybe that's why Dawkins is so angry."

"Always screw the black guy."

"At least Dawkins is alive."

"For now," said Henry.

Peter asked Henry to turn the frame over. That revealed the back of the engraving fitted neatly against the front matte, which pressed against the glass.

Peter pointed at the little tacks around the edge of the frame. "You see here, he's taken off the brown paper sheath that covers the whole package. And he's removed the inner backing which would have been a heavy-duty cardboard made from the same high-acid paper that they used for most other things back then."

373

"The engraving, too? Is that on acid paper?"

Peter nodded. "That's why it's so yellowed around the edges. Can't do much about it. But replacing everything around it with acid-free materials will make a big difference in its long-term survival."

Peter stepped back, studied, thought, scratched his head, looked around the floor, looked behind him. And there: the wastebasket under the worktable. It was stuffed with old brown covering and cardboard backing.

Peter reached, and Henry raised a finger—no touching without gloves.

The backing had been folded into four pieces and broken apart to fit in the wastebasket. Henry pulled out a piece and put it on the table.

"Just as I thought." Peter brought his face close to the cardboard. "See the ghosting?"

Imprinted on the faded gray cardboard was the square where the Lincoln letter had been secreted.

"The sun heats the engraving from the front, through the glass, cooks the letter against the acid backing, and projects an image of the iron gall ink onto the backing." Peter saw a pair of white cotton conservator's gloves at the corner of the table and put them on.

"Now you can touch stuff," said Henry.

Peter pulled the lamp over and saw the reverse image of the letter, almost illegible, and above it, half the outline of the envelope, which had been partially protected from sunlight and heat by the matting. He pointed out the signature. "'A. Lincoln.' As plain as day. If we studied this for a while, I bet we could read the whole letter."

Henry pulled out his phone and took a picture of it. Then he lifted the rest of the backing out of the wastebasket and laid it out on the worktable.

After a moment's inspection, Peter said, "At the risk of repeating myself, wow."

"What now?"

"A second letter. Look." With his little finger, Peter pointed to another square of discolored backing and more words.

Henry took another picture.

"Let's just take the backing," said Peter.

"How about we find the second letter. It must be here someplace."

"If it's here," said Peter, "it's in his sanctum sanctorum."

"Say what?"

"His special place. Every collector has one. It might be a safety deposit box or a safe right in the house, hidden in a wall or in the floor."

Henry looked around a bit.

"Don't bother," said Peter. "If we find it, we'll never be able to—"

Bing bong. Upstairs, the front doorbell rang.

"Stay still," Henry snapped from assistant into bodyguard, pulled his gun, stepped to the bottom of the stairs, and flipped out the lights.

They waited with the daylight leaking in the half-height cellar windows.

Then the doorbell rang again.

Henry cocked his head, listened, whispered, "Whoever it is, they're leaving the porch . . . . and . . . comin' . . . round . . . to the side." He gestured with the gun for Peter to come closer. "Do you know him?"

Peter looked up the cellar stairs. Sorrel had put a mirror above the side door for just this purpose, to see from the cellar without being seen.

"Motherfucker," said Peter.

"Who is he?"

"Professor Colin Conlon."

"Who?

"Well, if Volpicelli is the Red Sox, that guy is the Yankees."

"So that means one of them has twenty-seven rings and the other has two?"

"It means that Conlon is a jealous son of a bitch who wants to tell everyone what to do, and keep Lady T from getting tenure."

"Motherfucker," whispered Henry.

"And the Red Sox have seven championships."

Conlon turned the knob.

"I locked the door," said Henry. "Let's see if he has the balls to break in."

He didn't. After a moment, the professor pulled out his cell phone and made a call from the side of the house.

Peter and Henry listened for the sound of phones ringing upstairs or in the garage. None.

"He's calling someone else." Henry holstered his gun. "We better find out who."

The professor had his back turned and was leaning against the house.

So he did not see Henry whip open the door, grab him by the collar, and pull him inside.

"Hey."

Henry snatched the professor's phone and turned it off, locked the door, and pushed Conlon down the stairs.

Peter flipped on the light.

Conlon looked around and said, "Wow."

Henry looked at Peter. "'Wow,' he says. Another wowser."

Conlon looked at Peter. "You!"

Henry said, "What the fuck you doin' in here, man?"

Conlon recovered quickly. Peter had to give him that. He looked at Henry and said, "I might ask you the same thing."

Henry pulled out his Magnum and held it, pointing at the floor. He did that sometimes, just for effect. "I asked you first."

"I was on an important phone call with a rather volatile gentleman. You've heard of him. His name is Keeler." Conlon then made a show of straightening his club tie and wiping the dirt off the sleeves of his tweed jacket. "Keeler's searching for Lincoln's diary."

Peter said, "How did you learn about it?"

"I read Volpicelli's book."

"No, you didn't." Peter gave Henry a jerk of the head.

Henry put the Magnum against Conlon's skull. "Now, I had a bad day. Been drivin' all over Maryland, and my hemorrhoids is killin' me. I used to be a long-haul trucker, see, so hemorrhoids come with the territory, but I'm mighty cranky. So—"

"Those men on the telephone will be coming to find out why we were cut off."

"If they were close, they would've come themselves," said Henry.

"I thought you were above treasure hunts, Professor," said Peter. "How did you get into this?"

Conlon looked at the gun again and said, "Kathi Morganti."

"That's better." Henry lowered the Magnum.

"But she's on the other side," said Peter.

"Kathi Morganti told Dougherty, as sort of a peace offering to the Milbury camp, a way to stay on Milbury's good side, even though they're going around calling him the Communist Congressman because of this

VAT business. Dougherty told Milbury, and Milbury told me, because I am his advisor on all things historical."

"And you told Keeler? You're in bed with Keeler?" said Peter. "Liberal professor and disgraced lobbyist with a grudge against the government?"

"Money makes stranger bedfellows than politics," said Henry.

"Money *is* politics," said Conlon. "And Keeler was an excellent lobbyist. He came to me a month ago, when he first read about the Volpicelli book. I told him there was nothing to it. But two weeks later, dumb luck changed everything. Jefferson Sorrel went to a flea market and found that." He pointed to the engraving.

"But you and Keeler?" said Peter. "I still don't get it."

"I owed him. He did some excellent work for us when we were trying to get government funds for the Conlon Center for Studies in American History. It's named for my father, you know. And it's given me an enormous amount of clout."

"Enough to keep a woman off the faculty because she wouldn't sleep with you?" said Peter. "A gorgeous black woman, no less."

Henry looked at Peter. "That's why Lady T don't have tenure? Because this motherfucker couldn't get laid?"

"Pulitzer Prize–winning motherfucker, to you," said Conlon.

"Well, Pulitzer on this." Henry brought the Magnum back to Conlon's temple.

But the professor didn't even flinch. He said, "If my relationship with the congressman doesn't make me bulletproof, my Pulitzer does. And Peter Fallon knows it."

Henry asked, "Do you mean bulletproof literally or metaphorically, Professor Motherfucker?"

Peter was enjoying this good cop–bad cop game. He said, "Professor, you've got your fingerprints on the back door and the doorknob and the front doorbell. And we've got a body in the garage, belonging to Mr. Sorrel, whose house you have broken into."

"Body?" That changed Conlon's demeanor. The arrogance drained right out of him.

"So, did Keeler do it and then forget something?" asked Peter. "Is that why you're here?"

Conlon looked from one face to the other. "They asked me to come over here and see if I could get Sorrel to sell the backing for the engraving of *First Reading*."

"Why?" asked Peter.

Conlon said nothing.

"Why?" asked Henry, and he cocked the Magnum, even though it was double-action.

And Conlon said, "They found letters in the backings of the engravings of Jesus and Frederick Douglass that they bought from Dawkins up in Sharpsburg. But they need one more piece of the puzzle. So—"

"We beat you to it."

Henry said, "Now, you got two choices. You can promise me on your soul that when Assistant Professor Diana Wilmington comes up for tenure again, you are her champion, especially if she's written a book about the Lincoln letter. Or I can handcuff you to a heatin' pipe and leave you to answer to the cops when they come to investigate Sorrel's body."

"She deserves tenure," said Conlon. "She'll get it."

"Promise?" said Henry.

"Promise."

Henry made a gesture: Beat it.

Conlon turned and hurried up the stairs.

"She don't get it," called Henry, "I'm comin' after you."

"She'll get it." The side door opened and slammed shut.

After a moment, Henry said to Peter, "Everybody's fuckin' everybody else in this deal."

"Everybody's fuckin' everybody else in this *town*," answered Peter. "But I don't think that Keeler and his boys killed Sorrel. Otherwise, they would have taken the backing."

"Then who killed him?"

"The bruise brothers I met on the Key Bridge might be a better bet. Iraq security types know more about silent assassinations than guys like Keeler and his white-collar criminals."

"Yeah, and maybe it was just a heart attack."

. . .

From a pay phone on the Lee Highway, they called the police and tipped them to the body in the garage. Then they headed back to the hotel.

Henry gave the valet a twenty and told him to keep the car close.

J-Man let them into the suite then went back to whatever he was do-ing on his iPad.

Evangeline was in her bedroom, reading old newspapers on her com-puter, looking for references to any of the players they had been following.

Diana was sitting in the living room, studying the copy of *Fort Lafa-yette*, looking for clues as to the identity of the owner of that book, a woman name Molly Blodgett.

Henry looked around and said, "This is what I like. Everybody wor-kin' hard. Thinkin' hard. Doin' the hard thing to find the good thing."

J-Man said, "How come you like to talk so much, man, even if you ain't sayin' a thing . . . about a thing."

Henry laughed and looked at Diana. "Has this D-Leaguer been both-erin' you?"

"Not at all," said Diana.

Peter changed the mood with this: "Sorrel's dead."

"Dead?" Diana brought a hand to her mouth.

J-Man looked up from his iPad. "Now that's somethin' important."

Peter asked Diana, "What have you found?"

She shook her head. "Not much. This is a different kind of research. Not scholarly. Just hard. And dangerous, I guess."

"This is research for money," said Peter.

"Is he really dead?" asked Diana.

"Don't you worry about it," said Henry. "Just put it out of your pretty little Lady T head and get back to that computer. Let me and the J-Man worry about the bad stuff. Ain't that right, J?"

"True dat," said J-Man.

After a moment, Diana turned her eyes back to her computer screen.

Peter went into the bedroom.

Evangeline was sitting cross-legged on the bed. She looked up. "Did I hear the word 'dead'?"

He nodded. "The first casualty."

"Let's hope it's the last."

"Got anything?"

She shook her head, digested the word 'dead,' and said, "I can tell you what a bowl of she-crab soup cost at the Gosling Restaurant on Pennsylvania Avenue. I can tell you that Laura Keene is playing all week at Ford's Theatre, closing on Saturday night before Easter, but—"

"Keep reading."

"Any word from Antoine?"

Peter sat on the edge of the bed and checked his iPhone. "He just admitted that he's hit a blind alley."

"Peter, I don't want to be fearing for my life when I'm trying to look natural on camera. And we're filming at the Lincoln Memorial tomorrow, nine o'clock."

"Then that's my deadline." He massaged her foot. "I find this thing tonight or go home and leave you to work."

"Have you decided what you're going to do with that half-million-dollar check in your pocket?"

"Not yet."

"Until you do, you're on David Bruce's payroll."

"Now, this is what I like to see," Henry stepped in. "No-Pete and the E-Ticket, havin' a nice little married chat, even though they—"

"Don't say it," warned Evangeline.

"Don't say what?" Henry feigned shock. "I was just goin' to say, 'even though they ain't eaten yet.'"

"Oh. I thought you were going to mention the—"

"Wedding that wasn't?"

Evangeline threw a pillow at him.

"Best no-weddin' party I ever went to."

. . .

Over room service hamburgers and salads, they tried to make sense of what was going on, because it seemed as if everyone was feeding information in every direction

"Who do we trust?" asked Evangeline.

"Ourselves," said Henry. "And the J-Man."

J gave them a wave and a nod and toasted with his Heineken.

Peter drained a Yuengling, wiped his mouth, and cleared the table. Henry brought over a light. Peter got out a magnifying glass. Then he spread out the four pieces of backing that they had taken from Sorrel's wastebasket.

After about ten minutes of squinting and trying to read the old ink, backwards, off the cardboard, they had deciphered just a few words from that second letter:

Dear Mrs. Blodgett, I have be . . . asked by . . . Hutch . . . of a valuable item . . . son Zion . . . other letters as proof . . . if I can ever help you, I should. Yours, Noah Bone . . . by son Jacob

Blodgett. Diana said that the name on the endpaper of *Fort Lafayette* was "Molly Blodgett, and beneath it, 'Mother Freedom.'" The only other words written in the book, on the back endpaper, were, "This is the veriest rubbage."

Peter said, "No odd markings? No letters underlined on alternate pages, no acrostics?"

Diana shook her head. "No mumbo jumbo. Just a lady's strong opinion on a book by a Copperhead."

"Funny name, Molly," said Henry.

"Not really," said Diana. "It's my mom's name."

"But not her last name. The old lady that give all this stuff to Dawkins, her name was Esther Molly, right?"

"Right," said Peter. "According to Savannah Dawkins."

Henry said to Evangeline, "Can you look up Esther Molly? She just died, so there might be somethin' on her."

Evangeline typed the name into the search bar on her computer.

An obituary popped up right away. She scanned it and gave out the facts. Esther Molly, a lifelong Washington resident, a teacher of fourth grade in the city schools, mother of a son killed in Vietnam, and daughter of Zion Molly III, whose ancestors had lived and worked in the District of Columbia for five generations. And then, she read, "'Esther Molly always liked to tell people that her ancestors were the original sanitary workers of Washington, night soil men who cleaned privies and sold the leavings as fertilizer, a common practice in mid-nineteenth-century American cities.'"

"But how did the first name become the last name?" asked Peter.

Diana said, "Once they were free, a lot of slaves didn't want their masters' names. That's why you have so many Washingtons and Lincolns among black folks. They took the best names they could think of. And a lot of the children of slaves took their parents' first names as their last names. So, a son named Zion took his mother's first name and became Zion Molly."

"Zion Molly," said Henry. "I wonder what made him do the hard things."

Peter went to work with a few Web sites and found the address of Esther Molly, which had not yet been taken down. She had lived eleven blocks east of the Capitol, between F and H.

He said, "I think we should drive over there and look around."

"I'll call for the SUV," said Henry. "J-Man, you in?"

J-Man gave a little flip of his fingers. He was in. Then he punched up Google Earth on his iPad and showed them Maryland Avenue and Eleventh.

Peter took the iPad and "drove" down the street, past some big apartment buildings, a few long runs of joined row houses, all nicely kept with little gardens and good paint jobs in wild colors, lavender, yellow, some white to offset. All the houses had big windows, but a lot of them were barred. So there was some crime in the neighborhood.

Esther Molly's house was unpainted stone, three stories tall, four rooms deep.

Meanwhile, Evangeline was doing her own address search, turning up this: "Donald Dawkins lives right across the street."

"And he inherited the Molly property," said Diana. "Should we call him and tell him we're coming?"

Henry said, "Let's surprise him. It might cheer him up."

On the way down in the elevator, Henry said, "We get in that old house, look around, I bet we find a hidin' place for a valuable book in no time at all. It has to be there, right? In a wall or under the floorboards in the attic?"

Evangeline said, "It wouldn't be the first time we've found something like that."

Peter squeezed her hand. He liked it when she said "we" in the midst of the hunt.

On the third floor, the doors popped open, and a man wheeling a room service tray glanced in at them. He said, "I wait." He was short, dark-haired, Hispanic.

Henry said, "Hey, Ricky."

The man looked up, looked shocked, and the doors slammed shut.

Henry turned to J-Man. "That was Ricky the Rican, wasn't it?"

"I told you, man, I don't know no Ricky the Rican."

Peter said, "That guy delivered wine to our room last night."

"He sure looked like Ricky the Rican," said Henry.

"Like I told you," said J-Man, "I don't know no Ricky the Rican working in the Willard or anywhere else."

Henry and Peter caught each other's eye. Strange.

In the lobby, J-Man said, "I follow in my car, make sure nobody trailin' you."

That sounded reasonable, but Henry caught Peter's eye again, as if he was getting suspicious.

Henry and Peter had wanted to go alone, but the ladies insisted, saying that they would get through the old row house more quickly with four sets of eyes. So the four of them piled into Henry's Ford Edge.

. . .

They drove over Capitol Hill and out Maryland Avenue. At Eleventh they took a left. There was a playground on the corner. Some older kids were hanging there, smokin' and jokin'. They passed F Street and a large apartment building. Then Henry started to look for a parking spot. But as in most urban neighborhoods, parking was a competitive sport around here.

They found a spot up near H Street, the business strip, and walked back. Just for safety, and for a better look at things, Peter and Evangeline went down the east side, and Henry and Diana went down the other.

Dawkins lived in a wooden row house on the east, one of three joined façades, all gray, with porches that reached to the sidewalk. There were no lights in the Dawkins house, and because the street was well planted with trees, the streetlamps were shaded and the sidewalks were dark.

Esther Molly's stone row house, diagonally across the street, was much nicer than Dawkins's and much bigger. A building permit showed in the window. A pallet of chimney brick lay outside. A Dumpster filled almost all of the front lawn.

Peter said, "I don't like the sight of that."

"What?" said Evangeline.

"Construction work. Demolition plays hell with hiding places. Then he squeezed between a blue Nissan Versa and a Chrysler minivan and crossed the street.

She went around to the back of the Nissan, and they met Henry and Diana on the other side.

Henry said, "You seen J-Man?"

"He must've gotten lost," said Peter.

"Hell of a security guard," said Diana.

"Right you are, Lady T," said Henry. "J-Man knows this city like he knows the three-second lane." Henry looked around in the semi-darkness under the trees. "And how could J-Man be sayin' he don't know Ricky the Rican, when Ricky pushin' a cart right under his nose. Who'd you say he delivered wine for last night?"

"Kathi Morganti, the lobbyist," answered Peter. "She's working for David Bruce."

"David Bruce. We up against him, ain't we?" asked Henry.

"Up against him or working for him," said Evangeline. "Some of us haven't decided yet."

"Well, one way or the other, it looks like J-Man and his little Rican sidekick givin' us up to Mr. David Bruce," said Henry.

"Or to Bruce's security boys," said Peter.

Henry shook his head. "Like I said before, everybody's fuckin' everybody else in this deal."

"Sometimes literally," said Evangeline.

"What do you mean?" asked Peter.

"In all the excitement, I forgot to show you this." So she pulled out her phone and called up the picture of Kathi and William Dougherty.

"Wow," said Peter.

"Wow *what*?" said Henry.

"That closes the circle of deceit," said Peter.

A big Buick turned the corner at the end of the block and rolled slowly toward them. Its windows were vibrating to the powerful bass line beat of some rap song. There were four guys inside. When the car slowed, Henry slipped his hand into his jacket. And the blasting beat receded down the street.

"You better hope they don't set off any car alarms," said Diana.

Peter said, "Do we call Dawkins yet?"

"Nah." Henry had taken a claw hammer from the tool kit in his car. Now he pulled it from his belt. "Let's have a look first. You gals stay here till we reconnoiter."

Diana said to Evangeline, "Gals. Gals, he calls us."

"I'm old-school, baby." He and Peter went up the seven-stair stoop.

While Peter held a flashlight, Henry popped off a two-by-four nailed to the doorframe of Esther Molly's house. Then he tried the door. Unlocked.

Peter and Henry made eye contact. Bad sign. Either there was nothing in there, or someone was waiting.

Henry replaced the hammer and pulled out the Magnum, "I go first. You hold the light. If you see a shadow, hit him in the eyes with the beam. Blind him so I can get off a good shot."

"That's good," said Peter. "Shoot first, ask questions later."

Henry turned the handle and opened the door.

At the same moment, Peter's cell phone rang.

He grabbed it, looked at the caller ID: SAVANNAH DAWKINS.

Henry was opening the door, crying "Holy fuck!" and swinging out into midair . . .

. . . because there was no floor, no ceiling, no walls, no rooms, nothing. The interior was a void, except for new steel framing.

Peter dropped the flashlight, caught Henry by the belt, and pulled him back before Henry fell all the way to the dirt floor of the basement.

"Holy fuck." Henry grabbed the doorjamb and steadied himself while Peter held tight to his belt and answered the phone at the same time.

Savannah was whispering, "I . . . I . . . We need help. There's men in my house. Right here, right now. I'm in the bathroom, but they're here, and they're watching."

Bang!

She screamed, "No!"

It sounded on the phone as if someone had broken into the bathroom.

"Let's go." Peter pulled Henry after him.

They flew off the stoop and ran toward the Dawkinses' door.

They were halfway across Eleventh when they saw two flashes through the front window and heard two powerful bolts of thunder. *Boom! Boom!*

They stopped in the middle of the street.

Then came the scream of a woman inside.

Peter said to Evangeline, "You girls stay here."

But Evangeline wasn't moving. She was frozen in place on the sidewalk.

As Peter and Henry ran up to the door, Diana said to Evangeline, "I've heard that sound one time too many in my life. Gunfire, then a screaming wife or mother. Shit."

Then Diana started after the men.

Henry banged through the front door of the house, rushing to rescue a brother veteran from Vietnam.

Peter went right in after him.

The smell of gun smoke hung heavy and acrid in the air. The sound of Savannah's whimpering echoed from the hallway, directly ahead of them.

In the living room to the left, a big black man lay facedown on the sofa. At the end of the hallway, at Savannah's feet, a white man lay flat on his back.

Henry held the Magnum high, ready to fire, and stepped into the living room.

Donald Dawkins said, "Don't shoot."

Peter stepped around the corner and said, "Are you all right?"

Dawkins said, "They come in the back about half an hour ago. Started grillin' me and the missus about what all we sell at the Eastern Market. Real nasty. Then one of them got a iPhone message. They mentioned Black Irish, here, how him and his pals were comin'. Then they put out all the lights and started watchin' out the window."

Henry said to Peter, "That's when J-Man sent them a text, the bastard."

"Like we said," answered Peter, "everybody's fuckin' everybody else."

"Ain't it the truth." Henry kicked at the foot of the black man on the sofa.

Evangeline came to the door and peered in, as if she was afraid to step inside.

Dawkins said, "When they heard Savannah on the phone in the bathroom, it distracted them just long enough that I could get the sawed-off out of the sofa cushions."

"Sawed-offs is illegal, bro." Henry looked around the darkened living room and holstered his gun. "At least you shot them in the house."

"We would've dragged them inside if we had to." Savannah stepped into the parlor and wiped her tears. She was getting control.

"Yeah," said Dawkins. "We ain't stupid."

"Well," said Henry, "go take off them long pants and put on some Bermudas."

"Why?" asked Dawkins.

"If the cops see your sawed-off leg, they might cut you some slack on the sawed-off shotgun." Then he said to Peter, "You know these fellers?"

"They're the bruise brothers who picked me up on the bridge yesterday. Mr. Redskins and Mr. Fit, Andre and Jonathan. They work for David Bruce."

"Well, if they killed Sorrel, they paid."

"Y'all better go," said Dawkins. "We can handle this."

"One question." Henry gestured to the house across the street. "How come you didn't tell us?"

"What could I say? That I cherry-picked the good stuff, then sold the place and they brought in the wreckers to gut it. Whatever you lookin' for, if it was in Miz Molly's house, it's in some landfill now."

"We think it's a diary," said Peter. "Worth a lot."

"A diary? Goddamn. If I thought I threw away his diary"—Dawkins pointed to the picture of Lincoln on the wall—"I couldn't live with myself."

"And you ain't too easy to live with as it is," said Savannah.

"I'd sure like to read a thing like that," said Dawkins, "just to see what he had to say on whatever he was thinkin' about. There was truth in his thoughts and music in his words. Be a damn shame if we lost his words 'cause of me."

"Well, the diary may be gone," said Peter, "it may not. But you're cut in, no matter what."

They heard sirens in the distance.

Henry said, "We'd better go."

FOURTEEN

April 1865

Halsey believed that on Tuesday night, Lincoln would give a speech for the ages, another Gettysburg Address, which defined what they were fighting for in a few paragraphs, or another Second Inaugural, with its resounding call to mercy and resolve.

And though he was exhausted after his Monday adventures in the War Department, he had to hear it.

At dusk, he dressed in his soldier blues, begged a pass from the ward-master, and walked up Fifteenth, past the illuminated Treasury Building, its pillars glimmering with transparencies of ten-dollar bonds. He met Samantha in front of the State Department, which mirrored the War Department on the other side of the White House with candles in every window. The first Grand Illumination was under way.

She slipped her arm into his and together they walked toward the gas-lights and sputtering torches on the White House lawn, through a mist that floated like liquid anticipation in the air, into a close-packed crowd that smelled of damp wool and rye whiskey and a dozen ladies' fragrances.

Then, at eight o'clock, the window above the White House door opened, and Lincoln appeared from the shadows, almost a shadow himself.

The crowd began to roar, but with a tone and timbre far different from the previous day. Their cry was full throated and high pitched, joyful and angry, victorious and vengeful all at the same time.

Lincoln raised his hands for quiet. Then his secretary, Noah Brooks, appeared on one side of him with a lamp to hold over the speech, and Tad came on the other to catch each page as it dropped. And Abraham Lincoln began to read.

But he called down no rhetorical thunderbolts, raised no angry spirits, offered no powerful imagery or rhythmic parallels. Instead, he presented his listeners with thorny prose for the thorny problem of Reconstruction. He called it a task "fraught with great difficulties." He talked about the challenges of seating new legislatures, of the difficulties already faced in creating a government for Louisiana, and of Negro suffrage. He talked on . . . and on. . . .

People in the crowd grew restless. Some began whispering to their friends. Others drifted away. Undaunted, Lincoln forged ahead, as if he would outlast their boredom.

It was a good assumption, because that ghostly figure in the White House window had outlasted all his enemies and detractors, the Copperheads, the Knights of the Golden Circle, McClellan and Pinkerton with their inflated visions of Southern might, the Wood brothers and their Congressional allies, the Abolitionists and their radical expectations. Now, he would rise above them to do the hardest job of all, reuniting the broken nation. Vengeance might have been on the minds of many that night, but not on Lincoln's.

Then, Samantha was tugging Halsey's elbow. "Do you see him?"

"Who?"

"Up near the portico, right at the edge of the shadow. It's Booth."

Halsey looked over the sea of felt hats and ladies' feathers and—yes—there were the square shoulders, the firm jaw, the undeniable presence.

Booth was turning to the man next to him, a big man in a canvas coat. He was whispering into the man's ear, whispering hard and angry. The man shook his head once, then twice. Then Booth was turning, pushing through the crowd, in and out of the torchlight, his face flashing an actor's angry scowl. He brushed past, close enough for Halsey to smell the brandy.

Halsey was glad that Booth had not recognized him. He had had enough of Booth.

. . .

Over the next two days, Halsey plotted two things: to find McNealy before McNealy found him, and to get closer to the president. He failed on both counts.

He read the papers for mention of a presidential appearance. Perhaps Lincoln would go to Grover's to see *Aladdin; or, The Wonderful Lamp*, or to Ford's, where Laura Keene was playing all week.

And on Wednesday, Halsey walked by the shoeshine stand at the National Hotel. He wanted information about McNealy, because he now had information to give. He had read through Squeaker's ledger, studied the catalog of sins committed by men like Benjamin Wood, certain other senators, and yes, even old Doc Wiggins, the rebel sympathizer.

He approached on Pennsylvania, but Noah hardly glanced at him because Major Eckert and Police Superintendent Webb were sitting in the chairs, complimenting "the best shoeshine in town, a fine way to finish up after a fine lunch."

Halsey leaned against the corner in front of the telegraph office, opened a newspaper, and listened.

Eckert was saying, "We hear your middle son marches with the Colored Troops."

"He does, sir."

"When he comes back, will he work in the hotel again like his brothers?"

Noah stopped polishing and looked up. "Well, he dream of bein' a canal man."

"Canal man?" said Webb. "On a boat?"

"No, sir, at the lock house. He always want to work the lock and keep the records and spend the rest of the day lookin' up at Mr. Washington's monument."

"Not much traffic on the canal now," said Webb. "It would be a better job for a man whose back is broke from bendin' over shoes for too long."

"Yes, sir," said Noah. "That sure would be somethin'."

"So long as his sons kept in the shoeshine business," said Eckert.

Both men laughed. So did Noah. And two military officers came out of the hotel and got in line for shines. With celebrations every night, it seemed that everyone was looking to spiff, top to bottom.

So Halsey moved off and came back on Thursday, a gorgeous spring day with bright sunshine and warm temperatures, a day when the shoeshine business should have been brisk. But Noah's stand was closed.

Halsey asked the Negro doorman where he could get a shine.

The doorman said, "Sometimes Noah Bone just take a day off. He's plain tired out with worry 'bout his boy in the army. It wears on him, or so he say."

. . .

That night, Halsey and Samantha walked arm in arm onto Capitol Hill to see the final, grandest Grand Illumination. The mighty dome floated like a crown of light above the republican city, and every street below, a simple grid overlain by radiating diagonals, appeared as part of a light-bejeweled train covering the monarch of democracy. And every building along every street, from the lowliest Negro shanty to the mighty Patent Office, glowed with candles and gaslight. And out of every circle and square, red rockets were rising and bursting, like a confetti of light.

Samantha took Halsey's hand and said, "We'll have a life together, Halsey. I know it. In my soul, I do."

Halsey prayed that it would be so.

. . .

Sometime after midnight, Halsey was awaked by something landing on his chest, something small, cold, heavy.

"I believe that's yours."

Halsey popped up, saw his pistol on the blankets, then saw Detective Joseph Albert McNealy, legs crossed, arms folded, sitting in Walt Whitman's place:

"Nice little game you've got here. Soft bed, three squares, commode chair to shit in—"

"—bullet holes, fevers, amputations. You fit right in."

McNealy looked at the men in the beds on either side.

They were newcomers, both wounded at Five Forks. One of them was sleeping. The other seemed unconscious.

George Smith was snoring. He had not cried since Sunday night.

Halsey had decided that seeing the president changed things for him . . . or perhaps it was a good drunk.

Halsey pulled himself up on his elbows and looked at the gun.

McNealy said, "Go ahead, take it. It's yours. But don't think about shooting me with it. It's not loaded."

Halsey picked up the pistol and turned it over. Then he studied Mc-Nealy, who had not aged at all. Neither had his brown suit.

"I cleaned it and oiled it for you." McNealy pushed the gun under the covers. "Keep it. A man needs to protect himself on the dark streets."

Halsey said, "What are you after?"

"We had a deal."

"A deal?" Halsey remembered, but better for the moment if he pretended not to.

"You get the daybook and we rescue your reputation. Or I get the daybook and you give me Squeaker's ledger. Then we rescue your reputation."

Halsey said nothing.

"Of course"—McNealy pulled out a cigar—"it'll be harder to rescue now that you've shot down two men in cold blood on the Aqueduct Bridge."

"A setup," said Halsey, "telling me to track Doc Wiggins, then telling Hunter and Skeeter I'd be on the bridge. I was a fool."

"I never told you to trust me. I wouldn't trust me." McNealy bit the tip from his cigar and spit it on the floor. "But I wanted them dead, and you did the job. Knights of the Golden damn Circle, a group of lunatics who'd make the war go on even longer. They deserved killin' after what they did to Constance Wood. And if the soldier boys killed you in the process . . ." McNealy shrugged. "Instead, you've been a fugitive from justice for two and a half years."

"A fugitive fighting for his country."

"That'll count for something."

Halsey asked, "Do you have the daybook?"

McNealy nodded.

"From the beginning? From the day that you and Lafayette Baker went to the Squeaker's shooting scene?"

"Harriet Dunbar had it first."

"Had it?"

"She bought it from Squeaker that first morning. He showed her a page of it in the Willard. She went right home and told me."

"You?"

"I visited every other morning. She liked the way my beard tickled her thighs. Had a lot of feist in her for fifty. But that morning, she wasn't interested in my beard or my balls. She took two hundred in gold and went right back to Murder Bay and bought the diary. I bodyguarded her. Fucked her later."

Halsey tried to wipe that picture from his mind. "I saw her in the Willard the next day. It looked like she was waiting for Squeaker again."

"He liked her money, so he promised he'd sell other bits to her, out of his ledger. He may have thought he was doin' somethin' for the cause, gettin' a Confederate spy to give up her gold." McNealy lit the cigar. "She's no longer with us."

Halsey asked, "If you have the daybook, why haven't you used it?"

"Waitin' for the right moment."

"The war is over," said Halsey. "All the right moments have passed."

"Not if Lincoln hopes to rebuild the country. They're already carpin' at him over that speech Tuesday night . . . the Louisiana business, givin' niggers the right to vote—"

"Soldiers who fought deserve the vote," said Halsey. "Even colored soldiers."

"The Democrats'll want to keep the niggers down, which is what they wanted from the beginning. The Radical Republicans'll want vengeance on the South for startin' a war to protect slavery. The Democrats'll blame the Radical Republicans for startin' a war to free the slaves. It's politics. Except now we start backstabbin' again instead of frontstabbin'."

"Which side are you on?"

"My own, Corporal Lieutenant Whoever. Haven't you figured that out by now? My *own*." McNealy took a long puff of his cigar. "Just like every other man in this damn city, expect maybe for Lincoln."

"And every wounded man in this ward."

McNealy shrugged, as if he didn't care about any of them. "Lincoln will want the daybook to keep his early ideas on Reconstruction away from the public."

"So you want to bribe the president?"

"I'd rather do business with men who have more to lose."

"More than Lincoln?"

"Imagine you're a congressman. Benjamin Wood, say. You're happy that the war is finally over and you're still in office, ready to fight Lincoln's plans for nigger citizenship. Then a detective tells you he has evidence you've dodged your gambling debts for years, that you're a deadbeat hiding behind the honor of your office. Or you're a Radical Republican senator, ready to hand the niggers the keys to every front door in Dixie, ready to punish the South like Cain punished Abel. And the same detective asks you about a ring of little-boy smugglers."

"You don't care which side you blackmail, do you?"

"I told you a long time ago, I have no time for integrity." McNealy took another puff on his cigar. "This war has made me a corrupt man. But I'll swap the daybook for the ledger. I'll blackmail the men who deserve it. And you can do what you want with the daybook. Assuming, of course that you *have* the ledger."

Halsey did not tell him that it was in the sack under his bed. He said, "I know where it's hidden."

"How soon can you get it?"

"By tonight. Friday night. Do you have the daybook?"

"Not with me."

Halsey said, "Bring it here tonight. We'll make the exchange."

McNealy looked around. "Not here. Not on your ground."

"Are you afraid of a few sick soldiers?"

"We meet on neutral ground or not at all."

"No dark alleys," said Halsey. "No saloons where your friends can jump me."

"In the open, on the Tenth Street Footbridge, right over the canal. You come from the north, I come from the south. Even in the dark, you'll have a clear field of view. And you'll have the gun to protect you."

"And if you close my escape route—"

Just then Mrs. Cannon came along, muttering about men smoking and chattering in the dark. She stopped at the sight of McNealy, and said, "You again? Get out of here right this instant, or I'll wake up the wardmaster."

McNealy blew cigar smoke at her.

She huffed and scurried off.

McNealy seemed amused. He stood and said to Halsey, "The decision is yours. Meet me in the middle or not. Eight thirty sharp."

"And if not?"

"Wait for the Provost Guard, and start thinkin' of some alibis for—" He pretended to count on his fingers. "—six murders. You follow?"

"As I told you once before, 'Go where there is no path and leave a trail.' I've followed enough."

"Poetry. Once you were just educated. Now you're experienced. And still you spout poetry. Think of somethin' better."

.   .   .

Halsey lay awake the rest of the night, making plans and looking for pitfalls in the road that suddenly had appeared before him.

At first light, he wrote a letter to Abraham Lincoln:

> *Dear Mr. President,*
>
> *I have the honor of informing you that something you lost on April 16, 1862, may have been recovered by a friend named Halsey Hutchinson. He would return it to you at the first possible moment. When he or a representative approaches, he hopes that you will be receptive, especially given his personal difficulties in '62.*
>
> *Yours,*
> *Corporal Jeremiah Murphy,*
> *Armory Square Hospital*

Halsey had considered making the letter more anonymous, but the president might not bother with it, or his secretary might toss it. He thought also about signing his real name, but that might guarantee that the Provost Marshal got the letter rather than the president. So he chose the middle road as Murphy.

At six in the morning, he dressed and told Mrs. Cannon that he was going to take some exercise on the Mall and perhaps meet a certain lady on her way to work.

"I like your lady friend. But I can't say as much for your male friends when they come around puffin' cigars in the middle of the night."

"He's not my friend."

"Well"—she gave him a wink—"marry that girl, if she'll have you. Stay away from that other feller."

.   .   .

Good Friday 1865 had dawned clear but cool.

Halsey could see his breath as he paced in front of the ladies' quarters, waiting for Samantha. She emerged with another nurse around six thirty. He begged a moment, so Samantha sent her friend out to the barouche that was waiting for them on Seventh Street.

"I'll be right along," she said.

Halsey put the letter into her hand. "I need you to deliver this. I need you to do it this morning."

She looked at the address. "You want me to deliver this to the president?"

"To Major Eckert. He walks from the National Hotel to the War Department every morning at seven. Give it to him. Ask him to give it to the president."

"But—"

Halsey said, "McNealy found me. We've made a deal."

"A deal? Do you trust him?"

"No. But it's this or an arrest. He gave me back my gun as a gesture of goodwill."

"Goodwill from a man you don't trust?"

"He may be lulling me. And the gun had no bullets. He may think I can't find any in a few hours. But it's already loaded."

Samantha put the letter into her purse, waved the barouche away, and led Halsey to a bench beside the flowerbed. The tulips were closed tight in the morning chill.

And he told her his plan: to get the daybook as soon as possible and get it to the president as soon as possible after that. "All done and settled tonight, God willing."

"All tonight? Why tonight? What if we can't get close to him?"

"As long as I hold the book," he said, "I'll be in danger, and so will you. The Provosts may come after me, or McNealy's enemies, who may smell the blackmail he's planning. And trusting McNealy is a fool's game."

She looked off toward the Capitol dome, backlit by the rising sun.

He said, "Three years ago, I stood on the corner of Pennsylvania and Fifteenth as the president's carriage went by. I'd been carrying the book all day. I wanted to stop the carriage and give it to the president. But his wife was with him. She was dressed in black for their dead boy. I couldn't intrude. I've wished every day since that I stopped that carriage. I would never have ended up in this trouble."

"Well, one thing's for certain"—Samantha stood—"Mrs. Lincoln will be in a happier mood tonight."

.   .   .

As long as he was in the ward as Corporal Jeremiah Murphy, Halsey felt safe, so he napped. Midmorning sleep still came easily. He was still healing. Besides, whatever was coming that night, he would need his strength.

When Samantha's voice awakened him, the slant of light through the windows told him it was after noon.

"I waited for Major Eckert in the hotel lobby," she whispered. "He came down at seven. I stepped up to him and told him I was a nurse, and I had a soldier who needed to get a letter to the president.

"He said, 'Tell him to mail it' as if he were telling a streetwalker to stand aside.

"I held it out to him and said, 'It's important, sir. It's something that will matter to the president, so he wants to know the president receives it.'

"Eckert looked at the address and saw, 'President A. Lincoln, the White House' on the front. Then he turned it over and, Halsey, I swear that his brow furrowed suspiciously when he saw the name Jeremiah Murphy. Where had he heard it?"

"Stanton. It's the name I gave to Stanton the other day. I didn't think he'd remember, there was such commotion in the War Department."

"Well, Stanton must have told Eckert, because Eckert stood there, tapping the envelope on his fingertips, ruminating. . . .

"And then Booth appeared on the stairway. He was turned out in polished boots, with his hair and mustache pomaded, like he was getting ready for a performance. You could smell the perfume of it as he went past. He looked right at me, but he didn't recognize me. It was as if he was in a different world. Eckert barely glanced at him."

"A man who sees the president every day can't be too impressed with actors," said Halsey.

"Then Eckert put the letter into his coat and promised he'd hand it to the president."

"You did well."

"The president is now forewarned of you and of the daybook, which we can give him"—she smiled, reached into her pocket, and pulled out two theater tickets—"tonight."

The tickets had a preprinted header, FORD'S THEATRE, and the words DRESS CIRCLE on the side. Below that were the printed words: TIME and ATTRACTION. Handwritten next to them, *Friday, April 14, 8 P.M.* and *Our American Cousin.*

"The president and his wife are going," she said. "It's in the papers."

"But it starts at eight. I'm supposed to make the exchange at eight thirty."

"We'll think of something."

. . .

Later in the afternoon, Halsey begged a day pass from the wardmaster, who threatened to declare him healed and put him out on Monday if he spent more time walking the streets than resting and recovering.

Then Halsey went up to Pennsylvania, stopped in front of the National Hotel, looked around, and climbed into Noah's shoeshine chair.

Noah said, "Shine, sir?"

Halsey answered with his brogue, "Do you shine a soldier's shoes?"

"I shine any man's shoes who pay my price." Noah answered with none of the old jauntiness. And his hair had gone all white in two and a half years.

Halsey watched him work for a bit; then he looked up at the clouds that had come rolling in. "A sad sky for a sad day, the day they crucified the Lord."

"Yes, sir. A sad day for sho'. But a good Black Baptist still have to work."

"And your sons? Are they working?"

Noah raised his head. His old brown eyes were rimmed in little broken red vessels. "My boys in the hotel is workin'. My boy with the Colored Troops is . . . dead."

"I'm sorry, Noah." Halsey had hoped to proceed more cautiously, but the name just blurted out with the emotion.

"How'd you know my name? And how come you speak it in that gravelly voice?" The old eyes squinted down, then glimmered with recognition. "You . . . I thought *you* was dead."

"I'm sorry about your son. When did it happen?"

"Last week. I heard the night before last."

"How?"

"Secesh sharpshooter, down Roanoke Island. But . . . what's it matter?"

Halsey waited for the emotions to settle in both of them. He let Noah shine, and he wondered how to ask for help.

But as if he knew, Noah looked up and said, "Don't seem in my recollection that you ever think of nothin' in this chair but askin' me to help you somehow. Why you here today?"

"I need help. Again."

The hands stopped working. "I ain't much in the mood for givin'. I done give too much already."

"Are you still agin' any man who's agin' Mr. Lincoln?"

"Yep. And I'se agin' any man who lies to me or my boys, what boys I has left."

Halsey leaned down. "I need their help tonight."

Noah gave Halsey a long look, then spit on his shoes.

II.

On Good Friday, the city usually went quiet at nightfall, especially when nature enhanced the gloom of Scripture with a mist that deadened the sounds of carriage and hoof and shrouded the streetlamps in a cowl of gray.

Good Christians stayed at home. Waiters in restaurants stood idle. The theaters, if they opened at all, played half empty. Even iniquitous Murder Bay entertained fewer sinners.

But not that night. As Halsey walked from Ward A to the lady nurses' quarters, he could hear shouting, faint music, happy gunfire, as if nothing could dampen the spirits of the city, even after four days of celebrating.

Halsey hoped that he might celebrate himself. To sit in a theater again, to gaze up from the dark at the brilliantly gaslit stage, to hear a real orchestra instead of the brass and drum that had been so relentless in wartime, to laugh at the farcical goings-on in *Our American Cousin* . . . these would be wonders, especially if he went to the theater with the daybook—and his future—in his hand.

Samantha was waiting near the flowerbed. She was wearing the same powder blue dress and parasol she had been wearing on that long-ago July Fourth, but she protected herself from the night air with a navy blue cape of heavy wool.

Halsey was wearing a black suit from the donation bin, a white shirt, and a black tie, along with a wide-brimmed floppy black hat, perfect for pulling down over the eyes. She commented on how handsome he looked, and how "mysterious."

In the glow cast by the Capitol dome, a man-made moon above Washington, they went over the plan once more:

She would wait in front of the theater. She would try to find a spot at the front of the crowd that would gather to see the president alight. And she would tell him, even if she had to shout, that Lieutenant Hutchinson had to see him.

They could not count on the letter having reached Mr. Lincoln. So she would try to gauge his response. Eye contact or a spoken comment would be positive. If he went with his head down, focused on his own affairs or on his own company, she would mark that, too, and try at intermission to get close to him. But by then, if all went well, Halsey would be with her, enjoying the play, with the book in his pocket and Lincoln in his box, waiting to receive it.

There was no guarantee, they both knew, that anything would go well.

Then she asked again, "Why must it be done like this? Why not let me walk into the White House during some reception and simply tell the president your story?"

Halsey said, "I promised myself that I would put the president's private thoughts into the president's hands. This time, I will not fail."

He walked with her up Tenth to Pennsylvania and saw her to the good side of the street. She kissed him and hurried away.

. . .

Halsey returned to Ward A to collect himself.

Mrs. Cannon saw him walk in and held out a note. "This just come for you. A government messenger brung it, no less."

Halsey took the letter and went back to his bed.

The two men from Five Forks were already asleep.

George Smith was reading the paper by the oil lamp on his table.

It was just after eight.

Halsey pulled out a box of matches, lit his oil lamp, opened the letter.

When he read the header, *Executive Mansion,* he let out a gasp.

George Smith glanced up.

Halsey said, "It's all right." Then his eye dropped to the signature. *A. Lincoln.* The president had read his letter and answered!

Halsey scanned the page. And the words "presidential pardon" leaped out at him. Then he read more slowly, every word, twice. *A presidential pardon will be considered.*

It was all that he had hoped for.

He thought to run back to Ford's Theatre to tell Samantha that she could just enjoy the show, but he was seeing McNealy in a little more than twenty minutes. If he was late, McNealy might not wait. It might all fall apart. And once he had the daybook, it would all fall into place.

He pulled the pistol from his rucksack. He had loaded it in the middle of the night, with powder and ball. He had sealed each chamber with a plug of bacon grease to keep the moisture out. Now he popped the cylinder and, taking care that no one other than George Smith saw him, he put little copper percussion caps on the five nipples at the back of the five chambers. Then he popped the cylinder back into the gun and put it in his pocket.

George Smith said, "Do you need some help?"

"I wish I could count on you, George."

"If you're runnin', take me with you."

"When I do, maybe I will."

The former Frowner smiled at the mere thought of freedom.

Halsey folded the letter and slid it into George Smith's pocket. "This is what you can do for me. Take care of this till I get back. Don't read it. Don't tell anyone."

If things went wrong on the footbridge, and there was a good chance that they would, Halsey did not want to lose that letter. And after Samantha, there was no one he trusted more than George Smith.

. . .

What about Noah's two sons? Would they be waiting? Could he still trust them?

Halsey stepped out onto Seventh Street and heard the thwang of a Jew's harp. Jacob Bone was standing across the street, at the head of one of the many paths that wound through the darkness of the Smithsonian Park. He was playing a tune called "Kingdom Coming," about the year of Jubilo.

He stopped playing as Halsey approached. He looked Halsey straight in the eye. It was the gaze of a proud young man. "My daddy say you need some help."

"Just hide behind a tree and watch the south end of the Tenth Street Footbridge. Play your Jew's harp, keep your eye peeled. You see anyone other than McNealy—"

"I start in to playin' 'Dixie.' You hear 'Dixie,' you know they's trouble."

"That park is dangerous after dark," said Halsey, "so be careful."

Jacob pulled out a leather blackjack filled with buckshot. "Don't you worry. I know my way around. And my brother, Ezekiel—"

"The one who likes Dickens?"

"No. That was Daniel. He's gone for a hero now." Jacob looked down at the ground a moment. Then he said, "Our little brother's over at the corner of B and Tenth, watchin' from a saloon front where they's friendly to colored. He's playin' his harmonica. If you hear 'Dixie' from either way, there's trouble."

Halsey said, "If there's trouble, just move off. I promised your daddy this wouldn't be dangerous."

They walked a short distance together; then Jacob took a path into the Smithsonian Park.

Halsey crossed the canal on Seventh, then went west along B to the Tenth Street footbridge. He heard a harmonica playing "Lorena," a song about longing and love that the soldiers often sang. He could not see Ezekiel, but that was for the best.

Then, out on the footbridge, a cigar tip glowed orange.

Halsey took a deep breath, scanned the shadows and pools of light, then looked up Tenth, which appeared as two parallel lines of streetlamps, meeting somewhere in the far distance. A few blocks up on the right, Samantha must have been taking her seat in Ford's dress circle just then.

If all went well, Halsey would be joining her soon.

As he walked onto the bridge, he realized that McNealy had taken an advantage already. Halsey was framed by those Tenth Street lights. McNealy had come from the darkness of the Smithsonian Park, with its leafing young trees and the black hulking castle as his only backdrop.

The iron bridge echoed under Halsey's feet.

McNealy's hand went to his shoulder holster. But as Halsey drew closer, McNealy relaxed. He said, "I didn't recognize you in your suit. Strange to dress in black on your resurrection day."

Halsey stopped about five feet away. "The president dresses in black every day."

"He *should* dress like an undertaker. For him, every day for the last four years has been a funeral."

The bridge was arched. The men were now standing on either side of the apex.

McNealy said, "Are you alone?"

"That was the arrangement."

"So those niggers playin' music aren't friends of yours? They sure look like the Bone boys. What's left of 'em."

"They're watching for friends of *yours*."

"I don't have any friends."

"Not even Lafayette Baker."

"He's my boss but no man's friend. He's off in New York, scarin' a few more dollars out of the feed brokers who charge the government for sixty-forty, oats to corn, but deliver forty-sixty. Bad for the horse, bad for the government, good for the broker."

"The head of your service is a swindler?"

"He only swindles swindlers, but one thing's for certain—" McNealy puffed the cigar. "—he was a power unto himself till he tapped Stanton's telegraph line. Stanton wanted to fire him but shipped him off instead."

"So, he watches his own boss, but he's not watching now from the shadows"—Halsey looked around—"ready to spring once I hand over the goods?"

"He's not here." McNealy's eyes shifted. The whites of them flashed in the dim glow from the city lights.

Halsey slipped his hand into his coat pocket and gripped the pistol.

McNealy noticed and said, "Are you loaded?"

"You didn't think I'd come out here with nothing but a book to defend myself."

"I figured the gun would make you feel better. But that's a rare-caliber ball, thirty-one. Hard to get unless you know where to look."

"Not impossible," said Halsey.

"Even if you weren't loaded, you'd say you were." McNealy extended his hand. "Now, let's have the ledger. I don't want to stand over this stinkin' canal all night."

Halsey looked down into the water, as if he were thinking that over. He noticed something floating. A dead dog? A cat? He noticed something swimming. A rat? Definitely a rat. Appropriate, he thought. Then he looked at McNealy. "Diary first."

"I get the ledger, you get the diary. You follow?"

With his left hand, Haley slipped the ledger out of his breast pocket and held it for McNealy to see; then he let it drop back. "Three years old but still juicy. There's even dirt on Doc Wiggins, if he's still alive. He paid Squeaker to steal quinine. The South needed quinine to fight malaria."

"Now, most people in this city would like to put the war behind them and get on with things, including Doc Wiggins," said McNealy. "You should've killed that fat bastard when you had the chance."

And there they stood, on a gloomy night, on a slick footbridge, each waiting for the other to make a move.

Halsey cocked an ear, first for the low, droning twang of the Jew's harp, then for the harmonica competing with a piano in a saloon near the corner. Then he said, "We're out here for a reason. Who's watching us?"

"Everyone." McNealy's eyes scanned both sides of the canal. "Your nigger friends, Doc Wiggins and his boys, maybe the Knights of the Golden Circle, who'll be prayin' from now till Jesus that the South can rise again, maybe even the Wood brothers. Except for the niggers, they're all in Squeaker's book. That's why I want it."

Halsey said, "How do they know they're in the book?"

"Squeaker said so."

"You and the Squeaker?"

"I told you, we recruited our detectives wherever we could. I ran Squeaker before I ran you. He went to those meetings in the Wiggins barn. He kept a record of all their dirty doings and dirty secrets. What else he did—"

"Like killing my cousin?"

"—was his own business. We looked the other way."

Halsey was older now, not so easily shocked by the methods of men in business, politics, and war, but here was a government agency, sworn to protect Americans, allowing the Squeaker McDillons of the world to run loose.

"And you did all this for a higher purpose, I suppose," said Halsey.

"I did it for the money. War kills a lot of people, and it makes a lot more rich. Just ask your cousin. He was tryin' for the second and got the first." McNealy reached into his pocket and pulled out the president's daybook, showing it for about as long as Haley had shown the ledger.

Halsey said, "There are a million books like that in Washington."

"That's why we're standing here, because you grabbed the wrong one three years ago, the one that I could have used to blackmail half the powerful men in Washington. If I'd gotten it, I'd be rich now, rich and gone back to Ohio, to a little dirt farm where a very pretty mama sits waitin' with her little boys."

"Save the sad story," said Halsey. "Hold it out. Open it to the first page."

"You want to see the signature?" McNealy held the book open.

Halsey stepped closer, but he was still keeping his distance. *A. Lincoln* was clear on the upper right corner of the endpaper, just as clear as it had been to Constance Wood when it flopped onto the floor of the Smithsonian.

Halsey said, "Flip to the back page."

He remembered that the back page and the words, "The real problem with a general emancipation . . ." had been torn out. The words on the previous page mentioned sending the freed slaves back to Africa or Central America, and . . .

Halsey decided to be bold. Instead of pulling the gun from his right pocket, he pulled out a box of matches and struck one so that he could see the handwriting.

McNealy's brow furrowed. "What are you doing?"

"Reading the last page. I remember it as if Brady had taken a picture of it."

"Damn." McNealy blew out the match.

At the same moment, the Jew's harp stopped thrumming.

The sound of a rolling carriage traveled toward them from somewhere near the Smithsonian Castle.

The Jew's harp delivered a few notes from 'Dixie,' then stopped again.

Two yellow running lights flickered through the trees, marking the movement of the carriage.

Then the harmonica stopped. The sound of a short scuffle was followed by fast feet pounding along B Street and a young voice singing out, "I wish I was in the land of cotton, old times there am not forgotten."

McNealy shoved the daybook into his side pocket and pulled out his gun. "All right, stupid. Give me the ledger, now."

"Look away, look away . . . look away . . . Dixieland. . . ." The song was receding. Young Ezekiel was escaping.

McNealy said, "The match. It was the signal for Doc Wiggins to close in."

Then the carriage and its lights rolled to a stop at the south end of the footbridge.

And Halsey heard footfalls behind him, coming from the north. A big man in a tall hat walked out onto the bridge and stopped, blocking Haley's escape.

McNealy said, "That's Mr. Jeffords. He's your escort."

"My escort?"

"Give me the ledger and I'll tell you the next step." McNealy was carrying a Colt Wells Fargo, single action. He cocked it. He meant business. "Give me the ledger, or I will shoot you and take it and your nursie-girl will die."

"My nursie-girl?"

McNealy stepped closer. "The ledger. Now."

Halsey pulled it from his pocket but held it.

McNealy said, "That man behind you was in the barn the night that Constance was murdered. He's one of Doc Wiggins's associates. They've been plotting in this city for three years. And paying me for the privilege of doing their business, whatever it is . . . running deserters, smuggling quinine, cutting telegraph lines."

"Then you're a traitor?"

"I'm a profiteer, just like that cousin of yours. Except I've known where to make my money. I've also known that the South was doomed since Atlanta fell. And nothing anyone in Washington could do, good or bad, would change that, not with Lincoln resolved to spill every drop of blood left in America if he had to. So—"

"You played everyone?"

McNealy nodded. "You are gaining knowledge with your experience after all. I would like one more score, while my friends at either end of the bridge would like no evidence of their earlier wrongdoing. More than that, they know Squeaker's book contains evidence of the foibles of Benjamin Wood, who suspects them in the murder of Harriet Dunbar. If Wood has something on them, they should get something on him."

"An age-old tradition," said Halsey. "Did you kill her?"

"She had the daybook. She was going to give it to the Wood brothers just before the Democratic convention. She thought it would be a good tool to use in the election. No one else did . . . just then."

"So you killed her?"

"Her killer is now sitting next to your nursie-girl in Ford's Theatre. As soon as he knows we've made the exchange, he'll take the seven-inch blade in his sleeve and return it to his boot top, instead of sliding it between her ribs and into her heart and leaving her dead in the seat."

"So it's the ledger for the daybook?" said Halsey.

"No, it's the ledger for your nursie-girl." McNealy held out his hand.

Halsey knew now he should never have brought himself into this, but here he was. He had no choice. He handed over the ledger and kept his hand extended. "Now, the daybook?"

McNealy put the ledger into his side pocket and pulled out the volume that had started it all.

"Give it over," said Halsey.

McNealy smiled, showing teeth in that nest of beard. Then he held the daybook over the canal and . . . dropped it.

Halsey let out a wordless cry of shock.

The daybook fluttered down and splashed, right next to a dead cat . . . or a live rat.

McNealy was turning on his heels and marching toward the carriage at the south end of the footbridge. And he was laughing as Halsey had never heard him laugh before, laughing out loud, not the usual snicker or sneer, but a full-bellied roar.

Then McNealy shouted, "I have the ledger, Doc! We have a deal."

Halsey could not move. He felt as he had when he was shot, stood up straight from the force of the blow but just about to collapse.

Should he chase McNealy? Should he jump in after the daybook? But it had sunk already. So, he feared, had the future that appeared so bright a short time ago.

He took a few steps after McNealy and the voice behind him said, "Just stay where you are. We can see them from here. That's why the side-lights are lit."

Doc Wiggins sat in the carriage and his Negro driver held the reins.

Halsey turned back to Jeffords, who wore a top hat and a well-tailored claw-hammer coat.

"Once we know that Doc has the ledger and McNealy has the day-book," said Jeffords, "we'll go up and rescue your girl."

"The daybook? But McNealy just dropped it into the canal."

"That was a dummy, mostly blank, to make you play nice." The man looked beyond Halsey and said, "This here's a three-part deal. You give up the ledger to McNealy. He gives it to Doc, who gives him the daybook, which we took off Harriet Dunbar in her barn. And you get your girl."

Halsey watched McNealy and Doc Wiggins make their exchange in the lantern light. "So McNealy gets the daybook?"

"He figures he can get a fine price on it, because it shows what Lincoln was really thinkin' about the niggers when he started this war. Good oil to pour on a new fire, now that everyone's talkin' about reconstructin' the South with niggers as full citizens."

"And what else do I get? A bullet? A visit from the Provost Marshal?"

Jeffords said, "We wanted to kill you after the exchange, but Mc-Nealy said we'd do it this way and let you live. He says you've murdered a few people yourself, so you won't go singin'."

"Honor among thieves and killers, then?" Halsey reached for his pocket.

The man dropped a derringer from his sleeve and pointed it at Halsey's forehead. "Keep your hands where I can see them."

Suddenly, Jeffords's hat flew off and flew toward Halsey. At the same time, his arm swung wildly and his derringer went off.

Halsey felt the shot whiz past his ear. An instant later, the horse on the Wiggins carriage screamed and reared, hit in the haunch by a bullet. Then the horse bolted and went careening toward the lights of Seventh Street.

Jeffords was turning toward a shadow behind him, and something smashed him in the face. He stumbled back and collapsed.

Noah was the shadow. The something was a leather blackjack. He stepped over Jeffords and said to Halsey, "I told Ezekiel to go home. Jacob'll know to hide. Now, you just git what you come for."

"Thank you. Thank you, Noah."

"You said this wouldn't be dangerous. I didn't believe you."

Jeffords stirred, and Noah brought the blackjack down fiercely on the white man's skull.

Halsey turned and ran over the footbridge. It was not much more than thirty feet from end to end. In a few strides, he was over the arch and flying downhill.

McNealy still had a book in his hand and was raising the Colt Wells Fargo, pointing it straight at Halsey, who was trying to pull his Adams from his pocket.

McNealy pulled the trigger. The hammer snapped. *Click.* Misfire on a misty night.

Before McNealy could squeeze off another, Halsey flew into him, right at the south end of the footbridge. Hats flew. Book flew. Gun flew. They smashed off the wrought iron and spun out onto the gravel drive.

McNealy jammed his knee into Halsey's groin.

Halsey hit the ground and crumpled with the pain that shot up his flanks and exploded in his kidneys. Then McNealy aimed a vicious kick into his left side, right into the healing wound. The sound of it made a hollow thumping, as if Halsey were just a huge melon about to split apart.

McNealy began looking around on the ground. For his gun? For the book?

Halsey crawled to his knees and told himself that whatever pain he felt, he had to fight through it, get up, get out the gun, and . . . Goddamn but the gun and the fabric of a strange coat were all tangled. The barrel caught as he tried to clear it.

And McNealy kicked him again.

He fell onto his back but the gun tore free of the fabric. He raised it and pointed it, and another kick sent it flying into the shadows.

McNealy went to pick it up when they both heard the shrill screech of police whistles in the Smithsonian Park.

McNealy turned toward the sound.

And Halsey, despite the pain in his gut, lifted himself and drove his shoulder into McNealy, drove him backwards, drove him right over the low parapet wall. And they fell together, ten feet down into the filthy, black, crotch-deep water.

McNealy was underneath, so he cushioned the fall for Halsey.

But there was power in the little man. He burst from the water, lifting Haley all the way up and out, slamming him hard against the black, slime-covered granite wall on the south side of the channel.

Halsey wobbled.

McNealy pulled back with his right fist and shot it straight at Halsey's face.

But Halsey ducked, and McNealy's punch hit granite.

Halsey grabbed him by the lapel and pushed him through the water, through the shit and garbage and offal, and slammed him against the other wall.

McNealy swung with a leg and knocked Halsey off his feet. Then he flew knee first into Halsey's chest, grabbed his lapels, slammed him under the water, then pulled him out. "Did you think you could drown me, you Boston pansy boy?"

Slam . . . back under the water. Then up and out again.

"You come to Washington with your holy notions about savin' the niggers and savin' the Union, and good men on both sides end up dying."

Slam.

"And for what? For *what?*"

Slam.

And the fourth time he rose from the water, Halsey heard the police whistles directly above them.

At the sound, McNealy hesitated a moment, just enough for Halsey to gather his strength and throw McNealy off.

Then he scrambled to his feet, grabbed McNealy by his coat collar, and smashed him so hard into the south wall that McNealy's head almost snapped off.

"Hey, there!" came a voice from above. "Stop this."

Now it was Halsey who hesitated, looked up.

McNealy crawled to his feet, spat teeth and blood at Halsey, and leaped at him

Halsey sidestepped him and raised his fists.

"You think you can fight a street fighter?" growled McNealy, and he swung a wild punch that struck Halsey in the throat.

Halsey staggered at the blow, gasped for air, but managed to grab McNealy by the neck and gasp out, "I fought at Gettysburg, while you were swindlin' widows and sniffin' their cunts. I can fight you all night long." Then he tripped McNealy and drove him down into the water and held him under. "You follow?"

McNealy could not answer.

Halsey held and held in that strange light that reflected off the low clouds and made the surface of the canal look like grease.

He held and wondered why the police had stopped shouting, stopped whistling, stopped looking down. Where were they?

He did not look up to see. Instead, he held and held while McNealy struggled and thrashed.

Ten seconds.

No police.

McNealy kicked and grabbed at Halsey's arms.

Thirty seconds.

No splash, no nightstick, no gunfire, no whistles.

Sixty seconds.

McNealy drove a fist into Halsey's side. But Halsey held and held. And then . . .

McNealy went limp.

A minute and a half.

Another murder on Halsey Hutchinson. Seven.

He stood. He wobbled. He took a few deep breaths. He almost doubled over with the pain in his side and his throat. Then he saw an iron ladder that led from the water to the end of the footbridge. He started to climb and tried to prepare himself for whatever was waiting.

What he saw as his head rose above the low wall was a policeman's hat.

Inside the hat was a head. The policeman lay unconscious. His partner lay nearby.

And right in front of Halsey's nose, shining in the dim light, was McNealy's Colt.

He snatched it as he climbed out and looked around.

The runaway Wiggins carriage had disappeared into the night.

Noah had disappeared, too. And his son.

Halsey was soaked. He had not stunk like this since the dirty work of night soiling. The canal was worse than the bottom of a privy because it was never cleaned.

And now, he saw three shadows coming toward him from the direction of Seventh Street. They loped like wary wolves and spread out like a pack, one to his left, one to his right, one directly in front.

Three Smithsonian Park thugs. They might even have been the three that had menaced Halsey and Constance that first day. Whoever they were, they were bolder at night. For thugs, this was good ground at night.

One of them staggered a bit; two of them smelled of whiskey.

The one on the left, the sober one, said, "The niggers who jumped the cops were too fast for us, even the old one."

"Nothin' like a fast-legged nigger with a leather sap," said one of the others.

Halsey raised McNealy's Colt. "I'm armed, and these police will wake up soon."

The one on the left said, "Fuck them," and drove a kick into a police-man's head.

The one on the right said, "Good idea, Jed," and kicked the other one, then kicked again, then raised his arms, did a little dance step, and kicked again.

The one on the left growled, "Quit it."

"Those coppers are out good now, Jed. Out for the night."

And the two who smelled of whiskey snickered and giggled.

Then the one on the left said to Halsey, "We charge a fee for passin' through our park at night. And we figure, you owe for the rich man's car-riage, the two runnin' niggers, the cops, the feller in the canal, and your-self. So empty your pockets."

Halsey pulled back the hammer. "I told you, I got a gun." He also had most of the money from his hidden stash in the War Department.

One of them said, "You got a gun that misfired a minute ago."

"Yeah," said another, "must be this night air. Your gun got the vapors."

The two drunks snickered and giggled at that, too.

Halsey aimed at the big one on his left, the sober one, the leader. He prayed that the second chamber was better sealed. He squeezed the trig-ger and— *Click.*

"See now," said the thug, "the Lord don't want you to kill nobody on the day when the Jews killed him." And they started to close in, like a pack.

"What the Lord wants and what he gets," said Halsey, "are often two different things."

"The Lord's kind of like people, then, ain't he?"

Halsey squeezed the trigger again. *Bang!* The third chamber went off. The man's head snapped back and the force of the shot sent him over the parapet wall and into the canal.

Halsey pointed the gun at the others, but they were already running away, back into the woods from which they had witnessed the whole scene on the bridge.

Halsey stood in the silent darkness of Smithsonian Park, in the mid-dle of the Mall. He listened for more police whistles. He took a deep breath and willed his heart to stop pounding. It was a trick he had learned before going into battle.

He lit a match and looked around on the ground for the daybook. But he could not see it. And his pistol? Where was his pistol? Then one of the police groaned.

So Halsey moved quickly. There was one more thing to do.

He dropped back down the canal, into the filthy crotch-deep water, grabbed McNealy's body, and emptied all the pockets. He took everything: coins, watch, a small loading kit for his pistol, a barrel pen and notebook, a pocketknife with which he cut off the shoulder holster, a billfold containing greenbacks, papers, and a thin silver shield that read WAR DEPARTMENT DETECTIVE SERVICE. And perhaps most surprising, a small copper liberty head, like the one that Benjamin Wood had shown him in the Willard so long ago.

McNealy was a Copperhead. Or was it another ruse?

Halsey climbed the rusting wrought-iron ladder again.

When they came to, the police would find two dead men decomposing with the rest of the offal in the Washington Canal. And they would piece the story together: A man in a brown suit, without identification or money, had been waylaid by brazen toughs who had also attacked two police officers. The man had killed one of them, but the toughs had escaped with everything he owned, including his pistol.

Halsey looked again around the bodies of the police, wondering where the daybook had gone. Had McNealy even had it? Or did Doc Wiggins hold on to it? And that Adams pistol. Halsey could still be traced by that Adams pistol.

But no time for looking. One of the policemen was moving now. Besides, he had to get to Ford's Theatre.

He knew he couldn't walk into the dress circle soaked with stinking filth, shoes squishing, belly throbbing from the pain of McNealy's kicks.

So he hurried through the park toward the lights of his hospital, glimmering three blocks away.

He came around to the back of the ward, let himself in, and dropped all his wet clothes down the hole of the indoor privy.

Lights were out. Mrs. Cannon was busy at the front. The wardmaster's door was closed. A few men glanced up, but most were snoring or lost in their own worlds of pain. By the clock halfway down the ward, Halsey could see that it was quarter to ten.

He tiptoed to his bed, knelt, and shoved all McNealy's gear into his sack.

George Smith looked across the aisle. "Where are your clothes?"

Halsey brought a finger to his lips. Then he pulled out his soldier's uniform and put it on. His hair was still wet and stank of filthy canal water. He covered it with his kepi.

George Smith said, "Somebody just come lookin' for you. A darkie."

Halsey stepped across the floor and knelt beside the former Frowner. "Young or old?"

"What's wrong with your voice? You're croakin' more than usual, like you got a laryngitis or somethin'."

Halsey made a dismissive wave of his hand. He tried to clear his throat, bruised from the fight, and said, "The darkie, was he young or old?"

"Young. He snuck in the back. I said, 'What you lookin' for, boy?' He asked for you, and I told him I was your right friend. So he give me this." George Smith reached under his pillow. "I didn't look inside."

The daybook. Halsey took it and held it for a moment. Then he opened it to the front. There was the signature: *A. Lincoln.* A real signature, not the forgery that McNealy had shown him. Then Halsey flipped to the back and saw where the pages had been torn out.

This was it. This was his freedom.

And on the back endpaper, in pencil, in a childish script, was this: *Picked up with gun kep gun four pertekshun hope this helps m. Lincoln N & J*

N for Noah. *J* for Jacob.

Halsey said, "Do you have that letter I gave you?"

George Smith took it from under his pillow and put it into Halsey's hands.

III.

Ten minutes later, a carriage pulled up in front of Ford's Theatre. Halsey paid the driver with folding money and climbed down.

He had McNealy's Colt in his pocket. He had changed the percussion caps. He hoped that would help, but he had not had time to reload the three used cylinders. He did not want to start shooting in the theater, anyway, not with the president there. But he had to save Samantha. If these men had killed Harriet, they would certainly kill Samantha, too, if it served their purpose.

The big gas lamps lit the whole street and cast their light upward onto the high-fronted façade. Halsey felt the excitement just standing there, knowing that on the other side of that wall, there were fourteen hundred people, including the president, enjoying the play. And waiting for Halsey was the pardon he dreamed of. A few soldiers glanced up from their craps game, glanced at Halsey uniform, as if to ask, *What unit? Why out on the street?* Halsey reached for his hospital pass, but they went back to their game, as if the rules could be relaxed now that the war was over.

Halsey could not relax. After all he had been through, he did not think he had any more nerves left, but his heart was pounding, and his mouth was dry.

He had lost his ticket in the fight. Unlike his folding money, which did not run, the ticket had been soaked through and ruined. He peered in at the center entrance, where the ticket taker was still seated. How would he get in?

Just then, a familiar figure stepped out of the Star Saloon next door and stalked up the street: John Wilkes Booth.

He stopped a few feet from Halsey and made a bit of idle conversation with two people from the theater. Then a member of the Washington Cavalry Police came up, greeted Booth, and invited him for a drink in the Star.

Booth popped open his watch and said, "I'm afraid not. Keene will be onstage in a few minutes, and I promised to take a look at her."

Then Booth glanced over his shoulder and his eyes met Halsey's. His brow furrowed, as if he recognized this soldier from somewhere. Then, with that studied grace, Booth turned, leaped the step, and went into the main entrance.

Halsey decided to follow him.

The ticket taker held out his hand, and Booth pulled back in a show of melodramatic surprise, saying, "You would not want a ticket of me, would you?" And both of them burst into laughter.

Then Booth stepped into the narrow lobby, stopped for a moment by the door to the orchestra and cocked his head, as if listening to a bit of dialogue.

Halsey was thinking that if he told Booth why he was there, to save that fine young woman from Boston, who had greeted him and charmed him so well three years before, the actor might be willing to help him find her and protect her. At the moment, with his final expiation so close, he would turn to anyone for help.

But the ticket taker held out his arm.

Halsey stopped and said, in a graveled half-whisper, "I'm afraid I don't have a ticket, either."

"Then you can't—"

"I'm a great admirer of Laura Keene, and I've been away a long time."

Booth glanced at Halsey again, then turned for the staircase at the left.

Halsey said, "I'm a friend of Mr. Booth's, too—you could go and ask him. But since you insist, let me pay."

The ticket taker looked at the uniform, then waved him into the theater. "Find a place to stand. She should be onstage soon."

Halsey stepped into the narrow lobby. Doors to the right and left, leading to the orchestra, were closed. After the darkness that had enveloped him for most of the night, it was a shock and a strange pleasure to stand in this brilliantly lit space, with its yellow walls, cream-colored woodwork, and red carpet.

Inside, the audience was laughing at some silly line.

He listened for a moment, then started up the stairs on the left, which turned gracefully on their way to the dress circle.

At the top, he found Booth standing there, surveying the theater. The stairs came in audience left, so this was a good spot from which to peer across into the presidential box, audience right. The houselights were dim, but the stage lights filled the audience and lit the side of Booth's face.

Halsey whispered, "Wilkes."

Booth's head snapped round and there was another moment of—what?—recognition, shock, embarrassment, aggression. Halsey could not tell.

He smelled whiskey, but there was only sobriety on Booth's face, pure concentration. He said, "Can you help me, Wilkes? Can you—?"

"Help you?" whispered Booth. "No. I'm busy." Then he moved away, along the back wall, toward the other side of the dress circle.

A foolish idea anyway, thought Halsey.

On the stage, the farce creaked along. *Our American Cousin* followed the misadventures of American bumpkin Asa Trenchard in England. Mrs. Mountchessington and her daughter had determined that he was a rich man, well worth a marriage for money. Complications, of course, had been ensuing since the start.

Halsey glanced over toward the presidential box. He could not see Lincoln, who was seated well back, but he could see Lincoln's long left hand on the arm of his rocker, and the white flounce of Mrs. Lincoln's dress, too. And a younger couple were sitting in the box in full view.

Halsey remembered that Lincoln had been a great admirer of Shakespeare. He wondered what the president thought of this tripe.

Mrs. Mountchessington was saying, "Yes, my children, while Mr. De Boots and Mr. Trenchard are both here, you must ask yourself seriously, as to the state of your affections. Remember, your happiness for life will depend on the choice you make."

"What would you advise, Mama?"

Halsey scanned the dress circle for the powder blue hat and dress. He knew that she was here somewhere.

And the man sent to kill her . . . Was he sitting beside her? Behind her? Did she know of her fate, or was she blissfully unaware, still thinking that the only concern for the night was to get close to the president.

Halsey squinted in the half light and tried, systematically, to look at every seat, starting with the far side.

Was she sitting over there, beside those two army officers?

He noticed them because Booth had moved around the back of the theater, in and out of the little pools of dim light cast by the gas sconces, and had stopped right there and leaned against the wall, as if to watch the play—or the officers—for a moment.

Strange.

Halsey turned his gaze back to the audience and started to follow the rows again and, yes, there. Samantha was sitting in the front row, three seats in. An elderly lady and gentleman were sitting to her left. To her right was one of the six-inch iron columns that ran up through the building and supported the family circle above them.

Halsey stepped down the side aisle, so that he could look directly along the first row to get her attention. There were only seven rows of seats in the dress circle, so he did not have far to travel.

As he did, he glanced across again at Booth, who was showing a card to the man near the door of the presidential box, a civilian, a small man. Where was Lincoln's bodyguard? Halsey glanced into the box. He could not see the president, but Mrs. Lincoln had leaned into view. She was turned to her husband, and she was smiling and whispering like a giddy girl.

Onstage, Mrs. Mountchessington was babbling away to her daughter as they came to the realization that Asa Trenchard didn't have any money.

From the corner of his eye, Halsey saw Booth, pushing his knee against the door of the presidential box, then stepping inside.

Then Halsey made eye contact with Samantha. She raised her hands and smiled, as if to ask, *Do you have it?*

Halsey nodded and made a small gesture with his head. *Step out. Excuse yourself and step out.*

She pointed to the old lady on her left as if to say, *She took your seat.*

That meant the menace would come from her right or behind.

Halsey's mind was racing on three tracks at once. How to get Samantha out of her seat? Who around her was threatening her? And . . . Booth? Watching a play with the president? The Son of Kentucky and the great actor. King Lincoln and Richard III?

Halsey looked again at the president's box. All seemed as before, except that Booth had disappeared.

So Halsey studied the men seated around Samantha. And . . . one of them, behind her, was looking down at something in his hand. A carte de visite. *The* carte de visite? Halsey, in chin strap and uniform? Yes. The man raised his head again.

He was round-headed and burly. He filled the chair and spilled onto the ladies on either side and was likely a bit slow because of it. He studied Halsey, perhaps puzzled by the clean-shaven face, then he turned toward the back of the theater, as if searching for Jeffords. But Jeffords might still be lying on the footbridge, pockets picked, shoes stolen, head smashed.

Onstage, Mrs. Mountchessington was saying, "I am aware, Mr.

Trenchard, that you are not used to the manners of good society, and that alone will excuse the impertinence of which you have been guilty." And off she went.

Halsey glanced again at the president's box and suddenly, in the glittering lights and clashing emotions, he thought of the words Booth had spoken to him on an April morning at the shoeshine stand: *"Do not say son of Kentucky. This nation lies in perpetual winter, until Kentucky is removed from the seat of power."*

Booth wasn't going into that box to discuss Shakespeare.

But the man behind Samantha was moving. Toward her? Was he going to do it right then? Did he have a knife?

Asa Trenchard looked up into the dress circle, took a deep breath, and delivered his big line, "Don't know the manners of good society, eh? Well, I know enough to—"

Halsey thrust his hand across the two people at the end of the aisle and reached for Samantha.

"—turn you inside out—"

Halsey whispered, hard and low, straining his voice, "We have to leave. Now."

"—you sockdologizing old mantrap!"

From the corner of his eye, Halsey saw movement in the presidential box. And he realized in an instant what was happening. He tried to cry out, "Mister President!" But he could barely croak the first syllable before the house exploded with laughter.

In the same instant, the knife flashed in the hand of Samantha's assailant, and a light flashed in the president's box, and a pistol popped.

A pistol?

The man with the knife looked toward the sound.

Halsey felt Samantha's hand touch his. He closed tight around it.

Now there was a struggle in the presidential box, the sound of two men grappling.

The actors were looking up, and the audience was turning as Booth appeared in full at the railing. Even the man sent to murder Samantha still hesitated, and that saved her life.

Halsey pulled on her hand.

Booth swung a leg over the railing.

The theater had gone silent, except for the sound of tearing, of ripping, of rending.

Booth dropped to the stage, trailing the fabric of a flag that had caught on his spur. He landed and twisted his left leg, which broke as he hit. Halsey could tell. But Booth steadied himself with his hands and kept from falling, graceful even then. He rose, looked out, held up his knife, which glittered like a diamond in the stage lights, and proclaimed, *"Sic semper tyrannis."*

Halsey knew what that meant. "Thus ever to tyrants." And he knew that it meant something truly terrible.

He pulled harder on Samantha, all but dragging her along the front of the dress circle and into his arms.

Booth limped past the stunned actor playing Asa Trenchard and exited stage right, shouting, "The South is avenged!"

For a second . . . or two . . . or three, there was silence. They were all in a theater together, the stage brilliantly lit, brighter than day. They had just watched a new scene. Yes. That was what had happened. That was all. But this was a comedy. Booth had just played a scene from tragedy.

Then Mrs. Lincoln's scream pierced the still air, a scream sharper than Booth's knife.

People were moving now, to look around, to look up.

Mrs. Lincoln's scream became a wail: "Help! Help! Help!"

And the young man in their box shouted, "Somebody stop that man!"

Mrs. Lincoln's wail became a horrified shriek: "They have killed the president! Oh, God!"

And the whole theater exploded with screams, cries, sounds of horror more terrible than anything Halsey had heard in that final brawl at Gettysburg. Some men were clambering onto the stage; others were leaping for the presidential box. Chairs were collapsing and falling to the floor as people stood and turned and tried to do something. Help, pursue, escape. Men and women were stumbling, moving, milling, cursing, crying, and rumbling in every direction.

Halsey realized they had to get away, right away.

He wrapped an arm around Samantha and put himself between her and the man with the knife. But the crowd was now pressing in every direction, so there was no way that the man could get at them. Halsey dragged her to the door and started down the red-carpeted stairs as the doctors were rushing up.

. . .

They could not sleep that night. They wrapped themselves in blankets, sat on a bench in front of the ladies' quarters at the hospital, and listened to the cries and lamentations in the city.

Samantha wept softly.

Halsey held McNealy's pistol on his lap and watched the shadows, waiting for some attack that might come from Doc Wiggins or his men.

The gloom of the nation that dawn could not have been more personal. Halsey had almost taken his identity back. And Booth had snatched it along with everything else.

Halsey did not even tell Samantha of the pardon the president had promised.

It would only have meant more pain.

But several times during the night, he said, "I should have known . . . I should have known sooner what Booth was doing. I looked into his eyes."

Samantha tried to soothe him. "Booth is an actor. He knew what to hide and what to reveal."

"I tried to call out when I realized. But my voice is weak, and the laughter—"

"Booth waited for the laughter. He knew it would cover the cry of anyone who saw him at that moment, especially a man whose voice was damaged in the service of his country." And she touched his hand.

That soothed him more than her words.

Around seven, the barouche came to take Samantha up to Harewood Hospital. In some small ways, the work of the world had not stopped, could not stop.

Samantha said that she could not let sick men suffer the anguish of that day alone. She had to go.

Halsey decided it was safe. If Doc Wiggins and his men had what they came for, Squeaker's ledger, they no longer had reason to menace Halsey's nursie-girl.

So Halsey rode with her up to Seventh at G, got off, and walked across to Tenth.

A crowd had been on the street all night, waiting for word from the house where they had taken the president to die. A light rain had begun to fall. But the people did not seem to notice. They simply stood and waited.

Around seven twenty, a shriek of grief pierced the gloom. It was Mrs. Lincoln, crying out.

And a great sobbing groan rose from the street.

A few minutes later, as if horrible news traveled by some strange telegraphic electricity in the air, a church bell tolled . . . then another . . . then another.

Halsey stayed until they brought a long white box out of the house. Abraham Lincoln was in it. They put it onto a hearse. Then, accompanied by the infantry company that guarded the White House, the hearse rolled up Tenth Street, through the cold April rain.

Somewhere, a cannon boomed in mourning.

Halsey turned and headed back to the ward. He carried Lincoln's daybook and the Lincoln letter in his pocket. And he felt as if the world had ended.

FIFTEEN

Monday Morning

Peter Fallon walked down Tenth Street and stopped in front of Ford's Theatre.

It was four in the morning, the time when the ghosts owned the ground.

On that Good Friday night, there would have been soldiers, hangers, gawkers waiting for the president and his lady to emerge after the play.

Peter wondered if his own historical ghost, Halsey Hutchinson, the man he had now tracked across the Civil War, had been there, too, with the Lincoln letter in his pocket and that "something" in his hand.

And then, Peter saw Booth's ghost step out of the storefront to the right, the Star Saloon. He moved quickly, with long strides, and stopped to talk to a few of the ghosts on the street.

One of them invited him to have a drink.

Booth begged off. He said he had promised to watch Laura Keene, and she was due onstage in a few minutes. That was his story.

Peter wanted to tell the others, *Don't let him go in. Stop him now.*

Then Booth's ghost looked over his shoulder, right into Peter's eyes. His brow furrowed as if he recognized Peter, or feared that Peter knew what he was about to do. But Peter could not move. He could do nothing to stop Booth. There was no bridge to Booth, no river of time for Peter to travel.

And Booth seemed to know it. With that studied grace, he turned, leaped the step, and went inside . . . as he did every night for some street wanderer who happened to stop there in the hours before dawn.

A police car rolled by. Peter gave the officer a nod. The officer smiled, as if he had seen many people standing there in contemplation, just like that.

Peter's head was clear now. He could go back to reading the Washington *Daily Republican*.

. . .

In the suite, Henry was snoring. He had the Magnum on his lap. He had urged Peter not to go out, that the Bonnie Blue Flag boys might be out there, or J-Man. But Peter had gone anyway.

Evangeline had finally given up and gone to bed. She had an eight o'clock call for the shoot at the Lincoln Memorial.

That night, they had divided the task of reading the Washington newspapers, searching for anyone named Bone, or Molly, or Hutchinson, or Jeremiah Murphy. They had been working year by year. Peter went through 1865 before he took his break. Diana worked through 1866 and into 1867. Up in Boston, Antoine was reading into the 1870s until he sent an e-mail:

Got nothin'. Eyes crossed. Going to bed.

The chance to find that last lost expression of Lincolnian thought and eloquence was fading. Maybe Donald Dawkins was right. Maybe it was in a landfill.

But Diana was still awake, still working at her laptop.

"Any luck?" he asked.

"A few little bits. I wish there was a search engine that could go through every old newspaper and index it all."

"This is old-school research, the way we used to work. You read everything, even the advertisements. They tell you how people lived in the details. And we look for God in the details."

"Then try this for a detail." She picked up her notebook. "An ad from April 1867: 'Night soil collected, low rates, family business.' And here's the fine print: 'Only remaining son of Freedwoman Molly Blodgett, known as Mother Freedom, continues in business. Contact Mr. Zion Molly, Eleventh near Maryland.'"

"Wow." Peter sat on the sofa next to her. "That's where we were to-night."

"God's in the details. Don't know what it means or how it helps me to get tenure."

"Henry told you, the fix is in on that. Professor Conlon is now your champion."

"I want *real* tenure."

"Then read on. I will, too."

Peter grabbed his iPad, and an e-mail from Antoine appeared:

Dear Boss, Could not sleep. Thinking about you having all the fun in DC. Envious. So I went back to work. See the story, lower left corner.

Peter opened the link to page two of the *Republican*.

Washington Canal to Be Filled

The Mayor of Washington has announced the decision to fill the City Canal up to Rock Creek. The City Canal, from the Anacostia to the foot of Seventeenth Street, was opened in 1815. The connector was completed in 1833. It is believed that this will be a ten-year job.

"However," said the city engineer. "If we are to modernize Washington, we must eliminate this open sewer pit running through the city."

The only lock keeper's house is at the head of the Washington Branch, at the foot of Seventeenth. It is believed that the keeper and his family will be able to stay there for a span of five years.

"I sure do hope we can stay longer," said Noah Bone, the first Negro lock keeper. "My grandbabies been born here. And it's a fine place to live, with the river and the White House and the Washington Monument for a view." Bone was vouched for just after the war by Major Thomas Eckert, who convinced the city fathers that Bone, having shined the shoes and cleaned the boots of most of the major men of the time, having given one of his sons to the war, a son who dreamed of this job, should receive a sinecure.

Peter finished reading and said, "Aha!"

Diana looked at him. "What?"

He handed her the tablet. "I just had an aha moment. At least I hope so. Eckert knew Halsey Hutchinson. And he knew Noah Bone, who, according to what we could decipher from the ghosting from the second letter fragment, knew 'Hutch.' Halsey Hutchinson."

"And who also had 'a valuable item' for Molly Blodgett, also known as Mother Freedom." Diana paused, reread the piece, then asked, "So Noah is the bridge?"

"We can't be sure of all the connections, but yeah, an old black shoeshine. He's the real bridge."

"And now we know where he lived out his days."

"In a place run by the National Park Service."

Peter got up and shook Henry awake.

Then he went in and woke Evangeline and whispered, "Do you still have that picture of Kathi Morganti and William Dougherty?"

"What . . . what?" She rolled over.

"It may be a bargaining chip."

"Chips? No, I don't want any chips. They'll give you thunder thighs and—"

"Wake up, baby. This may all be over in a few hours."

. . .

They pulled up in front of Congressman Milbury's Georgetown town house at seven.

Henry and Diana stayed in the car.

Peter and Evangeline went to the door.

Some congressmen shared apartments, because they spent so much time on Capitol Hill or in their districts. But Congressman Milbury had planted his flag in D.C. over twenty years before, and from the look of his three-story town house, he liked to live well.

He came to the door in his bathrobe. His white hair was combed and his skin was shower-pink and smelling of aftershave. "What is this about?"

Evangeline said, "Do you remember me from the train?"

"I'm a politician. I never forget a face or a name. Now, why are you bothering me at my home at the crack of dawn on a day when I begin my campaign for a major change to American tax policy?"

"We have a deal for you," said Peter.

"You're the treasure hunter, aren't you? Dougherty told me about you. I thought we'd meet on Saturday night. I have a few things I'd like to talk over with you about your business practices."

Peter said nothing. Now was not the time to get annoyed.

Evangeline said, "We need your help."

"My help?"

"We need you to contact the NPS," said Peter.

"Why?"

"Because you keep a bust of Lincoln in your office," said Evangeline. "Isn't that what you said the other night?"

Milbury looked from face to face and said, "I'm not here to enrich you, Mr. Fallon, at the expense of our nation's heritage."

"There are some who say you're not here to enrich anyone except the tax collector," answered Peter.

Evangeline gave him an elbow. Then she said, "We only care about the truth, Congressman. And the hunt for this Lincoln treasure has gotten very dangerous."

"That's not my problem. Now, if you don't mind, I have a very important day." The congressman started to close the door.

Peter put his foot in it. "If the Lincoln diary is where we think it is," said Peter, "it's on government property. So you'll get all the credit if we find it, and we'll have to give it up."

"All the credit," said Evangeline, "and all the votes."

"Votes?" Again Milbury looked from face to face. "And what do you get?"

"The satisfaction of a job done," said Peter. "The satisfaction of giving Americans back a piece of their heritage."

"And no more killing," said Evangeline.

"Killing?" said Milbury.

"There are at least three dead," she said.

"Dead? Did you do it?"

"No. And the ones who did the first murder died in a home invasion."

Milbury said, "They were shot, I imagine. We have to get guns off the street."

Evangeline knew that Peter had some opinions about that, too. This was not the place for them, so she held up her iPhone and said, "Help us. It will enhance your reputation, put a national treasure into the nation's hands, and give you a piece of information recorded on this telephone that might be very valuable in your present battles."

But the congressman was not convinced. Poker, legislation, saving a priceless national document . . . he could play the steely-eyed game no matter the stakes.

So Peter said, "The ones who died last night—you'll see it on the news—worked for the man who's trying to bring you down. They worked for David Bruce."

"Can you spell 'scandal'?" asked Evangeline.

Milbury gave that some thought.

Evangeline said, "And we have more. You don't get it till we get what we want."

"I need more right now," said Milbury. "And even more later."

"All right," said Peter. "Try this: Professor Conlon is working for another set of rivals, not for you or the American people, as he has said so many times."

Milbury reddened. "That son of a bitch."

"So help us," said Peter. "You can even come with us. It should only take an hour. Then you can go on to Capitol Hill and whatever you have planned for America."

"Let me call Bill Dougherty, then I'll get dressed."

"Bill Dougherty, yes," said Peter. "Go ahead and call him."

Evangeline pocketed her iPhone and rolled her eyes.

. . .

"Congressman, this is highly irregular." The NPS ranger in charge was in his forties, ramrod straight, stiff brim hat, all business. His name tag read BARISON. He had four Park Police with him, too. "There are chains of command we're supposed to follow from the bottom to the top."

"I'm the ranking Democrat on the House Committee on Natural Resources," said Milbury. "I am the goddamn top."

They were all standing on the corner of Constitution and Seventeenth Street, in front of one of the oldest and most incongruous little structures in Washington, the stone lock keeper's house for a canal that had disappeared 130 years before. The Washington Monument loomed over them. The Mall stretched east and west. The morning traffic roared by.

"Now, open the door," said Max Milbury.

The ranger looked skeptically at the congressman in his trim blue committee-meeting suit, then more skeptically at the congressman's entourage, all of whom looked as if they had been up half the night: Peter and Evangeline, the pretty African American prof from GWU, and the black New York detective who was holding a tool kit. But Ranger Barison saved his most skeptical glance for the film crew that had arrived to shoot with Evangeline.

Abigail Lynne Simon said to Peter, "Just go in and start talking. You're miked. And we have a boom for wild sound."

The ranger said, "Congressman, this is on your head. Film crews are supposed to be permitted."

"They have a permit to shoot at the Lincoln Memorial. We'll write in the lock keeper's house, too," answered Milbury.

The ranger popped the padlock and used another key in the door lock.

Peter and Evangeline stepped in right after the ranger. The congressman followed. Then came Henry and the film crew. Diana stayed outside and peered in.

It was cold, damp, and smelly in the single room, about twelve by sixteen, with fireplaces at both ends. The place was filled with empty barrels, rakes, shovels, and other garden tools for the crews that worked the Mall. There were four windows downstairs. All were barred. One was boarded.

Henry looked around and said, "I bet if you were an old slave shoeshine man, this must have felt like a palace."

The ranger explained, "It was the lock keeper's house till about 1880. His job was to keep records, collect tolls, and when a boat was coming up from the lower canal, he would fill his lock with water, so that the boat could start uphill. The land rises from here. Then the boat would be towed up to Rock Creek and the next lock, and so on into the heartland."

"No carbon footprint on none of that," said Henry. "Now, do you got a cellar?"

The ranger shook his head. "No cellar. And poking around in a historic structure with whatever's in that tool kit is highly irregular, no matter what you're after."

Henry said, "Listen, my stiff-brim friend, we have come here to find something that is priceless to the American people, so I would appreciate a little help."

"He's right," said the congressman. "Now, if you don't have a cellar, you must have a crawl space."

The ranger pointed to the stones that made up the floor. "Those are laid directly on top of a slab."

"Has it always been storage, since the canal days?" asked Evangeline.

"No. It was a Park Police station in the thirties. And it was a comfort station in the fifties. Men's and ladies'."

Peter heard the sound of motorcycles roar by. He peered out the window. The boys of the Bonnie Blue Flag pulled up on the other side of Constitution.

Others were showing up, too. Kathi Morganti was peering in a window. William Dougherty had come up to the door and was craning his neck for a look inside.

"Word travels fast," said Evangeline.

Henry pulled out his hammer and tapped it against the palm of his hand.

Peter looked up at the joists above him. All exposed. So there'd be no hidden boxes in the ceiling. He asked the ranger, "What's in the loft up there?"

"More of the same."

The Park Police were now cordoning off the area.

Evangeline heard Kathi Morganti complaining as they moved her away from the window. Then she heard Diana's voice. "Officer, I think you should let that man pass."

A moment later, Diana poked her head inside the door. "Peter, Professor Conlon is here."

Milbury said, "Keep that hypocrite away from me."

Diana said, "You really ought to hear him, Congressman."

Conlon stuck his head into the lock house and said, "Good morning, all," as though he were addressing his class.

"Not for you it isn't," said Congressman Milbury. "After the grants I've sent your way, to betray me to work for renegades."

Conlon offered a letter. "The renegades found this in the back of the engraving of Frederick Douglass. They knew from that moment where the book would be found in a certain house, but they just couldn't figure out what house."

Milbury gestured to Peter. "He's the expert. Give it to him."

Peter took the letter and read, "Dear Mother Freedom—" His eyes dropped to the bottom of the page. It was signed *HH, hole man.* Halsey Hutchinson?

"Read," said Evangeline.

"Yes," said Milbury. "I have a hearing starting at ten."

"'Dear Mother Freedom, Nothing can ever repay you for what you did for me. And nothing can ever ease the pain of what you gave to America, any more than we can ease the pain of generations lost to bondage. But know that I am your friend. And if you or Zion are ever in need, go to the Bone family. Tell them to look in their house, in the knee wall, in a place where a man can awaken to see Washington and Lincoln, too. This letter and the letter from President Lincoln that I also include are all you'll need to show the world that you came honestly by what you'll find in that knee wall. Then find a fair broker, and you will get a fine price. You may or may not hear from me again. But I will go on to a righteous path.'"

"Wow," said Henry.

"The Bones and Mother Freedom," said Diana. "Building the piers to suspend the bridge."

"But where's the knee wall?" Peter looked around. "Upstairs?'

The congressman told the ranger to open the trapdoor, which was locked, and pull down the loft ladder.

Peter said, "Flashlight."

The congressman shouted, "Flashlight!" out the door.

A policeman handed one in.

Peter whispered to Henry, "Follow me up the ladder. Block the way for me. And bring that hammer."

Henry winked.

Peter climbed and stopped once he was halfway through the trapdoor.

He looked around: dust, junk, traffic cones, old boxes of . . . whatever, papers, records, the forgotten work of forgotten NPS bureaucrats. And four dormers where a man might slide a bed and still have a view, especially the dormers on the east side.

Peter lifted himself up. Henry popped up after him and stopped, so that his bulk filled the trapdoor opening.

The loft area was only a half story, so Peter had to scuttle, first to the front dormer, from which he could not see the Washington Monument. But from the back dormer . . . He pushed some boxes away and stretched out.

He imagined awakening there, on a low mattress. If he looked up, he would see the Washington Monument out the south dormer, close enough to touch. And if he sat up, he would see the White House through the north dormer, and perhaps imagine Lincoln there, peering through a telescope toward the smoke of battle on an August afternoon.

The book had to be here. So with the hammer head, he started tapping on the stonework in the dormer knee wall. *Tap. Tap. Tap.* Solid. Solid. Solid.

The ranger shouted up, "That's government property, mister!"

"Y'all relax," said Henry. "We're findin' history."

Tap. Tap. Tap. Solid. Solid. *Thunk.* Thunk?

Peter tapped that stone in several places. It sounded thin, like a piece of slate rather than stone. It was about a foot square, give or take a few jagged edges.

Peter looked back to the trap hole and told Henry, "Give me a screwdriver with a wide head." Then he went to work, using the screwdriver as a chisel, tapping gently on the mortar all around the slate.

"I'm warning you!" said the ranger.

"Relax," said the congressman. "Repointing the mortar will not affect the deficit."

Henry chuckled.

Finally Peter had worked all around the edges. He put the tools down and wiped his hands on his rumpled Dockers. He looked up at the Washington Monument. He glanced out at the White House. He looked down the Mall to the Lincoln Memorial, and he whispered, "Here goes."

He wedged his fingers, and the piece of slate slid off the wall. He caught it before it fell. The space beyond had been hollowed out.

And from across the floor, Henry said, "That sure looks like a book to me, No-Pete."

Peter gave Henry a big grin. "It sure does."

It was a small red leather-bound book in perfect condition. He opened it, and a letter fell out. He slipped the letter into his jacket pocket for the moment, because he was more interested in the book, and the signature on the endpaper: *A. Lincoln.* His mouth went dry. He wiped his hands on his jacket.

Then he opened the first page to the words, *March 3, 1861. Congress proposes Constitutional amendment . . .*

He flipped to the last page, April 16, 1862: *Immediate general emancipation is a thing I consider but am not ready to do . . .*

Peter whispered, "Yes, yes, yes."

And on the back endpaper, he saw a scrawl in pencil: *Picked up with gun kep gun for pertekshun hope this helps m. Lincoln. N&J.*

"Is that it?" whispered Henry.

"Stay right there." Peter had one more task to perform.

"What's going on up there?" cried the congressman.

Evangeline looked outside. Kathi and Dougherty had drawn together, each perhaps wondering who would be losing their job if their secret came out.

Up in the loft, Peter Fallon was using his iPhone to photograph each page of the diary. A few were brittle as he turned them, and he knew he should have been more careful. But by and large, the book was in excellent condition, the ink only slightly faded.

Click. Turn. Click. Turn. Ten pages. Twenty. Forty.

"Mr. Fallon!" The ranger stepped onto the bottom rung of the ladder.

Henry looked down at him and said, "Y'all just keep your place. You can't climb over me. I am what you call big-boned . . . and bigger bottomed."

The congressman shouted, "Mr. Fallon! What are you doing up there?"

"I'm authenticating."

And Evangeline laughed out loud. He had it.

When Henry's big butt started down, she waved to the film crew.

The camera pushed close to the ladder, to capture the moment that Peter descended and put the book into the congressman's hands. "May I present to you and the American people the diary of Abraham Lincoln."

"Holy God," whispered Ranger Barison in awe, as if now, he *got* it.

Peter said to Henry, "Tell the cops to draw their guns. This is worth twenty-five million, maybe more. We don't want anybody getting ideas."

"It's priceless," said Professor Conlon. "I told you that already."

"You're right," said Peter. "For once."

Evangeline said to the congressman, "What do you have to say?"

Comgressman Max Milbury's face reddened, and his hands shook with the awe of what was holding. And he said, "Mr. Dougherty... al... al... alert the media!"

. . .

Peter and Evangeline stepped out into the sunshine just as the four motorcycles roared away.

Keeler took off his Bonnie Blue Flag ball cap and gave them a wave. Peter waved back. Keeler had done the honorable thing after all. Without him, they might never have figured out where to look.

Then Peter turned to Diana and whispered, "Do you have a secure e-mail, one that you know hasn't been hacked?"

"I opened it last night. It's LadyT@gwu.edu."

Peter laughed, typed it in, and attached seventy-five of the most priceless pages any scholar in America had ever gotten a look at.

"Go up to your office now. The diary will go to the Library of Congress for conservation. There'll be all kinds of hoo-ha, but no scholar will get to look at it for months. I shouldn't do this, but what the hell. Go write your next book . . . Lady T."

At the same moment, Evangeline was walking over to Kathi Morganti. "Like you said on Saturday, you never know who you'll meet on the Acela to Washington. A literal power trip."

Kathi looked at Evangeline as if she might bite.

Evangeline tapped her camera and called up a shot. "I love to take candids."

Kathi looked at the picture of herself and Doughtery.

"True love or fake passion?" asked Evangeline.

Kathi said, "In this town, it's hard to know. But, I'm a mom. I showed you that picture of my kids on the train. They really do like Pop-Tarts."

Evangeline said, "This is none of my business. Which is not what we usually say these days if we can score a point on a political enemy . . . so." She tapped the DELETE button and the picture disappeared.

Kathi Morganti said, "Thank you."

And from behind them, William Dougherty said to the congressman, "I think we should get up to the Hill, sir, and get back to work."

"Yes," said the congressman. "This is an important day."

And Kathi said to the congressman, "Perhaps you should get back to your district instead, considering the poll numbers from last night."

Evangeline laughed at the Kathi-and-congressman version of the Washington give-and-take. It was starting up again because, well, that was what they did.

Evangeline took Peter by the sleeve and drew him away. "Nice work."

"I couldn't have done it without you."

Milbury had given the diary to Ranger Barison with instructions to take it directly to the Library of Congress. Now he sidled over to Evangeline and said, "You promised more information. Please tell me it's about a certain lobbyist who somehow figured out that we would be here this morning and came to annoy me."

"I have nothing on Ms. Morganti," Evangeline lied. "I was planning to rat out Professor Conlon. But Peter did it first."

The congressman glanced at Conlon, who was talking to Abigail Simon about getting "a few minutes of camera time." He said, "I think Conlon redeemed himself this morning." Then he called for his Chevy Tahoe.

Peter heard Henry growl, "Well, damn."

"What?"

"See the little dude in the runnin' pants, over in front of the OAS building? That's Ricky the Rican, takin' pictures, little motherfucker. He needs a talkin' to."

"It's over," said Peter. "Let him go. Just don't trust him on your next job."

"After runnin' with this crowd," said Henry, "I don't think I'm trustin' anyone ever again about anything, except my friends."

"A man can always use friends."

"Damn straight." Henry glanced at his watch. "If I leave now, I can be back in New York by one o'clock, and the Yanks are playin' a day game. See ya, No-Pete."

"Until next time."

. . .

An hour later, the film crew was setting up in front of the Lincoln Memorial.

The morning tourists were already gathering.

The Great Emancipator was gazing down.

And Peter was gazing out from the steps of the Memorial, wondering about the river of time running under the bridge that led them at last to that little stone house, wondering about Halsey Hutchinson.

Why had he given those Negroes the keys to one of history's kingdoms, the mind of Abraham Lincoln?

Perhaps they would never know. . . .

Sixteen

May 1865

After Lincoln's assassination, Halsey had hunkered another two weeks in Ward A, fearing discovery. Then they had discharged him. They were beginning the process of emptying the hospital, which would close and be torn down in August.

But Walt Whitman had returned and took Halsey into his rooming house on M Street.

He said, "The nurses think I offer hospitality to young men because I have ulterior motives. But I do it because I am a generous man. And a good friend to good friends."

And it was true. Halsey came to rely on Walt's friendship. And Walt, for "special" friendship, relied on Peter Doyle, the gentle streetcar conductor who had also had been in Ford's Theatre on that awful night.

Halsey did not tell Walt everything. He never told anyone everything about that night, not even Samantha.

But she pieced together much of the story when she read accounts, buried deep in the papers, of the mysterious deaths of two men in the city canal. One was a known thug, the other an unidentified gentleman who remained a John Doe until he was finally buried in a cemetery for indigents.

Halsey had spent those two weeks in the ward, expecting that Major Eckert would come through any day looking for Jeremiah Murphy. He did not.

And a greater worry was that Lafayette Baker, who had been brought back to direct the manhunt for Booth, would also loose agents to find the killer of Joseph Albert McNealy. But Baker had enough to do with

Booth, who remained at large for twelve days after shooting Lincoln. And Baker may never have known that the John Doe killed the same night as the president was one of his own men.

However, the climate of vigilante fear that Baker brought with him pervaded official Washington long after Booth had been run down and killed in a burning Maryland barn. It convinced Halsey that stepping forward with the daybook and the promise of a presidential pardon, in effect throwing himself on the mercy of a court that was hanging all of Booth's co-conspirators, would not be the best course.

Nor would it change the attitude of so many who were already planning to drive the freed Negroes into a new form of economic slavery, one from which they might never emerge.

Among that number was Dr. Joshua Wiggins.

At first, Halsey feared him the most. He waited for Wiggins to send his henchmen, so he begged Samantha to transfer to Armory Square, where he could protect her.

But it would seem that Wiggins and his henchmen were busy fighting among themselves, because Wiggins's name appeared in the paper two weeks after Lincoln's assassination. He had been murdered on his way home from a patient visit, stabbed neatly between the ribs and left to bleed on the street. But neither his watch nor his money were gone. The next day, a man named Jeffords was found murdered in his home in Georgetown, along the canal.

Halsey suspected the man who had killed Harriet Dunbar and threatened Samantha that night at Ford's Theatre. Had he killed over an argument among traitors, or had someone hired him? Benjamin Wood, perhaps, when he learned that Doc Wiggins had the ledger and was planning blackmail? Wood or his brother would enjoy using a man's own henchman against him. A quiet assassination, a quiet payoff, a quiet flight into the country.

Halsey worried less for Samantha after that, less for himself as well.

. . .

He grew his beard and went about the city as he had in the summer of '62, careful but confident that he had friends.

On a warm day in the middle of the month, he visited Mother Freedom. The old woman had been worn by her losses, but she still carried herself straight and proud. And she sang out a praise to the Lord the moment that she saw Halsey's face at her door.

Zion was not there that day. He had taken a wife and moved to another house.

So Halsey and Mother sat and drank tea and talked . . . of politics and books, of Mr. Lincoln and Frederick Douglass, of her dreams for her race.

When he rose to leave, she said, "You helped to set my people free, Halsey Hutchinson. You and my boys and all the other fine boys who fought. I knew when I saved you that the Lord set you on the righteous path, and you took it, just like you promised."

"But I'm still running for freedom myself," he said.

"You'll find it, son. You'll find it."

He promised her that he would be back.

It saddened him to think that he might not.

But he rejoiced with Noah when he learned, in the middle of May, that Major Eckert had arranged for the Bone family to move to the lock keeper's house on the Washington Canal. It had been the dream of a dead son. It would be the fulfillment of his family.

Some things, thought Halsey, worked out.

. . .

Samantha received her discharge from the Harewood Hospital in mid-May. They would be closing that one, too. The nation had spent millions more than it had to hold itself together. Now, it would skimp on the care of the men who had done the holding with flesh, blood, and bone.

In that way, it was like all wars.

And like all wars, the victors enjoyed a grand parade.

On a brilliantly bright May 24, the drums beat, the bands played, tens of thousands marched, hundreds of thousands watched, and for the first time in five weeks, the American flag flew at full staff above Washington.

Halsey and Samantha found a fine perch on the steps of the Treasury. From there, they could gaze up Pennsylvania, all the way to the Capitol, and watch the great blue phalanxes marching toward them, giant squares of bayonets weaving the air with flashing sunlight, thousands of men, parading proudly to the beat of drums and the blare of brass. Infantry units, cavalry units, artillery units with their limbers and guns, pioneers, engineers, support troops. For hours and hours they came on, an endless stream of manhood, from the cities and the farms, from the law offices and the counting houses and the logging camps and the fishing boats.

And after all they had been through, after all the terrible battles, after all the generals, from hesitant McClellan, who hated the sight of a dead soldier, to resolute and bloody Grant, who spent the young manhood of the North as if he would empty the Union vault of human capital, after all that, the Army of the Potomac had prevailed.

Samantha said, "It's too bad their leader is not here."

Halsey said, "He's watching, from somewhere."

And they knew that Walt would be watching from Fourteenth Street. So late in the day, they walked down into the crowd and found Walt and Pete Doyle right on the corner, a short distance from where Halsey had heard the report of the police superintendant that long-ago night.

Halsey stood there boldly now. He did not fear the crowds. In the crowds there was anonymity. In the bright sunlight, suspicions were wiped away.

When the Fifty-first New York marched past, they all screamed and shouted for Walt's brother, George Whitman, who gave them a great wave.

Then arm in arm, Samantha and Halsey strolled east on Pennsylvania.

They held each other close in those last days of May, because she was bound for Boston. But he knew he could never go back. As he had said before, there was no statute of limitations on murder. And with his father no longer alive, there was little reason to risk arrest in a place where he would certainly be recognized. His sister could have his inheritance. He would go West and have his freedom.

And as they walked, feeling the joy of the crowd and the power of the music in that late spring sun, they noticed a Negro standing on the corner.

He was wearing a kepi with the "Bugle and 54" on the crown.

It was Zion Freedom, saluting as the American flag went by.

Halsey went up to him. "Brother Zion?"

He looked at Halsey with tears streaming down his face. Most Negroes had been crying for weeks at the thought of Father Abraham's loss. But these were not tears of joy or sadness. Not surprisingly coming from Zion, they were tears of anger.

Halsey took Zion's hand and said, "It's been a long time. Did you ever get that Adams pocket pistol you always wanted?"

"I never did. And it's a good thing, 'cause I might've used it."

Halsey did not pursue that. He said, "Did Jim-Boy ever make it back?"

"He did, but not my brothers."

"They were good men," said Halsey. "They died for their country." It was an easy thing to say, because in those days, so many said it as a way to soothe so many more who needed to hear it.

But Zion answered through clenched teeth, "*Their* country? They died for *their* country?" Then he looked out at the troops marching past. "You notice anything?"

"I notice they look spiffed and polished and better fed than I ever was in two and a half years of fighting," said Halsey.

Zion looked at Samantha. "What about you, miss?"

She smiled and shook her head.

Zion said, "There's no colored troops. *None.*"

And Halsey realized that it was so.

"The white troops and the white folks want themselves a white march. They don't want to give a hundred thousand black men a bit of credit for savin' their damn country, not one damn bit. But my brothers bled just as red, and they died just as dead."

All that Halsey could say was, "That's not right. Not right at all."

Zion shuddered with sobs. "Damn near broke my ma's heart to learn the truth."

The drums thrummed, and the pounding step of the troops shook the ground, and right then, Halsey Hutchinson knew what he would do with the Lincoln daybook.

.   .   .

On the last day of May, he bade good-bye to Walt Whitman with an embrace and a kiss on the cheek. Walt gave him an envelope as a parting gift, "a little something I've just written." And the poet's eyes filled with tears, perhaps at losing a friend, perhaps because they filled with tears every day at the thought of losing Lincoln.

Halsey left Walt's rooms on M Street and walked over to Seventeenth, to the lock keeper's house. There were no boats in the canal. Business was slow, getting slower. Old Noah was sitting in a rocking chair beside the lock, looking out at the world.

"I'll be leaving soon, Noah," he said.

"You takin' that girl with you?"

"No. She needs to see Boston again. But she promised to come when I send for her, from wherever I land. There's a big country out there."

Noah rocked back and forth and said, "I'll stay right here. From my little bed in the dormer upstairs, all's I need to do is raise my head and I can see Mr. Washington"—he pointed to the stub of the monument in his backyard—"or Mr. Lincoln in his White House"—he pointed across the President's Park—"all in the roll of an eye. That's good enough for me."

"I have something that belonged to Mr. Lincoln, and seeing as I'll be traveling, maybe you'll hold on to it for me, for safekeeping. If I need it, I'll send for it. Or if my other friends in Washington need it, they'll be able to let you know. They're good folk who live out on Maryland Avenue."

"Is it that book? The one me and Jacob saved that terrible night?"

"You've earned a piece of it, for your sacrifice, for your friendship." As Halsey opened it to show Noah the Lincoln signature, an envelope dropped out of the endpapers. It was a letter that Halsey had written to anyone who found the book. He picked it up and slipped it back.

"And the other colored folks who helped me, they've earned a piece of it, too. If they ever come to you with a letter that has Lincoln's signature on it, just match it to the signature in the book and you'll know they're the right folk."

Noah took the book, looked at the handwriting of the president, and said, "I know just the place. And once it's hid, I'll have Jacob write a nice letter to your friend. He spells better than me."

"Mr. Lincoln would be glad to know that you have it."

"And since you're leavin'"—Noah pulled the Adams revolver from a little box beside the rocking chair—"you ought to have your gun back, for pertekshun."

. . .

That night, Halsey and Samantha stayed in the Willard Hotel together.
He had grown comfortable in his anonymity by then. She had grown comfortable in their love, unsanctified by matrimony but tested in so many
other ways.

So they loved in the big hotel featherbed and slept and loved again the
next morning.

They had breakfast in their room, with the sun streaming in the window.

And he pulled out the envelope that Walt had given him the day before.

"What is it?" she asked.

"A poem."

"Read it."

He scanned it and said, "But it's not exactly a love poem."

"Read it anyway."

So he cleared his throat and read, " 'O Captain! my captain! our fearful trip is done; / The ship has weather'd every rack, the prize we sought is
won; / The port is near, the bells I hear, the people all exulting, / While
follow eyes the steady keel, the vessel grim and daring: / But O heart!
heart! heart! / O the bleeding drops of red, / Where on the deck my captain lies, / Fallen cold and dead. . . .' "

Halsey looked up. "Should I go on?"

"Some other day." She reached out and touched his hand. "I wish you
could come with me. I have to go home for a while, beat a path to my old
mother's door."

"That's what makes you so good. You never forget the things that
matter. But I can't. So, as Emerson says, I'll go where there is no path and
leave a trail."

Later that morning, Halsey wrote a letter to Mother Freedom and put
it into a box that also contained the Lincoln letter and his Adams pocket
revolver. In the letter he told the Freedoms all that he had told Jacob. And
someday, he added, a letter from Abraham Lincoln would be a valuable
thing in itself.

They left the box in the hotel post office. Then he and Samantha
headed together to the train depot, a few blocks north of the Capitol.

Samantha had two trunks.

Halsey was carrying his rucksack and wearing a brown suit taken from the charity bin.

He was sure as he walked in the front of the depot that he saw bearded Lafayette Baker, scanning the crowd of comers and goers, looking for . . . someone. He would be glad to leave that city of intrigues forever.

They called her train first.

Halsey and Samantha embraced a final time as a big steam engine sent gray clouds of mechanized breath into the air.

He said, "Tell my sister I love her and someday I'll come back."

They kissed again and held each other for as long as they could. Then she boarded. As the train began to move, she dropped a window and called to him. "Find a place, and I'll come. I'll be there in the time it takes the train to travel. I promise."

He waved again and watched the train until it was out of sight. Then he turned to the message board. They were erasing the 10:30 Baltimore train and writing in the track for his Harrisburg train. From there, he would take a train to Cleveland, then Chicago, then . . . where?

Suddenly, Halsey Hutchinson felt very alone again.

As he walked toward a bench, he noticed a man in a wheelchair. Men in wheelchairs were common sights in Washington in those days. This man had a bag on his lap and a vacant look on his face. But he was familiar.

Halsey walked over. "George?"

George Smith looked up. He was frowning. "Jeremiah."

"How are you?"

"Fine. Your voice sounds better. Where's your brogue?"

Halsey knelt in front of him. "You're going home, are you?"

George Smith shrugged, as if he didn't much care. "No one to see me off, no one to meet me, either. My wife ran off when she heard I lost my legs. I told her I still had a dick, but— You need a friend?"

Halsey stood, thought for a moment, and said, "Can you ride a horse?"

George Smith laughed. "No, but I can drive a wagon, if you strap me in."

"A wagon? I suppose a wagon could take us a long way."

"A long way."

"Let's go change your ticket."

A few hours later, they were rocking northwest out of Washington, through the countryside where they had fought so ferociously, a countryside already gone green and soon to grow bountiful, a countryside healing itself.

It was late afternoon, but the sun was high. The longest days lay ahead, stretching before them like the continent.

Halsey began to hum. He was happy that the notes held together in his throat. He hummed the "Battle Hymn." He hummed it slow and low, and it sounded . . . beautiful.

Seventeen

Monday Afternoon

〜◎ "And that's a wrap," said the producer.

The shoot around the Lincoln Memorial was done. The story had been told.

So Evangeline walked up the steps and joined Peter on the perch he'd kept all morning.

The view took their eye along the reflecting pool, past the Washington Monument, all the way to the Capitol dome.

Peter looked and said, "Amazing."

"What?" She took off her shoes and massaged her feet. She didn't think Old Abe would mind.

"Amazing that it's so beautiful. There's something big about it all, no matter what kind of human foibles are on display in these buildings every day. Congressman Milbury is up under that dome right now, cooking up new ways to extend the power of the federal government. Meanwhile, David Bruce and Volpicelli are already into damage control, at least until Volpicelli turns against Bruce or the other way round."

"What was it Henry said last night?"

"Everybody fucks everybody else?"

"Crude," she said, "but accurate."

"And still—" Peter leaned back on his elbows and surveyed the scene. "—we get this."

"We must be doing something right."

They sat in the warm sun and listened to the chatter all around them as people saw the great statue of Lincoln for the first time. It comforted them both somehow, just to be there.

Then Evangeline she said, "Any thoughts on what you're going to do with that half-million-dollar check from David Bruce?"

"I can't really take it in good conscience."

"You weren't going to take it anyway, were you, and give those guys a tool to use in the spin wars?"

"There's not a lot to spin out of a man wrestling to do what's right, then doing his best. Diana finished reading the daybook, and she says that's the big theme on every page. And the theme of her next book."

"But the check?"

"I'll tear it up."

"Prove it."

Just then, a voice came from behind them. "I hear you found it."

It was Volpicelli. He walked down the stairs and stopped beside them.

"You're a little late," said Peter.

"Mr. Bruce has decided that you violated the terms of the agreement."

"I had no choice," said Peter.

"He'd like the money back."

Peter reached into his pocket and pulled out two envelopes—the check and the envelope that had fallen out of Lincoln's daybook that morning. In all the excitement, he had forgotten about it.

He handed Volpicelli the check and put the other envelope back into his pocket.

"Mr. Bruce wants you to have this in exchange." Volpicelli took a manila folder from under his arm. "It's the Lincoln letter. Since Sorrel never cashed the check, Mr. Bruce doesn't believe it was a proper sale. And he's an honorable man. He thinks you'll know what to do with this."

Then Volpicelli turned and started down the wide flat steps of the Memorial, as if he couldn't stand to be there any longer.

Evangeline watched him go and said to Peter, "He'd better be careful of Jan Bruce. She seemed to know what was going to happen to Sorrel before it happened."

"I was thinking that myself. But hard to prove. Hard to prove."

She stretched her legs in the sun. "What will you do with that envelope?"

He opened it, looked inside, ran his fingers on the Mylar. "Get some legal advice. Technically it belongs to Sorrel. But, if it's up to me, we sell it. Dawkins gets half the money, Diana's museum gets half, and a flea market paperback peddler by the name of Douglas Bryant gets my commission."

"I like it." She pointed to his pocket. "What about that one?"

He took it out and opened it and looked at the signature: "Halsey Hutchinson."

She said, "Wow."

And they read it together: "'May 30, 1865, Dear Sir or Madame, I leave this daybook here because the Negroes who inhabit this house deserve a link with the man who emancipated them. Until white and black can know each other as people, as equals in life and partners in the building of America, until they can march together after the nation's battles shall have been won, the work of Lincoln is unfinished. It will be for you to complete. I hope that when you read this, government of the people, by the people, and for the people has not perished from the earth but flourishes. So many, white and black, gave their lives to guarantee it. Halsey Hutchinson.'"

"I like him," said Evangeline.

Abigail Lynne Simon called up the stairs, "It's one thirty. If we leave now, we can get back to Boston tonight. We can drop you in New York."

Evangeline waved her on. "We're renting a car, taking our time. We need to be in Boston on Thursday for Peter's show."

Abigail said, "See you there, with a camera." Then she left.

Peter looked at his watch and cocked an eye at Evangeline. "One thirty?"

"Don't push your luck." Evangeline stood, slipped her feet back into her shoes, and pulled Peter up. "Let's walk."

They linked arms and descended the steps of liberty's great temple.